THE GOATS OF RYE GRASS HILL

“That is the land of lost content, I see it shining plain, the happy highways where I went, and cannot come again.”— A. E. Housman

"I'd trade all my tomorrows for one single yesterday."— Kris Kristofferson - Fred Foster

"Kids make you want to start life over."— Muhammad Ali

“It’s never too late to have a happy childhood.”— Berkeley Breathed

“Childhood is the small town everyone came from.”— Garrison Keillor

“This country is made up of small towns and big dreams.”— Brian Mulroney

"Friends are the family you choose."— Jess C. Scott

"My best friend is the one who brings out the best in me."— Henry Ford

“Animals, like us, are living souls. They are not things. They are not objects. Neither are they human. Yet they mourn. They love. They dance. They suffer. They know the peaks and chasms of being.” – Gary Kowalski

“Some people talk to animals. Not many listen though. That’s the problem.” – A. A. Milne

“Animals don’t hate, and we’re supposed to be better than them.” – Elvis Presley

“Let us close the springs of racial poison. Let us pray for wise and understanding hearts. Let us lay aside irrelevant differences and make our nation whole.” – Lyndon B. Johnson

"In a racist society, it is not enough to be non-racist. We must be anti-racist."— Angela Davis

"Kids aren't born to be bullies, they're taught to be bullies."— Matt Bomer

“It is not the monsters we should be afraid of; it is the people that don't recognize the same monsters inside of themself.” – Shannon L. Alder

“The true soldier fights not because he hates what is in front of him, but because he loves what is behind him.”— G.K. Chesterton

"What we do for ourselves dies with us. What we do for others and the world remains and is immortal." – Albert Pine

“This will remain the land of the free so long as it is the home of the brave.”—Elmer Davis

"A man's character is his fate."— Heraclitus

"It's choice - not chance - that determines your destiny."— Jean Nidetch

“The right choice is hardly ever the easy choice.”— Rick Riordan

“The cave you fear to enter holds the treasure you seek.” – Joseph Campbell

"Faith is unseen but felt, faith is strength when we feel we have none, faith is hope when all seems lost."— Catherine Pulsifer

“The turning point in the process of growing up is when you discover the core of strength within you that survives all hurt.”— Max Lerner

Aura Lee

When the blackbird in the spring,
'Neath the willow tree,
Sat and rock'd, I heard him sing,
Singing Aura Lee.
Aura Lee, Aura Lee,
Maid with golden hair;
Sunshine came along with thee,
And swallows in the air.

In thy blush the rose was born,
Music, when you spake,
Through thine azure eye the morn,
Sparkling seemed to break.
Aura Lee, Aura Lee,
Birds of crimson wing,
Never song have sung to me,
As in that sweet spring.

Aura Lee! the bird may flee,
The willow's golden hair
Swing through winter fitfully,
On the stormy air.
Yet if thy blue eyes I see,
Gloom will soon depart;
For to me, sweet Aura Lee
Is sunshine through the heart.

When the mistletoe was green,
Midst the winter's snows,
Sunshine in thy face was seen,
Kissing lips of rose.
Aura Lee, Aura Lee,
Take my golden ring;
Love and light return with thee,
And swallows with the spring.

W.W. Fosdick

THE GOATS OF RYE GRASS HILL

Joe Don Roggins

Rain Hill Publishing LLC

Paperback ISBN 979-8-9850821-2-8

eBook ISBN 979-8-9850821-3-5

Library of Congress Control Number 2022937274

Printed by Rain Hill Publishing LLC, in the United States of America

First printing edition 2022

www.joedonroggins.com

In memory of William and Mina Ebsen

ACKNOWLEDGEMENTS

This book is dedicated to the men and women
of the United States Armed Forces.

Army: "This we'll defend."

Marines: "Always faithful."

Navy: "Not self but country."

Air Force: "Aim high . . . fly, fight, win."

Coast Guard: "Always ready."

Space Force: "Always above."

United States of America: "In God we trust."

Gratitude eternal.

CONTENTS

CHAPTER 1

Morning Shadows

So much of life comes down to fate.

Every time I stood in Rye Grass Park looking at the statue, I felt a chill cross my temples, got a lump in my throat, and found it strange how the strongest faith can be so easily threatened by a twist of fate. The gentleman commemorated had played baseball for the New York Giants, circa 1916. He was a handsome man with an average build; a little under six feet, and perhaps 180 pounds. In the pose, he was staring down a batter: classic stance, ball in hand, hand in glove. His countenance was confident and determined. His eyes were riveted but kind. The artist had spared not a needle's eye of detail—from the sinewy forearms to the stitching of the plaid uniform and striped cap. I greatly admired Elias Gussard, the whole town did, and so did a great portion of the nation. Aristotle said, "You will never do anything in this world without courage. It is the greatest quality of the mind next to honor." Gussard was a man of honor.

At the height of his career, Elias Gussard left the ranks of professional baseball. He joined the United States Marine Corps to fight in World War I. Gussard became a medic. He was initially assigned to a support unit far behind the frontlines, quite likely due to his status as a sports hero. But not long into the fray, he requested to serve with the men in the trenches. There was no level of risk, no charge, no barrage, no volley of fire that would keep him from reaching and tending a downed soldier. His intrepid nature and skilled hands saved countless lives.

To my mind, this is a story as true as any. As much as possible, I have presented the account as seen through my own eyes. But there *were* times when relating events through the eyes and thoughts of others provided the most genuine representation. The historic and academic materials were drawn from many sources: books, magazines, articles, video and audio documentaries; as well as from personal letters, journals, and diaries. Observing discretionary protocols, some of the names of people and places have been changed. To maintain consistency and attain closure, it was necessary to do a little speculating, make some educated guesses, and fill in a few blanks. Entertaining at times, mundane at times, incredible but believable throughout, this is a chronicle of family, friendship, America, faith, strength, frailty, love, honor, and hope. It is a heartfelt portrait of a time, a place, and a people that had never been before and will never be again.

⚜

We look upon a battlefield: France, 1918, the Battle of Belleau Wood along the Marne River. A pitch-black night. No moon, no stars, no clouds, only a rolling mist. A faint wind whispered. French rockets left scarlet trails as they whistled and cracked. Flares hung from their silken webs, slowly dying as they drifted. A fireball lit up the muddy fields as though it were midday. It burst into bits of orange, gold, and blue. Not far off, thundering artillery-throated roars echoed across the river. From the mouths of dragons—coal boxes, crumps, and Black Marias—came fiery howls and deafening booms. The earth trembled and rippled the puddly mires. Impacts jiggled and splattered the mud for tens of yards.

It was an arena of silhouettes, shell-smashed trucks, flaming wagons; naked, frightened trees; iron posts tangled in barbs; horses blindly wandering. Soldiers: French, German, British, American, drudged and trudged, crawled and rolled, splashed and sloshed in chaotic advances and retreats. Rifles smacked; machine guns chattered. Men fell—screaming, writhing, groping, and still.

The German barrage collapsed the trenches. Their tanks rolled. Whistles, bells, gongs rang out. Trumpets blew their charge. In their weighty, cumbersome masks, the Germans massed and swarmed like insects. They threw grenades; they waved entrenching spades like battle axes. Shouts of "Gas, gas, gas!" flowed in terrifying waves. The allies donned their masks, fixed bayonets, turned, and countered. All became lost in the smoke and fog. Flares bathed everything in a blood-pink sheen. Allies without or slow to secure masks dug at their eyes. They gasped and gagged as the sulfur burned their throats and lungs.

Outnumbered by the hundreds, the allies turned in full retreat. Many lifted their masks to heave and vomit only to take in the caustic air. The Germans used cutters to snap the rolls of fence wire. Planks were cast upon the thorny coils. No Man's Land churned into a hellish bog of mud, and blood, and fire. Shrapnel took off a soldier's head, his life's blood gushed and sprayed. A blood-soaked American staggered and collapsed at the foot of a flaming tree. Through the mist, another soldier crouched as he ran; his extended arm brandished a red cross. The American medic knelt to attend the wounded man. "Let's take a look," he said and slung his medical pack into the mud. The suffering doughboy gurgled as he tried to speak. Face alighted by surrounding fires, the medic spoke with strength and compassion.

"Courage troop. Find strength in God." A volley of shelling drowned his voice.

The downed soldier gagged and spat up blood; the medic's gauze sunk into his chest. As the medic's eyes lost hope, the massive shadow of a spike-helmet fell upon him. The German thrust his bayonet; the blade pierced an outstretched hand; it ripped away fingers as it pulled back. Springing up, the medic lunged for the rifle. The men fought. The German caught an elbow to the jaw but held tightly to his weapon. He shoved the medic against a long-dead tree. The scream of a mortar split the air. It smashed into the earth, splattering sod, and spewing fragments, white and blue hot. The tree and the men were blown to kingdom come. Muscle, guts, gristle, and bone plopped into the mud like late-summer apples.

All of this came to me so vividly, so real as I stood in the park. I could hear every bomb, feel the cold mud, taste the ash, and feel myself retching at the smell of death. Yet, once a year I compelled myself to relive it—out of respect and in admiration. This recall proffered a catharsis of sorts, both emotional and spiritual.

I think I've read every book, magazine, and article ever written about Elias Gussard. Divertingly, and in contrast to the horrors of war, something I have always found especially touching about Eli's life was his love for the tender Civil War ode to "Aura Lee". I've always found it to be a hauntingly beautiful song. Gussard's wife, Annelise, would often sing it for him while playing mandolin. Sadly, the love of his life died of influenza during the epidemic of 1918, while he was warring overseas. This occurred only a few weeks before his own demise. It was said the light, which had always so deeply shone in Eli's eyes, went dim the day she passed; the limbic glow was never seen again.

Like Gussard, I grew up in the little town of Rye Grass, nearly three generations after the man himself. I'm sure that's why I've made such a concerted study of his life. He was our legacy, our native son—THE PRIDE OF RYE GRASS, WASHINGTON—so reads the message on the plinth of his statue. He was awarded the Silver Star posthumously. It is displayed in the Brayton Chapel, only a few miles east of town, along with some historic baseball artifacts from his days in New York.

Gussard's great-grandfather founded the community of Rye Grass just after the Civil War. Having a penchant for acquiring real estate, he became relatively wealthy. After leaving his family a substantial fortune, he donated a great deal of land to the town and surrounding area, including a church, rest home, and hospital just outside the town of Brayton. Even today, Brayton is not much more than a village, but the hospital, nursing facility, and senior living center thrive. In addition, this selfless man granted a beautiful hill of flowing ryegrass to the community of his hometown. It stands just a few miles to the south. The north side of the hill flows into a vast meadow of brilliant wildflowers, fed by artesian waters. The hill will live on as a place of peace, of nature, of refuge; in fact, it is now a state landmark. Topped by cherry, quince, and a sprawling horse-chestnut tree, this was once a Shangri-La for the young Elias—a place for picnics, summer antics, winter sledding, autumn contemplation, and perhaps a little spoonin' in the springtime.

Taking one last look at the statue, I beheld a proud countenance, with eyes full of compassion, and a smile that was engaging, yet strangely demure. A point of peculiarity: at the height of his fame, it became well-known that Elias Gussard persisted in the eccentricity of not wanting his picture taken. Few photographs of Elias exist. There is a verified anecdote that a whiskey distiller published an unauthorized baseball card of Elias, a uniformed close-up from belt line to cap. Gussard was a deeply religious man; he never touched a drop of drink. As the yarn spins, he was sent two complimentary copies of the distillery cards while away at war. He became enraged—mostly because of the whiskey-bottle advertisement printed on the back of the card. He ordered the cards to be burned, all of them, and he forbade that any others be printed—ever. To the best of my knowledge, no authorized baseball cards were ever published during his lifetime. Save for those required for official military and legal documents, Gussard never willingly posed for another photograph.

Sited on the west end of the park is another statue. It bestows acclaim for deeds and heralds the fulfillment of destiny. I'm not going to visit that one just now—I'll save that visit for the end of the story—when all is said and done. While I cherish the memories of these monuments, what follows is the interwoven tale of four men, four wars, four lives—and not to be forgotten, the societal contributions of four enigmatic goats. To expand, to reiterate, from morning shadows to twilight's last gleaming, this is a portrayal of joy and sorrow, love and hate, courage and cowardice, godliness and horror, honor and disgrace. Though set in America, it is a story of many people and many lands, a story of the worst and best qualities of humanity. I lived through most of these events, and as I write these words, I live them again. Over the years, my thoughts, feelings, and ideas have simmered into a curious contemplation of the human condition, presented here to rouse the powers within, to revive hopes and dreams; to confront doubts and fears; to forgive errs and imperfections, to cope with the aftermath of tragedy; to heal sufferings—especially those of our own making. Here begins the story: The Goats of Rye Grass Hill.

CHAPTER 2

Cal Brimiron's Amazing Goats

On a warm June night in 1963, a gibbous moon drifted through dark, ragged clouds. A '53 Dodge pickup pulling a livestock trailer rolled along a winding country road. The smell of spilled coffee lingered in the cab even though both windows were wide open. Bonnie Guitar's wistful rendition of "Dark Moon" played softly on the radio. The stretch of barbed wire fences and fields of tall grass seemed endless. The journey had been a long one, in terms of both time and distance. It had been, literally, a journey of America; a pilgrimage of faith, charity, and hope. At long last, the hallowed destination came into view: a small but steep hill of tall ryegrass. The truck's brakes squeaked as it eased off the road. A man stepped from the truck, walked past the glowing headlights, and removed a large canister from the passenger side. A chorus of bleating emanated from the trailer. If bleating sounds could be impatient, these bleats were impatient. The man opened the trailer door and withdrew four large bowls. He spread them out and filled each to the brim with water. The bleats came louder and faster. The man climbed into the trailer, and soon four goats, one by one, jumped down and hurried to the vessels. The animals lapped the bowls dry in seconds. The man said, "I figured you'd be thirsty, but I wanted to make sure we got here before morning." He refilled the basins. After the goats had fully slaked their thirst, the man led them up the rugged grade. The moon drifted into a clearing and shined upon their new home.

Cal Brimiron was a slightly stooped man of about 70 who walked with a bit of a limp. The four goats followed in a straight line, like regimented ducklings. Cal stopped and turned. "All right, go ahead." He swung his arm. "Run to the top!" Hopping and bounding, they reached the top in a wink. Most cumbersomely, Cal trudged his way to the crest. He continued toward a fringe of quince and cherry trees. The goats circled him, knowingly parting and bending the grass, setting the stage in their moonlit auditorium. The clouds drifted and darkened the land.

Cal wore a tattered jacket and baggy pants. A diametric crack crossed one lens of his teashade spectacles. His hair was silver and disheveled. The loving expression on his face phased from contentment to searching thoughts, to somber deliberation. The goats continued to circle and mat the tall grass. One by one, they settled and gazed up at the man. The pale, yellow moon insisted on a presence.

Though feigned, Cal cast a look of disappointment at one of the animals. "Now Tinker. Don't give me those woeful eyes." The small white goat shook her head; her peers bleated.

"Now, now, now. We all knew this day would come and there's no point in protesting—the moment is upon us. We're here and here we will stay. We may as well all accept it."

A large brown goat with floppy ears wagged his tail.

"That's it, Dandy! Lift our spirits."

Something rustled in the grass just beyond a massive horse-chestnut tree. A thin goat with long, slender legs rose and trotted toward the sound. Two birds flapped into the dawning sky, winging high and away, fading into the waning night.

"Ah, Willow, our selfless sentry . . . Grouse I believe, maybe quail. When they return, seek their fellowship. You chase off the field cats and they'll watch out for you." A burly, shaggy goat with a comical underbite and ram-like horns stood and dug his front hoof into the turf. He snorted and nodded approval.

"That's right, Henry—it's good to have friends, and you'll make a lot of friends up here on this hill—and even more down in the meadow. You help them and they'll help you. And Henry, my fine goat—we all know you'll protect this family. Never forget, we all need friends and neighbors. 'No man is an island'. That goes for goats too."

Cal gently scratched Henry between the horns. "You're just like your dad—rough and tumble on the outside, but an ol' softie at heart."

The sky had cleared. The moon was low, and the stars were faint. Cal scanned the horizon. The crack of dawn was violet and gold, and the scent of wildflowers sweetened the breeze.

"Beautiful. So very beaut—" Cal moaned, winced, and grabbed his left arm. His teeth clenched and he gasped. He let out a guttural wheeze and his knees buckled. Kneeling, grimacing, he looked to the heavens.

"Not yet. Not just yet. Just a while longer—my work is far from finished."

The goats stirred and bleated. They came close. One of them nudged Cal's arm. He managed a short breath, another, then a deeper one, and placed his right palm on his chest. He sighed, looked to the sky, and nodded gratefully. Cal reached out to the goats. With a single finger, he tapped each on the nose.

"Never you mind now. Just a little warning—keeping me on my toes. Help is very near, and I won't be long away." Cal sat like a yogi on the matted grass. "I'll rest a bit . . . just a bit, then we'll have a look around."

After sitting for nearly an hour, Cal stood slowly, unsteadily. The sun rested on the distant hillside, providing plenty of light. He walked the entire hilltop and the goats followed. All beheld the flowered meadow; three acres, maybe more. Cal reached out his arms and opened them wide. He made grand sweeping gestures and sang a "da-da-da" version of the Sleeping Beauty Waltz. The goats dizzily followed the motions. The glistening meadow filled their eyes. They glanced up at Cal and listened to his every word.

"Out there, and on into the woods, flowers dance to a robin's song. A cool mountain stream flows just beyond. And over there—look at that stand of cedars down the south side. They'll keep you from the cold and wet and shield away the wind." He pointed to the giant horse-chestnut tree, its branches full and green. "There stands our mighty guardian. A sky beneath a sky. No matter how mean and ornery that summer sun wants to be, it will never burn through that leafy dome."

Cal kneeled and the goats drew near; they lay down. Apprehension, uncertainty pervaded. The man caressed each of the goats in turn, meeting their eyes with his. "This is a good place, my old friends. Beautiful, bountiful, and safe. A good home for our family. And people from the town will soon come; they will care for you. Sometimes people need a good reason to find love in their hearts—they will surely find this love in you."

Cal rose and slowly backed away. The goats stirred and bleated softly. Cal reached out; his left hand told them to stay, his right hand told them to calm. Henry stood and lowered his horns; his hoof dug into the turf. When the others started to rise, Henry pounded his hoof and they settled back. Cal's head woefully bowed. He turned and waded through the tall grass. Looking back only once, begrudging each aching step, he disappeared over the rise. He heard the soft pleading of bleats and brays. Gradually they became louder with hints and tints of fear. The bleats faded as Cal neared the battered truck. The writing on the side of the livestock trailer read, CAL BRIMIRON'S AMAZING GOATS. The aged man wheezed and leaned back against the faithful carriage. Suddenly, he clasped his hands to his chest and winced—the pain was sharp, scalding, agonizing. It finally passed; tears rolled over his gaunt cheeks. He looked to the sky. "Give me strength. Give me time. There is so much more to be done."

CHAPTER 3

Ronnie Rix

Two hours later, five miles northwest of the hill, sat a farmhouse. The family living there had taken a long-postponed trip to the wilds of Wyoming. The word was they would return in a day or two. On their porch stood Elmer "Buddy" Foley, a boney, acne-faced young man; he had just turned 21. Buddy had a pack of Lucky Strikes rolled up in the sleeve of his dingy, armpit-stained t-shirt. He was cajoling his 13-year-old protégé, Ronnie Rix, to kick down the front door. Ronnie fidgeted and tugged at his royal-blue, Dodgers top. He hoisted up his baggy jeans and nervously mussed the unruly thatch on his noggin. Moving a little farther away, he judged the distance to the door. He leaned to the side, slightly dropped his hips, and raised a knee. The sole of his sneaker flapped, as he landed a lackadaisical kick against the center of the door. This half-hearted effort sent him tumbling backward. Buddy sneered and smoothed back his greasy pompadour. He spewed a loogie and flicked a smoldering butt onto the gravel.

"What the hell, Ronnie?! You ain't worth a gob o' snot! Here, let a white man show ya."

Buddy smashed the heel of his boot against the doorknob. The surrounding wood cracked. Buddy threw his forearm and shoulder into the door, splitting the frame and blowing the entrance wide open.

"I guess I need a pair of boots," Ronnie said.

"No, you need a pair o' balls!" Buddy rushed inside, expecting Ronnie to be on his heels. Ronnie hesitated and glanced back, following the length of the lonely road, dreading the approach of a vehicle, any vehicle. He stepped off the porch to get a better look. Walking past a wagon wheel, wooden saguaro cactus, and cracked steer skull, he finally found a spot where he could scan Rye Grass Road in both directions. From inside the house, Buddy started hollering. Ronnie hustled back to the porch.

"Get in here Rix! Hustle up . . .find the bathroom and get all the meds: prescriptions, aspirin, Alka-Seltzer, Pepto, hemorrhoid cream—anything new in the package . . . We can sell it on the way to Mexico—gas money."

"How'm I gonna carry it all?"

"Pillowcases, dummy . . . grab a bunch of 'em. Goll dang, I coulda done this better by myself. Use your head you little peckerwood . . . I've been teaching you this stuff for months."

Ronnie took a left, ending up in the kitchen. He turned back and hurried into a bedroom, emerging with a bunch of pillowcases. He tossed a couple to Buddy. As Ronnie searched the bathroom, Buddy ransacked the living room.

Buddy yelled, "Find the guns and ammo, huntin' knives, bows, arrows . . . any kinda weapon."

"Where?"

"Closets, numbnuts. Drawers, trunks, boxes. Christ almighty . . . Get movin'! We gotta split before Welski comes snooping around. You never know when that dork'll show up."

Rounding the last curve, unknowingly nearing a crime-in-progress, a near-antique, black-and-white police cruiser slowly rolled. Deputy Robert Welski noticed a suspicious truck parked near the porch, facing the road. He puckered his lips disgustedly, then squinted. "Ski", as he was best known, stroked back the fenders of his flattop. With a tan uniform sleeve, he put a quick shine on his badge. Ski saw no one outside the house. He twisted the knob on the radio to extinguish Johnny Cash's "Ring of Fire".

In a fading Texas accent, the deputy talked to himself. "Hot damn, look at that license plate—that's the one! I'll bet anything it's Foley. That fool is never gonna learn. This time his butt's headin' to county."

The police car crawled along a barbed wire fence and pulled up beside a mass of blackberry vines. With the car well-hidden, Ski bent low and stole up behind a pear tree. With military-trained stealth, he slipped up beside the house, making certain not to disturb the Snow White and the Seven Dwarfs figures on the beauty bark. He looked through the living room window, then quickly ducked out of sight. When he peeked again, he saw Ronnie coming into the room.

Welski whispered, "No, no, no . . . jeez. Who's that stupid kid? You're breakin' my heart you little fool. How'd you ever get mixed up with a piece of trash like Foley?"

Buddy dropped two crystal candle holders into a pillowcase. Ronnie set a cardboard box on the couch. He sought approval. "I filled it up. Pills, watches, fancy rings . . . and I found a box of bullets. Big ones, like for a rifle."

Buddy posed, "How 'bout the rifle?"

"Nope—no guns at all."

"There's gotta be guns, goofball. Everybody in these parts has guns." Buddy sighed, frustrated. "Probably in a gun safe somewhere... I'll take a look when I'm done with this junk... Man, we've been doin' this for months—months! And I don't think you've learned a damn thing."

"Are we gonna look in the barn and garage?"

"Ain't got time. That dope, Welski—he don't usually drive by here till around noon, but we can't count on it. I've been casin' this place like I told you. And you never can tell about a stupid Polock . . . You just never can tell."

Buddy kicked over a coffee table and magazines flew. He noticed a framed family photo on the fireplace mantle. He grinned and grabbed it.

"No cash, no guns, no packs of smokes. Just a bunch of stinkin' damn horse crap." Buddy gave the family portrait a poisonously precious look. "My, what a lovely family." He dropped it and smashed the glass with his heel. He tore the shade off a lamp, unscrewed the bulb, and threw it against a wall. Spying a stone ashtray, his destruction took a sinister turn.

"Take hold of that ashtray, Ronnie." Buddy gestured toward the console TV. "C'mon, man—show me that pitchin' arm!"

Ronnie looked at the TV, then looked at the floor. He said, "That's a really nice TV."

"Soooo what! It ain't gonna be nice for long."

"Let's just get outta here, Buddy."

Buddy needled. "You little pansy. This is part of your initiation. You gotta do some damage!" He raised a clenched fist.

Ronnie sighed wearily and shook his head "no".

Buddy gnashed his teeth, "Do it or lose yer teeth, punk!"

Ronnie picked up the ashtray, assumed a pitching stance, and drew back his arm.

"Watch out," Buddy warned. "TVs blow up. They throw glass all over when you smash 'em." Neither burglar noticed their "secret admirer".

Standing in the wide, arched doorway, Officer Welski cleared his throat and shouted like a drill sergeant. "Drop it! Drop it now!"

Heads turned. The ashtray thudded onto the carpet.

Ski stepped into the room. Ronnie froze. Buddy's eyes went right to Ski's holstered pistol. Ski stepped toward Ronnie. Buddy caught Ronnie's eye and slyly nodded toward the gun. Ronnie's eyes flashed toward the weapon, then darted away. Buddy went for a distraction. Lifting a crystal candle holder from a pillowcase, he raised it like a glass hammer. Ski treated Buddy to an *owly* bead. Quite subtly, he drifted a little closer to Ronnie. Buddy gave the lad another sly nod. Ronnie's lower lip quivered when he glimpsed the gun.

Buddy yelled, "I'm gonna split *yer* skull, Welski!"

Ski opened his arms wide, palms up, and sneaked a glance at Ronnie. He edged a little closer to the boy, took a triangular stance, and folded his arms. "Put that thing down, Foley . . . Put it down nice and slow."

Foley put a foot forward and faked a throw. Ski flinched. Buddy laughed.

Ski said, "Why don't we make this as easy as possible?"

"Easy? Sure, you bet, this hunk o' glass is gonna split your skull *reeeal* easy. Right between the eyes."

The officer held up his arms, palms forward as if surrendering, but prepared to block a blow. Again, he edged a little closer to Ronnie. Ski barked, "You get outside, kid! Go stand by the front gate!"

Ronnie took a step.

Buddy seethed, "You move Rix—I'm gonna beat your damn head in." Buddy's mouth twisted; his grin was icy.

Ronnie started to blubber. "I'm goin' outside."

Buddy threatened with the candle holder. Ronnie headed for the door. As he brushed past Ski, he snatched the pistol and backpedaled. Ski's eyes popped open *almost* comically; Buddy's eyes were reptilian. Ronnie's trembling hand pointed the gun at Ski's head. Hands still raised, Ski kept one eye on Buddy, while squaring up with the boy. As he spoke, he was amazingly calm.

"Give me the gun, son. You'll be OK, just give me the gun."

Buddy cajoled, "Shoot him, Ronnie. Shoot!"

Ronnie's finger eased onto the trigger, and he swallowed hard. Ski raised his eyebrows extra high.

Buddy demanded, “Pull that trigger, Rix. Take the shot or I’ll brain Welski with this thing, then I’ll take the gun . . . I won’t shoot you . . . I’ll kill you nice and slow.”

Ronnie lowered the pistol a might, pointing it at Ski’s chest. He closed one eye and looked down the barrel. Ski reached out for the gun.

Buddy coaxed, “That’s it, Ronnie, good move. Heart shot. He ain’t got a chance.”

Ronnie trembled again. Anger, hatred, fear crossed his face—his twisted expression fused.

Buddy connived. “We can go to Mexico, just like we said. You won’t have to go back to detention or live at that stinkin’ foster place no more. We’ll have it made down in Mexico. Total freedom! We’ll kick ass!”

Ronnie bristled, “Shut up, Buddy! Just shut your damn mouth! We can tie him up. Real tight. Take him back to the barn and hide his car. Nobody’ll find him for days . . . We can get clean away!”

Ski tipped his head curiously.

Buddy talked through his teeth, “We’re in this too deep, you little idiot! They’ll lock us up and throw away the key. You won’t go to *kid’s* jail after this—you’ll be in with them old bastards. Things happen to guys in there. I wasn’t kiddin’ about what I told you? Bad things, sick things happen every day.”

With stuttering dread, Ronnie said, “W-Will I r-really go there?”

“Hell yeah! After this—hell yeah!”

Ski remained silent, winked, wiggled his fingers, signaling for the gun. Ronnie shook his head "no". Ski nodded "yes".

Silence all around. Glances from one to another.

Ronnie asked Ski, "How long would I be in jail?"

Ski allowed a lengthy pause. "Probably not for too long—if you hand me that gun."

Ronnie fought the confusion; indecisiveness whirled. He pulled back the hammer and took careful aim at Ski's head. The boy choked on his words. "Sorry, Sir. I gotta do it."

Buddy's eyes bulged and his jaw dropped. Ski's expression was sour. Ronnie screamed, "I can't!" He threw the gun into the middle of the floor. Ronnie fled the room. Buddy threw the crystal and lunged for the gun. He rolled, jumped up, stood with feet wide apart, and aimed the pistol at the center of Ski's forehead. Deputy Welski dropped his chin. He bowed his head as though accepting defeat . . . awaiting his doom. He humbly offered his hands in abject submission.

Ski tried negotiating. "It's not too late, Buddy. You're a young man. Do your time . . . a couple of years. When you get out, you'll be able to turn your life around."

Buddy glowered. "Too late. And it's *definitely* too late for you, so you might as well shut your damn mouth. After I blow your brains out . . . I'm headin' down to *Meh-hee-co*!"

Ski's eyes pleaded with Buddy. The gunman's eyes were as cold as death. Ski's whimpering was pitiful. "So go ahead . . . go ahead, pull the trigger. You'll regret it for the rest of your life."

"I always figured you were chicken guts," Buddy scoffed. He secured the gun with both hands, grinned gleefully, and slowly squeezed the trigger. Click . . . click, click, click . . . Ski's voice was bold and reverent. "I haven't carried a loaded gun since Korea."

Ski was well prepared to dodge the gun. Buddy threw it. The deputy dove forward and tackled him. Buddy struggled, but Ski had him straddled. With a swift elbow to the jaw, Buddy was out cold. Ski rolled him over and cuffed him.

With Buddy trapped, kicking and hollering, in the back of the police car, Ski and Ronnie stood near the passenger door. Ski solemnly and somewhat philosophically lectured. "Listen, I know you were really scared. You were in a tough situation—life or death, as far as you could tell anyway. Anybody would have been scared. But you had the strength to defy that guy. He's nuts, he's dangerous, you know that as well as I do—but you showed you had guts. I don't know how the hell you ever got hooked up with Foley, but he's no good and never will be. So, take this as a lesson and trust that you found something inside yourself that most people never will. Now you gotta figure out how to do something with it."

Ronnie's attitude was nervous, impatient, but respectful.

Ski took a few seconds to choose his next words. "It took some real courage to throw that gun, even though you were scared to death, even though you ran, it took guts to take a risk like that—that showed genuine strength of character," Ski stroked his chin and continued, "but if you had made the decision to hand me that gun, that would have been something way more powerful—an act of honor. I don't remember who said it, but a really smart man once said, 'The only thing a person can have greater than courage is honor'. Those aren't the exact words, but it's the meaning of 'em that matters."

While Buddy continued to yell furiously and kick wildly at the barrier screen, Ski finished his sermon. "You're gonna come to a lot of crossroads in your life . . . everybody does. And some of those roads are gonna be scary and dangerous—probably more scary and dangerous than what happened here. Every time you face uncertainty and have to make the hard choice—especially when there's a risk or sacrifice, be sure you can live with it—if you can do that, you'll be a step closer to the end of your journey... Somewhere along the line you're gonna face something big, way bigger than yourself. And it can happen in a split second, you won't have time to think . . . Win or lose, live or die, you'll reach the point where you have to take action. Right or wrong, good or bad, you're gonna have to live with what you've done. It may take some time, but if you can find a way to do that—even if you have to forgive yourself—you'll know you have strength, you'll know you have courage, and you'll know you have honor . . . Once you've earned it, you'll have it forever."

The inevitable incarceration of Ronnie Rix was born of a devastating event that had occurred in September of 1960. Ronnie's mother, Mary, a nurse at the Brayton nursing facility, had taken a leisurely stroll to the banks of the Caulder River. For certain, the Caulder had nothing on the Mississippi; it was relatively narrow and shallow. In places, the rapids were swift, strong, and plenty *raftable*; occasionally, a nice swimming or fishin' hole sprang up; lots of rocky islands, great and small cropped up, providing platforms for picnics and fireworks shows; blackberries and huckleberries flourished throughout its trim of woods. The river provided a lush habitat for skunks, rabbits, bobcats, white-tail and mule deer, and more birds than you could shake a stick at. Then there were coyotes (often heard, seldom seen), and extremely rare sightings of bears and mountain lions. In the winter, ice built up along the banks, but the river never completely froze. In the summer, its waters invited wading, swimming, splashing fun, and could offer a bath—if you had a bar of soap.

A mile walk from her home, Mary would often take this pleasant trek to gather wildflowers and huckleberries. The family dog, Tonga, a black Lab, always tagged along. As do most Labrador Retrievers, Tonga loved the water. After the foraging, Mary would walk Tonga to one of the deep pools that formed between stretches of rapids during the summer months. Fetching a stick was Tonga's favorite game. But on this day, the cruel hand of fate had stirred up a strong undertow and the dog got caught in its grip. Mary ran along the rocky island calling her pet, but the current was churning and mighty. Up ahead was a snarl of debris, commonly known as slash. If pulled under the twisted branches and brush, Mary knew Tonga would drown. So, she went in.

Tragically, both became trapped beneath the slash and drowned. Ronnie's father had never been in the picture—reason never disclosed. So, orphaned at age 11, Ronnie was assigned to a state group home. After more than two years in this lonely, restrictive limbo, Ronnie decided to run. While hitchhiking, he was taken under the wing of ex-convict Buddy Foley. In the winter of '63, they began a burglary and vandalism spree that lasted nearly six months.

Buddy was sent to prison for two years. Ronnie was considered a juvenile and had to spend a year in "reform" school. While locked up, Ronnie became a voracious reader. Among his favorite books were *The Red Badge of Courage, All's Quiet on the Western Front, For Whom the Bell Tolls, The Naked and the Dead*—all accounts of war, courage, and honor. From a world history textbook, he learned of an ancient Greek concept called *eudaimonia*—reaching the ultimate level of achievement in any endeavor. Recalling the words of Deputy Welski, embracing the ideals of the ancient Greeks, Ronnie vowed to redeem himself . . . to cleanse his societal soul. He would approach every crossroad with courage . . . he would strive to attain the eudaimonia of honor.

CHAPTER 4

August 1965

To provide points of reference and a frame of context, what follows is a quick trip down memory lane 1965—from the perspective of youth and innocence. The Beatles, in Nehru jackets, played at Shea Stadium that August. A favorite movie for young people was *The Sound of Music*, though few males from ages 12 to 25 would have openly admitted it. Skateboards quickly became the rage; we all wanted one more than just about anything. Those who could "swing the deal" had three-speed, Sting-ray bikes with banana seats and sissy bars. But back in those days, my friends and I simply accepted such dream wheels were well beyond our means. Instead, we made "Frankenstein" bikes from parts found at the town dump.

Then there were Superballs, which were sold out wherever you'd go. If you were lucky enough to find one, the first time you bounced it over a house (as shown on the TV commercial), it was lost forever. Aurora monster models were also among the coolest of the cool—the cat's pajamas. And kids loved the new canned food sensation Spaghetti-Os. As for TV shows, the old west comedy *F-Troop* inspired a lot of backyard play and Liz Montgomery kept our eyes glued to the screen as the star of *Bewitched*. Lots of girls (and women) wore mini-skirts and white go-go boots. Boys wore surfer shirts and black Converse Chuck Taylor high-tops. And nobody could decipher the words to the year's number one song "Wooly Bully". It turned out the song was named after the pet cat of the Pharaohs' lead singer, Sam the Sham.

The terrifying Watts riots burned their way into history. Hurricane Betsy tore up the Bahamas, Florida, and Louisiana. Cassius Clay had just changed his name to Muhammad Ali. He later knocked out Sonny "The Bear" Liston with a "phantom punch". President Lyndon Johnson sent the first ground troops to Vietnam and criminalized the burning of draft cards. Ed White was the first American to walk in space. Gemini 5 splashed down after a record eight days in space. CIGARETTES MAY BE HAZARDOUS TO YOUR HEALTH had to be printed on every pack.

The Jets signed Joe Namath for $427,000; it was said no athlete would ever be paid more. We loved to watch the magical running of Chicago's Gayle Sayers. The Green Bay Packers were NFL champs. The Celtics ruled the NBA; these were the days of Wilt Chamberlain and Bill Russel. The Astrodome hosted the first indoor baseball game. In the World Series, the Dodgers knocked off the Twins four games to three.

This was the world we knew, and we gave no thought about it ever ending. Without a care, we foolishly took these time-fragile days for granted. As Ben Franklin said, "When the well is dry, we know the worth of water." But memories are magical; they flow forever in the bittersweet fountain of nostalgia.

Most of the acreage surrounding the town of Rye Grass was covered with spring wheat and ryegrass. Barring drought and fire hazards, the harvesting and shipping of crops provided plenty of work during the summer months. It was a great seasonal job for high-school boys. They could save enough money for all the little teen luxuries: record albums, cool threads, and junk food. Those with the discipline to defer their gratification saved up to buy a junk car so they could turn it into a hotrod with flame decals, and a human skull in the back window with eyes that lit up when you stepped on the brake. Yep, if you had a car, you had it made; you could drive your girl to the Union City drive-in theater and make out. From days of the first outdoor movies in 1933 to the George Jetson days of 1965, this was likely the primary reason teenage boys wanted automobiles.

⚜

Summertime. It was Thursday, August 19, 1965. In the middle of a hayfield strewn with wire-bound bundles, Ronnie Rix wore a Brylcreem haircut kids called the “Mormon-boy”. He was now 15 and a wiry 5’ 10”. Wearing his signature Los Angeles Dodgers t-shirt, he stood on a flatbed truck shading his eyes from a glaring sun. Even though it was still quite early, the heat was unpleasant; the thermometer would easily break 100 degrees before noon. The weather had been blistering hot for more than a month.

Ronnie dragged a hay bale toward the truck and heaved it high. He gazed across an amber sea of wheat and ryegrass, mildly sunburned and supremely annoyed. He did a radar scan for everything and anything incoming. A skosh of relief dawned on his face when he saw a pickup rounding a distant curve. The blessed sighting ignited a burst of energy, spurring Herculean strength, allowing him to buck and stack two more hefty bales.

The truck entered the open gate, rambled the dusty road, and parked not far from the flatbed. Dominique Toussaint, a man in the autumn of his years, stepped out of the passenger side. He gave Ronnie a wave and a nod. He was dressed in a clergyman’s frock, including a Roman collar, and lily-white gloves. His face was lean, deeply lined, and tanned. He had black, horn-rimmed eyeglasses and silvery hair cropped short; it was neatly combed and held in place with a few drops of Vitalis. His book-balancing posture made him a little above average in height. Another man rounded the back of the pickup, a Mexican gentleman in his mid-30s named Phil Trujillo. Trujillo's trousers had holes in both knees; his white t-shirt was stained with grimy oil and blotches of purple berry juice. A little shorter than average, he had a Pomade coif with a Superman curl, slicked back sidewalls, and a modest DA. His face was happy, his eyes smiled. In a native French accent, Father Dom introduced him. "Ronnie, this is Phil Trujillo. He just started working at the farm, and he's going to be doing a little bit of everything."

Ronnie nodded. "Nice to meet you, Mr. Trujillo."

"Just Phil," said Trujillo. "No mister, just Phil." Trujillo clapped his hands, "I hear you play a little baseball."

"Yeah. I've been playin' since I was, I dunno, about seven or eight."

Phil pointed at Ronnie's t-shirt. "A Dodgers fan. I'm from Fresno—I love that team!"

"My favorite, too. And I get to visit their home park in a couple of weeks."

"Holy cow, man! What's the story?!"

"Baseball—the West Coast Regionals. Anybody who made the All-Star team gets to go."

Phil acted like he was playing maracas as he danced toward Ronnie, "All-Star, let me shake your hand!"

Ronnie jumped down from the truck, looking bashful. He said, "Yeah, I play first base. I get to pitch a little, but the coach keeps me mostly at first."

"Well, first baseman, meet an old second baseman. I wasn't much of a slugger, but I could usually get on base. I never could pitch worth beans, though. Will you get to see the Dodgers?"

"No, they're out of town that week. They have a series with the Mets in New York. But we do get to see the Angels play the Giants . . .We'll be in the *knothole* seats, but I have no complaints."

"That's right, never look a gift horse in the mouth, man—any view's a good view."

Father Dom slipped a word in edgewise. He opened his palms and shrugged. "Where on Earth is Toby?"

Ronnie scowled, "Darned if I know. He was gone when I woke up. I told him, about ten times, we were gonna be balin' today." Ronnie put his hands on his hips. "I tell ya one thing . . . he ain't gettin' no Snickers bar."

"Certainly not. He knows our deal. Fair is fair."

"If I may ask," said Phil. "Who is Toby?"

Father Dom and Ronnie looked at each other and smiled. A brief silence. Father Dom gestured and gave Ronnie the floor.

"He's the grandson of a famous baseball player—Eli Gussard—from this town."

"Aye, aye, aye. This I did not know. He is royalty!" Phil raised his eyebrows," How old is Toby?"

"I ain't sure. To me he seems kinda old, but I don't know. . ."

"Toby is 33 years old," said Father Dom. "He lives out at the chapel with Ronnie and me. The three of us make a good family."

Ronnie started to speak, then hesitated and looked at Father Dom. "Go ahead, Ronnie, you can say."

"Well, Toby is sort of, oh, um, sort of . . .well, he's old, but he's like a little kid, maybe more like . . . he sorta has the mind of a child. And I guess I should tell ya he gets mad sometimes. He sorta throws baby tantrums." Ronnie struggled for his next words. "And you'll notice right off that he looks kinda different—some people even think he's scary-lookin' . . . like a, uh . . . Well, you'll see him."

Phil offered Ronnie a look of understanding. "It is all fine. He is like us all—a child of God. I would like to be his friend."

"I better warn you—if you ever work with him, don't ever underestimate him. He might look funny, but he's smart in a lot of ways. He can't talk real well, but he understands every word you say. And he takes advantage of people who think he's dumb. He's sneaky, and he steals."

"All very good to know, my friend. He won't get away with anything with me."

Father Dom counted the bales on the back of the flatbed. He walked in a semi-circle and pointed at the hay bales yet to be loaded.

"There's about 100 bales out there," said Father Dom. "Let's keep the loads at 40 a trip." He glanced up at the sun. "The weatherman says it could hit 106 today, so let's just do one load."

Ronnie put his hands on his hips. "If Toby was here, we'd have it loaded in an hour."

Father Dom asked, "Phil, do you think you could move those irrigation pipes and get back here by 10 or so?"

"Oh yes, easy."

"Okay. I'll take the Ford out when we get back and go on a search for Toby." He turned to Ronnie. "Do you have plenty of water?"

"Yeah, I got enough. And I have a jelly sandwich," Ronnie looked out at the daunting bounty of hay. "Maybe Phil should come back at 11 or so. Those darn things are heavy. Toby can throw 'em up there like they're rag dolls. If I'm on my own, it'll take till around 11. After that, I'm gonna ride my bike into town."

Phil and Father Dom headed back to the pickup. Phil saluted. "See you at 11, All-Star."

"Let's make this the last chore for the rest of the day, Ronnie," called Father Dom, shading his eyes. "And maybe we'll take tomorrow off too. The whole day!" The men drove off.

Ronnie went back to dragging and hucking bales of hay. After thirty murderous minutes, he leaned back against the truck for a breather. He had been so focused on his work he had not noticed the smoke massing in the northern hills. "Man, there's gotta be a fire up there. A big one." His ears perked to a faint rumble, then there was a blast. Unlike thunder, it did not build gradually or roll on and on. He stared at the hills for minute or two. "That was weird. They must be blowin' stumps . . . hard to believe, in this heat. . . Doesn't make sense." Orange flames blinked within grey-black plumes. "Jeez, the whole darn hillside's on fire. What the heck is goin' on up there?!"

Ronnie grabbed a red baseball cap from the seat of the flatbed. The white letter "M" was stitched onto the front. He pulled the bill way down and headed across the field to fetch a bale. His process: hunch over, drag a bale up to the tailgate, drop his weight, and groan as he heaved the itchy bundle onto the truck bed. After eight bales, he was soaked with sweat. At least an hour had gone by. Ronnie reached under the truck to find the discarded Mogen David bottle that held his water. He pulled the cork and swigged the bottle dry.

In the roasting heat, Ronnie did a double-vision, double-take when he saw the laggardly Toby Gussard peddling down the access road. He ran and met his tardy helper at the gate. Throwing his arms out and looking duly peeved he scolded, "It's about time, Toby. Where the heck were you . . .down at the stupid chicken coop again? Why don't you just move into that thing? It can be your private apartment."

Toby's potbelly filled out his overalls. His head was lopsided, and his ears were elephantine, and set a little low. He had a pimply rash all over his face. Toby appeared tall because he walked up on the balls of his feet, in a tip-toe fashion. Four of his upper front teeth were missing—in his case, a consequence of institutionalization; often mental patients with a penchant for biting (others or themselves) were required to have their *cutting* teeth pulled. Toby jumped off his bike. As he carefully pushed down the kickstand, his fingers formed a quick, compulsive net over the precious toys and trinkets in his handlebar basket. Without exception, he referred to himself in third person. With uncharacteristic exuberance, he said, "Toby come, Toby here. Toby work now, Ronnie. Toby work." He ran for a bale of hay. Carrying it back like a May Day flower basket, he tossed it high onto the truck bed. The truck bounced.

Ronnie's expression turned to suspicion. He knew something was not quite right. With one eye closed, he watched his helper's every move. Toby had deliberately been avoiding eye contact.

Ronnie wanted to get to the bottom of things. "You're acting kinda guilty or something, Toby. What have you been doin'?"

"Toby good. Toby work. Get all done. Get Snickers."

In Ronnie's mind, Toby was about as innocent as a fox with feathers on his mouth. Knowing Toby was on guard and would be hard to pin down, Ronnie decided to give him a little rope. He pretended to completely drop the subject and climbed onto the truck to stack bales. "Keep 'em comin', Toby. No messin' around. We got about an hour to get this done."

A few miles south stood a hill of tall ryegrass. Atop the mound, near a spreading horse-chestnut tree, stood a quaint wishing well and a small wooden shed. At the back of the shed, a stovepipe poked out of the wall; it was braced-up to form a chimney. A small oil drum sat on a rusty iron stand. In front of the shed were an aluminum feed bin and a wooden watering trough. Orrin Betters, age 11, red-striped surfer shirt, looked around expecting to see four merry goats competing for his attention. Their absence was beyond conspicuous. "They must be down by the creek," he thought. "They usually hear us and come running." Orrie carried a small wooden sign and walked up to the wishing well. He set the sign on the ring of the well, against one of the posts that held up the small, gabled roof. He stood back and read the board's message aloud: WISHES ARE THE WINGS OF DREAMS. He looked at the man who was peering up into the branches of a cherry tree. "What does it mean, Ski?"

Deputy Robert "Ski" Welski turned to take a gander at the sign. "I'm not really sure, Orrie. But I think your mom wants it to be deep . . . It reminds me of something a beatnik might have thought up in a poem."

"I don't think mom would make a beatnik sign . . . There's a beatnik place in Tacoma, close to grandma's house—'The La Boheme', it's called. I wanted to go in there, but mom wouldn't let me. She used to make jokes about the place."

"I don't blame her. All you'd see is a bunch of people sitting around smokin' and drinking coffee. Their idea of fun is playing bongo drums and reciting bad poetry—really bad poetry."

"Like mom's poems?"

"No, no—it's waaay worse than your mom's poems. Her stuff is award-winning compared to some of the kooky junk beatniks write. Sometimes they all sit on the floor and sway back and forth while they listen to each other's nutty ideas."

"Weird. Gosh, that's a really weird thing for people to do."

"What's weirder is their music—it's called jazz?"

"How does jazz sound?"

"Hmm . . .well, to me, it sounds like everybody's playing a different song."

"Beatniks seem like the kind of people grandma would say 'aren't all there'."

"That would be a compliment."

Orrie looked down the well for a long moment, then dropped his mother's sign into its bottomless depths.

Ski said, "Orrie! Holy smokes—why did you do that?!"

"You said mom wanted it to be deep . . . This well's the deepest place I know."

"Not that kind of deep! I was talking about—beatnik deep. Like Go-Man-Van-Gogh deep . . . Like, you dig what I'm sayin', big daddy-o?"

"Is that how beatniks talk?"

"Yep."

"I'm never gonna be a beatnik."

"I'm mighty glad to hear you say that . . . There's not that many of 'em around these days anyway—something we can *all* be grateful for."

At the wishing well, Ski vigorously cranked the handle that wound the rope and raised the water bucket. The lanky Texan set a filled bucket on the ground, then hooked up another and lowered it into the depths. As Orrie carried two splashing buckets toward the trough, four rowdy goats bounded over the hillside. They circled him—all trying to dip their noses in the water. Back at the well, Ski appeared anxious as he gazed at the distant hillside. "That sure is a lot of smoke—looks like it's coming from the mill.

"Let's just give 'em another three buckets, Orrie. We'll come back and fill the trough to the top later this evening. I gotta get up to the lumber mill and check on that smoke."

Orrie returned to the well with the two empty buckets; he hurried back and dumped two full ones. The goats lapped and lapped. Orrie stared at the hillside as Ski filled a final bucket.

Shading his eyes, Orrie walked across the hilltop to the brink of the sun-burnt meadow. "I think I see little fires glowing through that smoke. They look like blurry little tangerines. The flames must be spreading through the trees."

Ski said, "Yeah, that's a bad fire all right. I'm afraid Malman's mill might have burned to the ground by now. Nothing the firemen can do. They've probably gone back to town. But I'll still drive out there just in case somebody needs help—maybe a ride home."

"Will the fire spread into town?"

"No, it'll never get to town. The Caulder River and its banks are too wide. As far as I know, no fire has ever crossed that river."

"Will it burn up all the trees?"

"Probably a lot of them, but there's no wind, so the embers won't float too far. There are bare spots from old fires and some wide rocky strips of land. I don't believe the fire'll go any farther east than the trestle."

At that moment, a hole formed in the smoke, and after a few seconds, there was a resounding boom.

Orrie gave Ski a perplexed look.

Ski said, "That was dynamite. They keep it at the mill to blow stumps out of the ground. A couple of boxes must have gone off for us to hear it clear out here."

Orrie pointed. "Look! You can see more fire now."

"From bad to worse."

"I wish I could have seen that dynamite blow up!"

"That would have been a sight for sure."

Orrie turned toward the water trough and watched the goats drink their fill. He ran to the shed and came out dragging a half-bag of goat feed. He muscled it up and lugged it toward an aluminum tub. The goats gleefully hopped around as Orrie dumped the feed into the bin. When the animals started munching the grain, he headed back to the shed.

Ski said, "Hold off on that, Orrie."

"The tub's almost empty."

"We'll come back and fill it. We've gotta get back to the car. I'll drop you off with your mom, then go find out what's going on."

As they hurried down the hillside, Orrie complained," I don't see why you and mom don't want me to ride my bike out here anymore . . . Is it because of Toby Gussard?"

Ski lied, "No, not at all. Don't worry about Toby Gussard. He's never hurt, anybody. Anyway, he stays out at the chapel, most of the time."

"Good. He's really ugly—like a monster. Even worse than a monster cuz he's a real person."

"Now that's a terrible thing to say, Orrie. That man can't help the way he looks. My mother used to say, 'There, but for the grace of God go I'."

Orrie raised one brow and squinted one eye. "Okay, I guess I should just be thankful I don't have Toby's disease."

Ski and Orrie snuck away while the goats gobbled the grain.

CHAPTER 5

Outskirts

Stacked bales of hay covered about two-thirds of the truck bed. Toby grabbed the wire bindings of two bales and carried them like lunch boxes. He tossed them at Ronnie like pillows. Ronnie sidestepped the first, but the second knocked him flat. Toby laughed and ran to get more. Ronnie jumped up fuming. He yelled, "Yeah, that's *real* funny, Toby. Keep goofing around and you ain't gettin' a Snickers bar."

Hauling two more bales, Toby protested. There was a wildness in his eyes. "Oh no. Oooooh no. Toby get Snickers. Toby work. Toby get candy. Do be sine cup, Ronnie. Do be sine cup!"

"Just settle down. You want candy—settle down. And take it easy with those bales. Don't throw 'em . . . You do that and I'll use my Elvis karate on you." Ronnie did some flashy arm and hand movements and threw a kick as high as his head. He named-dropped Elvis because he knew Toby was a fan of the Mississippian—he always got super excited when Elvis did some karate moves in the movies. Fortunately, Ronnie had him buffaloed—he hadn't had a karate lesson in his life.

"No *karty*. You no hit Toby. No kick. Do be sine cup. Ronnie do be sine cup!"

"I don't know what the heck 'do be sine cup' means. You might as well quit saying it cuz it makes no sense at all . . . Just set the bales up here nice and easy."

Toby was very careful about placing the next hay bales on the truck. "Toby do good, Toby get Snickers. Ronnie no karty!"

"Okay, but you keep doin' good or you're gonna pay for it, buddy . . . Phil's gonna be here anytime and he expects this truck to be full."

Toby ran for a couple of more bales and hurried back. As he lifted one of the bales, he and Ronnie were startled by a muffled vibrating sound. A rattlesnake dropped out of the hay landing near Toby's tennis shoes. The snake rattled loud and fast. Far more scary than dangerous, it took a winding path toward the tall grass. It was a very slow-moving creature. Following closely, Toby easily kept up with the poisonous reptile, without regard for the danger. He reached down for its tail. He said, "Toby get snake. Toby get snake."

Ronnie jumped from the truck and yelled, "Stop! Don't touch it!" Toby keenly eyed the creature, but listened and drew back his hand, then just as quickly he reached again. A few feet away, the snake turned, coiled and lifted its head. It rattled furiously. Ronnie hollered, "Get away from it!" The rattlesnake struck at Toby, missing him by only a sliver.

Ronnie charged, knocking Toby out of the way; he hit the ground hard. Ronnie went down too. The snake struck at Ronnie and clung to his jeans. Ronnie tried to kick it free, but its fangs were hooked. Frantically shedding his pants, Ronnie hopped away. The snake detached and wound its way into the grass. Toby started after it. Ronnie blocked his path and yelled, “Stop! Now!” He displayed another fake karate move and Toby froze. “Get over by the truck!” Toby hesitated and started after the snake again. Ronnie growled and pointed. “Get over there by the truck!” Toby cowed and obeyed.

Ronnie wagged his finger. “Stay there!” He inspected his right leg, up and down, side to side. He rubbed at his calf. “At least it didn’t break the skin . . . Man, that was close.”

Ronnie and Toby were far too engrossed in their harrowing encounter to notice Phil and a fellow farmhand roll up in a pickup. Phil stepped out and his partner drove off. Ronnie quickly stepped into and hoisted up his trousers. With a puzzled look, Phil said, “Did you get ants in your pants?”

Ronnie was still a little breathless. “A rattlesnake. I almost got bit. Toby went after it, and I jumped in between. It snagged my jeans and hung on.”

“Is it still around?” said Phil, peering here and there.

“It took off . . . Toby should darn well know better. He’s been living out in Colorado, and I *know* they’ve got snakes out there.”

“Big ones. Prairie rattlers. The snakes here in Washington are smaller—Western rattlers.”

Ronnie acknowledged, then glared at Toby and scolded, “You know better, Toby! You could be dead by now. You and me both.” Again, Ronnie pointed and wagged his finger, “Go on! Get your bike and head into town.” Toby ran to his bicycle and hurriedly pedaled away. Ronnie yelled, “And don’t go around beggin’ for stuff!”

Phil offered, “There’s plenty of room for your bike. You can ride back with me.”

"Thanks," said Ronnie, "but I'd just as soon ride into town. I'll wash up in the park. I want to visit my friend, Wuzzie, at the cafe."

On the hillside overlooking the Caulder River, pine and fir trees flared from bottom to top. All around, branches crackled and crashed. The forest was a sea of flame, enshrouded by dense black smoke. Tornadic embers swirled like red-orange dreidels. Two-thirds of a flaming cedar toppled and slid down the hillside, splashing into the ever-shriveling river. The days had been windless for more than a month, a blessing of a sort. The fire moved slowly but burned with intensity—as did the morning sun.

Having descended the hill, Ski and Orrie walked up to a dusty, Alamo beige, Pontiac GTO—a '64, the year of the model's release. The 389-cc engine roared and thundered. Ski raced off in a cloud of dust. He switched on the radio just as the song "Telstar" by The Ventures was introduced. Orrie's eyes grew wide as Ski stepped on the gas. Fifty, sixty, seventy, eighty. Orrie turned up the music and they both started to laugh. Orrie stuck his head out the window and opened his mouth; his cheeks flapped; his lips vibrated. He stuck out his arm to feel it wildly undulate, then settled back into the seat. Ski let up a little on the gas.

Orrie asked, "How come Toby lives out at the chapel?"

"He's the last of the Gussard family, as far as anybody knows. The pastor out there in Brayton worked things out so he could stay as a ward."

"Like Bruce Wayne and Dick Grayson?"

At first, Ski didn't pick up on reference. He cogitated. "Oh yeah—Batman and Robin. Yeah, it's sorta like that. Good example."

Orrie rolled up the window and turned off the radio. "What happened to Toby's mom and dad?"

Reluctantly, Ski said, "They got in a bad car accident. It was a sad and awful thing. Toby's mom and dad were very unhappy people. And they became careless."

"How come?"

"It was a long time ago. Their son, Toby, set a house on fire and a man died. So, Toby was sent to a hospital in Colorado. His mom and dad never got over it. They just slowly wasted away.

"Toby stayed at that hospital for twenty years and when the time came for him to leave, Father Dom from the chapel out in Brayton and the town mayor, Charlie Figgs, arranged to bring Toby back home here to Rye Grass. He was given a room and a job and a chance to start a new life. Some say he was allowed to come back out of respect for his grandpa, Elias. That big statue in the park—that's in honor of Toby's grandpa."

"You mean, the baseball player?"

"Yep. That's Toby's grandpa. He got killed in World War I—about 50 years ago. It was during the Battle of Belleau Wood. The Germans had forced the American, French, and British armies into a retreat. Many soldiers were wounded and killed. Elias Gussard was a medic in that battle—do you know what a medic is?"

"Yeah, there's medics on *Combat*. I used to watch that show at grandma's."

"Well, Elias was helping a wounded soldier and got blown up by a bombshell. Whatever was left of him was lost in the deep mud."

"Why isn't it a statue of a soldier?"

"Baseball's mostly what people knew Elias for. He was one of the best Major League pitchers of all time. The town decided to celebrate his life with the image of something he loved, something that people loved him for. They figured that's what he would have wanted."

Orrie turned his head and became quiet. He said softly, "That was a good thing . . . that was the best way."

The GTO was sailing at a smooth 60 mph. Orrie and Ski came upon a black sign with the number 51 etched onto a white silhouette of George Washington. Orrie switched the radio back on. The song playing proved to be an amusing coincidence. Orrie was thrilled to be riding in the GTO while the tune "GTO" by Ronnie and the Daytonas was booming. And Ski surely loved his wheels. He had left the army in 1961—at the age of 27. He was wild and free, a paladin heeding the call of the wind. In '64, he poured all of his stashed Army pay into a masterpiece of a car. He chose the color Alamo beige; it was perfect for a native of San Antonio. Ski brought their speed down to 50, 40, 35. As they neared the city limits, Ski said, "See that totem pole up ahead, and that big eagle on top? That's the high-school mascot."

Orrie read the sign: THE RYE GRASS THUNDERBIRDS.

"The Mighty Thunderbirds—that's why your mom decided to rename the drive-in The Thunder Burger."

"Yeah . . . now I get it. At first, I thought it was a dumb name for a hamburger place."

"I tell ya, Orrie, you're gonna have a good time living here in this little town."

Orrie read a road sign: ENTERING RYE GRASS, POPULATION 1,560.

Ski surveyed the distant hills. Bearing a countenance of futility, he mumbled, "Look at that dang fire. There's no hope." He sighed, "But I'm gonna have to try drivin' up there anyway."

The town of Rye Grass was settled in 1866. It eventually became a steppingstone for the Columbia River basin, which butted up against the Cascade Mountain range. The Cascade Mountains form a barrier that divides Washington into two climate regions: the coast has a warm marine influence, and the weather is often rainy, but it's pleasant; the eastside has a weather pattern similar to that of the Midwest—hot summers and cold winters. North of Rye Grass is the Okanogan Forest, which spreads out wide east to west and all the way up into Canada. To the south, there is mostly prairie terrain, desert-like in places, and sparsely populated. To the east, along Highway 31, is the little village of Brayton. It's known for having a first-rate nursing facility and hospital with a rest home connected (still called an old folks home by most people). Next to the compound are acres of raspberries. The berry farm provides steady employment for the residents of the surrounding area and attracts many seasonal migrant workers. About 20 miles further down the highway is the little town of Wanoocha. Continue east and you eventually cross the Columbia River. From there the road blends into a rapidly expanding community known as Union City. Turn south and soon you're in Spokane, *The Biggest Little City in the Pacific Northwest*. To the west is an old stagecoach stop known as Weston. After that, there's nothing but a long, desolate drive to Interstate 90.

CHAPTER 6

Rye Grass

As you leave Brayton, driving east, you pass nothing but wheat fields, scroungy trees, and thorny blackberry bushes. Continue west for about five miles and you enter the small town of Rye Grass. To the north, you'll find forest-covered hills, a winding river, and after about 70 miles—Canada.

In 1965, there was a business district in the center of town: a feed store and a funeral home running parallel to Main Street. Heading west on Main you passed a movie theater/bowling alley, a beauty salon, an insurance office, a drug store, a tavern, a cafe, and a real estate office. At the west end of Main, on the north side stood the high school, on the south side was a drive-in restaurant. Continue west and you'd come to Maple Street, which intersected Main. There was an elementary school/junior high, a VFW building, and an athletic field to the north. At the south end, there was the town hall complex: the town council building, a post office, the police/fire station, a barbershop, and a church. Splitting the town in half, running north to south, was Rye Grass Road where stood a Mobile filling station, a general store, and public frozen food lockers. Finally, on Main Street, across from the businesses, was Rye Grass Park; it ran for two town blocks, from east to west.

Rye Grass Park was surrounded by a two-and-a-half-foot stone wall. The park featured a scattering of oak and maple trees, flowery bushes, picnic tables, barbecue pits, benches, horseshoe boxes, and a playground. At the center of it all, was a beautifully sculpted marble water fountain. It was seven feet high, gray-white, and displayed a winged angel pouring water into a serpent's mouth. This was one of many landmarks donated by the Elias Gussard Foundation.

At the east end of the park was the bronze statue of Elias Gussard. It's been said the sculptor had spoken to more than a dozen townspeople to help him visualize Gussard's image; in the end, the consensus held that the likeness neared perfection. The playground toys were at the west end of the park. In a lot of respects, they appeared to be relics left over from medieval times. Some were downright dangerous, especially the skyscraping Jack-in-the-Beanstalk slide and the at-your-own-risk merry-go-round. At least the swings were appropriate to the decade—and they were relatively safe. Also at the west end was a two-stall, cinder-block restroom. And lastly, in each corner of the crumbly, stone perimeter, a massive oak tree reached toward the heavens.

Ronnie Rix rolled through the east gate of the park on his Schwinn Sting-ray bicycle, which he had undeniably outgrown. It was a classic model with ape hangers, a banana seat, and a sissy bar. Ronnie had originally installed a speedometer but removed it when he heard Evel Knievel didn't believe in them. He leaned his bike against a tree and hung his red *Malman Loggers* cap on a handle grip. He pulled off his dusty, straw-spangled t-shirt. Most of the debris flew off during a vigorous shaking. The bare-chested lad jogged a few yards and ducked his head deep into the marble angel fountain. He raised up, shook away the water, then scooped handfuls of water to splash the sweat, and grime off his torso.

Ronnie did not see the two girls staring at him from behind a rhododendron bush. Connie Malman was 15, tall, pretty, athletic, and had long black hair. Her best friend Rhonda Stickle was a striking, blonde 15-year-old. Both wore modest cut-off jeans and white, Rye Grass High School t-shirts. Rhonda lowered her mirrored sunglasses to the tip of her nose.

Connie whispered, “The next time he ducks his head, I’m going for the cap.”

“OK. Once he comes up, I’ll run toward the statue and yell something. No, better yet, I’ll pretend to fan myself and say something in a southern accent—like a southern belle from Atlanta.”

As it happened, Rhonda didn’t need to bother with the Scarlet O’Hara routine because Ronnie stayed submerged for a long while, plenty of time for Connie to grab his baseball cap. When he came up for air, the girls were sitting on their bicycles on the other side of the stone wall. Connie waved the cap and laughed. Clowning around, Rhonda struck a seductive pose.

“Connie, you stupid skag! Give it!”

“Come get it,” Connie teased.

Ronnie started toward them. “Just drop the cap, Malman! Then get outta my sight.”

Rhonda jibed, “What’s a-matter, Ronnie. Ain’t you man enough to come take it.”

“Shut up, Stickle, you two-bit tramp.”

Rhonda cheered, "Two-bits, four-bits, six-bits, a dollar." She threw back her head in boisterous hilarity.

"Name-calling," said Connie. "Don't kids stop doing that in kindergarten?"

Rhonda said, "Normal people do. But Ronnie'll be doing it for the rest of his life."

Ronnie fixed a baleful stare on Connie, and then Rhonda. "If you weren't girls, I'd clean your clocks."

Rhonda could not resist. "Rough tough cocoa puff, pick your nose and eat the stuff."

"That's really nice language there, Stickle. Real ladylike . . . but I guess that's about your speed."

"My speed's 150 miles an hour." She pretended to rev a motorcycle. "Vroom, voruuuum!"

Connie laughed and waved the cap. "Here it is, Ronnie." She rolled up the cap and stuffed it down the front of her t-shirt. "All you gotta do is reach in and pull it out." She and Rhonda let out a resounding *Woo Hoo*!

Ronnie charged them, but they took off on their bicycles. He stopped and looked back at his bike and realized they'd be long gone by the time he even got mounted. Laughing as they glanced back, Connie yelled, "Come and get it, hotshot!"

Hands on hips, Ronnie raged. "You stupid skags! I hate your guts! You're skags! Both of you! Skags!!!"

Further down the road, a kitty-corner from the high school, atop a run-down restaurant was a sign reading THUNDER BURGER DRIVE-IN. Beside these words was another sign: a gigantic, cloud-shaped hamburger being skewered by a yellow lightning bolt. The dining room featured a big picture window. The sign on the door read CLOSED. Across the gravel of the vacant parking lot, rolled a beige GTO; the car disappeared behind the building.

Amid walls of knotty pine, were four booths, four tables, a Wurlitzer jukebox, and a pinball machine called "Gladiator". Tacked along one wall were the 45 rpm jackets of various rock n' roll artists: The Beatles, The Beach Boys, Elvis, James Brown, The Dave Clark Five, Petula Clark, The Ventures, The Rolling Stones, and Herman's Hermits. Posted near the front door was a Rye Grass High School football calendar. High on the wall above the service counter was the trophy head of a four-point buck; it was wearing a red hillbilly hat. Ski and Orrie entered the dining room through the back-corner door. Orrie went right to the pinball machine and pretended to play. Ski called out, "Rain, we're back. Where are you?"

Although 28-year-old Lorraine "Rain" Betters was very pretty, the first thing people noticed about her was the deep gouge on the left side of her face—a permanent scar. She wore a white uniform and apron. Her dark brown hair was in a ponytail. Her lipstick and nail polish were bright red. She came out of the kitchen with a leaning stack of pancakes and placed them on the center table, alongside a saucer of butter and a bottle of Aunt Jemima syrup.

Rain said, "Hurry up and eat. I wanna open for business early. The mayor put up a sign outside the Runnin' Bear last night sayin' the Thunder Burger is serving breakfast for lunch."

"I didn't know we were gonna do that."

"We weren't. It was one of his unfunny little practical jokes."

"That darn guy. With three jobs, you'd think that'd be enough to keep him occupied."

He's coming down here pretty soon to tell us what's happening with that fire."

Ski tried to smile. "Well, that's decent of him. And as for breakfast—if people can't afford burgers, I doubt we're gonna be selling many hotcakes."

"I just put a quarter in the jukebox," said Rain. "Why don't you guys play something?"

Ski walked to the record machine. "What do you wanna hear, Orrie?"

"'North to Alaska'. No wait—'The Battle of New Orleans'!"

"Good ol' Johnny Horton. I saw him play out in Tacoma a couple of times—him and Shotgun Red. That was back when I was stationed at Ft. Lewis. Ol' Buck Owens played out there a couple of times too . . . Man oh man, those sure were some good times." The turntable spun and a banjo introduced a novelty song about an 1814 American tiff.

Rain propped open the door to the early morning heat. "I still haven't figured out whether it's hotter with the door open or closed."

Ski went around opening the windows. "I'd say it's about the same. If we open things up, at least we'll get some fresh air."

A brown, '59 Pontiac with a cracked windshield pulled into the parking lot; its brakes complained as it ground to a stop. Ski and Rain walked out to meet Mayor/tavern owner/pawn broker,

Charlie Figgs. He slid his skinny, wrinkled body out of the car and pulled a pack of Winstons from the pocket of his bowling shirt. He offered to share. "Goin' once, goin' twice." Ski and Rain declined.

"Gonna hit the lanes today, Charlie?" joked Rain.

Figgs smiled and his eyes twinkled, "It's the only clean shirt I had!"

Ski gazed up at the hillside and said, "Doesn't look like there's much we can do about that fire."

'Nothin' we can do—nothin' at all. We didn't even take the fire truck up there. Lester tried to drive up a little ways, but the smoke got too thick—and it was pitch black."

Ski said, "There ain't gonna be anything left of that mill. I don't think even the tools and equipment will be salvageable."

"Nah, that whole place is a total loss. But Lester's got good insurance. He'll make out all right. He said he's actually lookin' forward to rebuilding."

Rain decided to let the men talk. She went back inside.

"Those clouds are billowing to the east. Must be a little breeze higher up," said Ski.

"That's usually the way of things."

"Has Lester got any idea of how it started?"

Figgs' hands went palms up and he shrugged. "He don't know. He said he blew a fuse up there a couple of weeks ago. He figured an old refrigerator in a storeroom might have shorted out. The outlets and switches he's got up there go back to the '20s. Rats, mice, sometimes squirrels'll chew on the wires."

"I suppose an electrical short is about all it could be. Buddy Foley's locked up, so we know he didn't torch the place."

"Him throwin' that dynamite—wasn't that somethin'!"

"Yeah, I heard about that. It was a couple of months before I moved up here. He got a year for it, didn't he?"

"Six months. They babied the little punk."

"Them doin' that just makes my job that much harder. At least the Bonnie and Clyde act'll keep him in there for a while this time."

"Think so?"

"Not really."

"I tell ya, he made a passel of money selling steelhead and rainbow trout. It didn't do him a darn bit of good, though. And he's still got it in for Lester for turning him in. Hell, Lester ain't the one that turned him in. The fool went around braggin' about it. And there were at least twenty witnesses. It's no wonder that after he got out, nobody around here wanted a thing to do with him. When he left town, he said he'd get back at Lester, if it was the last thing he ever did. Then, the next thing you know, he got out and started all that outlaw crap—thieving and bustin' things up—a genuine Jesse James."

"And that's where I came in. He told me he was gonna shoot me, burn me, stab me. I had to listen to his insults and threats all the way to the county jail. They kept him two days, then bussed him down to Tolawaka."

"Best place for him." Figgs flexed his brittle old neck. "When's he actually gettin' out? Must be some time soon."

Neither man had seen Rain wander back out. She blurted, “Soon? Attempted murder of a police officer? For land’s sake!” She rolled her eyes. “What’s this world coming to?”

Ski calmly said, “Rain, I’ve told you the story. The gun was empty.”

On the verge of tears, she said, “He didn’t know that gun was empty! If it hadn’t been empty, he’d have emptied it into you!”

Figgs got angry. “I agree, by God! That’s exactly what Foley would have done. They should throw away the damn key! He doesn’t belong out among decent people. Every time I think about it, I get so damn mad—”

Ski sighed, “Well, I gotta blame myself—at least a little. I should never have let Ronnie grab that gun . . . I was just trying to teach him a lesson. In the end, the one who learned the lesson—was me.”

Figgs fumed, “Buddy’ll never learn his lesson. He’s always been rotten to the core. And when he said he’d be coming back to get you and Lester—you better damn well take him seriously.”

Rain gave Ski a cold look. “You told me the *getting revenge* business was all over with.”

Ski exhaled in exasperation. He said, “As far as I’m concerned—it is over with. I never did pay it much mind in the first place. Just some spiteful words from a hot-headed kid. I don’t figure he’ll ever come back around here.”

Figgs stood in the doorway and looked up at the burning hillside. “That smoke is getting blacker and blacker. The air around here is gonna be full of pitch soot for two weeks.”

Figgs was getting fidgety. He pulled the wallet from his back pocket and searched its contents. Reaching the brink of frustration, he pulled everything out. “There it is.” He handed Ski a card. “You better call Tolawaka, Ski. If Fuller’s out, I can guarantee he set that damn fire. No tellin’ what else he’ll do.”

“Those people at the prison said they’d keep us posted. Maybe he messed up and got himself another year?”

Rain and Figgs got tight-jawed. Rain finally said, “Do what Charlie told you, Ski—call those people.” Ski nodded in agreement.

They all focused on the fiery hillside. Rain said, “Look, Charlie, there’s another one startin’ right over there.”

“I believe you’re right.” Figgs squinted at the sun. “We’re in a fix . . . I gotta admit—I’m a little worried about that breeze shiftin’ and drivin’ it west. Not much of a chance—but possible.”

Rain asked, “Will we get any help from the state; maybe the National Guard?”

Figgs shook his head, “Nah, no chance. There’s fires from Mexico, up through California, clear up into BC. We’re on our own. If you look east of where it’s burning now, you’ll see a lot of bald spots and lighter areas—that’s from past fires, heavy logging, plowing over and replanting. That’s where it’s all gonna slow down. It’ll burn out at the trestle—it always does.”

“Gosh, it really seems to be spreading fast.”

“That’s cuz things are so darn dry. I mean, it’s a real shame about Lester’s place, but other than that, we’re not losin’ much—a bunch of scrubby old trees that are no good for loggin’ anyway.”

“And you’re sure it won’t cross the river?”

"This town's been my home since the day I was born; no fire's ever crossed that river." He shaded his eyes and told a little lie. "At least that's *one* thing we don't have to worry about."

Rain leaned to one side and glanced around Figgs' shoulder. Her eyes grew wide. Nearly gasping, she said "Oh my God! Here comes Toby Gussard!"

Flustered by the sheer thought, Figgs hurried back to his car. "I can do without seeing that looney bird this morning. I'm making myself scarce—headin' back to the Runnin' Bear. Enjoy your day, folks." Figgs took off. Ski and Rain went back into the restaurant.

Rain glanced back. Toby was pedaling fast. "I feel like locking the place up."

"Oh, he ain't so bad. It's mostly his looks that scares people. I'll see to him. Everybody needs some attention now and then."

Orrie looked up from his pancakes. "What's all the arguing about?"

"Nothin', Orrie," Ski said. "Have some more flapjacks."

"Flapjacks." Orrie mused. "Sounds like something a cowboy would say."

"I'm from Texas—I am a cowboy!" Ski and Orrie laughed.

Rain whispered, "I think Toby Gussard is dangerous, Ski—with that weird little bow and arrows he carries around."

Ski muffled a laugh. "That bow wouldn't shoot five feet. He made it out of a dry old stick and a piece of yo-yo string. That sorry old thing'll probably break in half before the day's over."

Rain held her tongue, moved to the picture window, and tapped her fingernails against the sill. Ski stood in the doorway. Toby rolled to a stop in the middle of the parking lot, leaned his bike on its kickstand, and rummaged through the peculiar items in the handlebar basket. He looked up at Ski with a grinning, half-toothless maw. He had bound crow feathers around his head with a loud, green necktie. Toby pulled the crude bow over his shoulder and dangled it from the handlebars. He yanked at a strand of twine and loosed a coat-sleeve quiver from his belt. He laid the makeshift sheath on the ground; it was full of crudely whittled, crooked arrows. Toby rummaged through his junk and untangled a wad of yarn from around a large ceramic Santa Claus mug. He raised the mug high and declared, "This my favorite! Toby favorite! Oh boy, oh boy, oh boy!" He went back to foraging.

In a low tone, Rain said," He better not try bringing that bow in here. You're the law, Ski. You can take it."

"Yeah, I could take it. I could bust it up and throw it in the trash—but he'd make another one—maybe a better one. If he has to keep making new ones, he might actually make something dangerous, just by dumb luck. As long as he's happy with his goofy toys, we may as well just let him be."

Rain looked Ski square in the eye. "I also heard he sneaks around looking in people's windows. He's creepy . . . You've got to admit that."

"People around here are well aware of Toby Gussard. There's a hundred pairs of eyes trained on him when he's in town. Generally speaking, people are pretty understanding, and they trust Father Dom's discretion in giving him some leeway—he has to have some kind of life."

Some of the items in Toby's basket were stuffed inside a construction-worker hard hat. He pulled a plastic flute from the hat and played an erratic tune. He tooted, he babbled, his head bobbed up and down. He took a deep bow before an audience that only he saw, then held the flute like a microphone and began to sing the theme song to a television western called *Cheyenne*. He knew all the words and crooned like Crosby. Though parroting the lyrics, he carried the tune well. His performance was more than respectable.

Rain's jaw dropped. Ski chuckled. They were incredulous. Rain turned the CLOSED sign to OPEN. Both listened and thoroughly enjoyed Toby's rendition of the lonesome, baritone ballad.

Ski said, "The guy can hardly talk but he sings pretty damn well. I've read about such a thing. They call it—idiot somethin'. People have told me when he's down there at that old chicken coop, back behind the feed store, he plays with a jar of buttons and sings his heart out. I figured it was just a grinding of the rumor mill. But sure enough—we've seen it with our own eyes."

Rain still appeared ill-at-ease as she walked around the counter. "So, what has Father Dom told you about Toby and that hospital?"

"We've had lots of talks. The hospital claimed he was friendly and cooperative for the most part. They said he had a job making birdhouses. There was a little thrift shop on the grounds where the odds and ends the patients made were sold. Toby usually spent most of his money on candy, chips, pop—and weird junk like he has in that bike basket."

"So, no violence?"

"They said he'd get mad if other patients teased him. He'd holler and bite his forearms—that's why they're all scarred up. The dentist ended up pulling some of his teeth. But we were told he never went after other people . . . I know the town council has taken up the situation. But to be honest, we all know Toby's not the only oddball in this town. He's got his rights just like everybody else. He's a bona-fide member of the community."

Rain huffed and walked around the service counter. She lit a cigarette and headed into the kitchen. Toby wheeled his bicycle up to the front door. He pointed at the items in his bicycle basket as though he was taking inventory. Finally satisfied, he entered the dining room, walked to the counter and held out his big Santa Claus mug. He flashed a hopeful grin and said, "Coffee? Toby get coffee?"

Rain quickly walked up to the counter, "No Toby. No coffee. Father Dom has told you not to come into town begging for things." Rain gave Ski a hard look.

"That's right, Toby—you know better."

Toby frowned, looked down, and pouted. He spotted Orrie who tried to hide behind the Aunt Jemima syrup. Toby said, "Who dat? Who dat boy?"

Rain scolded, "You never mind—and no coffee!" She pointed to the door. "Now out! Scoot!"

As Toby quick-stepped out the door, he bit his forearm. "No more. Noooo more. Do be sine cup. Do be sine cup!" He bit his arm again. He let out a scream that could have raised the coldest of the dead, then scare them right back into their graves. Toby ranted all the way to his bicycle. He tore off, standing up, pedaling furiously.

Orrie joined Rain and Ski in front of the restaurant. Toby made a left turn after passing the high school. In a blink, he vanished. Ski looked at Rain, Rain looked at Orrie, Orrie looked at them. Ski said, "Well, I'm gonna take a little spin around in the black and white. Mainly just to let folks know I'm on duty." He pinned his badge onto his shirt pocket and headed for the back door.

Rain put her hand on Orrie's shoulder. "You keep away from that Toby Gussard, Orrie. Far away . . ."

"Don't worry. I'll keep *extra* far away from that ugly guy." Orrie yawned. "I'm gettin' kind of bored—could I go home and watch TV for a while?"

"OK, but be back here in an hour. And while you're there—vacuum, wash the dishes, feed Sammy, and take out the garbage."

CHAPTER 7

The Runnin' Bear

Painted at the top of the old west facade were the words RUNNIN' BEAR TAVERN, along with the scene of a grizzly bear on its hind legs chasing a terrified Indian brave. In one dark window was an Olympia Beer sign, in the other a Rainier Beer sign. Saloon-style doors were backed up by a standard door of solid oak. When the days and nights were hot, the main door stayed open, and the swinging doors swung. Buckets of pine-scented fragrance failed to mask the malodorous fumes common to a dive. Above the long mirror behind the bar were carvings. They replicated the "running bear" scene outside. Chaser lights framed the farce. At happy hour, the animated scene was activated. To the sound of growls and screams, a huge grizzly bear chased a terrified Indian brave. After each performance, the mechanism had to be reset by hand.

On a stool at mid-bar hunched 45-year-old Lester Malman. He was a ham-fisted, burly guy; unkempt, unwashed, and always drunk. His red baseball cap was pushed up off his forehead. There were egg-yolk and brown tobacco stains on the chest of his dingy *wife-beater*. Across the room, bartender/Mayor Charlie Figgs, early 70s, rearranged his pawn-shop showcase. The fake gold glowed, and the false diamonds sparkled. Lester drained his frothy beer while Figgs used his bowling shirt to polish the face of an imitation Rolex.

"Damn scratches ain't goin' away. I've tried Windex, floor wax and every other damn thing. 'Bout all I can do now is drop the price."

Lester spoke in a thick-tongued drone. "People don't want any of that crap anyway, Charlie. Garbage can's the best place for all of it."

Figgs moseyed behind the bar and filled a couple of beer glasses. "A real shame about the mill, Lester—wish there was somethin' I could say. At least you kept your insurance paid up." Charlie chuckled, "Like they say—you're in good hands."

"Yeah, you bet," Lester groaned. "Those guys are really on top of things—the only good thing about the whole mess. They're comin' up to make an assessment once those damn fires burn out. How the hell they're gonna assess a pile of ash and burned up buzz saws is surely a mystery to me. It's a total loss—a hundred percent."

"Your place is ruined for sure, Lester. Complete ruination."

"Thanks for the sympathy, Mayor. Makes me tingle all over."

Charlie smirked.

Lester took a swig and a gulp. "Don't pay me no mind, Charlie. Ruined—that's putting things mild. All that's up there now is enough roast squirrels to feed Fort Lewis."

Figgs strolled around the bar and draped his arm over Lester's shoulders. "Us old army buddies gotta stick together. We both fought in a big one and made it through. And I'm gonna help you through this. We can just be glad nobody got hurt."

Lester's voice cracked. "I blame myself. I knew that wiring was bad. I just kept puttin' things off and puttin' things off. And I shoulda done something different with that dynamite. There's a rock cave up there I coulda used. If there ever was a time I could spend a sober minute in my life, maybe I could get my head outta my hind end."

Lester pretended to pound his head against the bar. He moaned like an old bull. "Play something by Hank Williams, Charlie—bartender's choice."

Charlie scanned the selections as he shined up the glass on the jukebox. He finally decided on the fitting lament "There's a Tear in My Beer."

As the song got going, Lester laughed. "Whoa, yeah—good choice." He started singing along. Charlie harmonized. "When's that Queenie comin' in again, Charlie. A dance or two with her might be just the right medicine."

"Take some kindly advice, Lester. Best thing you can do about Queenie is leave her be. You know darn well she and Henny Perky have been shackin' up for over two years. Rile her up and she'll boot you outta here faster'n you can flick a booger."

"I believe she would for sure."

The woman of mention, Regina "Queeny" Causley, grew up in Rye Grass. She was 38, petite and lively. Though often cosmetically generous, she was considered quite attractive. People often commented on her big, blue eyes. Her Toni-Lilt bouffant never had a single auburn hair out of place. Generally, she wore tight Wrangler jeans and a floral blouse. Lester Malman was mesmerized.

A waft of heat and shaft of sunlight snuck into the room when the front door opened. Lester did a double take when Toby Gussard toddled in. Toby was wearing a dented construction-worker helmet. He grinned and presented his Santa Claus mug. “Coffee?” Lester flung a beer mug at the wall; a neon light fell and shattered—smokey snakes crawled into the air. Lester waved his hand, telling Toby to get out. Toby just stood there and grinned. He thrust forward his mug and repeated, “Coffee?” Lester jumped up and started toward him. Figgs was already out from behind the bar. The old man blocked Lester with a shoulder to the gut. Lester side-stepped Figgs and pointed at Toby.

“Get outta here, you goddam mongoloid.” Flecks of spit flew from Lester’s mouth. He seethed. “Go on! Get outta here *aforn* I knock the rest of your damn teeth out.” Lester reared back and wound up to throw a Popeye punch.

Toby ran like a scalded dog. Lester’s cowboy boots stomped out onto the sidewalk—the way a runnin’ bear might chase an Indian brave. Fleeing on his tip-toes, Toby kicked the stand and hopped onto his bike. He was halfway down the block faster than a sneeze. Lester yelled, “You better run, you ugly freak!”

A wheezing mayor Figgs was right on Lester’s tail. Lester held up, still boiling mad. Figgs came up alongside. “Simmer down now, Lester. I don’t want you giving out and droppin’ on me. You’re *like* to have a heart attack.”

Lester huffed, “I ain’t gettin’ no heart attack—not by a long ways . . . I’m just so sick and tired of the freak comin’ ‘round my place—I don’t believe he’s from this Earth, more like one of them mutants on that *Outer Limits* show . . . And why the hell does he always run around on his tippy toes.”

“Toe-walker, they call ’em. They get in a habit of doing that when they’re kids and their feet freeze that way.” Figgs counseled. “I’m surprised at you, Lester. That poor ol’ boy’s been cursed. And keep in mind, he’s a Gussard—a family you’ve always admired. He’s Elias’ grandson—like it or not.”

"I don't know that—nobody does! Who knows who that no-good mother of his had dealin's with. He probably ain't even a real Gussard. They should have thrown him off a cliff as soon as he was born—like them Spartans used to do." Lester looked across the street and stared at the statue of Elias Gussard. If ol' Eli hadn't been blown to bits, his body woulda busted outta its grave. I swear and I mean it—Lord have mercy on the dumb people!"

On the frying sidewalk, Figgs squared up with Lester. "Yeah, on that I agree, but you gotta calm down. Having pity on people like Toby is the Christian thing to do . . . Father Dom keeps pretty close tabs on him, and that hospital told us he was cured—or pretty close to it."

Sweating buckets, Lester walked up to the front of his F-100 pickup, balled up his fist and hammered on the hood. "Life ain't fair, Charlie! It just ain't fair." He headed back through the swinging doors. Figgs followed. Lester stretched and yawned. "I need a beer . . . I need about twenty beers." Plopping down on a barstool, Lester ranted, "That *mutanoid's* head looks like a butt with teeth—gives me the *heaves* just thinking about him."

"If there's a bright side to the situation, Toby won't be sneakin' around up at the mill no more—nothing left for him to get into."

"Yeah, I guess that's somethin'. I'd already had that little situation figured out anyway. I loaded up a shotgun with rock salt so's to blast his behind clear to east Georgia. That would have been the end of that . . . and no matter what anybody says about him bein' 'cured', I think he snuck up there to the mill and lit that fire."

"We all know the story about him settin' that house afire, but he was just a kid, and he's *touched*, if anybody ever was. Them doctors out in Colorado told us he went twenty years without any signs of messin' with fire. And I really do believe Father Dom's keepin' close tabs on him."

"Well, I'm glad you have so much faith and confidence. Me, I don't trust the retarded dummy for nothin'."

Figgs slapped his hand against his forehead. "Doggone it! I told Ski we should call that prison about Buddy Foley." Figgs dialed the Thunder Burger. Rain answered. "Say, this is Charlie. Did Ski find out anything on Buddy Foley?" After a few seconds, Figgs frowned and narrowed his eyes. "If that don't beat all . . . Those people don't know their ass from their elbow . . . OK, I better start spreading the word." Figgs hung up and scowled. With a disgusted sigh, he said, "They let Foley out Monday."

Lester hammered his fist on the bar. "That was three damn days ago! He coulda hitched up here easy. Holy creepin' Jesus! I take it back for blamin' ol' Toby. Foley set that fire sure as anything!"

"The timing's right . . . He made the threats . . ."

"I oughta go out and hunt that dirty bastard down."

"That's the law's job, Lester. I'd be mad too, but you don't want to be getting yourself into legal troubles. He ain't worth it. And Ski's already workin' on it."

"If I see him, he'll wish he never was born." Lester punched the palm of his hand.

"Anything you do—just make sure you're in the right. And the truth is—we don't know for sure if he'll ever come back around this town. He knows he ain't welcome."

"We'll I'm gonna do some lookin' anyway. I got nothin' else to do."

"Best to get your mind off it . . . Maybe talk a little baseball—who do you figure to take the series?"

Lester groaned, "Oooh, I figure Minnesota's gonna take it all. Maybe sweep it."

"Hmm . . . I don't believe it'll be a sweep, no matter who gets in. But Minnesota?"

"It's the pitchin', Charlie. Always comes down to the pitchin'."

"You bet—no argument from me on that."

In the interest of further distracting Lester, Figgs headed for the jukebox and played a bluesy country tune. As he walked back to the bar, the machine spun wax. "This Should Go On Forever" by Wanda Jackson wailed away.

"Man, I love the way that woman sings that song," said Lester.

Figgs drafted Lester another glass of suds. "That better be your last one today if you're gonna be coaching those kids."

"Season's over, Mayor. They turn in their gear and uniforms tomorrow, and I'll probably be drunk when they do. They've all seen me drunk before."

"You're right, you're right. I ain't got a mind anymore. But Ronnie does have that All-Star trip."

"And he darn well deserves it. He's a damn fine ballplayer. But that's his business from here on." Lester stood up and took a blurry-eyed look at the neon sign he had broken. "How much did me bustin' that thing set you back, Charlie?"

"Don't worry about it for now. I know you're good for it."

Lester pulled off his cap and scratched his head. "Some things just don't figure. Elias Gussard was a great man. His son Virgil, he drank a lot there at the end, but he was a normal man, a hard worker, good in school. He had everything going for him, all the ability in the world, but after he inherited his dad's money, he did nothing with his life—nothin'. And we all knew he married the wrong woman—Tula, they called her. I mean she was really good lookin', but as soon as she'd open her mouth, she was about the ugliest thing this side o' Tarnation."

"You ain't just a-whistlin' Dixie, Lester. No truer words were ever spoken."

"Now, add to that crankin' out a freak like Toby—Lord, it can't get no worse."

Figgs struggled to validate Lester's views while offering another perspective—standard bartender psychology. "At least Virgil treated Toby like a human being. All the way 'til he set that fire. But after that old man got burnt up, even Virgil couldn't stand the sight of him. If they wouldn't have had all that family money, Toby would have ended in some nut box out at Eastside. We'd never have seen hide nor hair of him . . . From what I heard—that private hospital out in Colorado was a pretty nice place, I guess that counts for somethin'."

"I never did pay much attention to all that. Never cared about it. Those were the years I was in the service—'42 to '46. And you know, as well as anybody, I wasn't the same man when I got home."

"You're still a young man, Lester. You don't have to end up in an early grave. Quit the drinkin' and you'll be flyin' right in no time." Figgs pulled a bottle of cheap wine from the back of the bar. "This here's what Tula drank—at least a bottle a day. And Virgil, he pretty much lived on whiskey. My late wife, in fact, most of the women in town, warned her all that drinkin' and takin' dope could cause all types of birth *de*fects."

"Famous last words . . . You can lead a horse to water."

"The shoe sure fits for her, but Virgil, he was a good man and I believe he did his best, all things considered. I warned him about his driving every time we crossed paths. Not a lot of folks know the whole story—ol' Sheriff Thompson kept it bottled up."

"I never heard the whole story. But I never did pay things much mind back in those days."

A family of four witnessed the wreck. Virgil was drunk as usual and found himself on a blind curve headin' right for 'em. So, it was either slam into them or a telephone pole. It was bad, *really* bad . . . And it left Toby all on his own—the last of the Gussards. As far as that poor devil goes, I don't think there's a thing anybody can do. The other day Father Dom was tellin' me he thought there was more wrong with him than what that hospital told us."

"Christ! There can't be *too* much more wrong with him!"

Figgs wearily shook his head. "I hear what you're saying. But then there's that Bible verse 'am I my brother's keeper'. To me, that means we all gotta watch out for each other."

"To me, it means Toby Gussard's dumb, ugly butt can rot in Hell."

Figgs looked to the ceiling and said, "I'm lost for words." He headed back to the jukebox to float Lester a not-so-subtle hint.

Lester started to wander the dance floor singing along with Hank Thompson's "Six Pack to Go". He expressed the lyrics with a genuine conviction. When the song ended, Figgs got him a six-pack and he went.

CHAPTER 8

Here and There

In a long, narrow room, resembling a 1940's soda fountain, Walter "Wuzzie" Washam, age 15, filled a tall, shiny coffee pot with water. The counter and stools had recently been upgraded with, then in vogue, bowling-ball red surfaces. Wuzzie had frizzy, orange hair. That, along with his scrawny, spider-monkey frame, earned him many a slung stone of outrageous nicknames. While his buddy Ronnie Rix filled napkin holders, Wuzzie reached under the display glass and replaced old, petrified donuts with new petrified donuts. Ronnie stared through the glass door and surveyed the park. He exhaled dejectedly. "Those skags really got me this time, Wuzzie." No response. He glanced to see if his friend was still in the room. "Did you hear me?"

"What?"

"Connie and that stuck-up snob, Stickle. They know I'll be in hot boilin' water if I don't get my cap back before we turn in our uniforms."

"I have no idea what you're talking about."

"When I was in the park, rinsing off at the fountain, Connie Malman, stole my baseball cap. And that skag Stickle stood there laughing her head off."

"So why don't you just take it back?"

"Reason one: She shoved it down her bra. Reason two: They took off on their bikes, and I don't know where the heck they went. Reason three: Do you think I want people to see me chasin' *her* around?!"

"OK, I get it. They usually come in here around two, two-thirty to drink Cokes and play the jukebox."

Ronnie looked over his shoulder to check the clock. "I've got a day of leeway, but if they stay holed up at Rhonda's house, I ain't got a chance."

Wuzzie clearly wanted to give some advice, but no words came to mind. He stroked his chin and strapped on his thinking cap.

Ronnie rambled, "Yep, I'm in hot water . . . my goose is cooked . . . my ass is grass . . . my . . . what's another one?"

Wuzzie's eyes rolled up toward the creative side of his brain, "Ummm . . . You're screwed, blued, and tattooed?"

"Yeah, that's a good one . . . I forgot about that one."

"So, what's the big deal about the cap?"

"The big deal is—Coach Lester G. Malman is nuts, Wuzzie. Sure, he's a drunk, but he also ain't normal. He's like—sick in the head in some way or another. You should see him before a game: he laughs and cries, tells us he loves us, then yells like a maniac. It's weird, man. Weird and kinda scary. Worst of all—he could put the kibosh on my All-Star trip."

"That'd be a real bummer, man. But you could just pay for a new cap. Problem solved."

"No, no, his brain doesn't think like a normal man, Wuzzie. You've seen how he acts. He'll blame me for being careless and not respecting team property. No tellin' what he'll do. One of his favorite moves is to scream at you like the devil's Dutch uncle, then twist on your ear and pull you around."

"That isn't right. He can't do that. It's assault."

"Yeah, who's gonna arrest him? People would just laugh and think the whole situation was cute."

"Yeah, but his own daughter's the one who stole the cap."

"That doesn't make any difference. And there's no way I'd ever tell on her. I ain't no rat. I mean Connie likes buggin' the hell out of people, but I'd never squeal on her. She'd probably get slapped around at home and locked in the root cellar. There's spiders down there—and that's one of the few things Connie's scared of . . . I heard her dad treats her like that sometimes."

"I've heard that story too. And that isn't right either; it makes me mad. Connie's a big mouth and she can be a bully, but she doesn't deserve to be treated that way. Nobody does." Ronnie started whistling erratically and Wuzzie said, "Man, this thing really *is* bugging you. Every time you get up tight, you start whistling."

"Yeah, people have told me that. I've got to admit, I am a little worried about not gettin' my cap back . . . Wanna go over and sit in the park for a while?"

"I'd better not. I told my mom and dad I'd keep this place open from eleven to eight. And I'm getting paid a buck fifty an hour—a quarter above minimum wage."

"I get minimum for bailin' hay; it's good enough for me—and it helps me build football muscles."

"When it comes down to it, I can close up anytime I want, but dad said he wants me to have a strong work ethic and learn responsibility."

"You already have a strong work ethic; in fact, more than anybody I know."

Wuzzie took a longing look across Main Street. The park was mighty inviting. "Maybe we can meet at the park later—if you come by and help me close up, we could go over there at around eight-thirty . . . I'd feel guilty about closing early. Dad's the only vet around since Doc Barth retired. He and mom work into the night sometimes. This is my summer project, and I don't wanna let 'em down."

"So how many customers have you had today?"

"Two . . . Well, only one that bought anything. Allie Davis and his mom came in for some black cherry ice cream. They buy two quarts to take home every Thursday. And Allie, he still hasn't got a haircut. It looks like he has a tropical grass hut on his head."

"Yeah, like everybody else they're tryin' to save money. It's hot as heck, nobody's got any money. You probably ain't gonna have any more customers for the rest of the day."

"Sometimes nobody comes in—sometimes for days in a row. It gets boring, man, I tell ya. But I've got the radio and some stuff to read. I keep startin' to write a book, a novel, but I just keep writing and fixing the same few pages over and over. I'm still on chapter one."

"What's it about?"

"A cesspool."

"What?!"

"Just listen to the idea—it'll make sense. The cesspool is like a galaxy for all these weird germs: bacteria, amoebas, protozoans. And, like, they have personalities. The highest evolution has got is these horrible tapeworm humanoid creatures. Anyway, there's stuff down there that nobody knows about—like landforms and oceans. I'm trying to figure out a way to get people down there—scientists who do research. I could go with an elixir drink like in Jekyll and Hyde or some kind of gamma rays like what happened to the Hulk. Or . . . I could make it easy and just say the people were already down there without any explanation—sort of a different version of Aquaman."

"Oh, it's a different version all right . . . You know, I'll bet there's a spare rubber room down at Eastside Hospital where you could set up a desk, get a bunch of pens and pencils, and write to your heart's content."

"Yeah, that's really funny there, Bob Hope . . . No, but just think about it for a second—it's a totally original idea!"

"I think I'd keep that idea to myself if I were you, Wuzz. You wouldn't want something like that to get spread around."

"If you've got a better idea for a novel—I'm all ears."

Ronnie rubbed his eyes and massaged the back of his neck. He wearily trudged to the door, "I'm gonna take a look around town for the skags, then head back out to the chapel and check-in." As he headed out, he started whistling.

Wuzzie offered, "If Connie comes in here today, I *would* try to get the cap back, but she can kick the crap out of me in about ten seconds flat."

Holding the doorknob, Ronnie turned and said, "Yeah, don't sweat it, man. I'll figure somethin' out."

Orrie unlocked the door to the little two-bedroom house his mother rented for $80 a month, a goodly sum for the humble hovel. After finishing his chores, he headed to the living room and switched on the TV. *Jeopardy!* was halfway over. He sat on an armchair holding his black cat. The living room decor featured the armchair, a couch with a bedspread to cover the holes, a lamp atop a turn-of-the-century end table, and a shelf with a few trinkets and books. A yellow floral drape covered one window; a bed sheet covered the other. He talked to his cat. "I hate the way they ask these questions, Sammy: "'A dessert featuring pastry and ice cream' . . . 'What is pie a la mode?'—it sounds stupid; it's all backward. Why don't they just say it the normal way?" The cat began to twitch its tail. "Mom says when you do that, you're making a decision. Well, I'm making a decision to give you some Friskies. Then I'm goin' over to the railroad tracks to set a new record for rail walking—338 steps. But first—I'm gonna have a big bowl of Cap'n Crunch."

Back at the Thunder Burger, Rain sat at a table covered with overdue bills, loan statements, IOUs, and fretted over the moths flying out of the cash register. She jotted numbers on a notepad and sighed between cigarette puffs. Ski delivered coffee and took a seat. He said, "So how's the ciphering goin'."

"It's goin'—like if we don't make a profit by the end of August, we'll have reached the end of our line of credit. We'll have to lock the door for the last time on the day after Labor Day. When the loan officer came out here last time, he was at his wit's end. He really wants to help us. He cried when he had to say, 'no more credit'. The man put his job on the line for us, and we didn't come through."

"It's tough all over, Rain. The woods closed last winter cuz of snow, then again this summer cuz of heat. The fields are drying up. If it weren't for the river and irrigation systems, the berry fields and dairy farms would go under—we'd be living in a ghost town. People are living on soup and spaghetti. I heard some are getting by on lard and salt sandwiches."

"That's awful! At least we're not quite that broke yet. But if the mayor would start paying you full sheriff's pay like he *said* he would six months ago—we might have a chance."

"Well . . . I know Figgs feels bad about it, but the whole town's barely hangin' on."

"I've never seen it this bad. There's not one job left in Wanoocha. A few people are gettin' work in Union City—a buck twenty-five an hour. That barely covers taxes and the gas it takes to get there. Welfare's all that's keeping people alive."

Ski looked over the papers. He stacked them all in a neat pile. "I could get 50 bucks for the Lombardi ball. Figgs would give his right arm for it."

"Figgs is talking through his shorts too, Ski. He's just as broke as the rest of us."

"I don't know . . . for some reason, I think he's got a little more money than he lets on."

All Rain could offer was a long, exasperated sigh. "Well, good for Mayor Figgs."

Ski glanced around the room, "Where'd Orrie go?"

"He's out walking on the railroad tracks. He pretends the rail is a tightrope and counts the steps till he falls off."

Ski laughed, "Now that brings back some memories."

Rain took another look at the paperwork. "If we could put up a couple of hundred against the first bank loan, we'd have a fighting chance."

Lost in their conundrum of concerns, the two did not notice the dusty, red and white, Plymouth station wagon rolling up. Phil Trujillo and his daughter Carmalita got out, leaving his wife Olive and youngest daughter in the sweltering back seat. "We'll be right back," Phil promised.

Rain and Ski warmly greeted their smiling customers. Ski reached out and shook Phil's hand. Rain shook Carmalita's hand and said, "Welcome. How are you today?"

"It's my birthday!"

"Goodness—happy birthday!"

Phil chimed, "She's an official teenager today."

"Thirteen!" said Ski, pulling a face of exaggerated surprise.

Beaming with a bright smile, Carmalita said, "Yes!"

Her dad beamed too. "We came for a little birthday treat—an ice cream and to play her favorite song."

Rain noticed Olive and Carmalita's sister sitting in the car. "Looks like you brought some friends."

“That’s my wife, Olive, and my youngest daughter, Juanita. She’ll have to wait till December for her birthday.” Rain hurried outside to invite them in. With a little hesitation, they accompanied her back inside.

Olive said, “Juanita knows we only have the money for Carmalita’s birthday treat today. But her turn will come.”

Ski drummed up some enthusiasm. “Have you folks had lunch?!”

“Some corn flakes this morning,” said Carmalita.

“Well let’s have a little party . . . Rain, let’s celebrate. We only turn 13 once.”

“We’re going to have to wait till payday to really celebrate—only a couple of days away,” said Phil.

“Nope. Have a seat. The celebration starts now; it’s our treat.”

Phil and Olive looked at each other and shrugged. Phil said, “Yes, OK, but we want to pay our way—we’ll be good for it Saturday. We’ll come in right after work.”

“Hmm . . . All right, we’ll respect your wishes. But dessert is gonna be *on the house*!”

The family sat at the middle table. Ski went into the kitchen. When he returned he delivered ice cream cones all around. He looked at Carmalita and said, “I hope our jukebox has your favorite song.” Ski started toward the jukebox.

Carmalita jumped up, “I have a dime. I’ve been saving it. I wished upon a star, so I know you’ll have it!”

With a face shining with hope, she scanned the song list up and down. Excitedly, she dropped the dime into the slot and pushed B7. A folk guitar introduced "Puff the Magic Dragon" by Peter, Paul, and Mary. The sisters glowed.

"Cheeseburgers and fries coming up," Ski said and headed back to the kitchen.

As "Puff" ended, Rain set the birthday tray on the table. All faces lit up. There is great joy in even the smallest kindness. Phil said, "Saturday is payday, I'll—"

Ski waved his hand, "Like I said, I respect your wishes." Ski started singing "Happy Birthday".

The family hurriedly finished lunch. "Back to the old grind," Phil said. Rain and Ski accompanied the family to their station wagon. Phil pointed and asked, "Is that your GTO?"

"Yep," said Ski. He brimmed with pride. "Bought it *brand-spankin'* new!"

⚜

At the top of Rye Grass hill, two snarling dogs had Tiny, the smallest of the goats, backed against a patch of nasty brambles. Her ruffled coat stood on end. She bleated in fear and her eyes gaped. Each time she took a step, a hunkering dog countered. The goat trembled. The dogs were feral and rib-showing lean. Their eyes smoldered. They bared their teeth as they snarled. One dog stepped closer, to distract, while the other prepared to pounce.

Down the hill, beyond the meadow, the three other goats wandered the dry creek where once cool water flowed. Willow's ears perked as she caught a sinister scent. Nimbly, she climbed the brown, grassy bank and raced between the trees. Wags and Toro lifted their noses and tipped their heads. They also raced into the trees. As they ran, they bounded high to see over the tall grass.

With its belly brushing the ground, the closer dog snapped at the small goat's foreleg. The other lunged, bit the goat's back leg, and rolled her down. Suddenly, a front hoof landed on the back of the dog's head. Another goat stood on its hind legs and slashed with front hooves; it struck the second dog on the nose and between the eyes. The largest goat brandished its horns and rammed its target in the ribs. Both dogs yipped and yelped as they streaked through the grass and down the hill. The small white goat hobbled toward the shade of the mighty horse-chestnut tree. The other three followed and stood fast as steeled and noble guardians. Angry, ears perked, they were prepared to take on all comers.

CHAPTER 9

Lon and Doug

Lon Fitzpatrick, age 12, dark-complected, shaggy brown hair, clad in a grubby Johnny Quest t-shirt and *kneeless* jeans, silently crept over railroad ties in pursuit of Orrie Betters, who was tightrope walking the steel rail. Abruptly, Orrie pivoted, and with an accusatory eye, confronted Lon. Lon feigned surprise at his discovery and said, "I was wondering when you were finally going to look back. I've been following you for at least five minutes."

"Why were you sneaking up on me?"

"I wasn't. I was just playing around. If I was a cougar, I'd be having you for lunch right now."

"Yeah, yeah, yeah, really funny." Timidly glancing around, Orrie said, "Are there really cougars around here?"

"Not really—well, sort of. Once in a while they come down to the river, but mostly they stay up in the higher woods. More toward Canada." Lon's bonding overture continued. "You just said 'yeah, yeah, yeah'—you must like The Beatles."

"Like beetles? I don't like any bugs. Why should I?"

"Jeez, don't you know who The Beatles are?"

"What are you talking about?"

"It's a band, man. Do you live on the planet, Neptune?"

"Yeah, ha ha, more jokes. I live here—I just moved here."

Lon stepped up on the steel rail parallel to Orrie. Beneath the blaze of high noon, they walked and talked.

"So, where'd you live before?"

"Tacoma. On my grandma's chicken farm."

"Tacoma's a big city. I was there once, but I didn't see any chicken farms."

"You must have been downtown. It's a pretty big place. There's lots of farms around Tacoma. Lots of 'em."

"OK, so you're a good ol' chicken farmer boy from Tacoma." Lon started flapping his elbows like wings and saying, "Bok, bok, bok."

Sufficiently annoyed, Orrie said, "You really think you're a comedian. Why don't you try to go on Ed Sullivan?"

"Ed Sullivan—then you must know about The Beatles . . ."

"I don't know anything about Ed Sullivan or The Beatles. I just know Ed Sullivan has a show."

"Man, you've *gotta* be from Neptune. Everybody watches Ed Sullivan . . . And The Beatles are the biggest thing on the planet?"

"The Beatles must play rock 'n' roll, like Elvis. Grandma says Elvis is a heathen. So, she would probably think the Beatles were heathens too."

"What the heck are heathens?"

"Pretty much any mean, bad people who do the devil's work."

"Well, I heard Elvis is pretty religious."

"Yeah, but grandma says, 'He doesn't have *me* fooled'."

"That's dumb, man. All Elvis and The Beatles do is sing."

"Yeah, I know. But it's the kind of music they sing. She only lets me watch Lawrence Welk. He has the Lemon Sisters and this blond, show-off lady who plays a piano. Almost everybody on there plays an accordion."

"So, what's the best Lawrence Welk song?'

"Hmmm . . . I think it might be 'Calcutta'. That's one of his main songs."

"How's that go?"

"It doesn't have any words." Orrie attempted to replicate the orchestral melody. "La la la la la—la la. La la la la la—la."

"Stop, stop! Please don't ever sing that again."

"Well, you're the one that asked for it."

"I should have kept my mouth shut." Lon brightened. "Now I see your problem . . . You've been spending your whole life on a chicken farm watching Lawrence Welk. . .You'd have been *waaay* better off living on Neptune." To Orrie, Lon's wit was flickering dim.

"Sheesh! You're never gonna shut up are you?"

"Nope. I'm gabby. I'm gabby and blabby."

"And a smart aleck."

"Yeah, that's me—a gabby, blabby smart aleck." Lon ad-libbed a silly song:

Yeah, yeah, yeah
I'm real cool
My name's Aleck
And I'm a smart fool

Orrie pivoted on the rail and spun in the opposite direction. "I gotta get back to the drive-in."

"Ohhh, so *you're* the new kid at the Thunder Burger. I heard there was a new kid."

Orrie shrugged. Lon stepped off the rail and started hopping over ties. "Hey, you wanna go with me and meet my friend Doug?"

Orrie looked intrigued, yet suspicious, "Is Doug weird like you?"

"Nah, he's a little punk. He's just nine, gonna be a fourth grader, but he's a good guy . . . most of the time."

Orrie joined Lon in hopping the railroad ties. "Yeah, I guess I'll go meet him." Orrie gave Lon a quick once over. "So how old are you?"

"Twelve. Startin' junior high."

"I'm eleven, startin' sixth."

Lon pointed at a nearby field, which was surrounded by barbed-wire fences. "Let's cut across." Orrie followed Lon's lead and they ran all the way to a pasture. Lon grabbed the top of a post, stepped on a middle strand, then the top strand, then vaulted over. Orrie was hesitant. He grimaced a little as he appraised the wicked-looking barbed wire. Not wanting to look like chicken doo, he put his foot on the lower wire. He got skittish when it sagged. He stepped back. Lon stepped forward and reached out. "You can do it—if you want to, grab my hand and I'll keep you steady." Orrie girded his loins. He placed a hand on the top of a post, then warily climbed the wire fence, strand by strand. As he started down the other side, his jeans snagged on the top wire. After unsnagging his britches, he was more than relieved to be standing on solid ground. But his complacent expression instantly turned to apprehension when a head-tossing horse trotted through a distant gate. Orrie started climbing back to the other side of the fence.

"Hold on," Lon said, "It's OK. That's just Dobbin. He's nice. Wave at him." They waved and Dobbin began swishing his tail. "See his tail. That's how he waves. We could probably ride him if we asked."

Orrie scrunched his nose. "Nah, that's OK. Let's just go to your friend's house."

Dust flew up as they ran through the tall grass, up and over the barbed wire, and down a dusty trail. They soon found themselves alongside the highway. Blurry heatwaves formed shiny pools on the asphalt, as far down the road as the eye could see. Not a car, tractor, or truck in sight: nothing but farmhouses, barns, and sunbaked fields. Town (Rye Grassers referred to the business district as *uptown*) was about a half-mile away. Panting in the desert-dry air, shading their bleached-out retinas, they drudged along, scaring grasshoppers, stepping over parades of ants, and pausing occasionally to contemplate Martian-like mantises.

"I'd better warn you, Orrie. Doug has a sister named Connie. She's really big. Some guys call her the Conster Monster."

"Whoa—she must be really ugly!"

"Nope, not ugly. Actually, she's kinda good-lookin', but it's how she acts. The meanest girl you'll ever run across no matter how long you live."

"Will she be at the house?"

"Yeah, at this time of the day—she'll be there. Her and her friend Rhonda watch soap operas and game shows 'til about two o'clock—then they go down to the park."

"Why don't we wait till they go to the park?"

"Let's call it a rescue mission. I try to get Doug away from her whenever I can. There's no tellin' when she might beat the crap out of him."

Orrie swallowed hard. "OK, if it's to rescue a good kid, I guess it's worth it. We can be just like Davy Crockett and George Russell."

Lon nodded and mused, "I used to have a coonskin cap."

"I still have one."

A ribbon of shallow, churning water wound between the burning hillside and the rocky bank. In places, piles of scraggly *slash* floated along with the current. Most years, even during the summer, the river flowed high, at least up to mid-bank level. But the river was low; stones and rocks, black and gray, jutted through the feeble current and silty islands had recently formed. Quilted shades of smoke blanketed the river well into the distance. Fiery branches tumbled, flaming trees toppled, sending avalanches of rock and dirt down the rugged slope. A blazing branch dropped onto a floating bulk of brush and grass; it ignited. Like a Viking pyre, it sailed toward the levy and got hung up at the edge of a sandbar. A little grass fire fought for life. Flits of flame peeked out, then vanished among the bank's boulders. A thin fiery stream snaked up the rocks, toward the rutted, bumpy road. Across the road, the withered woods, vulnerable from floor to canopy, whiled away, completely innocent, and ignorant of the stalking flames.

On the Conster Monster's front porch, Lon nervously rapped on the rattling screen door. His new friend, Orrie, stood alongside. Lon knocked louder. The boys held their breath. A minute passed. Lon pulled back the screen door and banged on the weighty front door. Seconds passed. Lon was about to knock again, but the hinges creaked, and the door slowly opened. Half-terrified, the boys fidgeted as they gazed up at the dreaded Connie Malman. Connie gave them a look that could have turned Medusa to stone.

Inside the house, a blue-gray television glowed in the dark. Connie's friend Rhonda called, "Who is it, Connie?"

Connie snidely replied, "Two little punks."

Lon avoided eye contact and stuttered, "Is D-D-Doug here?"

As Orrie studied Connie's face, his mind's eye saw a slavering vampire.

Connie squinted, "Who the hell are you?!"

"I'm Orrie."

With a high-pitched laugh, Rhonda chimed, "Whorrie? Did that kid say his name's—Whorrie?"

Connie managed not to laugh as she sourly replied, "Guess so . . . that's sure what he looks like."

Rhonda jumped up. "I gotta see."

Connie pulled the door wide open. Rhonda appeared and her eyes grew wide," Whorrie! Nice to meet you, Whorrie."

Lon repeated, "Is D-D-Doug here?"

Connie said, "Y-y-yeah, he's here. But he ain't c-c-comin' out. So beat it, you little stink wads."

Lon leaned sideways and peered into the dark room. He squeaked out a few words, "Hey, D-D-Doug?"

Connie's eyes blazed. "Get outta here now—or I'll tear off yer sacks and make you wear 'em for swim caps." Lon and Orrie backed away. Rhonda thought the warning was hysterical.

"That's a good one, Connie! Really original."

The boys swallowed hard. Connie extended her sharp fingernails and scraped them down the door frame. Suddenly, a shirtless, nine-year-old Doug Malman rushed past her and leaped off the porch. The startled Orrie and Lon followed him across the lawn and down the sidewalk. Connie and Rhonda stepped onto the porch laughing and making obscene gestures. Rhonda yelled, "You better get ready to wear those swimming caps!"

Orrie, Lon, and Doug ended up under the shade of a huge maple tree at the west end of the elementary school playground.

As they caught their breath, they walked around under the tree, looking for perfectly shaped whirlybirds—seeds that float and spin like helicopter blades, some of which eventually turn into newborn maple trees. The boys experimented with some whirlybird tossing. Controlling their flight patterns presented a challenge. They decided to have a contest. "Let's see who can land one on that mole hill," said Lon. "We'll each have to throw from the exact same spot."

Doug tossed the first whirler, but it landed way short. He yelled, "Crash landing!"

Lon said, "You gotta throw 'em higher, Doug. They'll catch more air and go farther."

Orrie said, "I've played with these things before. We'd throw 'em at recess if we didn't feel like playing soccer or four-square." Orrie tossed one; it landed dead center on the molehill.

Doug said, "Whoa, right on the money! You must have practiced a lot."

"Nope. Not that much. We never tried to aim at anything."

"Talk about beginner's luck," said Lon. He threw one way up in the air and it sailed well beyond the mole mound. He puckered his lips and blew a flatulent sound. "Oh well, you win, Orrie. Nothing like beginner's luck."

Orrie said, "Wanna try again?"

"Nah, it's too darn hot," said Lon. "I'd better head home. I've got chores to do."

"Me too," said Doug. "But I don't want to go home 'til Connie and Rhonda leave for the park. I might as well go home with you for a while, Lon."

Lon threw another whirlybird and said, "I love these things."

Doug jovially said, "If you love them so much, why don't you marry 'em?" Neither Lon nor Orrie laughed.

Lon said, "That's an old joke."

"So's your face," Doug quipped. "And we still laugh at it." Again, neither Lon nor Orrie laughed.

Lon said, "You got those stupid jokes from Connie—didn't you?"

"No, I heard Rhonda use 'em *on* Connie. And another one is—'You got a match?' then you say, 'Yeah, your butt and my face.'" This time Orrie and Lon did laugh.

"You got that backward, dummy," said Lon.

"Huh, your butt and my—oh, yeah—I guess I did." Doug slapped himself on the forehead.

Lon cleared his throat and moved the conversation in another direction. "The reason I like those *whirly* things so much is they remind me of helicopters. In fact, when I graduate from high school, I'm gonna join the army and be a chopper pilot. Then when I get out, I'm gonna be a welder. My dad used to be a welder—that's what my mom told me."

Orrie asked, "So what does he do now?"

"He got killed in the war. In Korea. I was only *one-years* old."

"That's terrible, Lon. I'm sorry that happened," said Orrie. "Ski was in the Korea war too. He never talks about it, but mom said he was in it. And it was pretty bad."

Doug said, “My dad fought against Hitler and the Japs, but he doesn’t talk about it either.” Doug paused for thought. “I’ll probably go in the army too. Maybe I’ll be a helicopter pilot like you, Lon.”

“Yeah,” Lon said. “It would be about the funnest job.”

Orrie said, “Grandma had a neighbor in Tacoma who was a welder. He went to a trade school called Bates. I could probably go there and learn to be a welder.”

An epiphany struck Doug like a bolt of lightning. “Why don’t we all go in the army? And when we get out—we can all be welders!”

Agreement on this practical goal was unanimous.

Thursday evening slowly blended into night. Underneath the Weston Bridge, Ski used a stick to poke around at scattered piles of trash. Orrie followed close. “Do you think Buddy’s been down here?”

“Doesn’t look like it. All these food cans and wrappers are old. I don’t think anybody’s been under this bridge for quite a while. Most of this stuff is from high school kids having keggers. Nobody’s got money for beer these days. So kegger days have been suspended.”

“What’s keggers?”

“One of the rites of passage for growin’ up—beer parties. It goes back to . . . possibly even caveman times . . . maybe back to the days of the Australopithecines.

“Australopith-ikins?”

“Yeah, they were little ape-men who lived in Africa—about a million years ago?”

“They drank beer?”

“Probably.”

Ski dropped his gnarly, wooden probe and took one last look around. “OK. The sun’s going down, the mosquitoes are out, the crickets are chirping, and there’s nothing here. Let’s head back out to the hill and visit the goats. We can finish filling their food and water tubs.”

CHAPTER 10

Brayton

In his upstairs bedroom at the Brayton chapel, Ronnie Rix awakened with a song in his heart. Sports posters, photos, and baseball cards covered the walls of his spotless room. Sandy Koufax, Mickey Mantle, Don Drysdale, Roger Maris, the Say-Hey-Kid, and the Los Angeles Dodgers team photo. There were also magazine photos of Elvis, Buddy Holly, Fats Domino, and Chuck Berry. Ronnie sat at a desk near an open window and paged through a high-school yearbook. He paused on a page featuring female athlete, Connie Malman: volleyball, basketball, and softball. Her dark eyes were mischievous, her smile was captivating. Ronnie closed the book and picked up the guitar leaning against his bed. He stood at the open window and looked across acres of berry fields to the smoke-shrouded hillside. He strummed along as he sang Woodie Guthrie's "Roll on Columbia", the folk anthem of Washington State.

From the bottom of the stairway, the French accent of Father Dom rang out. "Ronnie, Ronnie . . . Ronnie! I have some news."

Ronnie leaned his guitar against the wall and walked to the top of the stairs. "What? What's going on?"

"I need you to come down here. It's about the All-Star trip. Something has changed. We're trying to get it sorted out."

With a worried look, Ronnie descended the stairs. Father Dom opened his hands and took on a soothing manner. Ronnie followed him into the dining room, and they sat at the table. Father Dom quickly reviewed some notes. This was one of the rare times in his life he had to struggle for words—words to temper disillusionment and disappointment, words to provide guidance and assurance. Ronnie folded his arms as his fear turned to anger and brooding.

"It's bad news, isn't it? I'm not going, am I?" His face twisted in anticipation of prejudice and injustice. "It's because of my record, isn't it?" Ronnie stood and placed his hands on his hips.

Father Dom calmly gestured for him to sit and began to explain. "It's nothing about you. It's about another boy, another ballplayer, you know him—Kenny West."

Ronnie slumped in his chair. "Yeah, he's really good. A really good pitcher. Did he make the All-Stars too? I thought only one of us could go . . ."

"That's what we're trying to get to the bottom of . . . When they reviewed the paperwork and updated everything, the regional director said an error was discovered in the points calculations. The committee failed to count one of Kenny's strikeouts, which brings him to a tie with you. You both have 712 points."

"So, we both get to go?"

"No, there is only one position allowed from each league. This has never happened, not in all forty years of the competition. The original rules and constitution state that a tie may be broken by either a game or a coin toss."

Ronnie's fists were clenched, and his face was getting red. "It's not fair. I won the spot. They sent me a letter." He stood in protest, "They already made the decision." Ronnie started pacing. "It was their mistake—why punish me?!"

"I agree, that in one respect it is not fair, but not to give this boy a chance because of a mistake, an oversight—that would not be fair either."

"So, what then. I mean, the season's over—no more games. The plane leaves on Sunday."

"The regional commissioner has approved a playoff game. It would have to be tomorrow afternoon. Or we could agree to a coin toss."

"I'm sorry for acting like a baby, Father. But they said I could go—I got the letter! I'm really disappointed—that's all. And the way I acted; it wasn't at all honorable."

"There's no dishonor in expressing feelings. Our feelings shape our thoughts, and our thoughts guide what we do."

"Still, I'm fifteen, I shouldn't act childish."

Father Dom went to Ronnie and gently placed a hand on his shoulder. "The fairest thing they can do is give you the choice. The committee is allowing you to make the decision—do you want to toss a coin, or settle things on the field?"

Ronnie required no deliberation. "On the field!"

Ronnie ran from the room and through the main door of the chapel. He hurried down the steps and hopped on his bicycle. Across from the Jeffersonian-style chapel, old folks from the rest home jovially bid him good morning. He quickly glanced their way and waved, "I gotta get into town." On he pedaled, down the walkway and onto the highway. Father Dom stood on the chapel's front porch and watched Ronnie ride out of sight. He then crossed the lawn to meet with rest home residents and the patients of the nursing home. The buildings, grounds, and farm were collectively known as Brayton Gardens.

At an easel, angled to catch the soft rays of mid-morning light, Connie Malman gently brushed goldenrod watercolor onto a field of blooming daffodils. A weathered windmill stood lonely in the distance. Connie's room was a mess: clothes on the floor, an unmade bed, candy wrappers, crumbs on the carpet, and empty pop bottles scattered here and there. She sighed and examined the scene; she clearly disapproved. After an hour of self-effacing, artistic frustration, she dropped her paintbrush into a tall glass of inky water. She needed a fresh outlook. Without question, Connie would have given up her entire world of watercolor to be able to sing like Cilla Black. Indulging in a moment of fantasy, she became Cilla Black, on stage in London singing "You're My World" for the Queen. Returning to her muggy, mid-morning bedroom, she placed her paint tray alongside the murky water. She cleaned her hands, headed to a bookshelf, and pulled an oft-perused volume.

Connie sat on a wicker chair near the window and opened her high-school yearbook. The first page she turned to had been bookmarked. Photos of the Freshman class. She glanced at the class photos, then briefly focused on Ronnie Rix's picture before flipping to the sports section. There was an action photo of Ronnie standing at home plate, bat raised over his shoulder. She read the caption several times: "Dodgers, here I come!" She set the yearbook on the floor and picked up Ronnie's red cap. Though pulling the hat heist the prior morning had added some fun to the day, she felt at least a morsel of guilt. No matter, she planned to give the cap back later that afternoon.

Her window overlooked the roof of the back porch. The family's backyard was neatly groomed and burnt a toasty brown. A garage and shed, a hedge, and two apple trees blocked her view of the back alley. Angry fists of summer heat punched their way through the window. She scanned the smoky hillside, donned Ronnie's cap, tipped the brim forward, then returned to her easel. Reluctantly, she took a critical look at her daffodil painting. She frowned and huffed. "Pitiful," she said and left the room.

Against the back wall of the Thunder Burger was a pinball machine called *Gladiator*. It was right next to the Wurlitzer jukebox, which played 45 rpm records sideways as though defying gravity. With not a penny to their name, Orrie, Lon, and Doug had figured out a unique way to derive entertainment from the idle amusement device. They called the game: "Hulk and Puny Human". One of them would pretend to play Gladiator, one was a spectator, and the third guy was The Hulk. The Hulk's role was to walk up to the player, puff out his chest, flex his shoulders, then reach under the player's arms and, in a deep voice, say, "Move puny human—Hulk play!" The Hulk would then toss the player to one side toward a stack of cardboard boxes. This sent the boxes flying across the room. The trick was in the timing. The player had to synchronize a hurtling leap as The Hulk tossed him into the air. The spectator was the judge; he decided how *real* the stunt looked. The boys could easily spend an hour trying to perfect their act. Ski was amused, but Rain could only handle the hijinks for so long before telling them to "go outdoors". They weren't supposed to play at all when customers were present, but such audiences, of course, provided the greatest thrills.

After observing one final and impressive throw, Ski intervened. "Hey guys, I need you to run an errand for me. We need some hamburger meat from the frozen food lockers uptown—who knows where that is?"

"I do," said Lon. "It's next to the Mobile station; it's hooked onto Brownie's store."

Ski gave Orrie the key. "It's locker 267, way in the back and on the top row, so one of you will have to boost the other up. We need two packages of hamburger meat. Can you guys do that?"

"Yeah," said Lon. "It'll be fun! When I go in there, I pretend it's the Ice Age and a saber-toothed tiger is stalking me." Orrie and Doug locked eyes with a certain uncertainty. Lon looked at them with certainty. "It's fun, you guys. Not as fun as playing Hulk—but it *is* fun."

As the boys left, Ski warned, "And you better stay out of that park. There's a bunch of roughnecks that hang out down there—so you best steer clear."

"Oh man," Doug said in a hushed tone. "What if we see Toby Gussard? He messes around with the air hose at the Mobile station—'til they come out and yell at him. It's right next to the frozen food lockers?"

Rain hurried from the back room. "Orrie, if you see Toby Gussard—anywhere! You get right back here. Forget the hamburger."

"Don't worry, Toby won't get us," said Doug. "We can *easily* scamper from *his* sinister clutches."

Rain raised her eyebrows. "Umm . . . well, OK, Doug. You boys just be careful."

As they headed uptown, the boys played the *if-you-step-on-a-crack* game. Definitely not wanting to break their mother's back, they walked, ran, hopped, and skipped over the sidewalk, making sure not to come anywhere close to stepping on a crack. "Hold up," said Lon. "Let's change it. If you step on a crack, you break Toby *Gussard's* back!" From there on, they stepped on and jumped on every crack they could see. Walking past the high school, Lon told the hair-raising tale of a local legend. "I'll tell you somebody who's scarier than Toby Gussard. And scarier than Connie too. His name is Ronnie Rix. He's the toughest kid in town. He once beat up a kid so bad—the kid had to have surgery."

Doug confirmed, "I heard about that. That's been known around these parts for many a-year. Rix is the only kid my sister's scared of."

Lon rambled on and the legend grew. "Like I said. I know it's hard to believe, but the guy's a real-life juvenile delinquent. He's been in prison and everything."

Doug said, "The last kid Ronnie Rix beat up got his nose split in half, then his ribs broke off and jagged ends stabbed into his bowels."

Looking pale and wary, Orrie said, "I haven't lived here long, but this town is getting to sound like a really dangerous place: Toby, Connie, Ronnie, and Doug's dad. Half the people around here are scary and mean."

"It's not that bad—as long as you're careful. Just stay away from Ronnie Rix and Connie and you'll be OK."

Doug added, "And Toby."

"Yeah, don't go down by the feed store," said Lon. "That's where Toby usually is. He stays in a chicken coop—like it's his secret camp or something."

Orrie said, "Holy Criminy, that's really strange. In fact, I'm starting to think this whole town is strange. It's like a monster movie town."

"Yeah—it's unconventional," said Doug.

Lon gave Doug a quizzical look, shrugged, and said, "And it's gettin' more *unconventional* every doggone unconventional day."

The midday sun glowed red through the smoke on the horizon. Endless rows of raspberry bushes stretched right up to wooded banks of the Caulder River. Phil Trujillo stood in front of the crescent-moon door of an outhouse, smoking the last half of a cigarette. When he heard his daughter's panicked cry, he flicked the cigarette into the dirt. His Runnin' Bear Tavern matchbook lay on the arm of a cedar lawn chair. Carmalita yelled, "Bees! Daddy! Bees! Bees!" Phil's boots sunk deep into the soft soil, slowing him considerably. As he neared the crossroads to the berry fields, he could see men, women, and children running all over, shouting and screaming. The turbulent black cloud of insects attacked as a unit: black hornets, big ones, each able to sting many times.

On the dirt road near the outhouses, Toby Gussard stepped off his bicycle and removed his construction-worker hat. He proudly set it on a picnic table, then set to the business of rearranging the oddities in his bicycle basket. He glimpsed a smoky wisp rising from Phil's dying cigarette; his glee was unbridled. Toby hurried toward the smoke and reached for the smoldering stub. Delicately pinching the cigarette's end, Toby's lips gently brought it back to life. He glanced around, then snatched the matchbook from the lawn chair. Abandoning his bicycle and treasures, he sneaked toward the woods. After some guilty glances around, he felt confident no one was watching. He ran full out toward the trees.

Glowing cigarette butt in hand, he followed a narrow trail, treading on crackly twigs and brittle leaves all the way to the riverbank.

Out in the berry fields, Phil joined the others in swatting at the incensed insects. The men pulled off their shirts and caps, wafting away at the angry swarm. A huge, grey dome bulged from the bushes; it was one of three. Phil tapped the back of a young field worker and said, “Go get a couple of bottles of brake fluid out of the tool shed.” Phil winced with each sting. “Right inside the door!” The men dropped their shirts and hurried from the field, shaking the bees free of their arms. The hornets followed their every step, stinging the men anywhere, everywhere. Phil took the bottles of brake fluid from the young runner and headed for the nests. Badly stung men ran for safe areas. At a nearby picnic table, women mixed baking soda paste.

Gnashing his teeth, squinting his eyes, Phil dumped the heavy, oily poison all over the hives. Ignoring the acidic stings, he soaked the hives deep, then ran clear of the raspberries, and hurried toward a man spraying others with a water hose. As the cool water flowed over Phil’s back and chest, he was startled by new screams and terrified words. “Fire! Fire! Fire in the woods!”

At the wide picture window of Brownie’s General Store, Orrie, Lon, and Doug looked over the wish list display. Among the prizes were a skateboard, badminton and archery sets, a spread of comic books, an NFL football, squirt guns, and some Aurora monster models. Orrie pointed to The Creature from the Black Lagoon picture on a model box.

"Look, right there, *The Creature*. That's the one I want for my birthday."

After brief consideration, Doug said, "Yeah, I agree, that's a pretty good one."

Lon said, "Man, this kid named Robbie Roscoe, Earwig, we call him, has the Phantom of the Opera. See the prisoner, that guy looking up out of the dungeon . . . Earwig painted him green—with bloody scabs on his arms."

Doug and Orrie said, "Ohh, coooool!"

Orrie said, "That'd look pretty neat. I usually like to use my own ideas, but that's worth copyin' . . . I'm still gettin' the *Creature* first though."

Their eyes were next drawn to the skateboard and its $7.95 price tag. There was nothing fancy about it, just natural blonde wood, with black rubber wheels. But the guys were hypnotized.

Lon finally said, "Let's make a pact. An eagle-claw pact. We'll all put our money together and buy that skateboard."

Orrie and Doug nodded affirmatively.

Lon did some mental math. "So that's about eight bucks, the sales tax would be about, let's say 40 cents, to be safe, which means we should save up about $8.50."

Doug sighed, "Unless you guys have more money than I think you do, it's gonna take a while to save that much—even with three of us. I had a nickel a couple of days ago, but I spent it on cinnamon dollars—the two-for-a-penny. So, I got ten of 'em. Man, that was one heck of a good deal!"

With a bewildered look, Lon said, "I guess we all have to splurge once in a while."

Orrie admitted, "I've got twenty-five cents from doing chores, but I was saving it for playing the Gladiator."

Lon said, "OK, so we're basically broke. But we can work, and we can save . . . So do we want to make a pact right now for when we get the money." Orrie and Doug nodded with enthusiasm.

"Eagle-claw!" Lon said. The boys made grasping, taloned-fists and formed a triangle. They extended grasping hands until their knuckles met and together, they said, "Eagle-claw!"

White smoke filtered through the woods north of The Brayton Garden berry fields. Father Dom ran down the front steps of the chapel calling, "The pipes! Get the irrigation pipes!" A group of men ran into a wooden shed, came out with long, brass irrigation pipes, and carried them into the woods. A group of women did the same. Father Dom instructed as he ran alongside. "Take them back to the pump—the first pump." As the father returned to the irrigation shed, a distant siren wailed.

Residents and patients from the main complex and the surrounding cottages, some in wheelchairs, carried water in all sorts of vessels. Father Dom and a withered old man grabbed the ends of a long brass tube, then struggled toward the woods. Pausing once or twice, they finally reached the trail. Two younger men relieved them and hauled the pipe on toward the river. The farmworkers lined the pipes through the woods and parallel to the riverbank. Once the pump reached full flow, most of the fire had been doused.

High on the hillside, burning trees continued to topple and slide into the river. The field workers, patients, and residents watched the hill fire as they caught their breath; eventually, they filtered back through the dripping, soggy woods. The pipes were disengaged and returned to the shed. A fire truck crew finished off the flames along the levy road.

When Father Dom emerged from the woods, he saw a police car in front of the chapel. He extended gratitude to the crowd as they dispersed, then headed for the small church. Toby Gussard sat forlornly in the back of the police car, struggling to pull his handcuffs apart. He smiled and rocked back and forth, keeping perfect four/four time. Deputy Welski put his hands on his hips and displayed a sympathetic expression as he approached Father Dom.

The Father spoke to a gathering group. "Let's thank the Lord those pipes reached their mark. Had the fire moved a little more to the east or west—we'd have been in a real fix." He looked at Ski and whispered, "Count this as a wake-up call. I really don't think we could have evacuated in time."

On the walkway between the rest home and chapel, Mayor Figgs held a discussion with a group of volunteer firemen. One of the firemen said, "We've got to come up with some better ideas—and soon. Without that irrigation system, that fire could have spread into town."

"I agree," said another fireman. "If that fire had started a little further downriver—it could have burned at will—no stoppin' it."

"We got caught with our pants down, Mayor."

"All right, all right, you don't have to convince me. We'll put our heads together and come up with something. After living around these parts my whole life, I've seen the times change, people change, and the weather change—mostly not for the better.

Every year seems to get a little hotter and a little drier. But we'll abide and make the best of it. We always do."

An older lady began quoting Revelations. "Two women will be grinding at the mill; one will be taken, the other left."

Figgs mercifully interrupted the gloomy prognosticator. "Save it for Sunday, Annie. Save it for Sunday." He bid all good day and sauntered toward Ski and Father Dom. "Set Toby free," said Figgs. "Toby didn't start the fire—he's perfectly free to go."

Ski had his doubts. Taking chin in hand, he rubbed at some jailbird stubble. "It's sure lookin' like he did the deed, Mayor. We've got some pretty strong evidence. A pretty-near full book of matches. A burn on the tip of his finger. And he sure was doin' a lot of whoopin' and hollerin' while he watched the show."

Murmurs and grumbles from the lingering crowd rekindled uneasiness.

"I just got the official word," said the mayor. "A pile of slash caught fire and got hung up on the bank. It went right up through the weeds and grass, onto the road, then made its way into the woods. It was just a one-in-a-million freak of nature. Never would have happened if the river level hadn't been so low."

"Boy, I don't know, Charlie," Ski whispered. "Him having that matchbook—that's still weighing pretty heavy on my mind."

"Yeah, I know. I hear what you're sayin'. But we gotta go by the firemen's word."

"Well . . . OK. I guess that's that."

Father Dom said, "Let's let things be for now. I'll think it all through overnight."

Everyone glanced back at the woods. The smoke thinned. But still, across the river, dark clouds of soot billowed wide as they drifted over the hillside. Phil joined the group. Bee-sting lumps and bumps covered his face, arms, and hands. These were covered with dried calamine lotion. Phil said, "Damn, I gotta tell ya, those black hornet stings hurt like the devil! Meanest bees ever . . . A nurse tweezed out a few stingers, but most of 'em don't leave their stingers. It's about the nastiest bee there is."

Father Dom said, "There's plenty of ice in the freezer, Phil. We'll get some cold compresses on those stings and some more calamine. You're very lucky you're not allergic."

"No, I'm not allergic. I have been stung many times by many kinds of bees. I have never had much of a reaction."

"Thank Heaven for small wonders."

Phil winked at Father Dom. "A little Tequila might ease things up, but nobody in the whole camp's got a drop."

"Don't look at me. All I have is grape juice." The mood lightened.

Ski tried to pin Figgs down. "So, what's coming our way next . . . I mean, we all know this could have been way worse . . . and Toby havin' those matches?"

"I'll tend to Toby," said Father Dom.

Figgs did a little *soft-shoe* and tried to conjure up a joke. "I think Phil's got the right idea. I'm a little short on tequila, but there's a full bottle of Jack Daniels in the truck. Nothing to worry about."

Still a bit miffed, Ski said, "Would you like to certify that, Charlie?"

"The Jack Daniels? Sure, Old Number 7 is guaranteed at 80 proof."

A brief pause, then laughter. Ski finally chuckled a little then said, "I hate to be the skunk at the garden party, but I've got to admit—I'm still worried."

CHAPTER 11

Buddies

The low-wattage light bulbs on the ceiling of Brownie's Frozen Food Lockers flickered and emitted *clinky, tinky* sounds. The large room had the faint, sickly smell of frozen blood and fish. Orrie and Lon clad in sheer summer wear, Doug still without a shirt, shivered and shuddered. They shuffled along as a triangular unit, along the back wall. Ice puddles lay as scattered landmines loaded with plenty of slapstick potential. Accidently touch a steel pole and lose some skin. One of Doug's sneakers skated on an ice pool, he grabbed Lon, and they both landed hard.

Orrie squinted up at the label on a frosty locker door. "That's it, 267. Boost me, Lon."

Doug and Lon used their hands to form stirrups and lifted the wobbling, Orrie. He held the padlock as still as he could, poked and poked with the key, but the keyhole was clogged with ice.

"You're gonna have to work it in, Orrie," said Lon. "Grind the ice out."

"I'm trying. I'm digging at it."

"Warm up the key in your hands," Doug chattered.

Orrie groaned, "My hands are colder than the key!"

Lon said, "Cup it and breathe on it."

Doug's facial muscles were stiffening fast, his words almost unintelligible. It was assumed he said, "I can't stand it much longer."

Lon said, "We gotta get outside, Orrie. Get recharged, then we can try again."

"I've got it!" He dropped the lock onto the floor and clumsily rummaged through the rock-like packages, turning each to read the magic marker scrawlings. Hamburger, nope, nope, nope . . . There's no darn hamburger, not even one package."

Lon and Doug squealed, "What?!"

"None. No hamburger at all—nothing but stupid ground beef."

"Grab it!" Lon yelled. "Grab it, now! Hamburger *is* ground beef!" Orrie grabbed two of the icy packages. Lon and Doug lowered him to the floor. Like mechanical men, the three boys marched between the lockers. Were they made of metal, they would have clanked. Lon leaned against the push-knob of the main massive door; it was ice-sealed. "It's stuck—frozen shut!"

Doug's chattering words came out in fragments. "*Thiz nuth doe. Go inna star.*"

"Yeah, I remember it. Let's go." Lon led the other boys down the wall to a corner door that led into the general store. He twisted the knob. It was locked. He pounded, but nobody came. "Go back!" With their last ounce of energy, they made it back to the main exit.

In desperation, Lon slammed his shoulder against the plunger mechanism and the door gave way. The outside air hit them like a furnace. The intense heat rush was the stuff of hallucinations.

Lon said, "I feel like a marshmallow getting toasted in a campfire."

"I couldn't breathe there for a second," said Doug. "Now my skin's meltin' . . . like butter in a pan. But I'm still cold deep inside."

"It feels kinda good on my skin," said Orrie. "Like I'm in a hot air balloon floating over the African plain."

They flapped and rubbed their arms. They hugged them themselves, then raised their hands to the sun.

"I'm warming up a little, but I got no strength," said Doug. "I gotta rest a minute." He sat on the ground and leaned back against the building. The others did the same.

Orrie fondled the quarter in his pocket. After about a minute, he said, "If you can make it to the cafe, Doug, I'll get us some candy."

Doug's reserve battery kicked in. He stood right up. "I can make it."

"Get Milk Duds," said Lon. "The ones in the café are always stale—almost like jawbreakers. They last for about ten minutes each."

The legionnaires ventured forth, as though trudging the desert beneath a cruel Saharan sun. The cafe appeared, like an oasis, perhaps a mirage, but somehow, they gained new vitality with each sugar-craving step, eventually transitioning to a jog, then a lively trot.

Hiding behind a towering oak, in the corner of the park, Toby Gussard watched the boys rejoice in merry bonding. He wore a big smile and his eyes gleamed. He continually adjusted his positioning to make certain the boys did not see him. He gritted his teeth and excitedly clenched his fists, as though electrified. His gaze followed their every step, past the Mobile station, across the street, down the sidewalk, to the entrance of the cafe.

When they went inside, Toby turned his attention to a green Duncan yo-yo at the bottom of his bicycle basket. He pushed the other things aside and reached for it, but it was stuck halfway through a hole in the bottom of the basket. He doggedly worked it free, then inspected the basket. The damage was minor. Some of the solder had broken away. As he tried to bend the wires back into place, the hole only got bigger. So, he covered the hole with a toddler's book called *The Brave Little Steam Shovel* and said, "Do be sine cup!" Toby wound the yo-yo up and flung it up and down a few times. He tried a few tricks. When he tried to *walk-the-dog* he ended up dragging the yo-yo through dead grass and crumbled oak leaves. When he tried *rock-the-cradle* the string became tangled in a knot. Frustrated, he dropped the toy back into the basket. "Do be sine cup!" Toby rolled his bike out of the park and rode it across the street to the Mobile station. He pulled up beside the air and water hoses.

A mechanic wearing an oily pair of Mobile flying horse logo overalls hurried out of the garage. He yelled, "Get outta here, Toby! Get away from them hoses. Go on!"

Preening in the mirror behind the cafe counter, Wuzzie adjusted his soda jerk cap until he felt the angle was perfect. Then he turned, spotless towel in hand, and polished the red-marble counter. When "Needles and Pins" by The Searchers came on the radio, Wuzzie spun around and turned it up. All the while, Orrie, Lon, and Doug sat on stools ogling posters of ice cream sundaes. From behind the counter, Wuzzie leaned on his elbow and rested his chin on his hand.

"Did you guys figure out what you want, yet?"

Lon said, "We want *lots* of stuff."

"Do you have *lots* of money?"

Lon and Doug shrugged and looked at Orrie who immediately stood and displayed a quarter in his palm. "I should save this for the skateboard, but I might decide to buy something in here."

"You're gonna need a lot more than a quarter to buy a skateboard."

In unison, the boys happily chimed, "We know!"

"So, where's the other money coming from?"

"We're working on some ideas," said Doug.

"Like getting jobs," said Lon.

"Who'd hire you dumb little guys."

"Maybe a paper route," said Lon.

Wuzzie smirked and countered. "Get it line. If there was a paper route job out there, ten high-school guys would be waiting for it."

"I have a janitor job at the restaurant," said Orrie.

"How much does that pay?" Wuzzie asked.

Orrie held up the quarter.

"Every day?"

"A month."

Wuzzie laughed. "That's not a job. It's an allowance—and a pretty chintzy allowance."

"My allowance is fifty-cents a month," said Lon. "It's the most my mom could afford. But, for now, I use it to help feed Star."

"Star?"

"My dog."

For Doug, that brought up a sore subject. "I still don't see why you call him Star?"

"I told you fifty times—that white spot on the back of his neck."

"And I told you—that it doesn't look anything like a star!"

"It looks almost exactly like a star."

"Not even close."

"Oh yeah, smart shape-identifying expert—what does it look like then?"

Stymied, Doug finally opted for a geographical reference. "It looks sort of like . . . a state . . . sort of like—Nevada?"

"No way, buddy. Nice try. It looks *waaay* more like a star."

Mercifully, Wuzzie cut in. "Hey, you guys. I got a business to run here. So, are you gonna buy something with your measly quarter or what?"

Orrie said, "If I buy something, I want it to be for all three of us, so what could I get?"

Wuzzie let out a long sigh. "Penny candy, cookies, gum, pop, ice—"

"You got any of them stale Milk Duds left?" asked Lon.

"Hey, our stuff's not stale. Don't get smart or I'll kick you guys outta here."

On the wall behind the counter was a sign featuring a pretty mermaid in a sailor top and cap enjoying a glass of Green River soda. Orrie said, "It looks like you guys make Green Rivers?"

"Yeah, we make 'em. But nobody hardly buys 'em anymore—why would you?"

"Because we don't have those at the Thunder Burger. We don't have any of that green syrup stuff."

"OK, so you want three Green Rivers?"

"How much are they?"

"A dime—just like the sign says . . . It's right behind me!"

Doug asked, "How come you don't have the sunset, palm tree Green River sign."

"My dad likes the mermaid one—so that's what we got. If you don't like it, you can lump it."

"Gosh, I just asked a question—you don't have to get grouchy."

"So, three Green Rivers—thirty cents, plus a penny tax."

Orrie said. "I don't have quite enough."

"How about graveyards?" asked Lon. "We could buy two and get an extra glass."

Doug said, "They can't make graveyards cuz they don't have Dr. Pepper."

Wuzzie said, "Three parts Coke, one part root beer—that's Dr. Pepper. And yeah, we can make graveyards. But I ain't given' you guys no extra glass!"

Lon asked, "How come?"

"Cuz you can't go through life being freeloaders."

"Like Freddy on Red Skelton?" asked Doug.

"Yeah—a lazy bum. If you go around begging for stuff, that's what you'll turn into . . . Toby Gussard does that. He comes in here begging for coffee . . . You don't want to be like him, do you?"

A collective, "No!"

The boys sat quietly, gawking at the Green River sign.

"You little guys are getting on my nerves—are you gonna buy something or not?!"

Forthrightly, Doug ventured a solution. "I've got the answer! Rhonda Stickle. Do you know if she still wants a George Harrison bubble gum card?"

Wuzzie's salesmanship kicked in. "Matter of fact, she does . . . but it has to be a close-up . . . She'll give five bucks for it."

Doug looked at his pals, "That's mostly enough for the skateboard!"

Lon pondered, "Yeah . . . yeah . . . that would get us most of the way."

Orrie posed, "Who's George Harrison? And how would we get his card?"

Wuzzie and Doug flashed flummoxed mugs.

Lon explained, "I know it's hard to believe, but Orrie doesn't know about The Beatles. He never heard of 'em till I told him. On their chicken farm, the only music his grandma ever let him listen was on The Lawrence Welk Show."

"Lawrence Welk?!" Wuzzie went into a hammy dry-heaves act.

Lon explained, "We gotta buy Beatles bubble gum cards, Orrie. They're a nickel a pack, five cards in each."

Doug clamored, "Man, oh-man! That's good odds, Orrie! Real good odds!"

Orrie rolled the quarter in his fingers, then with pious indignation, put the quarter back into his pocket. "It's not the way of Jesus." Doug and Lon groaned.

Lon said, "Nothing in the Bible says you can't buy bubble gum."

Orrie paused to put the statement on trial. "I guess that's true."

Wuzzie encouraged, "Don't give up before you try. You could get the card with your first nickel."

Wuzzie pulled a box of Beatles bubble gum cards from the showcase. "We gotta keep these little jewels under guard. Hot items these days." Tantalizingly, he held up a pack. The boys gazed in wonder.

Lon urged, "Forget the Milk Duds, man. I mean—five bucks! It'd be worth the risk."

Doug added, "Yeah, at least it's worth a try!"

Orrie's brain calculated, then recalculated. His brow furrowed. He raised an eyebrow. He stroked his chin. He massaged his forehead. He rubbed his itchy nose. "Does it cost tax?"

Nope. No tax on a nickel."

"OK—one pack."

Wuzzie was moved to poetry. "You got the nickel; we got the pickle." He handed Orrie the package and the change.

The boys went to a table near the jukebox. Wuzzie followed them, dropped a coin in the juke box, and pressed some buttons. The song "Heart Full of Soul" by the Yardbirds filled the room. "Wait a minute!" said Wuzzie. "Those meat packages are starting to make a mess on the table." He went to get a rag and returned with an old newspaper. With the table clean and the hamburger packages on the paper, he approved the unveiling of the cards.

Lon, Doug, and Wuzzie watched intently as Orrie peeled away the wax wrapper. He snapped the pink bubble gum in half and gave one to Lon, one to Doug. Orrie flipped over a card; it was a close-up of Ringo; all but Orrie groaned. "Go ahead, Lon." Lon flipped the next card; Ringo was on the throne playing his drums.

Doug blurted, "What is this—the Ringo pack!"

"Hey!" said Wuzzie. "Ringo's a great drummer. And he sings pretty good too."

"I know," said Doug. "I just hate his cards. They're boring." Doug flipped the next card; it was Paul with his violin-shaped bass.

"That's a Hoffner bass," Wuzzie said. "If I played bass, that's the one I'd get."

"Me too," said Lon. "I know a kid who says he's got a Hoffner. They call him Earwig because he's . . . like, a creepy version of a Beatle—just like earwigs are creepy versions of bugs. He claims he has a Hoffner bass at home . . . I think he's lyin', but I *ain't* sure."

Doug and Wuzzie harmonized, "He's lyin'."

Lon said, "I kinda feel sorry for him. He's so fat he couldn't even do one pull up in P.E."

"That's too bad," said Wuzzie. "But he *is* lyin' though . . . Jiminy Crickets, a Hoffner bass—that's some serious money, man . . . Just think about it, a Hoffner in the hands of a kid like the Earwig—that would be a crime against humanity." No reaction. It appeared Wuzzie was the only attendee privy to the caustic nature of his remark.

Noticing Wuzzie's dismay, Orrie said, "Wanna pick one, Wuzzie?"

"Sure," he said, dryly feigning indifference. His card was a group shot of all four Beatles standing in front of a brick building.

Doug stated the obvious. "One to go . . ."

Orrie slowly turned the card. It was a full-body shot of George with his Gretsch guitar. The boys' initial hoorah lulled to a moan.

"Dang it!" said Lon. "If only it was a close-up. I can't believe it. Jeez, how much closer can you get?!"

Wuzzie went behind the counter and switched on the radio. The song "I'm Henry the Eighth, I Am" by Herman's Hermits sparked some good humor.

Doug said, "Connie has all the words to this song. She listened to it, like, 100 times before she got 'em all down. She and Rhonda like to sing it."

Thoroughly disgruntled, Orrie said, "I'm not buying any more Beatles cards." He handed Wuzzie a nickel and looked at his friends.

Lon said, "Milk Duds." Orrie and Doug nodded approval. As Wuzzie walked to the candy counter, Lon whispered, "I sure hope they're stale."

From behind the counter, Wuzzie looked out the window, smiled, and waved. His best friend, Ronnie, was approaching the cafe.

As Orrie divided up the candy, Wuzzie met his buddy at the door. Lon whispered, "Oh God! It's Ronnie Rix . . . Don't look at him. For God's sake, I hope and pray he doesn't see us."

Ronnie quick-stepped to the counter, plopped down and twirled on a stool. Wuzzie noted an apprehensive glint in the eyes of his friend. He assumed the traditional role of a barkeep: poor man's psychologist.

Ronnie snapped, "Connie and Rhonda—have you seen 'em yet?'

"No, I don't think they even walked past today. Like I said earlier, they don't usually come in here 'til around two-thirty."

"I just found out we've gotta have a special playoff game. I gotta get that cap back, man!"

"I thought the season was over."

"It ain't. I lost my All-Star spot. They messed up on figurin' the points. Well, actually, it's a tie right now. The Pirates are gonna be here tomorrow—down at the VFW field. That's the team with Kenny West, that *Triple-A-arm* guy." Ronnie put a crumbled dollar on the counter. "Gimme a Coke, man . . . make that a *cherry* coke."

Wuzzie mocked veneration. "Yes, Missa Benny!" He gave the cocktail an extra splash of cherry.

"I'm not in any mood to laugh at Jack Benny jokes, Wuzz."

Lon motioned for Orrie and Doug to follow him. They crept silently to a table partially hidden by *Barnacle Bill*, the pinball machine. Being the most exposed, Doug reached behind his head surrender-style and folded arms against his ears. He wanted to look as meek as possible. Lips zipped, the boys occasionally sneaked a peek at the older guys.

"You already know Malman's got my cap—stuffed in her stupid bra. It's probably all wrinkled up and ruined by now. I bet the bill's all curled up or bent."

Wuzzie's hand covered his mouth and he drummed his fingers. Sympathetically, he opened his palms. "What are you gonna do?"

"What can I do?"

"Just track Connie down and take it."

"Yeah, sure—out of her bra?! Like I'm really gonna do that. And like I said, I don't want anybody seeing me chasin' her around. Would you like people to see you doing that?"

"I wouldn't. I generally do my best to keep away from her."

"She thinks it's a game . . . And she knows her dad'll blow his top if he finds out."

Wuzzie looked at the ceiling and fidgeted. "Desperate times, man, desperate times." He glanced at Orrie, Lon, and Doug. The boys looked away. Wuzzie whispered and pointed, "Her little brother's right over there."

Ronnie squinted. "Yeah, the little punk hangs around practice sometimes. And I know the Chief, another punk . . . but who's the little blonde kid?"

"Orrie. His mom runs the Thunder Burger."

"OK, yeah, I heard something about a new kid. Whorrie—they've been calling him. Just what we need around here—another little pud."

CHAPTER 12

The Gauntlet

The cafe was stifling. Wuzzie took the fan from the back counter and set it on a chair next to the front door. He propped the door open with a folded magazine, then stepped back and held his arms wide like heat-detecting sensors.

Ronnie said, "Nice try, Wuzz. But I think that's actually making the place hotter." Wuzzie reversed his failed air-conditioning maneuvers and pulled the door tightly closed. He took a seat one stool away from Ronnie.

Ronnie whispered, "I'm cooking up a little scheme to get my cap back." He glanced across the room and fixed a bead on Doug; 'twas a very nefarious bead. He rose dramatically from the stool and swaggered in the direction of his intended dupes. Wuzzie followed. Ronnie barked. "Hey, you little circus freaks." He gave each boy a threatening look. Lon and Doug gawked, terrified. Orrie appeared oblivious. Ronnie glared at Doug and launched a threat. "You look *scared*, you little pud-butt. You *better* be scared . . . Where's your skag sister?"

Doug sounded sincerely apologetic. "I—I don't know. Sorry. But I don't know."

"Figures," Ronnie said. "I heard you were—the nice word is *slooow*. It must be true." The petrified boy remained silent. Ronnie leaned toward Lon. "How about you, Chief? Are you slow too?"

From behind Ronnie, Wuzzie gave the guys a *stay cool* hand gesture. Lon scrunched his face, shrugged, and said, "No. I'm not—I'm just a regular person."

Ronnie pressed. "D'you know the regular skags—Connie and Rhonda?"

"Ummm, yeaaah, I know who they are . . . but I haven't seen 'em."

"Haven't seen 'em? You're an injun, you're supposed to know everything that goes on in the woods. Sooo . . . I think you're holding out on me there, Pow Wow."

"No—really! I never seen 'em. Not since, maybe . . . two days ago . . . over in the park."

"You ain't much of an injun then, are you? A bear could sneak up on you easy—and bite half your butt off." Ronnie made a growling sound and pretended to bite.

Orrie laughed and looked Ronnie in the eye. Ronnie mocked him with a *goo-goo-eyed* lurch. "What are you looking at, little queer bait!?"

"My name's Orrie,"

"Whorrie? Oh yeah, the new kid from the drive-in. Yeah, Whorrie—that name's a perfect fit: Whorrie, the drive-in kid."

Lon and Doug had turned to stone. Orrie rebelled. "I ain't scared of you. And you yourself are a queer babe!"

Doug and Lon cringed. Ronnie and Wuzzie hooted and howled.

Ronnie stifled his laugh, "Queer *babe*? What the hell is wrong with you—it's queer *bait*!"

Orrie asked, "What's queer bait?"

"Queer bait is *you*, punk!"

Lon to the rescue. He stammered, "H-h-he doesn't know a lot of stuff. He used to live with his gran—"

"Shut up, Chief. If I want any dog crap from you, I'll squeeze your head. As a matter of *faaaaact* . . . that goes for everybody. Yep, you're a little trio of circus freaks—and you're all in this together. Just smart-mouthed little punks cruisin' for a brusin' . . . But I'll tell you what: You got one chance—and you better listen good." Ronnie clasped his hands behind his back and paced like an S.S. interrogator. He spun around and made a proposal. "I got a job for you . . . well, it's more of a command, from the Fuhrer himself—and I'm the Fuhrer! . . . Do your job and you get five bucks . . . yeah, that's right—five bucks! I'm a real generous guy. Don't do your job . . . I'll slug you in the guts till you get internal bleeding . . . I've done it before . . . I'll do it again."

Wuzzie turned away to hide a mile-wide grin. He pinched himself to keep from laughing.

Orrie was simply not getting the gist. "If we get eternal bleeding—we'll die."

"Whoa, little Whorrie the brainchild! I'm thinkin' you're startin' to learn how things work around here."

Doug and Lon felt like they were sunk up to their necks in quicksand. They wanted more than anything to go all the way under, to die and get it over with. And, finally, Orrie began to get the message.

"Well, I tell ya, Whorrie. I'm telling all of you little pudnuckers: You have a golden opportunity here. You have the chance to steal the Holy Grail. Yep, I'm throwing down the gauntlet . . . get the chance to retrieve the broomstick from the wicked witch. Succeed: You get five bucks. Fail: It's the hospital . . . or maybe . . . the graveyard."

At Connie's house, the blinds were closed, dark curtains covered the windows. The black-and-gray images on the TV screen flickered from dark to dim, from dim to dark. In a scene from *All My Children,* Erica Kane argued with an elderly physician. Lester wandered into the dining room where again he failed to suppress thoughts that gnawed at his heart and soul. The portrait hanging beside an heirloom china cabinet never failed to set emotion in motion. It was the picture of a woman with flowing hair, dark eyes, and a disarming smile. Though its presence was unbearable, it would always be a part of him, a measure of his worth, a validation of his being. He despised himself for loving her more in death than he had in life. On cue, the merciless agony twisted his face; his hand covered his mouth. He languished, he endured, for he knew love must go on for the sake of the living. Slowly recovering, he walked to the bottom of a stairway.

"Connie? Where the hell are you? Why ain't them dishes done? . . . Connie!"

Connie appeared at the top of the stairs. Lester spoke harshly, "Why ain't nothin' done around here? What the hell you been doin'?!"

Connie clasped her left elbow with her right hand. She looked away, then snapped back and stared Lester in the eye. After a testy, nostril-flaring inhale, she sourly replied, "I'll get to it, I always do."

Lester blustered, "You don't be gettin' smart. You ain't too old for a switchin'—that's what me and Aunt Gret got when we sassed."

"I know the story, Dad. And you both had to walk five miles to school, in the snow, with holes in your shoes."

"I can go out and find me a switch mighty fast."

"Yeah, I bet you would, you sorry old so-and-so."

Lester grabbed the rail and started up the stairs. Connie hollered as she ran, "You made mom kill herself—you alcoholic son of a bitch!"

Lester's feet hammered away. "Damn you, Connie. You watch your damn smart mouth!"

In the upstairs hallway, Connie neared her bedroom. Lester closed in. Connie slipped inside, slammed the door, and bolted for the window. Lester stormed in. As she climbed through, Connie bumped her head on the window frame; the window slid down onto her shoulder. Lester reached out and grabbed her arm. She pulled free and rolled onto the roof. Lester tried to follow, but the window was stuck; he pulled on the frame so hard that the pane cracked. He struggled his way onto the roof. Connie froze at the edge of the roof. Lester stepped toward her. She knelt, laid flat, and rolled off the side grabbing the eavestrough, which gave way under her weight. She landed hard but stayed on her feet. At the end of the roof, Lester wobbled and dropped to a knee. He considered jumping, then thought better. Instead, he shook a clenched fist, pointed, and yelled, "Yer gettin' it when you get home, Miss High and Mighty!"

The elementary school playground featured all the standards: swings, monkey bars, a merry-go-round, a towering slide—all atop a sizzling blacktop. The midday temperature was just a little above 100 F. The metal surfaces were as hot as frying pans. Orrie, Lon, and Doug sat on the steps outside the library, pretending to be cool, calm and collected, but the butterflies in their innards fluttered from toes to nose. When Doug stood up, he was shaky and weak at the knee. Orrie understood and sympathized. He said, "Boy, Doug, when I saw your sister standing in the doorway of your house, she looked like a muscle man—like that guy in the back of comic books."

"Charles Atlas. Not a bad comparison," said Lon. "I really wanna buy some of that stuff he sells. I bet my muscles would start popping out like Wylie Coyote's when he eats that ACME powder."

"I don't think it would work quite that good, Lon," Doug said, but didn't project much strength in his conviction. "At least I'm pretty sure it wouldn't. And you would probably have to do lots and lots of exercise."

"I was just kidding around, Doug. But I'm pretty sure it would work—eventually."

Orrie said, "If not, it would be false advertising. You could get your money back—almost for sure."

Lon gave his head a little shake, "Nah, I wouldn't need a refund. I'm sure it would work. Maybe that's the next thing I'll buy after the skateboard."

Orrie said, "Being a muscle man would be pretty neat."

The sun had shifted. It glowered and grimaced. The boys shaded their eyes. Doug examined his arm. "I'm pretty sure I'm gettin' a sunburn."

Lon said, "There's a little shade under the bicycle shed." They trotted over the asphalt and sat on the scratchy grass. Lon and Orrie checked their arms.

Orrie reminisced. "Last summer I got a sunburn so bad it made me cry."

Doug nodded, "Yeah, I've had 'em that bad."

"Me too," said Lon. "But not for a couple of years."

Orrie reflected on a miracle. "For my cure, grandma told me to pray with Oral Roberts. At the end of his show, he holds his hand up to the TV and you can touch it on the screen. So, I did it. I closed my eyes and prayed really hard for about a whole minute."

"Man, that was a good idea," Doug said, in soft-spoken wonder.

Lon asked dryly, "Did it work?"

"Yeah, it worked. It worked really good. I was completely healed . . . and it only took about a week."

"Wow!" said Doug, totally amazed. Lon was not quite so impressed, but he decided to button his lip.

Orrie said, "My grandma is very religious. Once I told her that this kid, Stevie Clayburn, would always say, 'Jesus peezus' when something went wrong. I asked her if he would go to Hell for saying that. She said he wouldn't, but that we shouldn't say it because it would displease the Lord. So, then I told her about this other kid named Shelby Cordle. He changed the saying to 'Jesus, Jesus, the big fat peezus'. Grandma kinda got mad and said Shelby would definitely be going to Hell."

"Gosh, that doesn't seem fair," said Doug. "It seems like there should be, like, an in-between penalty—maybe like going to the waiting room of Hell, you know, just to scare him . . . then maybe yell at him and let him go up to Heaven."

Lon said, "This whole conversation is boring and stupid, you guys. There's plenty of different things you could be talking about . . . But I do agree your grandma was being way too strict about the punishment."

"Yeah, and when you think about it," said Doug, "God probably thinks it's all pretty funny anyway."

"What?!" said Lon.

"Laughing's a good thing—right? The whole thing about God is doing good things. So, God probably laughs a lot. God probably has a better sense of humor than any of us."

"Actually, that kinda makes sense," said Orrie. "As long as it's not the kind of laughing that could hurt somebody."

"Oh, no," Doug clarified. "I never meant that kind of laughing. Just the good kind."

Lon called upon the voice of reason. "God's got a lot of serious things to do, you guys. He can't go around laughing at stuff all the time . . . This conversation's gettin' stupider and stupider."

Orrie said, "OK, next time I see grandma, I'll tell her your guys' opinion. And I'll tell her about the waiting room idea and the laughing, which will probably make her mad. But one thing I'm pretty sure about—she won't *ever* change her mind about Shelby Cordle—he'll be going to Hell for sure."

Lon interjected, "Ahhh! Enough! No more stories! We have to finish makin' our plan. A: We decided this was the best place to make our move. B: We know what we need to do. C: Now how are we gonna do it? The simpler we keep it, the less chance of making a mistake. So, who does what and when to who?"

Doug eyed the corner of the main school building. "I know it's hot, but if we go climb up on the monkey bars, Connie won't be able to see us at first. We'll be able to set ourselves up in a *strategic* position."

With a pained look, Lon said, "Strategic—you and your crossword puzzles . . . Anyway, is all this fuss really necessary? Our first idea was for me and Orrie to distract her, then for Doug to grab the cap. Simple."

Doug affirmed, "We need more strategy. Something could go wrong." Reluctantly, they moseyed across the blacktop and climbed to the top of the monkey bars, spitting on their hands, making as little contact with the scorching metal as possible. Doug pointed and said, "She'll be coming around the corner of that building, then head straight down the alley."

"Are you sure?" asked Orrie.

"I'm sure, I'm sure. Sure as sure can be. Every other day, at twelve forty-five, even if her chores aren't done, she goes to

Rhonda's house. And Rhonda comes to our house on the other days." Doug spoke with firm conviction. They all fixed their eyes on the corner of the building.

Sweat dripped into Lon's eyes and burned. "We've gotta get out of this sun."

Orrie asked, "So, what if today's different? What if Connie doesn't come by here at exactly twelve forty-five?"

"She *will*. I know her exact schedule. I keep track on a private calendar. When she's out of the house, I'm safe. I can go to the living room and watch TV and mess around and stuff."

"Yes sir, like clockwork, she comes by here every other day and twice on Sunday," Lon quipped.

Doug said, "Nope—just once every other day—and usually not on Sunday, cuz she walks by at a later time on Saturday and stays overnight."

Lon rolled his eyes. "We're counting on you, Doug. This is gonna be our only chance. If she doesn't show, we're sunk."

"She'll be here, Lon. That's not the problem. The problem is—if you guys don't distract her good enough, I won't be able to make the grab. And I'll probably get my butt kicked through the roof of my mouth."

Lon said, "OK, here's the emergency plan. If things get messed up, I'll throw a couple of rocks—not to hit her, just as a distraction."

"Good strategy," said Orrie.

"Yeah . . . that could work," said Doug. "Now, let's say I do make the grab—and that's gonna take some luck—then we've gotta hope she won't chase us because she knows Rhonda's waiting for her. But *believe me*, once they meet up—they'll both come lookin' for us—madder'n wet hens!"

"So, what could we do?" asked Orrie.

"Hide!" said Doug. And that was that.

Not yet in view, Connie walked along the alley next to the elementary school. She was only a minute from the playground. She gently massaged an abrasion on her elbow, then pulled down the brim of Ronnie's cap. Curiously, she peered at the fiery hillside, and compulsively counted each scattered blaze. "Unos, dos, tres, quatro, cinqo—no, sies. Six stupid little fires making all that smoke." She sighed and coughed. Finally, she rounded the corner that led to the playground—and right into the ambush. The boys' hearts were in their throats.

Lon whispered, "Thank God, she pulled the hat out from under her bra. That's gonna make things ten times easier."

Dreading the inevitable, Doug too spoke in a hushed tone. "This ain't gonna be easy, Lon. Don't even think that way. We've got to do everything perfect. And we're gonna need a lot of luck . . . You ready, Orrie?"

"Yep."

Doug said, "I got the bait—and the bait is me. And I've got a secret weapon. I'm gonna call her Constance—she hates that name . . . I'm countin' on ya, Orrie. . ."

Doug and Orrie monkied their way down the monkey bars. Lon remained on the very top bar. As insurance, he clutched a golf-ball-size rock in his right hand and another in his left. With a loud shout, Doug took the daydreaming Connie completely by surprise.

"Hey, Constance?" The other boys laughed extra loud.

She glanced his way. She scowled. Daggers streamed from her smoldering green orbs. Doug had awakened Godzilla. She said, "You might as well just walk over here and take your beatin' now."

Doug chided, "Maybe I don't feel like walkin'. Maybe I'll skip." Doug started skipping in a small circle and sang. "Skip, skip, skip to m' Lou, skip to m' Lou, my *Cahhn-stance."*

Connie fumed. "You're lucky Rhonda's expecting me, or I'd chase you down and pound your brains into jelly."

"What flavor?"

"Blood flavor!"

"Go ahead and try! Skip, skip, skip to m' Lou, skip the m' Lou, my Cahhn-stance." Doug stopped skipping and ran in place. With a Two-Ton Tony Galento accent, he said, "I'll moida ya, ya doidy bum. I'm gonna moitilize ya." Doug started thumbing his nose and shadow boxing.

Connie pursed her lips and squinted. She maintained the evil eye as she continued her path.

Doug flapped his arms daintily and tip-toed toward her. "I'm a magical fairy, Constance. I'm Tinker Bell. Won't you come and fly with me. Constance, Constance, *Cahhhn-stance*!"

Connie charged like a wildebeest fueled by a truck-stop coffee buzz. But her beeline attack came to an abrupt halt when Orrie burst onto the scene, set up a roadblock and pretended to direct traffic. The bewildered Connie's jaw dropped to the tarmac. In sheer terror, Doug stood at the edge of the playfield. The look on Connie's face was a mixture of outrage and disbelief. Orrie upped the ante on his traffic cop routine by inventing a parody to a song he'd heard earlier that day. "Connie, Connie, co Connie, banana bana bo Bonnie, fe fi fo Fonnie—Connie!"

Meanwhile, Doug had circled in from behind and was slowly creeping up to snatch the cap. Connie glanced back over her shoulder. Doug squatted and froze. Showing no sign of having seen Doug, Connie focused an evil eye on the serenading troubadour. Doug came up to a crouch, waved at Lon, then started closing in. Orrie continued to sing and added a little soft shoe.

From high on the monkey bars, Lon opened-up with laughter and a jeer. "What's that in front of you, Orrie? It looks like a giant dump truck. The road is closed—don't let it through." Connie gave Lon a look that turned his blood into slush and his spine into an icicle. But the lion's share of her wrath now fell upon Orrie. She seethed and she smoldered. She sneered and she snarled. "Time's up, little Whorrie. I'm gonna stomp your guts into the ground!"

Two steps and a reach away, Orrie taunted, "You are huge, and you are slow. And you are ugly too. You resemble a giant ground sloth." He began to shuffle his feet and circle to the left like the boxers he had seen on television. He threw a few left punches and transformed into *Cassius Clay*. "You can't catch me. I'm too pretty." He continued to dance in a circle. "I'm too fast . . . I float like a butterfly. . . And I sting like a bee. Bzzz, bzzz!"

Despite her surging fury, Connie summoned enough composure to assume a relaxed pose. Her hands went to her hips. Orrie kept circling, punching, and mouthing off. Connie kept turning on an axis. Her lips moved. She was counting and timing Orrie's clownish jabs. Doug continued to creep up from behind. Connie had synched-up with Orrie. When he threw his next jab, she grabbed his arm and slammed him to the ground. The back of his head hit the asphalt. Doug jumped on her back and snatched the cap. When she whirled around, Doug had raced away. So, Connie turned her attention back to Orrie, who was dizzily struggling to his feet. She kicked him in the floating ribs. He groaned and fell. She stomped on the small of his back. Lon jumped off the monkey bars clutching a rock in his right hand. The groaning Orrie rolled. Lon yelled, "Run, Doug! Run!" Doug hesitated. Connie dug her heel between Orrie's shoulders. Lon threw a rock at Connie but missed. Doug nodded to Lon, then took off across the playfield. Connie reared back and aimed another kick. Suddenly, she screamed and grabbed her thigh. Lon's stone missile had found its mark. Doug stopped and looked back. Orrie crawled toward the playfield.

Connie glanced at Orrie—*easy prey*; she'd get back to him. Still feeling the sting of the rock, she kneaded her throbbing thigh. Now, it was Lon she wanted, and she meant to have him. Lon saw Doug returning to help Orrie. He looked to join them. Connie did some quick hobbling to cut him off. Well aware of Connie's foot speed, Lon backed toward the monkey bars. With a smarting limp, Connie stalked him. Lon's head swiveled as he sought an avenue out. But even with her handicap, he knew she'd be on him within seconds; instead of bolting, Lon headed for the big slide. Connie closed in. Doug hollered and waved Ronnie's red cap, "Connie, here it is—your boyfriend's *ca-hap*!" Connie glared at him; it gave Lon just enough time to shoot up the ladder. At an altitude of about 12 feet, Lon was clearly safe from Connie's reach. If she climbed the ladder, he planned to swoosh down, run for his life, and eventually meet up with Orrie and Doug at their boxcar hideout. He knew it would be touch-and-go, but he also figured he could buy some time, allowing Doug and Orrie to get in the clear. Connie was in just as much of a quandary. She darted to the side of the slide, hopped onto the middle, and started to climb. Lon started back down the ladder. Doug and Orrie had backtracked, as not to desert Lon. Doug badgered, "Connie's a skag! Connie's a skag!"

Orrie wheezed as he yelled, "Hey, Conster Monster, you stupid skag butt!"

Connie pointed at Lon. “I’ll get you later, Chief!” She fumed. “And I’m gonna grind glass in your face!”

Orrie put an arm over Doug’s shoulder and gimped along. Doug strained to support his weight but was clearly on the verge of collapse. Connie breathed slow and deep, oxygenating her blood. Ignoring the agony of the drum in her thigh, Connie streaked toward Orrie and Doug. The boys realized that recovering Ronnie’s cap was no longer her goal. Beating them till their guts oozed out of their mouths and converting their scrotums to swimming caps now drove her demonic intentions. Envisioning this, Orrie and Doug instinctively parted; it was now every man for himself. Orrie was soon huffing and groaning. He dropped to one knee and held his side. Easy *pickins*. Connie zeroed in. Doug went in for a medevac. He squatted low, underhooked Orrie’s arm and tried to lift him. Using all his might, Doug brought Orrie to his feet; the two hopped and galloped as though in a three-legged race. Orrie winced with every step; one of his shoes came off, but he paid it no mind. Connie closed in.

Orrie groaned, “I feel like I got a knife in me.”

“We gotta run, Orrie. I *gotta* let you go again and we both gotta run—she’s right behind us!” As Orrie speed-walked, his moans would have scared a ghost. Pure fear numbed his pain; he clenched his teeth and ran for all he was worth.

Connie’s scream was venomous, “You little bastards! I’m gonna use your ugly little heads for soccer balls.”

The boys neared an eight-foot-tall cedar fence. They were trapped. Doug lowered his arms and interlocked his fingers. With a boost, Orrie ended up straddling the fence. “Yeow.” He laid his torso over the boards and reached down for Doug. Clasping Doug’s hands he dropped behind the fence.

Halfway over, Doug yelled, "OK, let go!" As he started pulling himself to the other side, Connie reached out and grabbed his shorts. Doug shifted his weight and let gravity take over. Connie yanked hard and reduced his trunks to dish rags; the togs lay to waste in her vengeful grasp. Orrie reached for Doug's hair and towed him rest of the way. Doug landed on top of him. Orrie gasped as the air rushed out of his lungs. Diaphragm paralyzed, eyes bulging, he feared he'd met his fate. After a desperate, resurrecting breath, he thanked God and Jesus as well.

From the other side of the cedar barrier, Connie said, "I hope you enjoyed your stomping, little Whorrie—there's a lot more where that came from. And Doug's gonna end up in the obituaries." Connie grabbed the fence top and tried to pull herself over, but the thin boards started to bend and crack. Backing up she made a short run and tried to vault over, but this time the ends of the two fence planks snapped off. She backed away, eyed the fence for a vaulting spot closer to a post. She gave it another try, adding a gymnastic move to hook a heel over the boards. A plank broke away and she fell into the grass. She exhaled, exasperated, and looked for a way around. She was facing a fifty-yard wall of wood that shielded the properties, mostly of retired people, from the schoolyard. Connie rubbed the big red spot on her thigh. She went up to the fence, hammered with her fists, and screamed, "You guys are dead! Yer two dead little punks! I'm gonna break your damn necks!"

Behind the fence, the boys cowered, terrified by the maniacal rant from the blind side. Doug whispered, "Stay quiet. She might think we already made it across the road." They scanned the sun-toasted lawn. Beneath the trees, the rotten pears and apples bled a sickly-sweet odor; their goo covered the grass and leaves. Twenty feet away, loomed a foreboding doghouse. Doug's bottom lip quivered; his face paled. "My God! Oh, Holy God . . . we're in Spike's yard."

"Spike . . . You mean a dog?"

Doug whispered, "Yeah, I mean a dog—and he bites like a shark!"

CHAPTER 13

Hedging Bets

For a few seconds, Deputy Robert Welski felt like a myopic bat when he walked into the cavern-dark Runnin' Bear Tavern. His pride and joy, a football autographed by Vince Lombardi, was tucked under his arm. On the black-and-white TV, which sat high on a shelf behind the bar, smiling American soldiers de-boarded a transport plane on an airfield in Da Nang. The first U.S. ground troops had arrived in Vietnam. Lester, Mayor Figgs, and Ski watched in tight-jawed silence. Figgs switched off the set and disgustedly shook his head, "That's the biggest mistake this country's made since the Civil War." Fiery-eyed, he fixed his gaze on Lester, then on Ski. "Do either of you think we belong over there?!"

Ski puffed through his lips, "I don't like it, but time'll tell, I guess."

Lester blustered, "Hell no! Hell no, we don't belong in another damn jungle war. Let the gooks kill the gooks." Ski and Figgs seemed taken aback by the harsh remark. "Yeah, that's right—I said it! Let 'em go to town on each other . . . and when there's only one left—gimme a gun!" Lester's eyes were wild. Was it dark humor or light insanity? Figgs and Ski couldn't tell.

"How 'bout a beer, Deputy?" said Figgs. "On the house."

"Well, officially, I'm on duty, but I been hankerin' for a beer all week."

Figgs handed Ski a glass of beer, then drew one for himself. He sighed, "Here we are . . . three men from three different wars: proven patriots, law-abiding citizens, good men, proud Americans. We served our country, did our share—but *we* had good cause. It was clear cut. Them kids goin' over there—and that's what they are—no mor'n kids: Some of 'em won't ever see home again . . . and it's all for nothin'."

Lester clenched his teeth and his fists, "And them kids that do get home . . . they ain't ever gonna be the same." Lester got quiet. He fought to holster his anger and choke back his tears. Gasping, he said, "Never be the same."

"Hell no, they won't be the same!" blurted Figgs. "But the big shots—they'll make out all right: Corporations get rich off war, politicians get re-elected, brown-nose generals puff out their chests and pin on a few more shiny medals."

Lester added, "The rich get richer, the poor get poorer . . . and if them kids don't die fightin' . . . they'll die a little at a time . . . with every passin' day."

Charles Figgs, Private First-Class, World War I; Lester Malman, Staff Sergeant, World War II; Robert Welski, Corporal, Korean War were three men returning to bygone battlefields, trapped in a limbo that never lets you go; it haunts your dreams, drains your will, erodes your faith, and sullies all hope. Though disillusioned and scarred for life, these men were part of a brotherhood, distinguished by their service; they were men bonded in a shared sense of duty, loyalty, and mortality.

Ski said, "Sometimes the whole world seems to be snowballin' downhill. I recall a time when a man's word meant something, and his life counted for something . . . at least it did back home. . ."

Figgs seized the moment. After four quick claps he lifted his voice and sang, "Deep in the heart of Texas!" The mood lifted.

"I'm right there with ya, Charlie," said Lester. "I always have liked Texas—and the people that live there. In fact, I never did meet anybody from Texas I didn't like . . . That being said, I remember once tellin' a lady that very same thing, and she said, 'Well Mister, *you* haven't met *my* ex-husband!'"

The men smiled and shared a chuckle. Then, like a bolt out of the blue, terror and hatred flashed in Lester's eyes. He choked on his words and stifled a sob. Figgs slid Lester a fresh beer and tried to offer a little comfort, "Believe me Lester, and it's coming deep from my heart—you got every reason to feel the way you do. None of us can imagine what you men went through in that filthy, rotten hole."

Ski sneaked Figgs an inquisitive look. Figgs signaled for him to hold off.

Pain, hurt, and wells of sorrow poured out as Lester spoke. "Fightin' Japs—that was a different thing than fightin' reg'lar men." Lester stood and stared at the back door. "In that pukin', puss-oozin' pit o' hell . . . I seen 'em . . . I seen what they did . . . I seen 'em . . . I seen 'em do it all . . ."

Figgs' words were solemn, sympathetic, sincere. "I've known you since you were a kid Lester; matter of fact, I held you as a baby. You've been to the other side of hell and back and they couldn't kill you. But I'm tellin' it straight, and right out as a friend—all that hate welled up in your heart . . . it's got you killing your own self."

"Yeah, I got hate in my heart. And what I hate is the stinkin', dirty, ignorant people I gotta live around. You want a list? Here's your damn list: I hate Japs, number one; Mexicans, number two; coloreds, Jews, chinks, gooks, injuns, queers, albinos. I hate A-rabs and Australian ab-o-rigines. I hate all the Toby-Gussard-lookin' freaks in this world, and I hate midgets—I can't stand a damn midget for nothin'!"

Charlie searched for a way out. "Sometimes you're a real hoot, Lester. I know you don't mean half o' that crazy stuff you're sayin'."

"You're right! I don't mean *half* of it—I mean all of it!" Ski and Figgs shared knowing expressions but didn't know how to express them.

Lester was breathless and his heart was hammering. "I gotta clear my head." He forced himself to stand proud, walked to the back door, and out into the parking lot.

The faces of Charlie and Ski were long, lost, and drained. The silence was not golden.

Ski finally mustered up a few words. "Well, Charlie, just like us, I imagine those boys over there in Vietnam figure they're doin' the right thing."

"Well . . . I suppose they might *think* they are anyway. Maybe that'll be enough to get most of 'em home." All at once, pride, ol' Glory, and ferocity lit up Figgs' mind. "But I'll say it again: Lester in '44, me back in '18, and you in '53—we all knew damn well what we were fightin' for!"

"I surely believe we did. We all should be mighty proud—and the whole damn world oughta be mighty grateful. And *shoot*, right now, maybe we don't understand what's goin' on over there in Vietnam . . . but those men fightin' over there—they have every right to believe in what they're doin'—and we all better damn well be grateful." Figgs nodded. He bowed his head as though contemplating the Gospel.

Figgs stepped from behind the bar and glanced at the back door. "Lester must still be out there. Normally, he lets you know when he's leavin' for the day."

"Is he gonna be, OK?" Ski considered heading out back. "He won't try to hurt himself, will he?"

Figgs glanced again at the back door. "Like I said, I've known Lester since he was a kid. But I've never seen him this bad. He's putting on that I-don't-care act about the fire, but I know he's torn up inside . . . No, he won't hurt himself—he loves them kids too much."

"That's a powerful motivation . . . but with his livelihood gone—what's he gonna do?"

"There's no worry about that. That mill's been a goin' concern for years. He's got some money squirreled away . . . But right now, more than anything, it's the men who've been depending on that mill for employment—that's what's bothering him more than anything. He had six or seven guys working for him, paycheck to paycheck. Now they've got nothin'. Helping men provide for their families—that always did make Lester feel like he counted for something. That mill was a saving grace."

"You can't beat that. When he comes back, maybe we can get him thinking about baseball or something different at least. I wanted to bring it up earlier, but the time never seemed right. I've heard from a couple of different people that Lester got a tryout with the Giants before the war. Is that just small-town rumors?"

"No rumor. He did. But he didn't make it. He was too slow, they said."

"I'll be darned. That's really somethin' . . . It's too bad."

"It's a cold, cruel world in a lotta ways. If we counted up the people who 'almost made it', they could probably form their own country." Figgs took a lingering look at some of the framed boxing photos behind the bar.

Ski had to squint because of the dim lighting, but he made out a likeness. "I'll be dogged, Charlie. Is that you?"

A little bashful and a little boastful, Figgs said, "Guilty as charged, Deputy—I did do some boxing in the service. And I wasn't half bad. I even had a couple of pro fights when I got out." Figgs walked back behind the bar and took one of the pictures from the wall. "Right out of the Roarin' 20s . . . Good gosh, was that ever a time."

Ski set the football on the bar and took the photo from Charlie. He handled the framed memoir with the greatest of respect. "So, what happened?"

"The war. Mustard gas. My lungs were burned, and I just couldn't go the rounds. Then I married a gal. Hard to believe she followed me all the way out here from Rhode Island. But she did and we were happy . . . I lost her in '58, a cold December day . . . Now you know the short, and not-so-sweet, story of my life."

"Sorry about your wife. A mighty hard thing to go through. It must be hard to be alone."

"We're never alone, Deputy. You'll understand that one day. You notice it in the little things—if you pay attention: a dish moves in the rack, a dove coos outside your window, a frog croaks on a frosty morning, a cloud changes shape. Our loved ones are always with us."

Ski nodded. "I'll start paying attention."

Figgs smiled and winked. "Now back to boxing. I'm not whining, but things haven't been the same since Marciano left in '56. To you, I'm sure that seems like the days of the pyramids. Too bad you never got to see Louis fight."

"I did see him. The heavyweight title on TV. I was 12, maybe 13. He knocked out Billy Conn."

"Right on the money!"

Ski paused in a search for words. "Well, that's one heck of a deal, anyway—you being a boxer. I got no doubt you can handle yourself. Nothin' like the fights, man . . . I can't remember—does Clay have a fight coming up?"

"Clay . . . I believe he goes by something different now."

"Yeah, I forgot—Muhammad *Alley*."

"As if he hasn't got people riled up enough over his big mouth."

"He does some hollerin' all right, but I really *do* think he could be bringing back the fight game."

"If he can do that—I'm all for him . . . Anyway, he does have a fight coming—Patterson, in November."

"Could be a good one."

"I believe so. But my money's on Patterson."

“I dunno, Charlie. After beating Liston twice . . . I gotta go with Clay.”

“Five bucks on it?”

“Well, I’m a little light these days . . . but we could make it a gentleman’s bet.” They shook on it.

“Now regardin’ the ball: Over the phone, you said you had a deal in mind.” Rounding the end of the bar, Figgs motioned for Ski to follow him to the pawn area. Ski grabbed the Packers ball and took it to the display case. Even in the gloomy cave of the Runnin’ Bear, the jewelry sparkled. The zircons mirrored the light, the true diamonds danced. Ski looked over the rings and pointed to a modest gem blessed with a tiny crystal glint. He said, “That’s the one. That’s the ring for Rain . . . Straight across for the ball?!”

“Good eye. That’s a real diamond, real gold. One carat. But even at a friend’s price, I’m gonna need a hundred.” The mayor’s expression was regretful, but business was business.

“I could go fifty-five, but for me, a hundred might as well be a million.”

“I’ll hold it as long as you need.”

“Hmm . . . fifty more bucks. I got nothin’ else to hock—I’m gonna need a while.”

“As long as you need. . .”

“What would a ring like that cost—new?”

“Five, maybe six hundred—probably more?”

Ski's eyes grew wide. "Man-oh-man . . . OK, hold onto that thing. I'll figure somethin' out."

They had not seen Lester slip through the back door. He had followed the whole negotiation.

Ski took one last look at the Packers ball. His fingers clutched the threads, and he faked a long pass. He handed Figgs the ball, which the mayor slowly rotated, examining every square inch. "Lombardi, Starr, Hornung, Taylor—"

"Don't worry, Charlie. That ball's as real as the air we're breathin'." Figgs was clearly enamored, but he didn't appear a hundred percent convinced. "I swear—it's the real thing. And I got the autographs in person—all six of 'em . . . Lombardi's signature alone makes it worth way more than fifty bucks."

"A '62 Packers football with six autographs. Fifty bucks . . . hmmm . . . very tempting . . . All right, I'll take your word, and I'll give you a pawn ticket good for a whole year."

"Fair enough." Figgs handed Ski the fifty.

The mayor removed the ring from the showcase and locked it in a small wall safe, then walked back to the bar with the football. "And I'm puttin' this big ol' jewel on its own little stand, dead center, back of the bar. As long as I have it—it'll be my pride and joy."

Ski lingered at the showcase, admiring Figgs' baseball card collection. His eyes locked on one particular card. "Hey, Charlie, what's this Elias Gussard card worth?"

Charlie headed back to the showcase. "Those are a dime a dozen. I just put it in there to honor the man. Just about all of the Gussard cards out there are drawings, like that one. There's a few grainy photo ones, but they're not worth much either. Most of 'em were made in the '40s and '50s."

"Is that story true . . . about Gussard: that there were some really nice cards made, with good, clear photographs—but they all burned up?"

Lester cut in. "It's true, Welski. You gotta brush up on your baseball history."

"It's kind of a long story," Figgs said. "There was a lawsuit and the cards had to be burned—all 498."

Lester butted in. "There were five hundred, but Elias was overseas when they printed the first batch. They sent him two cards and tried to get a release. He went off the handle, burned 'em up. Then he got on the phone with his big shot New York lawyer and a suit was filed—the whole batch had to be burned."

Ski was intrigued. "Somebody must have stashed a few . . ."

"Nope," said Figgs. "A security firm counted every single one. Papers were signed and the cards were burned in front of witnesses. It was a mighty big deal at the time."

"I'll be darned," said Ski. "I always thought it was a rumor cuz it didn't make much sense."

"He was a religious man, Deputy. No drinkin', no smokin'," Figgs said. "The cards were printed up for The Red Crow Whiskey Company. They put—"

Again, Lester butted in. "They put their name on the back of the card, along with a picture of a bottle of whiskey. Eli Gussard wanted nothin' to do with it."

Figgs added, "Yep, it's a true story. One of them sports stories that'll live on and on—another version of ashes to ashes."

Ski said, "Literally . . . Man, what do you think a card like that'd be worth today?"

Lester looked at Figgs. Neither had a clue. Figgs threw out a number. "I'd say bidding would start, at least—fifty, sixty thousand."

Lester said, "I'd say more like a quarter-million, Charlie."

"Yeah . . . I could see that."

"Jeez," said Ski. "An autographed copy of *The Old Man and the Sea* only went for two-thousand a couple of years back."

"There you go," said Lester. "You gotta keep up on your baseball."

"Hell," said Figgs. "I'll go ahead and *give* you one of them new Gussard bubble gum cards. Maybe your boy'll want one . . . Collector-wise—it'll never be worth more than a plug nickel."

"Don't matter. I admire the guy, so I'll be glad to take one."

Figgs headed for the showcase and reminisced. "The man left his family, his home, and gave up the greatest sport in the world so he could serve his country . . . In the end, he gave up his *life*. That was one *helluva* man . . . a damn fine American. Growing up with him was a pure joy. He was a good friend—my best friend."

"I'll bet you played a little ball together."

"Oh yeah. We played football and baseball. He was always a pitcher—from day one. Me, I got bounced around; finally ended up in right field . . . sometimes . . . those kinds of memories . . . it seems like they happened just yesterday."

"Then along came a war—did you guys ever meet up when you were over there?"

"Never did," said Figgs. "I was one of the last to go; by then, it was all but over. But I do still remember reading that first headline: ELIAS GUSSARD TO PITCH IN OVER THERE! That was really somethin'."

Lester stepped up to the pool table. Figgs handed Ski the complimentary Gussard baseball card. Lester started racking the pool balls; he cleared his throat. "That fifty bucks burnin' a hole in your pocket, Welski?"

"A bird in hand, Lester."

Lester guffawed. "Hey Charlie, we got Ben Franklin in the room."

Figgs said, "Ben Franklin was a smart man."

"Yeah, but I bet he didn't have a diamond ring; especially, the one in that safe." Lester pointed. "That safe right over there."

Ski said "And *safe's* the key word. I know that ring'll be safe in that safe. I've got half the money. All I need is a little more time."

"Time? Time's a-wastin'." Lester picked up a pool cue, reached out, and waved it at Ski. "Come on, buddy. You in love or not . . . ain't that woman worth takin' a chance on?"

Ski pulled the fifty from his pocket and handed it to Figgs. "Just to get it straight—it ain't you drawin' me in—it's just that you're makin' a little bit of sense for once—and that's the whole of it." Ski reached out for the cue.

Figgs activated the running-bear-chasing-the-Indian carving. Like little kids, the men watched it 'til it stopped.

Both on one knee, Orrie and Doug made a tactical survey of Spike's entire yard. They needed the fastest and safest path out of the front gate. Thrice they scanned the rotten apples and pears beneath the trees, the weed-infested flower bed dwarfing the gnome statues, the bucket and the hose next to the lawn faucet, the house's paint-peeled back wall, the tattered screen door hanging crooked on a loose hinge; Spike's doghouse, bowl, and chain; the stone sundial, the dying hedge; and the yawning, enticing front gate. The boys rose to a squat, then up to a crouch, then they crept. After two steps, Orrie crumbled, rolled on his side, and quietly groaned. He lay perfectly still and said, "It's like a red-hot poker—stabbing and twisting around. Ahh, ohh, mmm. I'm afraid to move." After an agonizing half-minute, relief came to his face. "Whoa, OK, it's gone. Completely gone. It doesn't hurt a bit—kinda like a light switch went off."

"I know the feeling . . . Connie must have kicked you in the kidney—that's one of her specialties. But don't worry, that pain'll come back when you least expect it. You're nowhere close to being out of the woods."

Taking shallow breaths, Orrie rose to one knee and lightly prodded his back. Gingerly, he got to his feet. "It really is gone. But I'm gonna try not to bend my back, not unless I absolutely have to."

"Yeah, that's the best way to go. Don't put any pressure on it."

The boys squashed a dozen rotten apples and pears as they walked. Every time Orrie stepped on one with his stocking foot he grimaced. About twenty feet from the doghouse was a large sundial. They approached the stone decor slowly, finally coming to kneel beside its sturdy base. All was quiet. Doug picked up a small rock, eyed the doghouse, looked at Orrie, and said, "I gotta do it. If he comes out, I'll distract him, and you go for that stick over by the faucet."

With nerves of steel, Doug tossed the rock onto the roof of the doghouse. No sign of Spike. "He's gotta be inside the main house," said Doug.

"But that screen door to the porch is partly open."

"I know. That worries me too, but the way I see it—we can either stay low and sneak along the fence and hedge, or we can just run all-out for the gate."

"I'm feeling pretty good. I think I can run for it."

Doug stood tall and hoisted his underpants up to his chest. He pulled Ronnie's red cap down tight, so it wouldn't fly off. He looked down at his bleached white briefs. "Do you think they'd put a kid in the delinquent hall for being outside in his underpants?"

Orrie felt Doug had a valid question and gave the prospect serious consideration. "I know there's some kind of don't-go-around-naked law, but I'm not sure about underpants. They could put you in there, I guess, but . . . hmmm . . . yeah, I guess they probably would. If I were you—I'd be worried."

Doug sighed, "Great."

Orrie removed his lone shoe and raised it as a weapon. "If that dog comes before I can get to that stick, I'll slap him right on the nose."

Doug rubbed his thighs and calves. "If Spike gets a hold of me, he'll rip my legs to shreds."

"He won't—I'll run for that stick and fight him off. I'll jab his ribs. I'll dance like Cassius Clay and use that stick like a sword."

Clearly not comforted by this valiant claim, Doug said, "Thanks for offerin', but I think chasin' Spike off would take a whole lot more than that."

"Well, doggone it—I'm sure gonna try."

One last time, the boys scanned the landscape. They fixed a gaze on the gate, gaping wide-open right the middle of the hedge. In their eyes, a twinge of hope eked from a deep gouge of doubt. Each boy gathered a lung full of air. Doug said, "Stay right on my tail—you gotta run like you shot outta the devil's keester!"

"I never heard of that—"

"You heard of it now."

Before the boys took a single step, a throaty, menacing growl threatened from behind.

CHAPTER 14

Predicaments

On a distant hill, the clamoring bleats of four pestering goats rang out. Ronnie held up a bulging grocery bag. The goats followed him under the big horse-chestnut tree. The animals crowded in as Ronnie sat cross-legged with his back against the mighty trunk. The goats pushed and nudged. Ronnie said, "You bunch of crazy knot heads. There's plenty here. Tiny, you wait, you're too pushy." Ronnie gave Wags a big slice of apple. "He gets one first because he's polite."

The other three goats nudged fervently. Ronnie reached into the bag for a handful of fruit slices. "Here Ghostie, Toro." As he gave the now-patient Tiny, the biggest and best of the slices, he noticed the bite on her leg. While the smallest goat munched her treat, Ronnie took a good look at the wound. "Hold still, Tiny. Hold still!" He gently brushed aside her fur. "Must have been a stray dog—coyotes never come up here . . . it ain't all that bad, but I'll have Wuzzie get his dad up here to take a look. He's a vet." All four goats got antsy and nervous. "Oh, he ain't gonna hurt you, you bunch of babies. He'll just bandage up her leg." Ronnie stood and tossed a couple of handfuls of fruit onto the fried grass.

"I wanted to visit you guys before I face the big battle tomorrow—it's all on the line—the Angels game, Disneyland, money for college, and they'll be sending up some scouts for my senior year."

Ronnie paced like a tiger in a cage. "Yeah, all I gotta do is face a guy who throws fireballs, rockets, and this weird spiral curve thing they don't even have a name for . . . It'll be hard enough just to get on base, let alone, the way I figure it anyway, knock one out of the park . . . fat chance of that."

Pulling a handful of fruit from the bag, Ronnie looked each goat in the eye and said, "Yep, my whole future is on the line; it's my way out of this stupid, boring little town . . . to me, except for you guys, this place is the edge of nowhere."

The goats crowded and nudged. "Bleat, bleat, naaaah, naaaah."

"If I don't knock it out of the park, I'm gonna end up workin' at the mill, and having my name carved on a barstool at the Runnin' Bear . . . So, you all better get serious now . . . They say you four shaggy old boogers are some kind of magical wizards—so tell me, Oh Great Wizards: Am I gonna do it? Am I gonna be an All-Star?!"

The goats bleated loudly, jumped high, and danced on their hind legs.

Ronnie scattered the last of the fruit slices here and there. As he walked down the hill, he said, "All right! That's *all* I needed to know!"

While Ronnie was talking to the goats, Orrie and Doug were held at bay, frozen, and blind to the snarling dog at their backs; Deputy Welski was chalking up a pool cue; Rain was watching Father Dom and a nurse guide old folks to booths and tables at the restaurant; Figgs was watching Lester drink; Connie and Rhonda were walking toward the Thunder Burger.

The drive-in was packed for the first time since Rain had taken over. Shortly after inheriting the place from her uncle, she was informed he had fallen nine months behind on the lease payments. Hard were the times: a harsh winter had shut down the woods and hurt the crops; a summer drought came along and shut down the woods again; the lumber mill had been all but closed; the cattle farms were struggling as never before—some of the spreads further south had to have water trucked in for the livestock. Thanks to the Brayton irrigation system, migrant families and dairy farmworkers still had gainful employment. Everybody else was on the verge of pulling up stakes and heading for greener pastures. But there were no greener pastures; Snidely Whiplash had foreclosed on McDonald's farm; and the boy looking after the sheep had nothing to cry wolf about.

As the nurses tended to the seniors, Father Dom and Rain set up an assembly line of ice cream sundaes. Father Dom scooped ice cream into paper bowls while Rain followed with toppings, whipped cream, and a cherry for the top. Father Dom turned to fill cups with soft drinks and coffee. Rain started delivering desserts. Connie and Rhonda walked in and went directly to the jukebox. Rhonda played "Baby Love" by the Supremes and started dancing. The room lit up. The girls made the rounds talking and laughing with the old folks. Rain handed each of them a strawberry sundae. She said, "Girls, stick around. You two are the cleanup crew." A lady in a wheelchair pulled a camera strap from around her neck and asked for a photo with Rain, the girls, and Father Dom. Rain waved at Father Dom who was in the kitchen cleaning the ice cream counter. He happily trekked over for the group photo.

The old lady's eyes twinkled when the nurse returned her camera. Rain and Father Dom returned to the kitchen.

Father Dom picked up a hand towel and went back to wiping the ice cream counter. When Rain joined in, she noticed chocolate syrup spots on one of the Father's gloves. "That glove will stain, Father. It'll take some bleach. And there's a smudge on your collar too. In ten minutes, I can have them white as snow."

"I'll be fine, Rain. I have plenty more where these came from. They're all part of the uniform: frock, the collar, the gloves, and a gold pocket watch. I've found these gloves a softer touch when I help folks with chair transfers and such."

"All right," she relented, having become accustomed to his stubbornness. "Anyway, Connie and Rhonda are going to help me clean up. So, I'll let you tend to your flock. Thanks so much for helping."

"Thank *you*! It was a wonderful day out for all."

As Father Dom headed back to the dining room he asked, "Where's your partner in crime?"

"Doing his rounds. At least I hope that's what he's doing. He shouldn't have much policing to do. Most days around here, we don't even get a cat-up-a-tree call. So, he'd better have a good story." Rain touched Father Dom's arm. "If you hadn't helped out, I'd have drowned in a swamp." Father Dom winked.

Father Dom and the nurses accompanied the happy crowd out the door. Connie and Rhonda cleared tables and wiped up. They straightened the furniture and refilled the napkin holders. Rain recounted the cash, then put it in the register. She said, "Check the ashtrays before you go, girls."

"OK," said Connie. "Then we're heading out."

As she made her way to the food-prep room, Rain called, "Thanks ladies, you earned your sundaes." A little annoyed and a little concerned over Ski's failure to check in, Rain ran some hot water into the sink and glanced at the clock. She scowled. "He should have been back at least an hour ago."

Three moody men lurked within the neon and shadows of the Runnin' Bear Tavern. Patsy Cline's "San Antonio Rose" hopped and bopped inside the jukebox. Lester swigged down another beer. A game of pool was about to begin, with $50 on the line. Figgs readied a quarter on his thumbnail. Lester said, "Call it, Welski."

Ski said, "Tails."

The coin went up, twirled, took one big bounce, two little ones, and spun until heads came up. "Go ahead and rack 'em; I'll take stripes," said Lester. Ski placed the eight ball in the middle of the triangular frame, then spread the stripes and solids around evenly. Ski broke. The cue ball hit the formation dead center; the other balls scattered into a well-spaced pattern. There was a little clustering near one of the pockets, and the eight ball had settled against a bumper. Lester drained his beer. "The drunker I get, the more accurate I get." He took a bead on the cue ball and struck it with both power and precision. A striped ball shot right into the pocket. Lester had a lot of *easy-as-pie* shots, but instead of dropping them, he pretended the cue was a rifle and performed a military drill. The shot he finally chose required a snap of the wrist; Lester hit it clean. The cue ball banked twice, then nudged a striped ball into the pocket. This left him with a choice of three, piece-of-cake, shots. From there on, he may as well have been shooting fish in a barrel. He dropped stripe after stripe.

The eight ball was beautifully aligned with a corner pocket. "I'm gonna let you sweat it Welski. I'm gonna take a quick leak, do little spinnin' on a stool, listen to some tunes, have couple o' beers, then polish off that eight ball."

"Just take your shot, Lester, I gotta get back to the restaurant."

Figgs said, "And no more drinking, Lester. You gotta get those kids ready for that game tomorrow."

"Ready for what game?! They turn in their *unies* tomorrow. You gettin' senile?"

"Didn't you get a call?"

"What are you talkin' about?"

"You got a game tomorrow—against Pemmican, with that Kenny West kid. The idiots running the show messed up. It turns out Ronnie and West are tied for that All-Star spot."

"I ain't in no mood for jokes, Charlie."

Welski stepped in. "No joke, Lester. They were supposed to call you."

"I ain't hardly been home cuz of that fire . . . So, hell no! Nobody called me. This is a load of BS. Ronnie got that spot. He got the letter—a signed document!"

Ski and Figgs exchanged looks, compared notes, and nodded to confirm the situation. They turned to convince Lester.

Ski said, "I know it's kind of hard to believe—almost like we're playing a practical joke. But league management screwed things royal."

Figgs said, "I guarantee you, I argued with those fools for most of an hour. They just kept saying the numbers were the numbers. The games on—tomorrow at one o'clock."

Lester huffed and puffed. "You guys *are* serious . . .damn! . . . So, do the kids know?"

"The word's gettin' around," said Figgs." Some of the VFW guys are making calls and even going door-to-door. And they're doin' a little work on the field—spreadin' some lime."

"Damn! Ronnie's got his work cut out for him. That West kid's struck him out at least ten times over the last two years. Dammit. Kenny damn West, fifteen years old—that kid could play Triple-A ball . . . I gotta figure this out."

Miraculously, Lester started acting like he was half-way sober. He grabbed a pool cue. "Oh well, first things first. One last beer, Charlie."

"You been drinkin' since dawn, Lester . . . I don't do this very often, but today—I'm cutting you off. You gotta get those kids together and get ready for that game."

Lester flashed an expression of comic indignation. "Well, Mr. Hoity Toity, I got a bottle of whiskey at home—so I'm gonna cut myself from off to back on."

Figgs shrugged.

Ski sat on a stool and lit up a Winston; Figgs slid him a cup of coffee and said, "You better have a couple of cups too, Lester."

Lester scowled and howled. "Coffee ain't gonna do me no good! Can't you tell—I'm drunk out of my mind—I do believe I'm turning into a werewolf!" He howled again. "Lon Chaney, Jr.!"

Having reached the end of his patience, Ski said, "Take your shot, Lester!"

Fake-staggering to the table, Lester's pool cue bumped the multi-colored swag lamp, which caused his hulking shadow to wobble and sway. In the manner of a snooty British butler, he said, "My word—you're in a bit of a sticky wicket, old chap." He daintily tapped on a far corner pocket. Ski's expression was unreadable. Lester backed away from the table and re-demonstrated a clumsier version of his West Point rifle drill. He passed gas all the way back to the table and folded over with hilarity. "I love fartin'!"

"Take your shot, Malman!" Ski said with a hint of anger.

Lester made goo-goo eyes at Ski and said, "Are you *ruffy* the tough man, or *tuffy* the rough man?" He laughed heartily, leaned over the table, and again tapped the far corner pocket. Feigning silly grogginess, he lined up the shot. Slowly, dramatically, he drew back the pool cue, making eyes at the seductive eight ball as it lay naked and vulnerable. "Say good-bye to yer fifty bucks, Welski."

With a resounding *crack*, Lester struck the white ball, which *smacked* into the eight ball, which shot into the pocket like a bullet. But then, quite unexpectedly, the cue ball continued to snail along, getting closer and closer to the forbidden corner pocket. By the laws of physics, the ball should have come to a dead stop, but it didn't; it was like a magical string was gently tugging at it. Finally, it did stop—but only after oozing into the pocket like thick honey. Coordination and faculties impaired, Lester had shot himself in the foot. Astonishment! Ski's eyes shined; his hand covered a wide smile.

"Scratch!" declared Figgs, joyfully waving the cash. He handed the money to Ski, along with a small, velvet box. Making no eye contact, Lester skulked out the back door. Ski flipped open the velvet box and admired the sparkling jewel.

Still stunned, Ski said, “Man, I just can’t believe he scratched on that last shot. It was a piece of *fudge cake*—how the hell could he have missed?”

The eyes of Charlie Figgs twinkled. “Mr. Welski, I’ll tell you a little secret. I’ve seen Lester sink an eight ball a thousand times. That last shot . . . that was just his way of saying congratulations!”

All Orrie and Doug could see was the Promised Land through the gateway that lay before them. All they could hear was the fearsome growl of the dreaded Spike. Orrie swallowed hard, slowly raising the tennis shoe he held in a death grip. With all due temerity, he slowly turned to face his fate. The terrifying creature Orrie’s eyes fell upon was a trembling, old dachshund with a little grey beard. Spike barked hoarsely and snarled with brown, broken teeth. Orrie and Spike shared a primal gaze. Summoning both courage and conviction, Orrie raised his arms high and roared like an angry bear. Spike offered two pitiful woofs, then awkwardly hobbled away. Doug and Orrie trotted through the gate. They headed east along the highway, a quarter mile from town.

CHAPTER 15

From Three to Six

Carrot, lettuce, and onion scraps littered the counter of the Thunder Burger's cramped prep room. Like sudsy icebergs, pots and pans rose out of the water in a sink as deep as it was wide. Above, a finicky lightbulb winked and blinked. Deputy Welski walked sheepishly into the room and said, "Sorry you got swamped, Rain. But I do need to spend some time with the public every once in a while. A few friendly words can keep things on an even keel."

"So, you've been doing some critical PR work? PR, of course, standing for pool racking. How many times did you rack 'em up today Ski—while I was sloggin' away trying to save our financial hides?"

"What makes you think I've been shooting pool?"

Rain rolled her eyes. "Well, for one thing, blue chalk dust stands out really well on a tan shirt!"

Ski brushed away the chalk and stepped toward her. She turned away. She huffed and sighed, then went around him and walked into the kitchen. He followed. She said, "Well, at least, Father Dom, Connie, Rhonda, and I pulled in enough money to pay this month's rent."

"That's great! And we've still got a couple of weeks to catch up on the bills." Hoping to stave off a warranted tiff, he revived a little white lie. "Anyway, I ended up helping the mayor out on a little project today. He guaranteed that once that full-time sheriff job opens—it's all mine."

"Not that old story again."

Ski spotted a broom leaning against the ice cream machine and started to sweep. "He really means it this time. He's been going through next year's budget with a fine-tooth comb, and has a few—"

"Figgs just loves to kiss that darn Blarney Stone, doesn't he?" Rain turned and tossed her cleaning towel on the counter. "Go ahead and tell me another one." Drumming her heels, she marched toward her man. She squared up and put her hands on her hips. "What are you gonna be when you grow up, Ski? You're basically just playing cowboy lawman—complete with a dime-store badge. You have so much more potential. You know, anytime you want, you can get in that GTO and head down Route 66, right behind Todd and Buzz . . ."

"Now don't start that baloney."

She made an engine revving sound and said, "Peel out, burn rubber, smoke 'em, roast 'em—ride off into the sunset on a stick pony—your destiny awaits."

Ski put his hands on his hips, then he folded his arms, he reached out with open hands. "My destiny is standing right in front of me. And I'll never let her go."

She backed around the main counter and bolted out the front door. He raced behind her. She turned her back. He spun her around. They embraced. And they kissed until the blazing sun drove them back into the shade. Ski took her by the hand, pulled her toward the jukebox, and took a magic quarter from behind her ear. She smiled.

"On the radio, when I was driving back, the DJ announced this song. He said it had just turned number one." A happy little oboe introduced the pop-rock waltz "I Got You Babe". They danced till the lingering of the last note dissolved.

Every summer the railroad company left empty flatcars and boxcars sitting idle on the tracks not far from the Thunder Burger. The boys did not understand exactly why, but playing inside the boxcars added a joyful variety to the monotony of a small-town summer. And there were at least twice as many flatcars as there were boxcars. *King of the Flatcar* was one of their favorite games. The objective was to be the only guy left standing on a flatcar. This meant pushing everybody else off, which usually resulted in abrasions, contusions, and lacerations. But these injuries were well worth the pain and misery if you could claim the title: Hobo King.

The boxcars served a different purpose. They were secret hideouts—places to eat cookies, candies, and chips; to drink bottles of pop or cups full of High-C orange drink; to sit on, roll down, or jump around on big piles of sand. The sand had a fine texture and packed well. If someone brought a jar of water along, you could mix up a little mud and build some mighty impressive sandcastles.

It was late Friday afternoon. Orrie and Doug sat on a pile of sand in the dark corner of a Northern Pacific boxcar. The car was strewn with pages from old newspapers, twine and string, burlap bags, crushed oyster shells, rotten potatoes, moldy hamburger and sandwich scraps, candy wrappers, worn-out shoes, and dirty socks. Standing at the edge of the open boxcar door, Lon vigorously shook the sand from a burlap bag. He took the bag, along with a coil of twine, to the middle of the boxcar. He tugged at a corner of the sack, but it wouldn't tear. He tugged to the point of frustration, then worked the material back and forth. "This stuff is too tough to tear. I'm gonna have to cut it with something." Lon roamed the boxcar looking along the walls and squinting in the corners to find a cutting edge—metal, glass, a sharp rock; he wasn't fussy. Orrie and Doug combed the floorboards inch by inch. Eventually becoming frustrated, Lon jumped out of the boxcar. He looked along the rails and between the ties.

As he walked the tracks, Lon sang Rusty Draper's "Freight Train" and kept his eye peeled for Indian arrowheads. In those days, to kids, every small, triangular rock was a potential Indian arrowhead. Although he just needed something sharp, finding an arrowhead would have been a thrilling bonus. Eventually, Lon found an empty beer bottle. He struck it against a rail, examined the shards, then selected one that reminded him of an Indian arrowhead. Taking great care to avoid the sharp edges, Lon pinched the glass between the fabric of his t-shirt for safe transport.

He hurried back to the boxcar and placed the fragment on the floor. As he climbed into the car, he said, "I broke a beer bottle and got a nice, sharp, piece of glass." Using the point of his tool, he twisted and cut armholes in the stinky, burlap sack. Next, he artistically tailored the garb into a V-neck masterpiece. He then used a piece of twine to create a neckline fastener. While Lon labored with inexplicable delight, Orrie and Doug crawled across the sandy floor, pretending to be prospectors, dramatically dying of thirst. Imagining swollen tongues and sunken eyes, they wretchedly reached out toward a shimmering mirage. Lon stepped forward to proudly display his contribution to the world of fashion. “Ta dahhh . . . a custom-made tunic!”

Orrie and Doug were far from impressed. But the nearly nude Doug stood and accepted the tunic appreciatively. He pulled it over his head and slipped his arms through the holes. The fit was a little baggy, but passable. Lon double-wrapped twine around his waist and secured it with a double-knotted bow. Doug began wiggling, twitching, and scratching.

“This thing smells like skunk cabbage, and it itches!” Doug said.

Lon said, ‘You got no choice, Doug. You can’t go home cuz your dad’s probably drunk and he might pound on you. You can’t go around in your underpants coz you’ll get sent to reform school . . . This is the best we can do right now.”

“Why don’t we just stay here until it gets dark?”

“Because we’ve got to get the cap to Ronnie by four o’clock—and it’s getting close.”

“You don’t have a watch. How do you know what time it is?” asked Doug.

“Partly by the sun, and partly by a good guess . . . To figure it out, you decide which way’s north—that’s 12 o’clock—then you look at how the shadows fall. To be accurate, you draw clock marks in the dirt and stand a stick in the middle. The shadow of the stick shows the hour.”

Orrie said, “That sounds pretty neat. I’m gonna try that later.”

Lon walked to the boxcar door. “Come on, you guys—we don’t have any time to waste.”

Doug frowned upon his gown with a gagging disdain. "This thing is horrible. It itches, it's dirty, it stinks *really* bad. It's embarrassing! Could I just wait here?"

"Oh yeah, sure, and be bait for Toby Gussard. What if he was to come around?"

"Don't' say another word—let's get outta here."

Wearing the precious red cap, Orrie decided to give Doug some social and emotional support. He walked up close and examined the tunic from various angles. "I really like it. It kinda looks like something Robin Hood would wear."

Lon said, "Yeah, that's a good point."

Doug whined, "It looks dumb! And it's *incredibly* itchy."

Lon said, "Incredibly? Jeez, right out of the Sunday crossword puzzle?"

"Sure is—it means this thing is really, really itchy . . . Connie got me a crossword puzzle book for Christmas, and I have done every puzzle three times. I can't do it anymore because the pages are too worn out from the eraser."

Lon said, "Connie actually got you something for Christmas?!"

"Yep, every year. Christmas is the only day she's nice. Not Thanksgiving, not birthdays, not Easter—no other day—just Christmas."

"You'll get used to that tunic pretty soon, Doug. It makes you look like a strong, powerful guy," said Orrie. "Like a guy who would fight a dragon."

Doug squinted and pursed his lips. "Do you think I was born yesterday?"

"No, really—I wish I had one."

"Shurrrre you do."

"Look, Doug," said Lon. "It'll all be worth it when we get that five bucks!"

Orrie added, "More than half enough for the skateboard!"

Doug squirmed and adjusted the tunic. He said, "Actually, it doesn't itch that bad right now. I guess I'm gettin' a little used to it."

The boys had no idea, lurking outside the boxcar, hidden among a cluster of fir trees, straddling his bicycle, was the dreaded Toby Gussard. He clutched his bow and held an arrow in his right hand. Grinning widely, sans upper incisors, he stared curiously at the boxcar. He rolled up right to the edge of the tree line. The evergreen branches now provided only partial cover. Moving into the open, Toby nocked his warped arrow. In the past, Toby's arrows had been blunt at the tip, but the head of this arrow had been whittled to a sharp point. Pulling the bow to full draw, he aimed carefully and let the arrow fly toward the boxcar door. It wobbled as it glided in a slight arc, finally landing on the wooden floor. Toby fought to control a wheezy laugh. He covered his mouth; his eyes were full of devilment.

Inside the boxcar, three pairs of eyes fell upon the arrow and those three pairs of eyes grew to the size of saucers. In a hushed tone, Lon said, "Toby Gussard!" All three ran to the massive boxcar door and tried to roll it shut. They shoved with all their might, but it would not budge. Lon continued to push while Orrie and Doug looked for a handle, lever, clip, knob—anything to release the door. "It must be locked from the outside," said Lon. "Somebody's gotta jump out and pull the lever."

"Toby might be out there!" said Doug.

"That's why we've got to close the door!"

"Go ahead, Lon—you know how to do it."

"I went out already—to find that piece of glass."

Doug said, "I ain't goin'. Toby could grab me! He might haul me to his lair."

The clock ticked. The fear mounted. Cowardice wrestled courage. Terror extended ghoulish talons.

In a half-gasp, Orrie said, "I'll do it."

Lon advised, "Just pull the lever all the way up."

Orrie jumped out of the car and spotted the lever near the bottom of the door. He scanned the area, then pulled on the handle. It was stuck tight. Orrie glanced around and thought he'd seen a tree branch move. With a two-hand grip, he threw all his strength and weight into his effort. Finally, the lever gave way. There was a rustling in the trees. Orrie hopped back into the car. All three boys pushed, and the door slammed shut. Lon pulled the inside lever. The door held tight.

After a few seconds, there came a knocking . . . a thumping . . . a pounding . . . a loud hammering. The locking lever squeaked and began to move. Lon grabbed it and pulled it back into place. He held the handle in a crushing grip. There came resistance. He whispered, "Somebody out there's pulling on it!" Orrie and Doug grabbed the support struts and held on. Lon said, "He's pulling hard. I can't hold it! Shove! Shove hard!"

Leaning into it with all their weight, the three boys held the huge door tight. All was quiet. There was no resistance. After a minute, Lon said. "OK, let's let up, but if you hear something—shove with all your might."

"Can we lock it?" asked Doug.

"This lever thing won't hold. I don't know if there's another way. There must be some way, but I'm afraid to let this thing go. I'll wait for another minute."

Orrie said, "Did either of you see Toby?"

"I didn't see him, but that has to be one of his arrows," said Lon. "Nobody else in town is retarded enough to make something like that."

Doug said, "I didn't see him either . . . It could have been someone playing a joke."

"I didn't see him. But when I was out there, I think a tree branch moved."

At that moment, the boys heard a light knocking at the door. They went into action. "Push. Brace your feet!" said Lon. Next came a thump, thump, thump. The locking lever rattled. They felt pressure and the door rolled slightly and opened about an inch, but they were able roll it back into place. The resistance let up; it stopped. A few seconds passed, then the handle rattled again. A tremendous force yanked and pulled at the door; it rolled a little. There came a straining sound. The door rolled again, and fingertips curled around to the inside. The boys' feet slid . . . they dug in and leaned against each other. They resisted for what seemed an eternity. Finally, the fingers pulled out and the pushing stopped. The boys listened intently for the slightest sound, awaiting their next battle of strength.

Outside, among the trees, Toby threw back his head and laughed in the manner of a braying donkey, then he honked like a goose. Using both hands, he slapped himself on both sides of his face, then repeatedly punched himself in the forehead. Finally, he pulled back out of the trees. He flailed his arms and yelled, "Do be sine cup! Do be sine cup!" He screamed and babbled as he pedaled away.

Inside the dark, spooky boxcar, the boys held the door tightly closed for another five minutes. Lon held the lever with vigilance, but his hands were cramping. He let up. All three boys let their aching arms hang as they shook off the lactic acid. They breathed as though they had run ten miles. Slowly, the fear subsided, their minds cleared. They settled into an edgy comfort but made certain not to stray far from the door.

With a little hope and a lot of doubt, Orrie posed, "Do you think Connie and Rhonda could have been the ones out there?"

Doug confidently assured, "No. Not Connie or Rhonda. They never come around these boxcars. Sometimes there's weird railroad guys that hang around here and do work. Connie and Rhonda don't like 'em. They call 'em railroad pukes."

Lon said, "No, it wasn't Connie or anybody else. It had to have been Toby."

Doug said, "It's been a while since we heard anything out there—do you think he's gone?"

"Only one way to find out," said Lon. "Let's pull the door open—just enough for me to look around." The guys rolled the door open just enough for Lon to get a good view. With eyes peeled, he kept a patient watch. They kept quiet for a full ten minutes. Sounding relieved and confident, Lon said, "OK, let's roll this thing open."

Doug jumped out of the boxcar and said, “Toby knows about this place now. We’ll have to find a new hideout.”

“Yeah, we got no choice,” said Lon. “Let’s get the heck outta here.”

As Ronnie and Wuzzie prepared to leave the cafe, the radio reported a temperature of 104. Wuzzie grabbed a jacket. Ronnie said, “What are you doin’?”

“It’s new. I wanna break it in.”

“That’s nuts, man. It’s one-oh-four.”

“Oh well.” Wuzzie locked the door and the two crossed the street. The cruel sun speared through the leafy canopy of the park. Finding the coolest spot possible, the boys sat on a picnic table at the east end. Ronnie playfully tugged on the sleeve of Wuzzie’s brand new Nehru jacket.

“Man, you must be hot in that stupid-lookin’ thing,” said Ronnie.

“It’s not so bad.”

“Tell that to your soggy armpits, bud. I think it’s gotten hotter the few seconds we’ve been sitting here.”

“These jackets are designed to resist heat. People in India wear ’em, and it’s way hotter over there—all year ’round.”

“Yeah, well people in India also die in the Black Hole of Calcutta—and that’s just the one hole we know about. There’s probably lots of black holes over there—and everybody trapped in 'em are probably wearing Nehru jackets."

"Ha, ha, Mr. Sarcastic, King of Comedians . . . Go ahead and laugh. I might feel a little warm, but at least I look cool—way cooler than you."

"Keep telling yourself that and maybe one day you'll believe it." Ronnie gave the jacket a slow, appraising once over. "There's *no way* you could have bought something like that at Brownie's. Where the heck did you get it?"

Wuzzie opened a few buttons. "This town is just full of smart alecks. I saw an ad in *Teen Beat*. The Beatles wear 'em. I sent to San Francisco for it."

"That figures. Jeez, I hate to say you're a dork, but—you know . . . if the shoe fits."

"Sometimes I'm a cornball, but a lot of cornballs and dorks do egghead stuff. And, while I'm sure you're gonna laugh—I'm an egghead and I want to be a nuclear physicist."

Wuzzie looked surprised when Ronnie looked impressed. "Wrong. I'm not gonna laugh. I am all for guys having goals. So, what makes you think you can accomplish something like that?"

"I've got brainpower—at least better than average. I've got as good a chance as anybody."

"From this little town, and this little school, you don't have a snowball's chance in Hades. The high school doesn't even offer a physics class."

"I'm learning about it myself with library books. Nuclear energy is the way of the future and physicists lead the way."

"It seems like all physicists do nowadays is make bigger and bigger atom bombs. They want to set the world on fire. At the detention center, I read about this thing called overkill . . . like, the Russians have huge bombs that can kill all the life in the world nine times. But America makes smaller bombs, and way more than the Russians. They can saturate the world and kill every living thing at least sixteen times."

"That's insane!"

"No kiddin'—tell me something I don't know."

"Well, if that's the way things are—I'd rather have the Russians blow up the world so I only have to die nine times—that would be way better than having to die sixteen times." The sheer thought of this filled the boys with mirth; they laughed till they couldn't breathe. At that moment, the world did seem completely insane.

Ronnie said, "I don't get it. The smartest people in the world think up stuff like this. It's like they're bratty little kids: I got more than you, mine's bigger than yours, mine's better than yours . . . it's like—there isn't really an adult world."

"Nope, I agree—a hundred percent. An adult world does not exist."

"And the people in our government, our fearless leaders, actually passed laws that approved building weapons like this. I mean, maybe a couple to protect ourselves, but enough to kill everything on Earth sixteen times . . ."

"It's supposed to be part of a plan to scare the Russians and stop the spread of communism."

"What the heck is communism? The Russians are people just like us and think about it—do you think the Russians really want to kill all living things, including themselves and their kids—even one time, let alone nine times. It's a bunch of baloney."

"Baloney or not, people are getting killed over it—over in Vietnam. There must be something to it."

"Well, I tell ya, real or not real, if I get drafted for Vietnam —I'll go over there, do my job, then come home and go to college."

"I feel pretty much the same way. And there's always a chance that fighting a war can bring peace to the world."

"Mr. Smart Aleck says, 'Peace on Earth will come . . . when all the people leave'."

Wuzzie repeated the thought to himself several times and finally said, "Peace on Earth will come when all the people leave. Actually, I think that's more cynical than smart alecky."

"By golly, you may be right."

Wuzzie rotated his arm and looked at his watch, which he wore face down to keep the face from getting scratched. "It's three-thirty on the nose."

"Those little punks probably ain't comin'."

"Those little punks probably aren't even alive. If they tried to pull your cap outta Connie's t-shirt, she would have stomped their guts out by now. They were probably too scared to even go up to her . . . I sure would have been."

Ronnie's expression was one of practicality. He said, "Yeah, I wish you could stand your ground against her, but she could beat you senseless . . . You wouldn't have near enough brains left to become an assistant nuclear scientist."

Wuzzie accepted the assessment. He pulled a bag of marshmallow peanuts out of his Nehru jacket and offered some to Ronnie. He took a scoop-shovel load, gobbled three at a time and said, "How many of these do you think you could stuff in your mouth?"

Wuzzie examined one of the soft, orange candies. "Eight, nine, maybe even ten."

"Go ahead and try. I'll hand 'em to you, one by one, and keep the official count. Probably nobody else on Earth would try to do this, so you'll have the world record."

"Hmm, maybe it will become an Olympics event someday . . . I accept the challenge."

Wuzzie started by opening his mouth wide and pushing a candy peanut into the hollow of his left cheek. The next one went into his right cheek. After putting two more in his cheeks, he forced one under his upper lip, but it slipped out, so he forced it in tighter and farther under. He managed to trap one behind his lower lip—the total was now six. Ronnie happily handed him two more. He fit one into the mid-hollow. As he started pushing in another, he began to laugh. Even though his face was getting red, and it was hard to breathe, he forced number eight into his mouth. Ronnie handed him number nine. Suffocating, face crimson, eyes bulging, he blew like a volcano. The mucous-soaked confections lay on the ground in slobbery globs. More laughter. Ronnie said, "Man, you got *sooo* close—you had number nine in your hand."

"I'm thinking if I ever try it again, I'm gonna smash the peanuts flat—then I might be able to arrange them in layers."

"Marshmallow peanut smashing—the first ingenious idea of a budding nuclear physicist." Ronnie surveyed the entire park in hopes of seeing Orrie, Lon, and Doug. "Those kids wanted that five bucks really bad. If they woulda got the cap, they'd be here."

"It's three forty-six."

"OK, no cap. I'm dead—what saying haven't we used about me being in trouble. The last one was—I'm screwed, blued, and tattooed."

"Did we use, you're a had dad, already?"

"Probably. If not, we'll count it right now . . . what's another one?"

"You're . . . ummm . . . ohhh, let me see . . . hmmm . . . I can't think of any. . .wait a minute . . . *estoy en problemas*—it's Spanish."

"I'll take it: I'm *estoy en problemas*."

Ronnie ate the last of the marshmallow peanuts. He breathed into the bag, pinched it closed, then smacked it—*pow*! He sighed, stretched, and yawned. Wuzzie yawned too.

From behind, someone cleared his throat. When Ronnie and Wuzzie turned, the bright faces of Orrie, Doug, and Lon beamed. Doug proudly waved the Malman Loggers cap. Wuzzie's jaw dropped. Ronnie's eyes lit up.

Wuzzie said, "I can't believe it!"

As Ronnie took the cap from Doug's hand, his eyes fell upon the burlap tunic. "What the heck have you got on? It smells like cow crap."

Doug said, "I'm a knight."

Wuzzie declared, “A Knight of the Order of the Pig Sty.” He and Ronnie laughed.

Ronnie examined his cap, inside and outside. He donned and adjusted it. “No worse for wear.”

Filled with excitement, Orrie held out his hand. Ronnie ignored him, jumped off the picnic table, and mounted his bike. Wuzzie did the same. Ronnie said, “Time to buzz, Wuzz.”

Orrie approached them, again holding out his hand. “Where’s our five dollars?”

Lon stepped up, somewhat less self-assured. “Yeah, where’s our money?”

In the background, Doug said, “We had a deal.”

Casting the boys a fleeting glance, Ronnie said, “Man, it’s sure good to have my cap back. And just in time for practice.” He and Wuzzie rolled past the boys as if they were invisible.

Wuzzie mumbled, “Once you told me that if a guy’s word’s worth nothin’, then the guy is worth nothin’.”

“Yeah, I did. But that stuff doesn’t count until tomorrow.”

Wuzzie smiled at the silliness and shook his head. “I’ll ride down to the field with you, then I gotta get back to the cafe.”

They pedaled out of the park and cruised down Main Street, heading for the practice field.

Brows furrowed, eyes blazing, faces red as beets, the boys began to holler. Orrie’s infuriated voice burst upon all ears. “You fuckers!”

Doug and Lon's jaws dropped. Eyes agape they looked at each other, then riveted their gaze on Orrie. A gradual smile blossomed, as Orrie realized he'd said *the word*. Hysterical laughter followed and they all fell on the grass—yelling and hollering, calling Ronnie all sorts of foul names. Instead of crying their eyes out, they were laughing their heads off. Lon gained composure first and said, "Come on you guys, we gotta settle down. I don't know why we should be laughing so much, we just got cheated and cheated bad—we put our lives on the line for that money."

Doug said, "Maybe we're laughing about how stupid we were to trust that guy."

"I was laughing to get the anger out of me," said Orrie, "but most of it's still there."

"We're all mad. But I have an idea about how to get back at him, and . . . make him give us our money. We'll have to work together. It will be tricky . . . and it could be dangerous."

At 4:55 pm, a black and white police car pulled into the driveway of Lester Malman's residence. When Deputy Welski stepped from the vehicle, he noticed the blinds were closed and the curtains were drawn. A sliver of light could not have penetrated the dungeon-like realm. Ski walked up the steps and crossed the porch to the front door. He pulled back the screen door and knocked courteously. Face directly in front of the peephole, he smiled and knocked a little louder. He called, "Lester. Lester?" He hammered with the side of his fist. His voice grew gradually louder. "Lester. Lester—you in there? It's time for practice. Lester!"

Slowly, Ski turned the knob, opened the door just a crack, and said, "Lester? Lester, you OK?" He fully opened the door. The room was still quite dark, so he slipped inside. The TV glowed bluish-grey, black, and white. The five o'clock news was starting; the opening theme blared. The doorway allowed just enough light for Ski to see Lester lying on the couch. He emitted a startling, ragged snore. On the floor near the couch was an empty whiskey bottle; Lester's hand dangled inches away. Ski appraised the situation and said, "Sleep well there Sleeping Beauty. I'll head down to the field and see if I can help out." He switched off the TV and walked out.

Ski backed the police car onto the street and headed west, toward the VFW baseball field. The sandlot diamond and scrubby outfield butted up against the elementary school playfield. The respective grounds were separated by a tall, cyclone fence. On the field, the Malman Loggers were having batting practice. The players were all dressed the same: blue jeans, white t-shirts; and black, high-top, Converse All-Star basketball shoes. It was clear Ronnie Rix was directing the show. "Rotate in, Bobby." Ronnie walked toward the pitcher, "How's the arm, Allie?"

"Good, but I'm gonna save some fastballs for tomorrow. I'll throw, maybe five or six more, then take a break." Like all the players, Allie Davis was in his mid-teens. He was short, stocky, and his blonde hair looked like a haystack. Generally known as a "mellow dude", on a baseball diamond, he pitched at a fever pitch.

A radio at peak volume started playing "Gloria" by Them.

Ski came out of the parking lot and walked up to the first baseline. He said, "Hey Allie! Why don't you let me throw Ronnie a few curves?"

"Yeah, sure—you're welcome to it," Allie met Ski halfway, handing him the ball and his glove. Ronnie trotted behind the backstop and pulled a Louisville Slugger from the rack. After a little flexing and a few practice swings, he stepped up to the plate. Out of habit, he choked up on the bat, and nodded at Ski.

"I'm comin' with some heat, Ronnie. But I only have about three or four good ones in me."

Ronnie lifted the brim of his cap, wiped his brow, then lowered the cap just enough to block the sun. "Burn 'em in here!"

Ski's windup wasn't all that bad considering he hadn't thrown a baseball in a couple of years. Right down the pipe. A swing and a miss. The next pitch had a little more on it. A swing and a miss. Ski gave the third pitch all he had. Ronnie fanned the air; his frustration was obvious. Ski said, "I can guarantee you—that West kid is gonna be throwing faster, straighter, and trickier than I ever could. "You're way too tight, Ronnie. It's like you're made of wood. You've gotta lighten up. Relax and let the energy flow. If you tighten up tomorrow, that West kid will eat you alive."

Annoyed, but appreciative, Ronnie moved back from the plate, rolled his shoulders, and flexed his neck. He took a couple of slow, deep breaths. He bent and twisted at the waist.

"Relax your jaw," Ski said. "Don't clench your teeth."

Ronnie stepped up to the plate, clearly more relaxed, and with determined countenance. Without a windup, Ski offered Ronnie *egg in his beer*. He swung hard and connected; the ball sailed high and foul, just off the third base line. Ronnie rolled his shoulders, flexed his neck, set his feet, and raised the bat in perfect form.

Ski gave it all he had, right down the center of the strike zone. There was a loud *crack*. Everybody watched the ball climb, arc, and vanish into the sooty sky. It fell well beyond the elementary school fence. A beautiful sight.

Ski said, "Bring it in everybody." The players gathered around the pitcher's mound. They talked among themselves. They were irritable, uneasy; it was hot, and they were tired. Squabbling broke out.

Ronnie shouted, “Hey, shut up and listen!” Silence. “Start thinkin’ about the game.”

Ski concocted one of his little white lies. “Coach Malman had a bunch of paperwork to do because of that mill fire. He asked me to check in on you. You just had a really good practice on a really hot day. Looks to me like Coach Malman has taught you well.”

“Yeah, we know our stuff pretty good,” said Ronnie.

Allie Davis said, “We’re with you, Ronnie. We’re gonna take ’em to the cleaners.”

The whole team cheered, clapped, and chanted, “Loggers, Loggers, Loggers!”

CHAPTER 16

Friday Night

One might easily romanticize that the Jeffersonian architecture of the Brayton Nursing Facility, bathed in a crimson twilight, would have put Monticello to shame. Inside the main building, the recreation room was brightly lit. It was a little too warm for comfort, but lots of fans blew, and the local weather consensus forecast cooler days ahead. The window blinds along the north wall were pulled up and the sheer, nylon curtains had been drawn aside. Along one wall was a sink, a watercooler, a wastebasket, some cupboards, and shelves. On the shelves were books, paperback novels, popular magazines, a variety of puzzles, games, and boxes full of arts-and-crafts. There were also plenty of pens, pencils, and crayons, along with a ream of drawing paper and some coloring books.

Olive Trujillo sat at a table with hospital patients and rest-home residents. They were engaged in needlework. On the table were bundles of yarn, spools of thread, thimbles, various pins and needles, embroidery hoops, loops, and sewing frames. Olive's daughters, Carmalita and Juanita, sat at a nearby table with a group of people, some in wheelchairs, doing jigsaw puzzles.

The old folks loved it when the girls visited. A man with salt-and-pepper wavy hair, wearing a VFW pin, rolled up and began to sing Perry Como's "Turn Around".

At other tables, men, young and old, played checkers and chess. A wizened old-timer in a bathrobe laughed merrily as he took Ronnie's queen off the chessboard. The man said, "Like I told ya—keep your eye on that queen. Now you've got to pull your nuts out of the fire."

True to form, Ronnie pretended to feel foolish after deliberately sacrificing his most powerful game piece. "Gosh darn it, I knew I blew it, right after I took my hand off . . . I keep getting distracted when I think about that game tomorrow."

"I don't blame you. And I'll be there!" The man's eyes twinkled. "I'll be there with bells on—a whole bunch of us will." He laughed, slapped the table, then helped Ronnie round up the chessmen.

Toby sat at a circular table near a window. He strived diligently to color a picture of Woody Woodpecker. Demanding painstaking realism, he fretted over which crayon to choose. Charily, he picked up a maize crayon and colored Woody's beak. While Toby worked, he rocked in his chair and parroted the words of Foghorn Leghorn and The Three Stooges: "I say now, boy, I say now boy, I say now, boy, I say now boy". He squeezed his eyes tightly. "I can't see, I can't see . . . Whatsa mattuh? . . . I got my eyes closed." He began quacking. Father Dom approached him and said, "Let's finish Woody later, Toby. It's time to set the tables."

"Set tables. Dinner time," said Toby. He sprang up and put the crayons and his Woody Woodpecker picture on a shelf. "Good bread, good meat, good God, let's eat!" He clapped with enthusiasm and followed Father Dom out of the room.

Big band music was coming from a hi-fi in the back of the dining room. From the kitchen, the cooks waved at Father Dom and Toby as they entered. With the help of Ronnie, they transferred dishware and utensils from cabinets to tabletops. There were two sets of long tables separated by a half-dozen smaller, round-shaped tables. Ronnie started filling water glasses. Toby placed trays of bread and butter on credenzas.

The fully ambulatory filed into the dining room in a steady stream. Patients on walkers, on crutches, and in wheelchairs were accompanied by nurses and attendants. Father Dom and Ronnie rolled food carts to each table. The menu: roast beef, mashed potatoes, gravy, green beans, and ice cream. Coffee had to be kept in the kitchen until ready to serve; otherwise, Toby would guzzle it, even if scalding hot. To keep him out of mischief, Toby was assigned to eat his dinner alone at a corner table. He was to remain there until excused to bus other tables.

At the round tables in the middle of the dining room, Father Dom, Olive, and Ronnie assisted nurses and attendants with the handfeeding of patients. "In the Mood" started playing on the hi-fi and one old gentleman, in the interest of stealing the spotlight, broke into a hip-shaking rhumba. One of the ladies eating puree coughed and sputtered. And, as usual, everyone's eyes lit up when the ice cream was served.

Friday night was movie night. At 7 pm, the inner halls of the hospital and the residence wards were deserted, as all able-bodied had gathered to enjoy a motion picture. The auditorium was spacious. On one side of the stage was the flag of Washington State, on the other, Old Glory. A reel of 35mm film fluttered in the projector, sending flickering images onto a theater-size screen. *Drums Along the Mohawk* was the feature. The audience was entranced. Midway through the showing, Mohawk Indians, feathers aside their rising crests of hair, half-naked and smudged with war paint, shot fiery arrows over the high walls of a formidable log fort. In the front row, Toby Gussard rocked excitedly in a creaky, old chair. He mimicked the men on the catwalks who were tamping powder into flintlocks. He laughed and gestured wildly as fiery arrows flew and burned into the wooden battlements. One row back, Ronnie Rix, thoroughly vexed, begrudgingly watched Toby act out the movie.

Toby's voice rang. "Wowee! Arrows. Burn. Burn arrows. Wowee!" Unbridled, he glanced over his shoulder. "Look Ronnie, fire arrow. Burning. Burn wall." Toby got to his feet. "Toby, Indian." He let out a curdling war whoop, then pretended to shoot arrows at the screen. He whooped again.

Sourly, Ronnie said, "Shut up, Toby. You're buggin' everybody. Just sit down and watch the show."

Abounding with a gaiety that verged on mania, Toby's obnoxious antics persisted. The rest of the audience shushed and chastised him. Father Dom approached. He made a quieting gesture. Toby ignored him and pointed to the screen; he let out another whoop. Father Dom scowled, pulled him up by an arm, grabbed the scruff of his neck, and ushered him into a hallway. Cheers echoed. Ronnie followed Father Dom and the grumbling Toby down the hall, outside and across the lawn to the chapel. Head bent in shame, Toby ascended the steps. On the chapel porch, Ronnie yawned and stretched. "I think I'll go to bed too."

"Good idea," said Father Dom. "Charge up those batteries."

"I've been thinkin' about this game all day," Ronnie said glumly. "I'm thinkin' I don't really have much of a—"

"Take account of yourself, young man." Father Dom's white gloves waved away the doubt. "You have the strength, you have the skill, and you have your calling. After all that talk about courage and honor, you should be raring and ready to go. The brass ring taunts and it's well within your reach."

"I know . . . but jeez—that West kid pitched three no-hitters this season—at least three!"

"Ronnie, you must *realize* you're at one of those *crossroads of destiny* you're always going on about—one of those sovereign rites of passage."

Ronnie's brain wandered amid caverns of gloom.

"So, what is it you intend to do?" Father Dom asked.

Ronnie huffed and sighed weakly. He fidgeted, hugged himself, bowed his head, put his hands in his pockets. Did some trunk twisters, took a deep breath, and looked off into the distance. He crossed his arms, then put his hands on his hips. Finally, he nodded with a sense of purpose. Garnering pure determination, he looked Father Dom square in the eye.

"I'm gonna hit that dang ball a *country* mile!"

In the otherwise empty dining room of the Thunder Burger, Orrie, Lon, and Doug sat at the booth nearest to the Main Street window. Unblinking, they watched the blazing hillside, looking away only to dip their French fries in ketchup. Orrie pitiably eyed Doug's burlap garment. He said, "That Knights of Templar Cross Lon painted on your tunic looks really neat."

Doug pulled the burlap away from his chest to get a bird's eye view of the emblem. "Yeah . . . I like it. And it's so big that other people will really notice it."

Lon bit his lip to fight off a smile. "You'll stand out in a crowd for sure!"

"I wish I could see it better—a head-on view." He stood and tried to catch a reflection in the window, but it was not favored by the lighting.

"Don't worry. You'll see it all you want before too long. And it'll make a great collector's item."

"I know it, especially cuz I'm wearing it to the game tomorrow. That will make it even more special. It will be our team's good luck charm."

Orrie said, "Remember Doug, if you change your mind about wearing it, you can try on some of my clothes when you stay over tonight. My pants won't fit you, but my shirts probably will."

"Hmmm. Nah, I like this tunic. It hardly itches anymore, and I think the smoky air is deadening the smell. But if I do keep it to start some kind of a collection, I'd better wash it."

Lon said, "Maybe you'd better not wash it. It could fall apart. And I'm pretty sure the cross symbol would wash off."

Orrie said, "He could get it dry cleaned."

Lon said, "Dry cleaned? That would cost way too much, and besides, I don't think any kind of dry cleaner would even consider touching that thing . . . Really, all we need to do is spray it with some Lysol."

Doug brightened. "And maybe sprinkle on a little Old Spice."

"That'd be perfect," said Lon, unable to completely suppress his chuckle.

The sun was setting. The blanketing smoke veiled and unveiled the stars. Orrie pointed to the hillside fires. “Those fires are forming something . . . you know how clouds do; it’s like, I dunno . . . a dragon. A dragon’s face with big, bloodshot eyes.”

“Bloodshot eyes—like my dad’s,” said Doug. “Maybe it’s the Lester Malman dragon.”

The boys laughed.

Lon said, “Look at that row of trees burning just below—they’re startin’ to look like sharp, pointed teeth . . . It’s starting to snarl.”

“Yep. That’s my dad when he’s mad; it’s the Lester Malman dragon for sure.”

Lon asked, “So what’s Lester Malman gonna do when he finds out you’ve been running around this late?”

“Probably, swat my butt. Sometimes I get butt swats, or my ear twisted. And that ain’t fair—all Connie ever gets is yelled at.”

Lon said, “So your dad doesn’t really lock you guys up in the root cellar with spiders and rattlesnakes?”

“Heck no! He’d never do that. Anyway, we don’t even *have* a root cellar. Now Granny and Jed Clampett, they have a root cellar, but there from way down south.”

Lon jovially recited a limerick of olde:

Way down yonder in Aberdeen
A bobcat jumped in a sewing machine
The sewing machine it ran so fast
It put 99 stitches in the bobcat’s (he whispered) *ass.*

Orrie said, “Jesus doesn’t want us saying stuff like that, Lon.”

"Maybe not. But I don't think he'd want you to be calling Connie an ugly skag butt and saying the F-word either."

"I suppose not. But I was mad."

Doug said, "That's OK, Orrie. Don't worry about it." Doug cleared his throat. "And now gettin' back to the business of people saying our dad's mean to us; it ain't true. He might be mean to everybody else, but not us. It's just that people in this vicinity are exceedingly prone to exaggeration."

Lon sighed, "Oh boy, more fancy words."

"We might as well just get used to it, Lon . . . Doug has developed quite an inquisitive vocabulary."

"Now don't *you* start!"

Doug mumbled, "Extensive vocabulary."

Orrie pled, "I can't help it. It's rubbin' off on me. I keep getting this crazy idea I should start doing crossword puzzles. Like maybe it could, uhh. . . *benefit* me in the future–you know, like in school and stuff."

"That's a crazy idea all right. Both of you should just talk normal. Otherwise, you may *acquire* the *osputanious* reputation of being *dorks*!"

Doug interceded, "Hey, I thought you guys wanted to know the truth about my dad."

Lon said, "We do, Doug. Go ahead."

"Dad gets mad sometimes . . . and says mean things sometimes. But he still loves us. He wants us to work hard and show good manners."

Orrie said, "I'll bet your dad's hard on you because he wants you to be tough as nails when you grow up."

Doug closed one eye and entertained the thought. "I guess that could be. Connie's already tough—even tougher than most of the men around here—so I guess he doesn't really need to pull her ear. As a matter of fact, I think Connie could have a good chance of being a lady wrestler. Even a champion—like The Fabulous Moolah."

"Yeah!" said Orrie. "The Conster Monster could be her nickname."

"Oh, that would be perfect!" Doug said.

With a twinge of dread, Lon said, "Speaking of the Conster Monster, when you think about it, getting butt swats and your ear twisted ain't all that bad when you consider she wants to grind glass in our faces."

All three boys fell into a pensive repose, gradually drifting into deep contemplation. Mirroring, they locked their fingers behind their necks and looked up at the ceiling. Each rocked in time as the song "Travelin' Man" by Ricky Nelson bebopped out of the jukebox. Finally, they returned to the here and now, finishing their burgers, picking the last bits and crumbs from the wrappers, then using their straws to vacuum the interiors of their milkshake cups.

On the walkway in front of the restaurant, Rain gazed at the silver sheen falling over the moon. She remembered the childhood joy of watching the stars wink and blink, but tonight the twinkling wooed an inkling in the melancholy sky. She swayed dreamily as "Stranger on the Shore" by Acker Bilk played softly on the juke box. The fires on the hillside burned orange and red as they crept east. Ski slipped up behind Rain and whispered, "Hi." He pulled at his clingy, sweaty t-shirt. She massaged her temples. Careworn trifles pricked and nipped at the star-crossed night. Seduced by a stellar wanderlust, Ski mused, "Starlight, star bright, I hope I see a ghost tonight."

"A ghost is about all you're gonna see. I'm starting to think we won't see another clear night till winter."

Ski gave her a side hug. "I still feel mighty bad about leaving you in the lurch earlier."

"I've handled worse . . . sorry I ran off to pout. That's something I'm trying to break myself of."

"Everybody needs to run away from things from time to time. It keeps us sane."

Rain rubbed her arms. "I could swear it's getting cooler. It's really noticeable now that it's dark. And there was the brush of a breeze a second ago."

"Let's see: two nights ago, it was 102, last night it was 101, tonight is 100 on the nose . . . yeah, it's getting cooler."

She giggled and pointed at a little dust devil. "See what I mean." Ski smiled. "We need rain," she said, and reached her arms to the heavens. "Hey sky, Rain wants you to *raaain*!"

Ski said, "On a night like this, we'd have more luck praying for pink and purple snow." He gave Rain another side hug.

Excitedly, Rain said, "Let's set up a hot dog stand at the baseball game tomorrow—we can mix up some lemonade, and I've still got apples from the 4th. I'll bet I can get three pies out of them."

"Sounds good. We'll drape that stars-and-stripes bunting over the counter and, if I can find those markers, I'll draw an Uncle Sam poster on some butcher paper." Ski stood at attention, saluted, and started singing "America the Beautiful". Rain harmonized. The boys stepped through the door and added their voices.

Posters of British Invasion musicians covered three of the light-pink walls. The Dave Clark Five poster was surrounded by twinkling lights. This was Rhonda's favorite group and their hit "Because" was her favorite song. The panoramic mural of a winged unicorn, flying over a waterfall and under a rainbow, adorned the fourth wall. The mural had been meticulously hand-painted. The artist had added a border depicting each evergreen tree indigenous to the locale: pine, fir, cedar, and hemlock. Connie reclined on Rhonda's bed—a queen-size replica of the one designed for Barbie's dream house. It was covered with a silky-white, lace-trimmed comforter, and above, a frilly canopy. Rhonda sat at her vanity thumbing through Life magazine. As she turned a page, she caught a glimpse of herself in the mirror and leaned forward to take a closer look.

Connie said, "If you keep warming that mirror, you're gonna fall through it, Alice—all the way to Wonderland."

"I'm getting a zit, smarty. If you were a real friend, you'd go get me the rubbing alcohol and a cotton ball . . . Well?!"

"OK, don't have a hissy fit. Where is it?"

"First bathroom. Towel cabinet, lower shelf."

Connie returned with the pungent elixir. "Don't you have any *Clearasil*?"

"I'm out."

"Heaven help us!" Connie said, then flopped back onto the bed.

The Beatles song "All My Lovin'" came on the radio. Rhonda turned up the volume 'til the windows rattled. Jumping out of her chair, she went into a go-go dance, featuring her own choreography. She shouted over the music, "Come on, Connie! I know you love this song. Dance with me."

Connie brooded in red-eyed silence. Rhonda turned the radio volume way down. Her enthusiasm drained as she sensed her friend's deep pain. She went to her side. Connie droned, "I can't take it anymore, Rhonda. I swear I'm gonna be on that bus outta here tomorrow night."

At first, Rhonda took a dismissive approach, hoping to lighten the mood. "Yeah, I know—you're running away to California, and you're gonna work at Disneyland, and blah, blah, blah—"

"Don't make fun of me, Rhonda! You don't know what it's like. My dad is worse than you think—he's a creep. He's unbearable."

Rhonda walked to the vanity and turned off the radio, then returned and sat on the end of the bed.

A nervous habit, Rhonda tugged the back of her hot-roller curled hair. "You don't think I know?!" Rhonda said, in a near nasty tone. "He's rude, crude, and full of hate. You've heard the stuff he says to me—'Hubba hubba, ding ding, baby you got everything'. . . and what about when he makes fun of my name 'Hey Rhonda, can I Stickel ya?' He's a cur—a letch—a cad."

Connie smiled weakly and shook her head, "Oh, that's only when he's drunk."

"Uh, pardon me, if you haven't noticed—he's always drunk!"

"Since mom died—yeah, he's always drunk . . . and what scares me is—I'm gettin' to be just like him—mean, rude, hateful. If I was old enough to buy booze, I'd probably be an alcoholic by now . . . nobody'll ever love me." Connie started to cry.

Rhonda scooted close and softly patted her knee. "I know it's bad; it's really bad sometimes . . . but I don't have it so good myself, Connie. Sure, I have a princess bedroom and spending money—but nobody loves me either."

Connie sat up and hugged her. "I do—you know you're my best friend . . . You can come to California with me. Tomorrow night. Let's do it, Rhonda. We'll fix 'em. We'll show 'em all."

Connie stood, folded her arms, and paced. She went to the window. After a few seconds, she turned and leveled with her friend. "Here's the truth, Rhonda—most of the other girls think you're totally spoiled, and your life is a fairy tale. They're jealous. They might smile to your face, but any one of them would stab you in the back if they had the chance."

"I don't doubt it . . . Some fairytale—the world's most rotten fairytale. I've got no family at all. My parents' home is wherever the next jet sets down. I'm Rapunzel, only I live in a dungeon, instead of a magic tower."

Connie looked around. "I dunno Rhonda—this is a pretty nice dungeon. And Rapunzel didn't have a swimming pool outside her window." Connie gazed down at the sky-blue pool. "Why don't we go swimming for a while?"

"Nope. Mrs. Agnew won't let me even get close to that pool. Even if she's out there to keep watch. She's so afraid I'll drown. Jeez, when we lived in Alameda, I learned to scuba dive. I was ten years old." Rhonda sighed, "Thank God we have air conditioning. It would be stifling in here without it."

Connie quietly said, "At least Mrs. Agnew cares about you. She wants to keep you safe. And she knows she's too old to help if you got a cramp, or choked, or bumped your head."

"Sometimes I wish I *would* drown!" Rhonda surveyed her room; she looked up, down, and all around. "I'm sooo tired of this . . . All of it—every bit! It's babyish—I've outgrown it. I hate it."

On the end of the bed, sat a stuffed rabbit with big, floppy ears. Connie started to talk baby talk. "*Ow could ooo tay dat 'bout Wabby?* It makes ho sooo sad."

"Leave *Rabby* out of this." Rhonda took the stuffed toy from Connie, hugged it, and said, "*Chee is dust a innocent witto kweecho.*"

Connie walked to Rhonda's vanity, turned the chair around, and faced the middle of the room. "The final curtain to my life in the horrid little town of Rye Grass is closing, Rhonda. You've got to decide—are you with me? . . . Are you coming with me to California? The bus pulls out of here at ten-forty tomorrow night."

"If I do go . . . I want to go in disguise. That way nobody would recognize us in missing person photos. I'll wear one of my mom's wigs." Rhonda formed a picture frame with her hands and held it up, viewing Connie from different angles. "I know just what you need."

Rhonda jumped up and rifled through drawers. She gathered brushes, combs, scissors, spray bottles, tissues, curlers, barrettes, bows, and bobby pins. She placed everything on a small table near the window. She pulled a fancy, wicker chair across the room, and said," Come on. We need to make some changes. I'm going to give you a new look."

"You ain't cutting my hair."

"Sometimes your hair looks like a rat's nest, Connie. You need a little off the top."

"Rat's nest? If you rat your hair anymore, it'll turn radioactive. And that dye job—it looks like you dumped a quart of Clorox on your head."

"Hah, hah. You know Marie does my hair. I think I look good." She tousled her flowing locks. "I'm hot stuff around these parts . . . and when I get through with you—you're gonna look hotter!"

"You ain't *touchin'* me, Delilah."

Rhonda turned the radio way up. The DJ was saying the weather would be getting cooler over the next week. She walked across the room, like a model down a catwalk, and took Connie by the hand. Connie resisted a little—very little. Rhonda guided her onto the wicker chair. Though the sun had not set, a gibbous moon peered through frays in the sky's smoky veil. Rhonda picked up a comb and a pair of styling shears. The Beach Boys started singing "Help Me Rhonda". "It's an omen!" Rhonda said. The girls sang along.

As Rhonda set to work, Connie focused on the hillside fires. "Those fires look like they're forming the shape of a face. A devil's face—you can see the horns growing."

"Shush. Sit up. And stay nice and still. You're gonna have to trust me on this."

"How can I trust you? You don't know what the heck you're doing."

"Hah. Little did you know—I spent a whole Saturday afternoon at Marie's last year. While you were playing stupid basketball, I was watching every move she made. I can cut hair like you don't even know."

"If you mess up my hair, you're gonna be sorry, Rhonda."

"I won't mess it up. Jeez, you're like an old fishwife sometimes."

"What the heck is a fishwife?"

"A mean, crabby lady who doesn't appreciate her friends. So, if you don't want to be a fishwife—appreciate me!"

"I'd appreciate it if you'd take some of your mom's Midol."

"Shut up."

Connie started to get up, Rhonda held her shoulders. "If you don't sit still, I *will* mess up your hair." Noting Connie's mounting impatience, Rhonda sped up the process. Her scissors flashed and twirled.

"You're taking too much off!"

"No, I'm not." Rhonda glanced down at the haystack of hair piling up on the newspapers. Impulsively, she put her fingertips to her lips, and for just an instant, looked alarmed. Quickly, she laid a new layer of newspaper over the bounty of shorn locks and felt she was back in control. She squinted and inspected her work from a variety of angles. After a satisfied nod, she continued snipping away. Connie stirred and adjusted her position. "Hold still. I'm almost done." Suddenly, Connie ducked her head, leaned away, and stood up. She tried to tousle her hair. Nothing tousled. She ran to the vanity, let out an *eeky* scream, and plopped down in front of the mirror. She began pouting and grabbed a hairbrush. Forcefully, painfully, she dragged the brush across her scalp, hoping to add a little length. "You butchered me, Rhonda." Again, she dragged at her bangs.

"It'll grow back. Anyway, I did you a favor—you're mod, chic, debonair. It's the new you!"

Leaning close to the mirror, Connie scrutinized the wasteland that had once been a forest. She picked up a hand mirror for a view of the back. "You gave me a stupid pixie cut, Rhonda!"

"Uhhh . . . yeah, silly—that's exactly what I was going for!"

Connie fussed and mussed. "At least you could have left me some bangs. I look like Audrey Hepburn!"

"Exactly. Like I said, that was the plan all along. I wanted to surprise you. No more rat's nest—you look like a beautiful movie star: stylish . . . elegant . . . alluring."

Connie rolled her eyes. "You're so full of crap." Again, she tried to brush her bangs down. "My bangs are almost gone—look at my forehead! It's an *eight* head!"

"It is not—such a fuss! Just wait till people see you. You'll get so many compliments. And why? Because you're fashionable, glamorous, and completely up to date. In Europe, the pixie is back—soon it'll be in New York, Los Angeles, then up here. I guarantee you the pixie will be the number one fashion statement of '66. You're way ahead of your time."

Connie gazed into the mirror, raised her eyebrows, faked an approving nod. "Yeah, you gave me a real modern look. It's the rage in Paris, I'm sure. And I *would* really be up to date, if it was *1954*!"

"It'll grow back, Connie—in all its full, luxurious splendor. And it will probably—oh, shoot—it's 9:30 already!" Rhonda rushed across the room to her television, turned on the set, and spun the channel dial. "We almost missed Peyton Place!"

Lester's head drooped as he sat at his kitchen table. He had not planned to fall asleep. From time to time, a nightmare visited him in wide-awake flashbacks. Sometimes in dreams. The Philippines, 1945. A prisoner of war camp.

A sizable, three-corner tear in the tarpaper above revealed a starry night. The surrounding grounds and outlying jungle lay still. But within the dark detention barracks, there were suffering moans, delirious murmurs, and restless mumbles. Then there were the squeaks and smacks of rats nibbling at the limbs and face of a dead prisoner—a man who had been severely beaten days before and had likely passed the night before. Lester Malman winged a woven thong and the rats scurried. Once a large, powerful man, now bony and emaciated, Lester struggled to his feet. He teetered woozily toward a prone body; it was caked with putridity—the dried slime of diarrheic voiding. The hair was matted and stiff with dysenteric vomit. Lester dragged the bloated body to the doorway. He winced as he bumped his ulcerated arm; the throbbing, burning pain lingered. In a phlegmy whisper, he called, "Guard, guard." Prisoners stirred, some grumbled, some spoke the crazed words of feverish hallucination.

Drawing close, the guard pointed his rifle at Lester's head. The bayonet jabbed his scalp. "Pick up. You carry," said the guard in harsh, broken English. He motioned for Lester to drape the man over his shoulder. The body was soggy, dead weight; but Lester managed the lift. The guard waved at the tower sentry as they walked toward a chained gate; he unlocked and dragged it open. Lester could barely muster the strength to carry the dead man. But he dug deep and somehow managed to push on toward a pit layered with rotting corpses.

The guard closed the gate behind them as Lester wobbled along on failing knees. Through etherized eyes, he could see the silhouettes of the roughly hewn, sharpened poles that formed an abatis around the camp. The entire compound was obscured by long, bending razor blades of grass. At the pit, Lester searched for a spot to drop the body. The guard growled and gestured with his bayonet. "There, take there!" Lester's knees went weak; he staggered a few steps. The guard closed the distance and jabbed him in the ribs.

Lester heaved and wretched as he neared the common grave. Mounds of decaying corpses half-filled the eight-foot ditch. Lester hesitated. The guard drew near. "Drop man!" As Lester slipped the body down from his shoulder, he twisted awkwardly, pretending to stumble. Dropping his weight, he took a short step and threw the body onto the guard. The startled soldier fell backward; the corpse's torso broke open as it landed on top of him. A burst of fumes overcame the guard; he vomited convulsively. Lester scrambled to grind a handful of grit into the guard's eyes. Blinded and still retching, the guard managed to fire a shot. Gaining his feet, blinking away the grit, the soldier peered through the sites of his rifle. But Lester had already made his way into the jungle.

From the tower, a wide beam streamed and washed back and forth all the way to the grave pit. It flashed over the gardens and across buildings, repeatedly bathing the entire camp in blinding light. In a slow, rhythmic pattern the light moved away from the prison, merging in overlapping bands, illuminating the fields all the way to the tree line. The guard pushed open the abatis gate and twenty Japanese soldiers poured through, holding their breath as they passed the horrific hole. Into the foliage they charged, roaring insults and threats, probing with fixed bayonets. After entering the dense undergrowth, they spread out. Despite the near-full moon, the jungle was very dark. Most of the soldiers carried flashlights, but they did little good.

About 200 yards ahead of his trackers, Lester came upon a clearing. He considered taking the easier path toward the river but surmised the Japanese would search there first. Instead, he turned east, into the denser recesses. As he slipped through the foliage, bearing cuts from the wicked grass, brushing against sharp leaves and thorns, he knew the drops and smears of blood would shine in the faintest light. On a branch sat a monkey; in the grass, crawled a snake; in the trees, the birds stirred as they roosted.

The soldiers meandered in a wide, serpentine path; eventually, reaching a river to the east. Although Lester had made a clean escape—he was lost, at times, groping his way, depending only on his sense of touch. He stopped to catch his breath and contemplate his next move. North, he decided. He made his best guess and headed in that general direction. Lester was aware that the northern part of the island was unmanned, unfortified. To compensate—pits, booby traps, and landmines were spread strategically throughout the area. There was nothing he could do but play the odds. Lester walked cautiously, taking care to turn and weave, avoiding most of the grass cuts. At this time of night, snakes were out, lots of snakes—on the ground and in the trees— constrictors, venomous, and some unidentifiable. A small python dangled from a tree limb. Leopard cats and civets roamed the area; occasionally, they screamed and growled, but rarely did they bother people. Perhaps, the deadliest creature in the jungle was the giant, red-headed centipede—extremely poisonous; usually, they dropped out of nowhere. Tonight, this subtropical realm was strangely silent. Lester's nerves were frayed; his heart raced, thumped, and hurt.

He did not see the glow of the campfire until it was too late. He froze. Shadows moved around the fire. Faint voices and quiet laughter sifted through the trees. A twig snapped. "Hands up!" Lester immediately complied. Fingers laced behind his head, he turned to face two small men. One raised a machete, the other pointed an M-1 rifle. Filipino resistance fighters. They ushered Lester toward a hearth where a dozen men were gathered.

"American? British?" asked a guerrilla.

Lester nodded and said, "American." The Filipino guerillas grinned; their faces showed warmth. One of them offered Lester a canteen.

Lester awakened with a breathless start. The guerillas, the campfire, and jungle were gone. He was thousands of miles away from the jungle, slumped over the kitchen table of his humble home. Various items spread across the table: military awards, insignia badges; staff sergeant stripes; candid photographs of jovial pals and drinking buddies, picturesque snapshots of the Philippines, and Hawaii. Off to the side, was a polished golden ring, sporting three sparkling diamonds. Alongside were photographs of Lester and a very pretty woman—in one photo she wore a wedding gown. Beneath these precious memories were pages from newspapers carrying the headlines: "Malman Survives Palawan", "Freed From The Philippines", "POW—Malman's Own Words". Lester sorted the pictures of his wife and placed them in a row. Looking over these things, his thoughts came and went, fragments flashed, each stirring unique blends of emotion. These cherished keepsakes gave him comfort, while ironically tearing him apart. Lester forced a dull church key into a can of Olympia beer. He continued to browse his remembrances, one after another, lingering for a time on some, just glimpsing at others. Occasionally, he would clemently hold an item and shed a tear. Lastly, he picked up the diamond ring and the photo of the woman with flowing dark hair. Dressed in her wedding gown, she smiled with loving eyes; this was the happiest day of her life. Lester gazed at the photo with bittersweet longing; he held it to his heart. Tears streamed. His face convulsed hideously. Lester brushed the photo and the ring aside and buried his head in his hands. His body trembled, he whimpered and sobbed, as another little part of him died.

CHAPTER 17

Saturday Morning

As Ski, Orrie, Doug, and Lon trudged up Rye Grass Hill, the goats met them midway and frolicked in dizzy circles. All endured the acrid smell and taste of smoke; though relatively faint, it was still duly unpleasant. The morning sun burned bright and hot. On the hilltop, the goats roamed and mingled, each trying to get the lion's share of attention. Doug rubbed the sleep from his eyes. Ski cranked the handle of the well. Suffering the close quarters of his patent-leather dress shoes, Orrie stood at the crest of the hill overlooking the parched, scraggly meadow. "It'll be nice to see it when it's all green again."

Ski said, "We do have a little wait ahead of us, but I agree, it *will* be worth the wait. It's really beautiful up here in the spring. The wildflowers, heather, scotch broom, the blossoms all over the trees—for the goats, it's a wonderland. They couldn't have a better place to live."

Once again, Lon yawned. He said, "I hardly ever get up this early. I usually stay up till mom gets home from workin' out at the hospital. She gets home at about eleven. We stay up and watch old movies."

"How long's your mom been a nurse out at Brayton, Lon?" asked Ski.

"Since before I was born. Maybe about 15 years. She really likes working out there."

Orrie started a follow-the-leader game with the goats. They trotted in line as he ran through the grass. Extending his arms like an airplane's wings, he said. "Roger, wilco. I'm coming up on strong turbulence. I'm gonna have to take 'er down."

Doug joined Ski at the well. "Thanks, Mr. Welski. Thanks for lettin' me stay over with you guys."

Ski handed him a full bucket of water. "We were glad to have you. Go ahead and dump that in the trough, then come back for another one."

Lon grabbed a bucket; Orrie flew in for a landing and grabbed another. When Doug returned for another load he said, "My dad's been gettin' so mad lately, I'm kinda gettin' afraid of him."

Ski said, "Stay clear of him for a while, Doug. He's still getting over losing the mill. I'll talk to him later when I see him at the game. I'll get things worked out for you and Connie."

"My dad's always been really proud of that mill. He doesn't say it, but he's especially proud he can give guys jobs . . . It used to be great in the old days when mom was still here. Connie and me, we loved camping out up there. But we don't get to do it anymore."

"Your dad's a good man, a good man goin' through some mighty bad times . . . He was a brave soldier you know."

"Yeah, mom told us. She told us a lot of times . . . She said he had a sickness–he couldn't help it. And she told me and Connie we should always love him."

"Your mom was a smart lady. You can bet she loved him too." Ski pulled up another full bucket. Each time an empty was returned, he had one ready to go. Orrie and Lon were on their way back.

A sadness came over Doug's face. "Yeah, I guess mom was pretty smart . . . me and Connie, we miss her. Sometimes I cry about her. Connie does too; she tries to hide it, but I know she does." Doug became quiet.

All three of the boys picked up another bucket. Ski said, "OK guys, that should do it for water. Let's dump another bag of that feed in the trough."

Suddenly, two goats rushed past the wishing well. The smallest one nudged the one with the floppy ears. Orrie pointed and said, "Look! They're playin' tag! See? I was telling the truth. Tiny bumped Ghostie, so Ghostie's it. She knows she's it—and she's after Toro."

Ski said, "Well, I can see they're having a lot of fun, but goats aren't nearly smart enough to play a game like tag. They're just runnin' and hoppin' around. It sure is a sight."

Orrie said, "It's not just hopping around. They really are playing a game. Just watch close."

Ghostie nudged Toro, then bounded into the high grass. Lon shouted, "They *are* playin' tag!" The boys jumped and cheered. Ski studied the scene and scratched his head.

Doug said, "Toro's it!"

Toro looked confused. His playmates had disappeared. At that moment, Wags shot out the grass, ran headlong in Toro's direction, then zig-zagged away. Toro dug a front hoof into the turf and lowered his horns. He bleated in frustration. Wags reappeared. So did Tiny and Ghostie. Toro charged.

Orrie yelled, "He's after Wags!"

Doug said, "Wags was teasing him—that's why."

Wags rushed past with Toro on his heels. Ghostie and Tiny readied for evasive action. Orrie said, "They're playing tag, Ski—I told you!"

"I'll be darned. Hard to believe, but I'll be darned if they aren't. Ain't that somethin'."

Tiny and Ghostie trotted under the shade of the big horse-chestnut. Wags walked from the grass and joined them. Toro emerged from the grass, stared at the other three, snorted, and conceded the game. He too came to rest under the shadow of the leaves.

Orrie was exuberant. "They can play soccer, too. And they can play leapfrog!"

Doug and Lon found the claim credible; they looked rightfully amazed. Ski pulled out a pack of cigarettes and lit one up. He said, "And I suppose they can sing 'Old MacDonald Had a Farm'?"

Orrie's was a face of proud satisfaction. He met Ski's eyes. "Nope . . . but they can sing 'London Bridge'." Lon and Doug's eyebrows raised, and their mouths opened wide.

"Why do you think they're able to do all these things, Ski?" Orrie asked.

Ski wrinkled his brow, then dropped his cigarette and ground it out with his boot. He returned to cranking the well handle. "Nobody knows where the goats came from, Orrie. They showed up the first summer I moved here—summer of '63. It's always been a big mystery."

"Maybe they're from outer space," said Doug.

Lon laughed, "Yeah, Martians raised 'em to have superbrains and brought 'em here for an experiment to study the human race."

Doug and Orrie seriously considered the possibility. Ski said, "I can almost hear that 'Out of Limits' tune—*do do do do, do do do do*." The boys were familiar with the popular riff and joined in.

While the goats rested, Ski repaired the frayed rope and the hook attachment on the well crank. Doug and Lon carried and dumped the rest of the water buckets into the trough. Orrie swept up the grain from the floor of the shed. Eventually, the guys and the goats gathered near the well. Ski said, "Say your goodbyes, and let's haul on outta here, gentlemen." The boys gave the goats a farewell pat on the head, then ran to catch up with Ski. As they descended the hill, the goats watched intently. Ski and the boys took notice.

Orrie said, "I think they're watching out for us."

Doug said, "They'd fight off mountain lions to protect us if they had to."

"By golly," Ski said, "I do believe they would."

The sky grew dark as a cloud of black smoke rolled across the sun. The group watched as the heavenly orb turned from baby pink to bright blood. Lon said, "Man, that sun looks *red-in-the-face* mad. This is gonna be the hottest day ever."

Doug stopped and turned. He shaded his eyes and fixed a bead on the goats. "Look at them standing up there, all close together. They sure look happy . . . It's like we're part of their family, and they're part of ours."

Ski said, “I think you’ve got something there, Doug . . . Having a family is about the best thing there is.”

In the Rye Grass Cafe, Wuzzie sprayed Windex on the storefront windows and Ronnie polished the red-marbled countertop. Wuzzie asked, “Do you think we’ll be going to Vietnam?”

“Hard tellin’.”

“Do you think you could actually stab a human being with a rifle bayonet?”

In a voice cooler than Elvis or James Dean, Ronnie said, “’Til it poked out the other side.”

Wuzzie’s quick smile turned to concern. “No. I’m serious. Sometimes I worry about it . . . I don’t think I could do it.”

Ronnie studied his friend. “Yeah, I get what you’re sayin’. In your case, the way you are now—I’m thinkin’ maybe you couldn’t.”

“I know *you* could do it. You’re used to it, after all those guys you beat up.”

“Don’t believe everything you hear, Wuzz. I’ve never beat anybody up. Not one person. I’ve never even *hit* anybody.”

“What about when you were in Prescott Hall?”

“Nope. The trick is—just get some stories goin’ and people’s imaginations will take care of the rest.”

"Sorta like Pecos Bill."

"Yep."

"Well, I plan on going' right to college after high school. I heard college can keep you out of service—it's a law."

"Maybe. But I wouldn't count on it; they could change that law anytime."

"And there's that 4-F thing. I heard about this rich kid whose dad paid a doctor to keep him out of the army. The doctor wrote a note that said the kid had some kind of ingrown toenail fungus—some stupid excuse along those lines."

"I don't doubt it . . . Oh no! I have a skeeter bite. I need a crybaby note."

"Gosh, my butt itches. You gotta disqualify me, Doc."

"A guy'd be better off to just go over there and get killed rather than do chicken-guts stuff like that. If you live in America, you defend America. If you claim to be a man, you gotta act like one."

Wuzzie started cleaning the glass on the jukebox. Ronnie put red-checkered coverings on the tables. Wuzzie said, "Yeah, I could never lie or chicken out. I'll go for sure if they call me, but I still don't think I could kill anybody . . . I've been worrying about that for quite a while."

Ronnie thought for a few seconds. He said, "There's a cornfield behind the cottages out by the chapel. I was thinkin' we could make some dummies out of feed sacks and set 'em up like scarecrow soldiers—like Viet Cong out in the jungle. We could make stick rifles with bayonets and practice stabbing 'em."

"You know . . . that could work. I read about something like that in a magazine. People do it to cure phobias—like a fear of heights. You do what you're afraid of a little bit at a time . . . It could work!"

"Do the thing you fear, and the fear will disappear."

"Who said that?"

"Lots of people have said something like that. I just made a rhyme out of it."

"That's a pretty good one. Sayings like that get people thinking about things—a little more than they usually would."

"Like—'Look before you leap' and 'fools rush in'."

Wuzzie raised his hands as though standing on a pulpit. "'The Lord by wisdom hath founded the earth; by understanding hath he established the heavens.'"

"Proverbs?"

"Yep. But I can't remember the number that goes with it."

Ronnie sighed and gazed out the window. "Who knows—maybe you or I will say something wise someday, and people will be quotin' us a hundred years from now."

"That'd be cool."

Smoothing out the last of the tablecloths, Ronnie said, "Anyway, I think doing something scary, just a little at a time, could work pretty good. I can get my hands on a little bb gun out at the chapel. There's one in a closet. It's locked up, but I could get to it."

"And we could make dirt-clod grenades. Remember when we used to do that—throw 'em on the road and they'd break all apart."

"You bet. We'll do it. It sounds pretty awful to say—but we could probably get really good at learning how to kill people."

"We'd just be doing the kind of stuff you learn in basic training. My uncle Bud told me you have to throw live hand grenades—sometimes guys get nervous and drop 'em. Then there's the part where you have to crawl under a bunch of barbed wire while they shoot real bullets two inches over your head."

Ronnie assured, "If other guys can do it—we can do it."

"Jeez, it does sound pretty awful to be practicing how to kill people, but if the enemy's trying to kill you, you've got a right to kill them. Getting a head start so we can get used to it is actually a pretty good idea."

"You bet—we're in this together. If we have to fight in a war, we're gonna be ready. We'd better do some strength training too." Ronnie made a muscle with his bicep. "Does my muscle look bigger than the guy's on the Arm and Hammer box?"

"Uhh . . . turn to the side a little bit. Uhh . . . I think his is a *little* bigger."

"Hmmm . . .Well, at least you're bein' honest."

Wuzzie said, "Talking about *honest*—that man of honor stuff you've been talking about—I think you've been making some progress on that lately. But you gotta stop doing things like pushing those little kids around and gypin' 'em out of their money."

Ronnie nodded his head in agreement and casually added, "Maybe so—but I figure it's only natural that becoming a man of honor is gonna be a gradual process . . . it's gonna take some time. And those kids gotta go through the little aches and pains of growing up—just like the rest of us."

Contriving their war-preparation plan had the guys believing they had taken another step on the road to manhood. They met in the center of the room and engaged in a firm handshake, then Ronnie put Wuzzie in a headlock and gave him a Dutch rub and five knucklehead noogies.

Rhonda entered her bedroom with a towel wrapped around her head, still wearing her pajamas.

Connie asked, "Why'd you put your pajamas back on?"

"It's still early and they're comfortable. How was that bed in the guest room?"

"Good. The mattress is a lot more solid than the one in the other room."

"I figured you'd like it."

While Connie watched *The Bugs Bunny Show*, Rhonda hatched a new brainchild. She started moving all the furniture in her bedroom against the walls. Connie cast a quizzical glance. "What are you doing?"

"I'm making a dance floor. Help me roll up the carpet. We'll put it over next to the mural."

"It's 10:30 in the morning, goofball. I never dance before noon."

"Ha, ha. Come on, take that corner."

The girls rolled away the carpet, exposing a polished hardwood floor. Rhonda went to her stereo and pulled a 45-rpm record from its sleeve. She snapped a plastic adaptor into its center and placed it on the turntable. Next, she went to her dresser and pulled out a pair of thick, woolen socks. Changing her socks while standing she said, "I made up a dance. It's like nothing you've ever seen."

Connie groaned. "Oh boy, hit the spotlight. There's nothing like watching a spaz girl dance in her pajamas."

"Go sit over . . . ummm, pull a chair over by the door. You need to see this from the side to get the full effect."

Yawning and rubbing her eyes, Connie set the wicker "barber" chair in front of the bedroom door. "OK, I'll watch your stupid dance, but you're gonna owe me."

Rhonda did some warm-up stretches. "Last winter I saw this old movie with this band leader named Cab Calloway. He, like, wore a white suit and these, I dunno, faggoty-lookin' shoes—they seemed sort of like silk slippers. Anyway, he could slide around in them."

"Yeah, yeah, OK, sliding around in faggoty shoes—please just get it over with."

Rhonda did some warm-up steps, a few turns, and a sache. "Cab Calloway, like, stood up on his toes and started alternating his knees, then started to walk, but then slid back. He moved up and down on his toes; it seemed like he was walking forward, but he was sort of sliding and wasn't going anywhere."

"Uh huh, yeah, that really makes sense."

Rhonda did some deep knee bends and toe touches. "It reminded me of the Red Queen race where you run and run but stay in the same spot. Only I changed it so you do go somewhere—it looks like you're walking forward, but actually you slide backward."

"You do realize I will be making fun of you . . . and you're giving me a whole lot of ammunition."

Rhonda ice skated to the stereo. "You need a big band sound. My mom has this song called "Midnight in Moscow"—it's perfect!"

"Yeah, they play that on the radio once in a while—it's an OK song."

"It's great for dancing. All kinds of dancing. It works especially well for "The Silky Way"—that's what I'm calling my new dance . . . for now."

The jumpy little tune "Midnight in Moscow" by Kenny Ball and his Jazzmen started up. Rhonda walked across the room and started rolling her hips; she did a series of swing steps, then transitioned to her innovative concoction. She straightened to full height and began walking forward on her toes, then settled back onto her heels. It appeared she was walking forward, up and down, while riding backward on an escalator. As she neared the mural wall, she spun and continued her dance to the middle of the floor where she took a hammy bow. Connie laughed, swayed from side-to-side, clapped, and cheered. She jumped up and started dancing freestyle. Rhonda pulled her to the middle of the floor and tried to teach her "The Silky Way".

When the song ended, Connie said, "It isn't really as spazzy as it looked. Actually, it takes a lot of coordination. But it does feel really weird trying to move your body like that. When I first saw you do it, I thought you were just clowning around."

"So, if I improve it a little, smooth some things out—do you think it could catch on?"

"Not in a million, billion years. I don't think anybody in the whole world, of their own free will, would want to be seen doing something like that in public. Not even if their life depended on it."

With slight indignation, Rhonda said, "Well, thanks for all the encouragement, *friend.*"

"I'm not saying it was bad—it was just, like, super-deluxe oddball strange. I could, maybe, see trained poodles doing it at a magic show."

"You have no appreciation for the Arts, lady."

Although "The Silky Way" died there and then in Rhonda's bedroom, little did either girl know that someday, "The Silky Way" would be called "The Moonwalk".

Out in Brayton, a ways down the road from the chapel, at the far end of the berry fields, Toby Gussard skulked toward a huge horse barn. He crept up to the door of the attached workshop. Carrying a long, curved stick, he quickly slipped inside the building and twisted the knob of an archaic light fixture. In a dimly lit corner, Toby cut notches in both ends of the long stick, knotted the ends of a thin strand of jute, then bent and strung his new weapon. Composed of ash—a light, flexible wood—this was a relatively well-crafted bow. He took aim and twanged the string; he smiled, well-satisfied. He pulled some old paint cans from under the workbench and reached back for a handful of handmade arrows. They were sturdy and reasonably straight by Toby's standards. Their blunt ends were notched. Toby placed a nail in a vice and used a hack saw to cut off the flat end. He pushed sharp nail points into the end of each arrow and sanded the jutting dull heads into points. As he examined each shaft, he trembled with excitement and tapped the sharp points with his thumb. "Ow, ow, ow. Wowee!"

Toby trod lightly to the workshop door and peeked outside. No one around. He hurried back to the corner of the room, kneeled, and carefully pried up one of the floorboards. He lifted a cigar box from the sub-floor and gleefully viewed the contents. From the box, he took a flat, red Prince Albert can and sprinkled the contents onto the floor: stick matches, easily two dozen, and a Bic lighter. He set two matches aside, then returned the rest to the can. Next, he brought up a can of lighter fluid and set it aside. Finally, he reached down and pulled out two handfuls of matchbooks—most of them were labeled *Runnin' Bear Tavern*. After compulsively lining them into four perfectly spaced rows—he leaned back and admired the display. In routine fashion, he hid his treasures, save for the two stick matches and the can of lighter fluid. Toby stood up, grabbed the bow and arrows, as well as a few strips of white cloth. Slowly opening the door, he looked left, right, left, right, then straight ahead. No one in sight. He closed that door and opened the inner access door to the barn, closing it tight after he entered.

Toby scoped out a target for his new and improved arrows. He settled for a dusty, battered old horse saddle draped over the rail of an animal stall. He backed off five paces, wrapped a strip of cloth tightly just below an arrowhead, then squirted on a little lighter fluid. Toby fit the notch of the arrow onto the bowstring and lit the cloth. Hurriedly, he drew back the bow and sent the fiery arrow deep into the tough leather of the saddle. He tilted back his head and let out a series of eerie war whoops, ending the celebration with a chilling shriek. The sound echoed within the walls and wailed up through the cupola.

CHAPTER 18

Foreign Wars Field

Way out beyond left field, Rain hung the red, white, and blue bunting over the counter of a hot dog stand. Ski put three crystal pitchers of lemonade on display. Charlie Figgs hustled across the grass, making a beeline for Ski. In confidence, he whispered, "Tolawaka gave me a call about an hour ago. There's a new warrant out for Buddy Foley. They figure he stole a car the same day they let him out."

"Nice of 'em to give us all this timely news. He could have shot both Lester and me in the back by now."

"I gave 'em an earful. But everybody I talked to just covered everybody else's butt."

Eyes stinging from smoke and sweat, Ski scanned the fire-spotted hillside. The main blaze had moved well east, nearing an old railroad trestle where all past hill fires had eventually burned out. "You figure Foley set that fire?"

"Could have. And he could stay up in those hills, or in the woods along the river, eatin' berries and pine squirrels for about as long as he wants. We'd never find him."

"Sounds like a mighty lonely prospect. But I don't think he'd stay up in the hills for long. He'd come down to the woods and hold up in some old shack or barn—like he did with Ronnie."

Figgs held his chin and searched his thoughts. "Makes sense . . . We *are* in a pickle. Maybe we oughta just settle back and let him make his next move."

"With everybody and his brother here at the game, it'll be easy to get the word out. I'll make the rounds and let everybody know. It wouldn't hurt to tell Dodd to put a blurb in the newsletter for the next edition."

"I'll get a phone tree set up. Maybe Rain would help with that."

"That'd be good . . . Man, this is all we need." Ski took a gander at the gathering crowd. "There's Brownie, Tom Sparks, ol' man Higgins . . . After all of this is over and done with, I'll round up a few guys and go out and do a little more searchin'. Just knowing we're looking might be enough to drive him outta here."

"And there's another little complication: Lester said he might just take the matter into his own hands—go, all-out vigilante."

"Great!" Ski said sarcastically. "Good thing you let me know. I'll talk to him . . . And to think, back in May, I believed we were gonna have a quiet little summer."

"Lester'll be mighty hard to discourage. It's the kids he's worried about—Connie and Doug. He isn't real comfortable with thinking there's somebody out there laying for him. If something was to happen—"

"No need preachin' to the choir, Charlie. I'll help Lester figure things out. No need to worry about the kids either."

Fans crossed the gravel parking lot toward the scrubby VFW baseball field; everybody called it Foreign Wars Field. They carried folding chairs, coolers, and makeshift lawn umbrellas. Many of the rooters wore sunglasses, caps, or sunbonnets. The smoke-tainted scent of *Sea & Ski* and *Coppertone* hung like honey in the air. Slowly, the derelict bleachers filled. You had to be careful—sit on the wrong crack and you could end up with a nasty blood blister on your behind. Everybody else had to settle for a tolerable spot on the itchy, brown grass.

The Malman Loggers sported bright red caps and jerseys and worn-out blue jeans. They milled around behind the backstop. Ronnie Rix coasted in on his bike. The other guys rallied around him. He clowned around a little, then sat on the player's bench. He tightened up his shoelaces and the other players did the same. Charlie Figgs took his umpire vest and mask from a box near the backstop. Through the chain-link fence, he addressed the home team.

"Why don't you guys take the field for warm-ups? Deputy Welski will get things goin' 'til Coach Malman gets here."

Ski's badge glinted beneath the glare of the sun. He took the mound. The fielders were in position. There was a batter at the plate, one on deck, and one in the hole. Ski tossed an easy pitch and the ball sailed high into center field. Ronnie started some chatter. "Nice swat, Benny!"

⚜

Rhonda came out of her walk-in-closet with a blouse on a hanger and a box of *Kellogg's Pop-Tarts*. She tossed Connie a silver packet and said, "Here's breakfast!"

Connie tore it open as soon as she caught it. "Ahh, strawberry—my favorite!"

Rhonda pulled off her pajama top and replaced it with the blouse. It was white with short, frilly sleeves and it tied at the midriff. She swayed her hips and looked for approval. Connie folded her arms and rolled her eyes. Her wolf whistle had a sarcastic tone. "Nice to meet you, Sue Lyon."

"Sue Lyon . . . I'll take that compliment any day!"

"This isn't *Night of the Iguana*, Rhonda—it's *Day of the Ballgame*. And you look like a floozy."

"I do not. Once I put my cutoffs on, you'll see . . . I'll cut one of mom's blouses in half and make one of these for you if you want."

Connie held her palms out like stop signs. With a stern look, she said, "I ain't wearin' nothin' like that . . . Think about it, Rhonda: There's gonna be a bunch of guys there, you know, like, teenage boys with lots of pent-up desires."

"Tell me something I don't know. I've been countin' on it. I want to see their eyes pop out like telescopes."

Connie groaned, "Go find something decent to wear."

Rhonda hurried back to the closet and came out wearing the shortest, tightest pair of cutoff jeans in her wardrobe. She mussed up her hair and cake-walked across the room. "I think I'll go with some diamond posts, sugar pink lipstick, and a ton of mascara." Her devilish eyes darted; she tipped her head and smiled slyly.

"You're not really going to go out in public like that, are you? I mean you're kidding, right?"

Rhonda hid her *come-into-my-parlor* intent. A femme fatale in sheep's clothing, she baited a little trap. "Oh, I think I'm a long way from kidding . . . You'd be surprised at what a little *floosiness* can do . . . If you really, truly, want to get back at your dad—a get-up like this would definitely fix his wagon."

Connie walked to the window, leaned on the sill, and gazed into the depths of the sky-blue swimming pool. "To be or not to be," she mused and turned to Rhonda. Connie put her hands on her hips. "I know you think you're tricking me—but you're not."

"OK. Whatever you say."

"I just hadn't thought of the idea, yet."

"So, should I get the blouse?"

After one last little battle with her conscience, Connie said, "Go ahead. I'll take a pair of your mom's *hundred-dollar* jeans too."

Back at Foreign Wars Field, the hot-dog stand was much hotter than the hot dogs. Rain smiled and waved at the Trujillo family as they weaved through the crowd. Orrie, Lon, and Doug sat on a bench in front of the stand. They sipped lemonade and talked out of the sides of their mouths like lieutenants of Al Capone.

Lon said, "When Ronnie gets on deck—that's when we'll make our move."

"On deck?" asked Orrie.

"When he's the next guy to bat. While he walks to the plate, Doug and I will start our fight."

Doug asked, "Just to make sure—you want me to attack you over by third base as soon as Ronnie steps up to the plate?"

"Yeah, but call me a stinkin' injun first. Really loud. And when everybody's watching us fight, Orrie can go for the mitt."

Orrie gave Lon a quizzical look. "A stinkin' injun. You know, I've been wondering, Lon—how come so many people call you Chief?"

"Cuz I'm a little dark complected—that's all it takes around here."

Doug said, "Sometimes they call him Tonto or Geronimo."

Lon added, "Sitting Bull, Running Bear, Cochise."

Both curious and trying to be helpful, Orrie asked, "Injun Joe?"

"Yeah . . . but not that much."

Doug said, "Once I heard Ronnie call you Chief Warhoop."

Lon looked at Orrie. "That's from the Cleveland Indians. Ronnie hates that team."

"Are there any real Indians around here?" asked Orrie.

Lon said, "No. They mostly stay on the reservation—the Colville Indian Reservation."

"Probably cuz people would call them names," said Orrie.

"Not probably," said Doug. "That's exactly what does happen. And the names are way worse than what they call, Lon."

Lon stood up and said, "We gotta get back to business. Remember, Orrie, it's *really* important to grab the right glove—the first baseman's mitt is long, with no fingers."

"I'm not dumb, you know. You drew a picture of it, and I saw him wearing it. I'll find it, don't worry."

"You've got the hardest job, Orrie. If you get caught, it will look like you're stealing."

"I can do it. I can picture myself—like a falcon swooping down on its prey."

Doug said, "Good comparison, Orrie. You can do it, man."

"Just don't get nervous and give yourself away," said Lon. "Slow and steady. Slip the mitt under your shirt and walk away like your normal self."

"Should I start whistling—you know, like I'm all happy and all innocent?"

"No!"

On the other side of the ball field, the Pemmican Pirates' bus rolled into the parking lot. Trailing the bus were Connie and Rhonda. As the girls sauntered along, Rhonda's radio played "Pretty Flamingo" by Manfred Mann. They were both wearing their "floozy" outfits, complete with gaudy makeup. Connie wore dangling hoop earrings. Rhonda wore her winged, rhinestone sunglasses. Making certain to maintain the occult status of her *pixie* cut, Connie adjusted a floppy yellow sunbonnet. And she carried a large *Nordstroms* shopping bag. Rhonda stepped back and ogled Connie's backside. "Good Lord, my mom's jeans fit you like a glove!"

"A little tight, but waaay nicer than anything I've got."

As the girls passed the Pemmican players bus, windows slid down. Taunts, teases, whistles, jeers, claps, and cheers began. A wide-grinning player yelled, "Hey blondie, go back to your street corner." Laughter rang.

Another player shouted, "What's the goin' rate?"

"A nickel!" Shouted another, followed by more whistles, laughter, and cheers.

The taunts kept coming. "I bid ten cents!"

A shaggy-haired boy thrust his head and shoulders through a window. "Hey twinkle twat, wanna see what I got?" The bus roared and started to rock as the players bounced up and down.

The girls hastened, but suddenly Connie turned back. Her lip curled and she pointed at the kid with shaggy hair. "Sure, Pee-Wee, why don't you stick it out and rotate on it!" The tide turned and all hilarity spotlighted the crimsoning heckler.

Rhonda was mortified; her face had gone scarlet. Connie pulled her behind the groundskeeper shed. Rhonda blustered indignantly, "I'm going home right now!"

Connie reached into the clothing bag. "Let's have a snack first."

"Forget you! We're gettin' outta here! The guys on that bus are a bunch of creeps."

"True, but we proved we can stand up to them. They're punks—immature, just like the guys at school. And besides, I think you're really gonna like this snack." Connie pulled out two extra-large white t-shirts and draped one over Rhonda's head.

A red-tinted sun glowered. The layered smoke increasingly irritated eyes and throats. Wheezes, sneezes, and coughs formed a respiratory orchestra. Through it all—a perspiring, sunburned, calm-before-the-storm crowd, cordially engaged. Home team supporters numbered several hundred. A smattering of visiting fans mingled among them. Uncharacteristically sober, Coach Malman stood at home plate. The Loggers gathered near. "Take a knee, men. We got one matter to deal with before taking the field. Surreptitious glances. "What's the penalty for being careless with team equipment."

The team answered, "Duckwalks!"

"Duckwalks. We all know the deal." Lester's visage was one of oversold disappointment. "Ronnie, by now everybody in town knows you got your cap stole the other day."

Ronnie waved the cap. "It's right here."

Lester lectured, "You made the whole team the butt of jokes, young man. In every nook and cranny of the town. By team rule, you gotta pay the price. You already know the drill."

"Here?! Now?!" Ronnie threw his arms wide, but Lester's scowl abruptly ended the protest.

The rest of the team whispered and mumbled, eyes down. Lester turned toward the infield and made a circular gesture with his index finger. Ronnie gave his teammates an unconvincing wink. Their faces showed sympathy, empathy, and ire. Ronnie squatted on the first baseline, locked his fingers behind his head, flapped his folded arms, quacked, and waddled toward first base. The smoldering eyes of his teammates burned into Lester's heart. Lester met their swollen eyes. "Gentlemen. You all know Ronnie's All-Star spot is on the line. You all know he plays best when he's mad . . . If this doesn't make him mad nothin' will." A couple of guys affirmed with nods; the rest were non-committal.

As Lester proceeded with the questionable disciplinary tactics and dubious method of inspiration, the crowd's discontent escalated. Aspersions and catcalls: "What the hell is wrong with you, Coach?"; "Lester, are you nuts?!"; "He's a Nazi!"; "That's enough!"; "You're a monster, Malman!"; "These are kids, you idiot!" There were also a few *spare-the-rod* sentiments, but very few.

Ski approached Father Dom and said, "Do you think I should step in?"

Father Dom said, "Let it play out. A higher power looks on . . . As I recall, you're the one who planted the seeds of crossroads and virtue."

"Yeah, I did for sure. But this is a crossroads I didn't see comin' . . . I mean, I'll bite the bullet this time cuz, like they say, the Lord works in—"

Father Dom smiled. "Mysterious ways."

Walking along the first baseline, clad in Kelly green, Kenny West, tall, tan, and handsome, proudly led the Pemmican Pirates toward the visitor's reserve. The head coach trekked alongside. "Plenty of heat left in that arm, Kenny?"

"Way more than these guys can handle."

The coach smiled and veered away. He went down the line of players stoking fires of resolve. Reaching his assistant he said,

"Tommy, they want you to *ump* first base and right field—their guys have the rest."

"I figured they'd need me to do that. I'm pretty sure we've got this one in hand, so, if something's close, I'll give them the benefit."

"I agree. We don't want any questions about Kenny's right to the All-Star bid."

As the Pirates neared their bench, Ronnie had duck-walked halfway to second base. His opponents merrily spewed teases and taunts accompanied by bursts of laughter: "Quack a little louder, duck boy!"; "It's his mating call!"; "He sure knows how to squat!"; "He's doing his duty out there"; "That's what he does best!"

Kenny West frowned. He turned and yelled, "Shut up! Everybody!" The Pirates abruptly calmed and, in fact, became virtually silent. As they continued their walk, a bigmouth shouted, "Give that duck a quacker!"

Kenny stopped, turned, and strolled down the line. A loud *smack* split the air when he cuffed the bigmouth on the back of the head—the player's cap went flying. "You knock that crap off and keep your big mouth shut!" As Kenny returned to the front line, there was not a peep.

The coach trotted up to investigate. Satisfied things had been settled, he guided the Pirates to their bench. Two managers followed, lugging a cooler and a garbage can full of bats. As the Pirates got squared away, Umpire Figgs approached. Kenny confidently stepped up, removed his cap, and extended his hand. "Nice to meet you, Sir. I'm Kenny West."

Down at the hot dog stand, Connie and Rhonda stood before the patriotic bunting, talking with Wuzzie. Rain wrapped up three hot dogs; the teens reached out for lunch. Wuzzie crunched on the fast-melting ice left in his soda cup. Rain said, “Do you girls realize you’re wearing more make-up than party clowns? . . . Nice earrings though.”

Rhonda said, “We have costumes too.” She raised the long t-shirt up to her chin. Rain offered a discerning eye. Wuzzie’s eyeballs flashed to high beam. Rhonda laughed heartily. A pink-faced Connie tugged her friend’s shirt down.

Connie said, “Please excuse this crazy person . . . Thanks for lunch.”

Rhonda elbowed Connie and whispered, “Your dad just looked over here.”

“Did he see us?”

“I’m not sure—we’re pretty far away.”

“Let’s not take any chances . . . We’ll mingle.”

The girls quickened their pace and vanished like chameleons.

CHAPTER 19

Loggers vs Pirates

The scoreboard was set—Loggers 0, Pirates 0. The first of seven innings (the standard game length for the 15-and-under category of the Gussard Memorial Baseball League) was in the offing. Orrie, Lon, and Doug walked toward the players' benches. Spectator after spectator stared at Doug's grubby tunic and its sweat-distorted Templar Cross. They gawked, smiled, whispered, pointed, chuckled, and leaned away from the smoke-and-fish-guts smell. One man said, "Young man, you may be better off with a clean shirt and a pair of trousers."

"This is my knight tunic—it's a good luck charm. And it makes me distinctive."

Lon said, "Distinctive—oh boy! The college professor's back in town."

"Yep. It means rare, unique."

"Distinctive," said Orrie. "I'd say more like dis-*stinky*-tive." Lon laughed, Doug didn't.

All three boys froze as they watched the Loggers' pitcher wind up for the game's first pitch. The Pirate popped a Texas leaguer well up into the smoke, ordinarily, a base hit. The ball briefly disappeared. The third baseman took a few backsteps, reached high and the ball dropped into his glove. One away. Allie Davis, the tubby, usually jovial Logger hurler, was grim and steely-eyed. He visibly ground his teeth and he looked three-days constipated. With machine-like precision, he let three rockets fly—abashing the Pirate batter and battering the catcher's mitt. A grounder to Ronnie at first base ended the inning.

The Pirates took the field. Kenny West threw nothing but fastballs, making the first two batters look slow and feeble. The Loggers' third slugger stepped up; on deck, Ronnie took some easy practice swings. He and Kenny locked eyes. Expressionless, Kenny glanced at the shortstop, then he nodded to the catcher. Kenny burned one in—strike one! Getting edgy, Ronnie took a couple of wicked practice swings. Out of nowhere, a ruckus brewed, not far from third base. The shouting and hollering turned the crowd's attention. Kenny held back the pitch.

Doug did his best to sneer. "My dad says you're a stinkin' injun. He don't want me playin' around you no more." Lon tackled Doug. They wrestled and pretended to punch each other. Orrie scooted along the backstop and scooped up Ronnie's mitt. It magically disappeared under his surfer shirt. Despite a twitch or two of facial guilt, Orrie pulled off an inconspicuous getaway. He hustled toward the parking lot.

To the great relief of Lon and Doug, Father Dom intervened and ended the farcical fight. He sent Lon to the hot-dog stand. Before sending Doug in the other direction, he took account of the youngster's garb. The Father could not have shown a more flummoxed expression. He smiled wryly, raised his eyebrows, and kindly said, "Goodness gracious—I'm not even going to ask." He directed Doug to watch the rest of the game from behind the backstop.

The game resumed. Kenny West blew the third batter into oblivion. Ronnie had wanted nothing more than to step up to the plate. He made his disappointment evident, dramatically facing the bleachers and dropping his bat. While the other Loggers took the field, Ronnie scoured the grass for his mitt. He scurried around like a chipmunk. Lester walked toward him, arms wide, fingers splayed, face just shy of demonic. "Ronnie, what the hell are you doing?!"

"My mitt's gone . . . It was right here next to my bike! I know I left—" Ronnie's voice broke up. Lester's scowl subsided. His eyes softened. Umpire Figgs caught his attention and gestured toward the field.

"Time out, Charlie. Ronnie lost his mitt."

They looked up, down, all around. Figgs tapped his wristwatch. "Game's on, Lester, mitt or no mitt."

Lester motioned for Ronnie to join him near the bench. He opened a moldy old satchel and tenderly removed a beaten-up first baseman's mitt. He dusted it off and handed it to Ronnie. "It's the one from my tryout with the Giants. I feel pretty proud it's gonna be used for one last game—especially a big game like this, and more so that you're the one using it."

Ronnie reverently gazed at the relic. Lester gave him a side hug. As Ronnie took the field, the cheers built to a crescendo. Lester's eyes glistened.

In the parking lot, Orrie moved stealthily through a maze of cars and trucks. When he took a turn between two pickups parked next to the VFW hall, he found his way blocked by the side of the building. Turning back, he found himself looking directly at the gap-toothed grin of Toby Gussard. Toby's eyes grew wide. He grunted and laughed like a loon. Toby pointed to the lumpy mitt hidden under Orrie's shirt. "What boy got?"

"Nothing." Orrie knew he was trapped. Fight or flight energy built toward a blastoff.

Toby stepped forward and reached. "Give Toby." Orrie hugged the mitt against his belly. Toby pressed the issue. "Do be sine cup!"

Toby lunged. Orrie tossed the mitt clear over the bed of a pickup, jumped kangaroo-high, and pulled himself over the side of the truck. Toby's hand grabbed at thin air. Orrie rolled across the bed of the truck and scrambled over the other side. He snatched the mitt from the gravel and instantly transformed into the wing-footed Mercury. Toby swung himself onto the truck bed and watched Orrie run out of sight. "Do be sine cup! Do be sine cup!"

Wild-eyed, Toby jumped off the truck and ran for his bicycle. With a running start he hopped on and peddled with teeth-baring spite. The green Duncan Yo-Yo in his bicycle basket fell through the bottom and the string became wound in the front spokes. This sent Toby headfirst onto the rocks. Stunned, he struggled to rise, rubbed at his gravel-grazed forehead, and raged at the sky. He yanked the yo-yo string free, screamed again, took a running start, and tore a path around the corner. Orrie had disappeared.

The scoreboard atop the elementary school fence still showed Loggers 0, Pirates 0. Ronnie stepped up to the plate. Kenny nodded to the catcher, then hurled a heater that singed leather. Ronnie's swing was so late, and so flailing that he nearly fell. Kenny smiled impishly. Ronnie recovered and saw Kenny's arm rise high, circle away, and follow through with a wrist twist; a curve was on the way. It looked like it would be way outside, so Ronnie held back. The ball curled in and nibbled the corner. "Strike!" yelled Figgs.

From behind the backstop, Lester said calmly, "Relax, Ronnie, relax. Flex your neck. Shrug your shoulders. Breathe slow . . . just relax."

Ronnie choked up, slipped both hands to the bat's hilt, then up about an inch. He and Kenny were the bull and bullfighter in a Mexican standoff. Ronnie swallowed hard, gulping down a chunk of his confidence. The windup flashed, in the blink of an eye, a fastball bulleted into the catcher's mitt—*smack*! Ronnie swung in frustration, staggering backward like Buster Keaton on a tightrope. Spontaneous laughter broke out, followed by a hum of conciliatory support. Ronnie endured his walk of shame, looking gloomier than the Mighty Casey. Spectators nearby continued to console. Ronnie did his best to shrug things off, but his discouragement was undeniably on display. As he rounded the backstop, Lester gave him a pat on the back. "Next time. It'll come. Try stepping forward in the batter's box, right up to the line. He won't expect it. That'll make him think twice about throwing a curve or a slider. He's afraid of you—take my word for it."

His hang-dog expression and doubt-filled eyes were the only responses Ronnie could muster.

Tightly clutching the golden-fleece mitt, Orrie raced past fences and down a series of pot-holed alleys. The neighborhood was understandably uninhabited. Crossing lawns and side streets, he soon spied his boxcar refuge. Toby had discovered this hide-out, but that was of no consequence; it was the perfect place to stash the mitt—deep beneath the sand. Orrie flew across the deserted highway, streaked across the narrow grass way, and hopped up onto a railroad car coupling. He glanced around for the slightest sign of Toby, then jumped down and ducked behind a big, iron wheel. From there he could see the distant crossing where he, Lon, and Doug had planned to meet. He could also peer over the coupling to see the stretch of highway east of the trees. At that moment, Toby wheeled into sight. Bon vivant and nonchalant (in his own peculiar way) he rolled the highway, glancing from side to side. When Toby had ridden completely out of sight, Orrie climbed into the boxcar. He pulled an old newspaper apart, wrapped the mitt securely, then took it to the top of the sand mound. Scooting down into a corner, Orrie scooped out a hole, about a foot deep, and buried the ransom package. After carefully scouting the area, he headed for the railroad crossing rendezvous. His friends were nowhere to be seen. Unnerved and antsy, Orrie waited a few minutes, then ran back to the baseball field.

As the scoreboard came into view, Orrie noticed the contest had moved into the fourth inning. The score was still Loggers 0, Pirates 0. The Pirates had two away and the count on the inning's third batter was three and one. The Loggers' Allie Davis hurled a fireball. The batter missed by a whisker. "Streeeerike two!" Facing a full count the pitcher signaled his intentions. The batter displayed a gritty grin, ready to swat at whatever came his way. It was a slider. It came in low and a little outside. The Pirate reached for it. Crack! The ball climbed and climbed. The right fielder backpedaled; the runner rounded first. The fielder offered a futile raise of his glove as the ball sailed high over his head, and over the fence. To the clamor of his fans and teammates, his face aglow, the Pirate regally rounded the bags. The next batter grounded out, retiring the side. The Loggers trotted off the field, the Pirates trotted on. The scoreboard showed Loggers 0, Pirates 1, the bottom of the fourth.

Allie Davis joined Ronnie behind the backstop. He said, "We're all with you, Ronnie. I never figured that kid had a chance of hittin' that lousy pitch." Allie dragged an index finger over the grit gripping his eyelids. "This dang smokey sweat's burnin' the heck out of my eyes."

"It's OK, Allie. He got a lucky hit; it's all part of the game."

"It still makes me feel like some kinda candy-ass pansy."

Ronnie chuckled. "You might look like a teddy bear, but you can throw harder and run faster than anybody on our team—you're no pansy."

"Well, that guy ain't gettin' nothin' else off me—none of 'em are!"

"That's right—tear 'em up." Ronnie looked toward the hillside. "The next time I get up, I'm blastin' that ball clear across the Caulder River."

The fourth inning ended with the first two Loggers striking out and Ronnie undramatically popping up on the very first pitch. The fifth inning began with the pink-faced, sweat-dripping, teeth-grinding Allie Davis, again taking the mound. He lifted his chin like a fearless matinee gladiator. His shifty eyes had the hitter blinking nervously. He fired three fastballs into the catcher's mitt; it was like John Henry driving railroad spikes. Allie yelled out, "Next?!" Stepping to the plate was easily the smallest player on the field—a Munchkin with chips on both shoulders. Davis cannoned the next pitch right down the pipe; the mini-Pirate blasted a line drive right into Allie's ribs. The pitcher dropped; he curled up and groaned. The runner raced to first, and the catcher held him there. Ski, Figgs, and Lester had gathered around Allie Davis. Ski and Lester helped him to his feet and walked him off the field. The audience applauded in both sympathy and appreciation. Behind the backstop, Ski gently touched Allie's left side; the boy winced. Ski whispered to Figgs, "I think there's a broken rib." Figgs nodded and arranged a ride to the Brayton hospital.

Lester called the right fielder to cover first. The fielder and Ronnie traded mitt for glove and Ronnie took the mound. A new right fielder hustled into position. Whistles and cheers accompanied each move. At first base, the Munchkin ventured a generous lead off, but a twitch from Ronnie scared him back. After two wild pitches, Ronnie kicked up some dirt and pounded a fist into his glove. He turned on a little high heat, a little low heat, and three batters went down swinging. The Loggers talked it up as they headed in. The Pirates took the field with nary a word—in deference to Kenny West's cool confidence.

While Rain was watching the game from the hot-dog stand, Orrie, Lon, and Doug arrived at the counter looking like lost pups. She set three paper cups side by side and filled each with two ounces of lemonade. "That's the last of it. I'm closing up." The boys each gulped their drinks in a single swallow.

Orrie asked, "Can we use the stand as a secret hide-out?"

"What in the world could you be hiding from?"

"Nothing. It's just a saying. We just want to stay in here for the fun of it."

"OK. Since we're closed, I guess so. But you better not be up to any monkey business."

"We're not. We just want some privacy."

"I do declare, the biggest thing to happen in this little town all summer, three-hundred people out there cheering, and you three want privacy."

All three boys nodded *yes*.

After taking a few steps, Rain turned and said, “No monkey business—I mean it!”

Orrie started *ooking*, *awking*, and acting like a monkey. Lon and Doug joined in on the joke. She mockingly furrowed her brow and went on her way.

Doug asked Orrie, “Is she mad?”

“No. I don’t think so. She’s just feeling hot like the rest of us. And she’s getting kind of tired.”

“I’ve been wondering, Orrie. I don’t want to butt into your guys’ business, but what happened to your mom’s cheek . . . that scar?”

Orrie scowled. “That was from Denny. She went on some dates with him, but I never liked him. I used to tease her and sing ‘Denny, oh Denny, he’s my lucky penny’—and she’d get mad. Grandma didn’t like him either. He was a mean little army guy with a skinny mustache. Always trying to act tough because he was small. Grandma called him a banty rooster. Anyway, he punched mom once—with his wolf ring on.”

“God!” said Lon. “That’s awful!”

Doug bristled and raised a clenched fist. “I’d punch him right now! Right in his stupid face!”

“It’s OK,” Orrie said. “He got in trouble by the police. And by the army too. I think grandma called them and he had to go to jail.”

“Good,” said Lon. “I hate that guy.”

The boys sat on the grassy floor of the hot dog stand discussing their quandaries and precarious circumstances.

"So why do you think Toby Gussard keeps trying to follow us?" Doug posed.

"He tried to grab me in the parking lot," said Orrie. "That was the scariest thing that ever happened to me. Thank God I got away! I think he might want to beat us up for some reason."

"We never did anything to him—none of us," said Doug.

"He's just weird," said Lon. "He's like one of those retarded guys you see at the county fair in Union City. Retarded guys don't usually need a reason for what they do—they just do weird stuff."

"That sorta makes sense, I guess," said Orrie.

"My dad calls those guys pinheads and balloon heads—and some of 'em mongoloids."

Lon said, "Yeah, kids at school call each other those names. Along with moron and idiot . . . Retard's probably the most popular one."

Doug recollected, "Last year, at the fair, a siren went off. Connie and Rhonda told some old ladies that a guy from the retarded home jumped off the Ferris wheel and tore his testicles off. It didn't really happen, but the old ladies said something like, 'Oh, my bless*ed* Jesus!'—Connie and Rhonda thought it was funnier than heck."

"What's testicles?" asked Orrie.

"I better not say. Jesus could be listening," said Doug.

Lon added, "You better look it up, Orrie. It could be in a crossword puzzle someday."

"Maybe I will," said Orrie. "And I will *obscure* it from you."

"So, what. I don't care what it means—and I never will."

Doug shrugged his shoulders and turned to Orrie." Why did you go back to that boxcar? Toby knows we go there."

"I know, but I was real careful. I thought it would be a good place to hide the mitt. At first, I ducked behind a wheel next to a coupling and watched Toby ride his bike down the highway. He went into town. I waited 'til he was clear out of sight, then climbed up and buried the mitt—way back in a corner, under about a foot of sand."

"Good goin'," said Lon. "Those were some smart moves."

Doug asked, "Do you guys really think Ronnie will pay us a ransom?"

Lon said, "He will. He'll give us the five bucks. He loves that mitt. He probably sleeps with it and kisses it every night." Lon pretended to hug and kiss an invisible mitt. "Mwuh, mwuh, I love you mitt. Oh, how I love you! Mwuh, mwuh, mwuh."

As their young hearts rang with laughter, a commotion on the field demanded their attention.

"The crowd's gettin' louder and louder," said Orrie.

Lon jumped up and said, "Let's go see what's goin' on." They left the stand and weaved their way to a good vantage point.

Innings five and six had basically been more of the same—strikeouts, ground outs, pop-ups. There was one close call out in centerfield, but it was foiled by the outstretched arm of a lanky Logger. At the top of the seventh and final inning, the tables were turned when Kenny West stood at the plate facing his nemesis. West's *coffee-toned* tan looked a little milky when the shoe was on the other foot. But he was game enough and sent a couple of foul tips into the parking lot; unfortunately, his final swing ended with a hollow rush of wind. Still, considering Kenny had a no-hitter going, he was able to mount the mound with a pinch of pomp and a smidge of ceremony. Someone in the crowd called out, "Finish 'em off, Kenny!" West doffed his cap.

Everyone at Foreign Wars Field was looking at the long, black scoreboard: Loggers 0, Pirates 1, the bottom of the 7th, no balls, no strikes, no outs, no one on base. The sun beat down, smoke filled the air, and the crowd was as quiet as a toasted marshmallow. The end was near . . . it was all on the line: the agony and the ecstasy, the pride and prejudice; the blood, toil, and tears; the best of times, the worst of times; the fate of the Mudville nine; the braggin' rights; and the imminent crowning of an All-Star—the stuff of which bittersweet tales of glory are woven. And for Ronnie Rix of Rye Grass, Washington . . . it was another crossroads on the way to achieving an ancient Greek heralding—The Eudaimonia of Honor.

Umpire Charlie Figgs took a small brush from his pocket and stepped around the squatting catcher to dust off the plate. As he came eye to eye with the batter, he winked and whispered, "Bunt." The player subtly nodded. Figgs whisked the plate clear of dust.

Fireball! Swing! Miss. Fireball! Swing! Miss. Kenny West feigned boredom and faked a big yawn. Having saved these shenanigans for the final scene, Kenny arrogantly raised his chin, then turned and directed a silly pout at the Loggers. The batter grumbled, gnashed his teeth, and lifted the bat over his shoulder like a lumberjack's ax. Figgs cleared his throat.

Kenny preceded his windup with some ape-like mockery. With an extra whirl, he exaggerated his wind-up and threw a tight, inside comet. At the last second, the Logger lowered his bat. *Thunk*! The ball crawled away from the plate. The catcher dove and flipped the ball to the oncoming West. The runner flashed toward first. West caught the ball with his bare hand and whipped it toward the outstretched first baseman. The runner started his slide a little early. The first baseman's toe strayed away, then returned to kiss the bag. The first-base umpire crouched. Dust and grass flew up and floated down. The ball smacked hard into the first baseman's mitt. The official literally had his nose in the play. He hesitated . . . the decisive pause was agonizing. With bellowing conviction, he threw his palms out flat and wide. "Saaaafe!" The hometown fans drowned out their own noise.

Standing side by side, Rain and Father Dom danced with little jumps of joy. Rain pulled the red ribbon from her ponytail and flounced her hair. Father Dom reached up with his dusty white gloves to remove his priestly collar. With his sleeve, he dabbed at his brow.

Rain giggled. "Goodness, Father, without that collar, you're nearly naked!" Father Dom smiled.

Ski snuck away from his third-base post and gave Rain a big hug. He said, "Out of lemonade?"

"All out. And we sold a whole six hot dogs. Actually, I gave them away. We are officially closed for business."

No longer clowning, Kenny West tucked his glove under his arm and applauded his opponent with sportsman-like respect. He stared at the runner glued to first base and said, "Nice trick, kid. But it'll only work once." He set his stance and offered a provocative nod, daring the next batter to approach the plate. The crowd reacted with shouts of disapproval. The fans simmered after the first strike. The Logger player knew the fastballs would be coming and he knew they would be on the money, so he had to take his cuts. His swings were a week late and fifty bucks short. Feeling lower than a hog's jaw on market day profoundly understates the young man's dejection.

Figgs marched majestically to the pitcher's mound. He beckoned to Ski, Lester, and the Pirates' coach. Figgs and the visiting coach compared notes. Ski and Lester double-checked. The men nodded in agreement and dispersed. Ronnie was talking to Wuzzie behind the backstop when Lester approached. Wuzzie made himself scarce, then slowly wheedled back around to eavesdrop. What he heard dropped his jaw; he hurried back to the parking lot to share the news with Connie and Rhonda. On the mound, Kenny West stood with folded arms, looking impatient, and for the first time, appearing nervous.

Wuzzie streaked across a strip of grass bordering the parking lot with eyes fixed on the flatbed truck where Connie and Rhonda paced like caged tigers. Breathless, he sprang onto the truck bed. Dangling on the shy side of dread, Connie removed her sunbonnet and twisted it into a knot. Rhonda tilted her sunglasses to the end of her nose.

"It's like this," Wuzzie said. "Ronnie has to hit a home run—that's the only way he can get the All-Star spot—the *only* way!"

Rhonda started swooning in song. "And it's one, two, three strikes you're out—"

"Hush, Rhonda! This is serious," Connie said. "This means everything to Ronnie."

"I don't get it, Connie. It's just a boring little baseball game. What's the biggie?"

"Everything! It's Ronnie's whole future. His chance to get out of this stupid little town."

"Yeah," said Wuzzie. "He can get a college scholarship, get on scouting lists, go to Disneyland—lots of neat stuff."

Rhonda droned, "OK, I get it . . . And if he fails to hit a little round thing with a big stick, he will end up wasting his life working at the dirty old mill."

"That's right—the dirty, stinky Malman Lumber Mill." Connie's emotions were high and on the rise.

Wuzzie's expression was one of foreboding. Newfound baseball fan Rhonda rallied with a hackneyed old cheer. "Ronnie! Ronnie! He's our man! If he can't do it, nobody can!" Connie's expression wallowed in a dreary mire. But Rhonda and Wuzzie's exuberance was contagious.

Rhonda, Connie, and Wuzzie gave the truck's shocks the workout of their springy, bouncy lives. All three shouted, "Ronnie, Ronnie, Ronnie, hey!" over and over. Within seconds, hometown rooters had joined the chant. "*Ronnie, Ronnie, Ronnie, hey*!"

CHAPTER 20

Showdown

When Ronnie stepped up to home plate, he seemed oblivious to anything but the task at hand. He was calm, respectful, and totally focused. By the same token, Kenny's manner was one of cordiality and good sportsmanship. Neither bore evidence of ill-will or awkwardness; it was simply a matter of two young, talented athletes getting down to business. Umpire Figgs picked up a megaphone and strode to a spot between second and third base. He said, "We've all had the pleasure of witnessing baseball at its best, in some of the worst conditions we've ever seen. Let's show these young men lots of well-earned appreciation." The entire crowd clapped, whistled, shouted, and cheered for well over a minute. "This batter-pitcher duel will be the last play of the game—the winner will become our league's All-Star representative!" More cheers and applause. Figgs shouted to the sky, "Let's play ball!"

With an owl-like stare, Kenny laid down a threat. Ronnie nodded and returned an even more owlish gape. Neither blinked. The Logger runner inched away from the bag. With the waft of an eyelash, Kenny scared him back.

If the dry grass could have grown, all would have heard it sprout. Then came the noise. It started with a single voice; eventually, both teams were chanting their mascot names. Before long, the rhythmic voice of the crowd mimicked the pounding of war drums, which slowly built to a crescendo, then faded away. But the chanting of the players lingered.

The base runner led off at the perilous distance of four feet; a distraction more than anything. Kenny ignored the ploy. Ronnie sensed motion from behind. The catcher had moved well to the right side of the plate. Disbelief came over Ronnie's face. Hurt and angry he looked back at Figgs, whose expression changed from helplessness to disgust, back to helplessness; finally, drooping into sadness and settling on disgust.

Lester headed for the Pirates bench. "Lester!" yelled Figgs. "Get back! I'll boot you outta here for sure." Lester glared at the visiting coach and folded his arms. His hands moved to his hips; his eyes were baleful.

Ronnie issued Kenny an overt challenge by raising his bat to near vertical and waving it in defiance. West's eyes grazed the gaze of his nemesis, as he casually slung the ball way out of range. Sourly, Figgs clicked his counter; he scowled and took a discerning account of the Pirates' coach. The coach raised his eyebrows, shrugged his shoulders, and opened his hands. Figgs begrudgingly called, "Ball!"

West's next pitch was a little faster, but so far outside the catcher's reach that he had to scramble for it; meanwhile, the Logger runner was able to sprint for an easy steal. Status: Count 2 and 0, a man on second. Kenny's decision to walk Ronnie was no longer in doubt.

The crowd became a massive swarm of sun-burnt, stirred-up hornets. Boos. Groans. Shouts: "Pitch to him,

West!"; "Play the game!"; "You're a punk!"; "Have some pride!"; "Prove yourself, West!"; "Throw the damn ball!" The boos grew louder. Gestures appeared. Thumbs down, pointing fingers, fists, middle fingers, hands punching palms. Beer cans and pop bottles flew onto the field. Father Dom scowled. He raised and waved his arms, then walked across the grass and began retrieving the debris. Rain followed suit. Others followed her. A collective calm returned.

Lester's fists were white-knuckle clenched. Figgs could plainly see the man was reaching a boiling point. He pulled off his face mask and called the two coaches to a point midway between third base and home. Ski walked in from the outfield and the first base umpire crossed the infield. Lester spoke first, his first word verging on rage, "You—". Figgs shot a hand in front of Lester's face.

"I'm running this show," said Figgs; he looked at the Pirates' coach.

Ski stood silent. Arms folded. Expressionless.

"We've got to be reasonable here," said the visiting coach. "Kenny pitched to your man twice. Fair and square. Ronnie had his chance."

Lester's head looked like a Donald-Duck anger thermometer, which would have exploded had not Figgs lifted a cautionary hand. "Reasonable is—we've got a special situation here. You know how much is on the line—"

The Pirates' coach said, "On the line for both boys. We're following the rules. The ball is in Kenny's hands; it's his life, and it's his decision."

Lester's big fists were clenched again. Figgs caught Ski's eye. Ski touched Lester's arm and said, "Let's talk." Lester was stubborn. Ski nudged. They headed for the home team bench.

Figgs claimed the last word. "OK, it's your boy's call. But I hope to God he can live with himself."

In ritualistic form, Kenny and the catcher set themselves up for the third act of an intentional walk. The crowd started up again; the ballpark became a barnyard full of roosters and hens. Bok, bok, bok; clucks, cackles, and squawks. People walked around flapping elbow wings. Ronnie tapped the end of his bat on the plate. The catcher again moved two strides to the right of the plate. Kenny took a deep breath; his eyes were a little red, a little puffy, and genuinely sad, but he clearly intended to toss the ball way out of range. Lester paced; suddenly, on impulse, he rounded the backstop and kicked up a dust cloud. He poked a finger at Kenny, then turned and yelled at the Pirates' coach. "You better do something about this!" The coach waved him off. Lester looked directly at Kenny—the young man took a fearful step back. Lester warned, "Pitch to him, buster! Throw the damn ball, hotshot, or I'm comin' out there."

Figgs blocked Lester's path. Ski headed their way. Figgs said, "Back off, Lester! Back off or you're outta here!"

Lester ranted, "This is poor damn sportsmanship! People here came to see a ballgame!" He pointed at Kenny. "Respect the game, young man. You wanna be an All-Star—act like one!"

Ski and Figgs sandwiched Lester between them. Cool and calm, Ski said, "I feel the same way you do, Lester. Damn near everybody here does. But this moment here . . . it belongs to these two boys—we gotta let them work it out."

Lester blurted, "It ain't right! It just ain't right! This is bush league! Bush league!" He tore up, choked up—unable to speak a word. Lost, empty, forsaken, he slowly trod behind the backstop, resigning himself to watch, sullen and mute, aback the crosswire mesh. He closed his eyes as the crowd chanted, "Bush league! Bush league!" Their support gave him some comfort and, for what it was worth, validated his stand.

Figgs pulled the umpire mask over his face and stepped behind the plate. "Play ball!"

The Pirates' catcher continued to squat well to the side of the home plate. Ronnie had stepped as far to the front of the batter's box as he could get away with. Kenny had his glove hand trapped under his opposite arm; his free hand stroked his chin. The wheels in his head went round and round. Standing on the precipice of his life's finest moment he somehow felt cheated, self-betrayed, empty, ashamed. He feared all the clucking, squawking, chanting, and jeering now echoing through his head would haunt him forever. His fear turned to anger, and the anger to arrogance. Giddily, he assumed the stance of a basketball player at the free-throw line and pretended to give the ball a couple of bounces. He let the ball go in a beautiful rainbow arc, letting his hand follow through with a wave goodbye. The catcher stood and made a breadbasket catch.

Such audacity and unbound arrogance. Astonished and disgusted by such a pompous affront to the game's legacy, people from one end of the park to the other began to murmur and mumble. The hum grew louder and louder. Reborn were the boos and jeers, hollers and shouts, poultry impressions and rude gestures. Kenny tipped back his head and laughed. He removed his cap, bowed, and cupped a hand to his ear.

Perhaps the mind of Father Dom alone knew the truth of the boy's torment, the near unbearable languor in anguish. The clergyman had seen it many times—the desperate, despaired manner of people behaving exactly the opposite of what was in their heart. And he also realized Ronnie's emotional plate was filled with heaps of his own brand of suffering. Standing at the father's side, studying his face, Rain began to understand. She had also seen such stories play out. Secretly, silently, they prayed.

Kenny gazed up at the sun. He pretended to sway and swoon, as though on the verge of fainting. With an air of indifference Kenny turned toward the plate, knowing he could easily claim the grand prize and wash away the dream of another. All he needed to do was casually toss the ball to the catcher. With the count at 3 and 0, facing the final pitch, Ronnie realized this was another crossroads. A disturbing vision invaded his thoughts: He was back in the farmhouse with Ski and Buddy Foley; he had a gun in his hand. Trapped, eviscerated, terrified. Back to the present. "That's enough!" Ronnie whirled in a half-circle and hurled his bat against the backstop. He tore off his cap and stepped on it, grinding it into the dirt. Eyes down, he stormed away toward the parking lot.

Figgs started to follow but thought better. He called out, "Ronnie! Ronnie, come on back!" Ski jogged past Figgs. Ronnie quickened. Rain ran to catch up with Ski. She grabbed his arm and held tight. Respectfully, they reigned in their nurturing natures. They stood and watched. Suddenly, from behind a relic of a van, Connie appeared. She charged at Ronnie, blocked his path, and shoved him in the chest.

"You get back there, Ronnie! Get back there and finish the game!"

Startled, somewhat lost for words, stunned by Connie's *pixie* cut, all Ronnie could do was utter, "Huh? What?" Connie noticed him notice her hair.

"Don't you say a word, buddy!" Connie pointed to the field. "Now get back there! If you run away now you'll be runnin' for the rest of your life. You'll be a little nothin' man from a little nothin' town and you'll be worth? . . . That's right—*absolutely* nothin'!"

One out of anger, one out of shame, they glared at each other with faces as red as pickled beets. Connie could have turned and punched her finger through the windshield of the Volkswagen at her back when she pointed and commanded, "Get back out there on that damn field!"

Only slightly recovered from Connie's scolding, Ronnie drearily headed back toward the field, strangely gaining strength with each step, preparing to face one of those life-defining crossroads. As he came back into view, a resounding cheer went up. Ronnie raised his head and waved a hand high. He scanned the field and glanced at the scoreboard: Loggers 0, Pirates 1. He made eye contact with the base runner who was bright-eyed, antsy, and raring to go. He glanced at Kenny and sensed that his foe's melancholy was, perhaps, more sullen than his own. Kenny stood alone on a mound of soil, knowing the spoils of his next pitch would be far more tart than any proverbial grape. Then fear clawed at the thoughts of both young men; it funneled into bottled anger and fumed into grit and determination. Amidst the clamoring throng, a life's dream at hand, Kenny West was the loneliest being on the planet. One road leading to triumph, the other to humiliation, Ronnie faced a circle of mirrors, soon realizing his only choice, no matter the outcome, was not strength and courage . . . it was self-respect and honor. Beneath a blazing sun there was darkness, amongst a frenzied crowd there was silence. Umpire Figgs handed Ronnie his dusty cap.

As he took his practice swings, Ronnie picked out faces in the crowd, the faces of people he knew would offer a pat on the back and a sincere "good job", win or lose; people who had come to respect him, who had forgiven him for the destructive acts and thievery of a misspent youth; people who genuinely cared about him and wished him the best. Perhaps it was the first time he had allowed himself to appreciate having friends, and to truly believe he deserved them. Quite to his surprise, he came to discover the best thing about growing up in a small, country town was the acceptance, comfort, and love of a community. He realized that one day he would be the one leading tomorrow's children toward crossroads of their own. Then came to mind, four scruffy, old goats on a nearby hill. He decided he would visit them soon after, to enjoy their company and talk things out. He now cherished such things from an enlightened perspective— this made a baseball All-Star title seem a paltry trifle. But even in those tender and contemplative moments, something inside wanted nothing more than to see that *damn* ball go sailing over the fence.

Motionless on the mound, West's eyes closed, and his soul searched. Ronnie stepped into the batter's box. Even through the haze of smoke, Ronnie could see Kenny fighting back tears. When a drop glistened on a lower lash, he blinked it away. His expression softened. A confession and an apology sifted into his mind. In expressing these thoughts, he ardently articulated, hoping Ronnie could read his lips. But, in the stillness of the moment, Ronnie completely understood. Kenny said with words that showed it in his eyes: "I'm sorry, Ronnie. I really am sorry."

Ronnie acknowledged with a nod, then settled into his sweet spot, ready to shoot for the moon. Again, the Pirates' catcher moved well off the plate and socked the center of his mitt. The crowd groaned and booed, but nothing could stop the inevitable. Kenny waited, checked the runner at second, then took a moment to scan the entire scene. He was creating a memory, though tarnished and hollow, this would be evidence of personal integrity and a test of life's worth; the right or wrong of it wallowed in ambivalence. His eyes lingered on the scoreboard: Loggers 0, Pirates 1, the bottom of the 7th and final inning. He removed his cap and dragged a forearm across his brow. Ronnie stood, as proud and noble as any bronze statue; his brain flooded with fight-or-flight adrenaline. Kenny and Ronnie locked puffy, reddened eyes. Then subtly and strangely, Kenny nodded at Ronnie. He gave the catcher a sideways head toss. Ronnie was perplexed. So was the catcher. So was the umpire. The crowd murmured. Kenny thumbed the catcher to get behind the plate. The crowd whispered, murmured, mumbled. Kenny stared into Ronnie's eyes and nodded with the gravest intent. His words were true, his voice was bold. "It's comin'!" Ronnie waved his bat. With a slow, deep breath, he settled his body and focused his mind.

At any given moment, our physical existence and emotional state may become as one. At this given moment, emotional stakes could not have been higher. Figgs backed up a step, to get an optimal view of the strike zone. Lester curled paralytic fingers through the backstop fence; his jaw ground and he spit chew. The runner on second timidly led off. Ronnie flexed and choked up on the bat. Absolute silence. No one moved. Kenny rose to his full height and set for a windup. Ronnie saw everything in slow motion. West wound up, drew back his arm and with a fierce, guttural exhale, hurled the ball with all his might, right at the down the pipe—a bull's eye! Ronnie's swing was more instinctive than trained. It was too slow, at least it looked that way at first, but strong emotion intoxicates; it distorts time and space. *Crack*! Perfect swing, ideal impact. The ball climbed and climbed; it seemed to vanish. It hung on the edge of forever, high above center field, lost in the smoke. The outfielders wandered, confused, and blind. The crowd held fast in breathless wonder. When the ball came into sight, it seemed to float and spin like an autumn leaf; it whirled closer and closer to the fence, a delusional illusion. The center fielder had backpeddled to the perimeter's edge. All he could do was leap and reach. He was well lined up, the ball fell directly toward his glove—whether by a whisker or whether by a country mile, it didn't matter—the ball cleared the fence, and, for the little town of Rye Grass, Washington a new baseball legend was born.

The crowd erupted in body, mind, and spirit. Yelling, cheering, laughing, crying, dancing, singing—everything but the ticker tape. With the first score in, Ronnie surreally rounded the bases with the trotting gait of Babe Ruth. Lester, lost in time and space, focused on the scoreboard: Loggers 2, Pirates 1—Final. For the first time in many years, he was sober as a judge. The coach picked up his moldy satchel and walked away unseen. Totally alone, he would soon drown in the moody, murky river of a bleeding soul.

On the flatbed truck, Connie, Rhonda, and Wuzzie bounced and screamed as though on a trampoline during a San Francisco earthquake. Rhonda jumped on Wuzzie's back and they tumbled onto the grass. Connie leaped beside them; she pulled them to their feet for a three-way hug. The berry field workers strummed guitars and played trumpets. Ski lifted Rain with a hug and whirled one time around. The coaches and players walked down the line uttering the traditional and obligatory: "Good game." Father Dom smiled a kindly smile and strolled among the flock. Umpire Figgs took care of business, stowing gear, and tending to officiations.

Leaving the mirthful pack, Ronnie headed to the table where Kenny West sat, his right arm submerged in ice. With his cap tipped high, he leaned back, woeful and worn. A little sulky, a little pouty, Kenny brightened as Ronnie approached. He stood, shook the cold water from his arm, and offered a firm handshake. Though it took some effort, West finally managed a genuine smile. Ronnie's words were solemn, appreciative, and heartfelt, "You're a man of honor, Kenny West."

When Kenny realized Ronnie's admiration was sincere, a lump rose in his throat. His eyes, as well as his voice, said, "Thanks."

Ronnie said, "I wish we both could have got that All-Star spot. You deserve just as much as me."

"Oh well . . . I think my dad's more broke up about it than I am. He's the one that figured out we were tied in points . . . Don't really matter that much, the best days are ahead . . . for both of us."

"Boy, I sure hope so."

"Nobody's ever hit a home run off me—nobody. If I was the one votin', I'd have voted for you—no lie, man—I'd have voted for you. I laid into that pitch with everything I had, and you hit it just perfect . . . You knew what was comin', didn't you?"

"Yeah, I kinda figured . . . and I also figured you were getting a little too big for your britches."

"You figured right." Kenny smiled with humility. "You sure figured right." He sat back down and iced his arm.

About to leave, Ronnie asked, "You play football?"

"Nah, you?"

"Yeah. Double days start the day after I get back . . . I like baseball better though."

"You're a smart man—baseball's the best!"

Ronnie nodded, gave Kenny a little wave, then headed back for some pats on the shoulder and some manly handshakes. A Logger teammate came up from behind and handed Ronnie the homerun ball. In the interest of comradery, he feigned a look of grand surprise, took the ball, and shook his friend's hand. He cherished his gem from that moment on.

Not far off, Father Dom was talking with Ski and Rain. Ronnie jogged toward them and presented the ball to the Father. "Do you think we could put this in the chapel showcase—next to the Eli Gussard stuff?"

Father Dom took a discrete gander at the ball and, with slight reservation, said, "Only under one very special condition."

"What's that?"

"It truly deserves to be there but . . . not without your autograph."

"You bet!"

CHAPTER 21

Hangin' 'Round

Alone at a quiet corner booth, Ronne Rix listened to "I Gotta Know" by Elvis Presley and waited for his complementary Thunder Burger meal: a deluxe cheeseburger with a slice of ham and an endless basket of fries; usually, he had a Coke, but today—a large chocolate malt. He slapped the bottom of a Heinz ketchup bottle and stood it on its cap. Rain delivered the meal on a tray and Ski placed the shake on the table. Although he knew the food was free, Ronnie dug into his pocket. "No dice, partner," Ski said. "You made us all proud today. You're crossin' those crossroads like nobody's business."

Rain laughed, "The Eudaimonia of Honor looms on the horizon . . ."

Ski said, "Yes sir, I do believe it's within your grasp, Mr. Rix."

Ronnie wanted to laugh but couldn't because he was starving; his mouth was literally watering and he was afraid he would slobber. He put his hand to his mouth to prevent a *faux pas*, then humbly said, "Thanks, you guys. Man, oh man, am I ever hungry." He clutched the three-inch-thick burger in the talons of an eagle and gnawed with his beak—mayo, ketchup, relish, and mustard oozed all over his hands.

When Ski and Rain realized they were standing there with twinkling eyes and cute smiles, Rain motioned for them to head back to the kitchen. On the way, Ski said quietly, "I don't think there's anything for *you* to worry about, but Brownie called. The store got broken into while everybody was at the game."

She put her hand to her mouth. "Land's sake."

"He's still taking inventory and told me he's 'really scratchin' his head'. The place was all torn up but not that much was taken. Mostly destructiveness was all. Doesn't make sense."

"Nothing stolen?"

"Not much. No clothes, no food, no valuables. It looked like just a bunch of candy bars. The thief must have eaten a few when he was tearing stuff up—there were wrappers on the floor."

"So, are they still looking for Buddy? Do they think—"

"Naw, there's no way Foley could have had anything to do with it. He'd have taken guns and ammo. That stuff wasn't touched. It would have been easy pickin's—the whole town was at the game."

"Toby?"

Ski smirked, "That's what I was thinkin'—mostly because of the candy bars. He could have gotten in through the frozen food lockers. Brownie said he might have forgot to lock the connecting door. The only good news . . . Toby will eventually tell on himself—so the case is basically closed." Ski chuckled. "Another day in Mayberry."

"It's not all that funny, Ski."

"I know, I know . . . And here I thought it would be a nice little summer evening . . . We won the ballgame, everybody's happy, it looks like this hot spell is about over." Ski looked at the Coca-Cola clock. "Dang near five o'clock. I told Brownie I'd be down there by four-thirty to fill out a report." Ski gave Rain a quick kiss then left through the back door, talking to himself. "Then tomorrow, I better go out looking for Foley . . . ahhh, heck with it, that can wait till Monday . . . Jeez, these kinds of things happen once every third blue moon and today had to be the third."

Laughing, yakking, horsing around, Orrie, Lon, and Doug approached the Thunder Burger. They entered through the dining room door and stopped short when Ronnie looked up. His expression said, "I'm going to kill you." After getting that message across, he went back to eating his meal as though the boys didn't exist. The boys walked on feathers all the way to the booth near the door. Lon whispered, "One of us has to go over there." Foreboding lurked, suspense lingered.

Orrie, Doug, and Lon would have gladly faced doomsday rather than approach Ronnie; however, each of them realized the time was now or never. Hands twisting a napkin, eyes darting about the room, Orrie begrudgingly said, "I'll do it."

As though pardoned by the governor, Doug and Lon silently rejoiced. When Orrie strode the centerline of the room, it may as well have been the final scene from *High Noon*. At first, he appeared to be headed for the jukebox, but he slowly summoned the nerve to veer in Ronnie's direction. Orrie stopped and pretended his feet were nailed to the floor; there was no backing up. Ronnie's eyes narrowed. He leaned back, and with a sarcastic gawk adopted the chesty tone of Lurch the Addams Family butler. "You rang?"

Timidly, Orrie confessed, "We have your mitt."

Ronnie's eyes flashed. He started to stand but noticed Rain noticing him. He remained seated. Rain feigned obliviousness. She busied herself at the counter. Ronnie spoke low and slow. "Go get it. Go get it right now!"

"Go get our five bucks."

Ronnie lifted his chin, bit his lip, steepled his fingers, cracked his knuckles, folded his arms, made intense eye contact and said," Where's my mitt?!"

Steeling his nerves, Orrie reached out, palm up, an amazingly steady hand. He said, "Five dollars please."

Ronnie huffed and sighed. He looked up at the four corners of the room, one after another, as though rounding the bases. Mind milling and mulling, Ronnie finally leaned left, reached into his right pocket, and pulled out a crumpled five-dollar bill. He crumpled it tighter, held it above the table, and said, "Bombs over Tokyo." He dropped the money and Orrie whisked it up.

Orrie said, "It's in the second boxcar, in the sand pile, in the corner, about a foot down."

Ronnie said, "There better not be any sand on it."

"It's wrapped up good. No sand."

As Ronnie stood, he issued each boy a menacing stare, then with a friendly gait, headed out, bidding Rain a cordial farewell. Slyly, he shot one last scowl at the boys. They visibly gulped. When the coast was clear, Lon said, "Eddie Haskell just left the room." They giggled.

It was an extra-happy happy hour at the Runnin' Bear Tavern. The place was packed—every seat taken. People were spread from wall to wall—standing by walls, leaning on walls, and pounding on walls. Fuzzy neon signs glowed through a rolling mist of burning tobacco. Lester pressed two jukebox buttons and Hank Williams' "Jambalaya" blared. He daintily slipped in front of a blue-jean barmaid as she passed. He grabbed her hand and gave her a spin. She slapped out and bristled all the way to the bar where Charlie Figgs pulled frothy drafts until the tap chortled. "Damn, I gotta change the keg again!"

The barmaid rested an arm on Figgs' shoulder and spoke directly into his ear. "Charlie, you get Lester out of here or I'm leaving."

Figgs lifted praying hands. "Come on, Queenie, have a heart. The guy's just lost everything—the wife, the mill, his kids are hiding from him. Right now, coming in here is all he's got. He needs to be around people. He needs you and me."

She rolled her eyes. "Yeah, OK. But keep him off me, or I'm gone, no matter what!"

Lester spun the song "I've Got a Tiger by the Tail" by Buck Owens. He gave Queenie the eye and a loaded eye at that. Queenie wasn't about to be a target. She had to shout above the noise. "Charlie?!"

Figgs said, "Don't worry. I'll run interference—now help me change this keg."

"I don't get it. The town's broke. Who's paying for all these drinks?"

"Me . . . I got a lot of tabs goin'—most of 'em are mine. Be sure to keep reminding everybody we close at nine."

"Last call 8:30?"

"That'll work."

"I don't know why the hell, or how the hell, you're payin' for all this—but the tips have been really good, so I'm not complainin'."

"This town hasn't had a big-time celebration in a coon's age. We have an All-Star! It's never likely to happen again, so I'm glad to foot the bill. Things'll pick up. Let's just have some fun tonight."

Queenie put a hand over her mouth and shook her head as she and Figgs watched the obnoxious fool on the dance floor. Tonight, Lester was all about flaunting social graces. And the crowd loved it—hoots and hollers!

Lester's fancy boots did a Texas ten-step that could have won a blue ribbon at the county fair. He did a figure-8 around the floor, then slipped up to the jukebox and played "Oh, Lonesome Me" by Don Gibson. At that moment, the man most considered to be worse than the plague, had become the man of the hour. He had delivered the town an All-Star and the crowd was only too happy to celebrate and pay homage. When Lester resigned to do some heavy drinking, the frolicking slowly fizzled.

Henny Perky, 42, a lanky Natasha Fatale in pedal pushers, came through the swinging doors with two companions, both in their 20s, both very pretty. One wore tight jeans, a Harley Davidson t-shirt, and Kookie Byrnes hair. The other wore a pink blouse and some borderline-bikini cutoffs. They sat at a table with a RESERVED sign. Queenie hurried over with three bottles of Bud. Her pal Henny stood and gave her a hug. The friends said, "Hi." Other than scant glances, they were mostly ignored. But these were Queenie's friends, so all due respect was bestowed. Being part of this big celebration, for their girl's night out, was a good chance to unwind and have a little fun.

The jukebox was idle, the dance area empty. A member of the new crew hip-rolled to the music box and punched in "The Race Is On" by George Jones. Henny and her friend joined their bold companion. The three engaged in a little barn dancing. Queenie set down her tray and joined in. A smiling woman, a dead ringer for Dorothy Lamour, sidled up and started two-stepping. Most unexpectedly, a dozen women: young and old, jeans and skirts, blondes and brunettes, hit the floor and do-si-doed to Jones' twang. Tables were pushed back to make room. The honky-tonk cake was out of the oven and the ladies were spreading the frosting. When Lester's numb brain caught up to what was going on, it was like watching a zoot-suit clad cartoon wolf pop out his eyes to the sound of an ahooga horn. As the tune galloped to an end, cheers, yee-haws, and applause set the place abuzz. The rollicking had returned.

Carrying a heavy pan of potato and onion peelings destined for the dumpster, Rain did not expect to see Ski's police car still sitting behind the restaurant. When she pushed the screen door open, she saw Ski sitting in the driver's seat with his head leaning back and his hands covering his face. She had learned not to disturb him at such times. The episodes usually ended within minutes; other times they would go on-and-on, usually at night. These traumatic visions had to run their course, and she knew there was nothing she could do or say. As she eased the door closed, Ski re-lived a Korean-war haunting.

More of an outpost than a camp, the compound shivered at the mercy of fierce winds funneling down from the Siberian tundra, characteristic of winters in North Korea. The tents flapped and billowed. It was eight below beneath a sky of dying diamonds. The breath of sentries hung in the frozen air. Perhaps a mile beyond the barbed wire perimeter stood an outcrop of hills, stark and silent as death. To the south, about a half-mile, was a small native village, maybe twenty huts.

In the flicker of a gas lamp, Corporal Robert Welski swung his legs out of bed and stepped into his boots; he laced them tight. He warmed his hands over a pot-bellied stove before slipping into his woolen gloves. He pulled a heavy sweater over his head.

"Keep it wired tight, Bobby," croaked a grunt from his sack. He then broke into a dry, hacking cough.

"Everything's gonna be tight out there," Welski replied. "Two damn hours of it."

"It'll seem like two damn days," said the grunt.

"I've got fuel and woodpile duty."

"Lousy post, man—over by the hills; it's the worst."

"That's the breaks."

Welski zipped his bulky jacket and raised the hood. He pulled the string tight around his eyes and nose. He grabbed his M-1, tested the mechanism, and loaded the clip.

"You know to pee on the bolt—comes down to it?" the grunt asked.

"Old wives' tale, man. I'll just work it free now and again."

"Hope you don't have to use that thing."

"You and me both, man. You and me both."

Welski had to fight the wind as he pushed open the door. The cold air rushed in like floodwater. The door fought closing. Welski held the knob tight, leaned into the gusts, and pulled till the latch clicked. Already, his eyes ached, and his teeth hurt. He trudged past the tents and huts and headed toward a central bunker. When the sentry on duty spotted him, he teetered on frozen legs and uncovered his mouth. He forced words through paralytic lips.

"Watch them hills, Bobby. Watch for tiny lights; they'll rise, dip, and sway—kinda like little fairies. At best you'll get a glimpse, but a glimpse is enough. This is the sort of night them bastards'll come."

"Got it."

"You see somethin'—no warnin' shots. Shoot to kill and we'll come a-runnin'."

"Got it." Welski's teeth chattered.

The camp was in blackout. Though the starlight was dim, the thick frost sparkled just enough for the wind-whipped, starch-stiff sentry to make it back to his tent. Once Welski's eyes had adjusted, the visibility was surprisingly good. He scanned the peaks of the sinister hills. Some were pointed, some were round, all were ominous. Welski's dry lips were not quite cold enough to numb the sting of a new chap split. He lowered the rifle from his shoulder, folded his arms around it, and hugged it tight against his body. At times he had to muffle a cough, he could not see the smoke of the tent stoves, but he could smell just a hint with every cross breeze. Welski paced from one end of the fuel bunker to the other, looking around the corners, scanning the huts and tents, but mostly watching the hills, terrified he would see the slightest speck of moving light. And there it was . . . or was it? He squinted, stepped forward bringing his rifle to the ready.

"Not tonight," he whispered. "Please don't come tonight."

He walked toward the perimeter fence, surveying the hills and grounds with every step. Other than the tree line at the base of the hills, there was no cover around the camp. Tiny snowflakes swirled as he backed toward the fuel barrels. Movement. He turned slowly and raised his rifle. He held his breath. Shadows shivered in the gusty wind; a wind that was sad and hollow. A shuffling sound—near one of the woodpiles. A small log rolled from one of the stacked cords. Just a piece of wood. He sighed with relief and his breath billowed. Again, he scanned the hills.

Another log tumbled from a woodpile. And another. A moving shape. Someone was inside the perimeter. The hunkering figure crept behind the wood stacks.

"Who's there?!" Welski snapped. "Who's out there?!"

He aimed his rifle and walked parallel to the columns of firewood. Contrary to orders, he warned, "Show yourself! Hands up!"

A hooded form appeared, carrying something bulky, hurrying toward the fuel barrels.

"Stop! Stop!"

The figure paused, turned its head, then hurried on, toward the fuel bunker.

Welski took careful aim. No more warnings. He followed the figure in his sights, held his breath and squeezed the trigger. The rifle cracked. The figure landed hard on the frozen turf. Soldiers, half-dressed, some barefoot, emerged from the tents, rifles in hand. Welski approached the crumpled form. It was wrapped in a ragged coat and scarf. The hood had blown away. The head was half gone.

A soldier knelt beside the body. He gasped, "It's an old woman."

Welski dropped his rifle and pulled back his hood. His face paled and shriveled. Tears flowed and turned to ice.

The soldier shook his head and spoke softly, "Looks like she was stealing wood to keep her family warm."

Welski put his hands over his face. He sobbed in the agony of unforgivable guilt.

⚜

Ski's eyes opened to a dusty windshield and the view of a quaint little town. With his fingertips, he wiped the tears from his cheeks. The frozen hills of Korea melted away. The hills of home blazed. Ski turned the key in the ignition and rolled onto Main Street. When he switched on the radio "White Silver Sands" by Don Rondo was playing. Quickly, he upped the volume and tried to sing along. He prayed the flashbacks would never return. From a block away, he noticed a slew of cars lined up outside the Runnin' Bear, but this came as no surprise. At the Mobile station he made a right turn and pulled up to Brownie's General Store.

⚜

With a critical eye, Rhonda beheld one of Connie's water-color paintings. Meanwhile, Connie pulled clothes from every drawer and stuffed them into boxes. Rhonda gave her a puzzled look. "Connie, are you paying any attention at all to what you're doing?"

She said, "More than I need, but I don't ever want to come back here—ever! I'll sort everything out when we get to your house."

"You've got four big boxes there. How are we going to carry them?"

"Doug's stupid little red wagon. I know what I'm doing, Rhonda. Why don't you help me?"

"Suuurrre. I'll be glad to. Want me to put the kitchen sink in a box?"

"Noooo, I want you to pull my windbreaker and a couple of sweaters out of the closet."

Rhonda rifled through the clothes hanging in a small closet. "Blue windbreaker, white sweater, and let's see . . . how about this Bavarian—"

"No! The pink pullover. We're not going to Austria!"

"OK. I've got it, now let's get out of here before your dad gets back."

Connie started rattling through a jewelry box. "He won't be back—not 'til morning. After every game, he ends up at the Runnin' Bear. He stays there till after they close."

"Good. I just don't want there to be any chance of him coming in here making rude comments about my butt or boobs or anything else."

Connie groaned. "Oh, he never said anything about your butt and boobs."

"How about that *hubba hubba* stuff! And you know darn well he's called me *stacked*!"

"Hah! I've seen you in P.E. Don't worry—you're definitely not stacked."

Rhonda made the classic raspberry sound. "At least I don't stuff or wear falsies like half the girls at school."

Connie examined a pair of earrings. Rhonda was not quite finished. "You're gonna stand here and say your dad doesn't say rude stuff to me." Connie held the rings up to Rhonda's ears.

"Yeah, I know. He says rude stuff to women, but only when he's really, really drunk."

"He's always really, really, drunk."

"I've already admitted he's turned into an alcoholic creep."

"And that's exactly why I want to get outta here!"

"Jeez, Rhonda, you don't need to freak out!"

"I'm not freaking out. I'm just trying to protect myself . . . I wish there was something I could do . . . Maybe my parents could adopt you."

"You know I can take care of myself, Rhonda, but thanks just the same." Connie drifted into a wistfulness. "When I was a kid . . . it seems so long ago when mom was here—he was different . . . he was a nice guy, a good dad. Every summer we would go up to the mill and pick huckleberries. We'd play hide-and-seek in the woods, and sometimes sleep out under the stars. Back then we were a happy family, most of the time anyway. He'd have war memories and dreams sometimes; they made him angry, and sad, and scared. It was a terrible thing to see. But after that truck loading thing, he started getting mean, spiteful sometimes. And he started drinking more and more. He was too stubborn and ornery to admit it, but I know he was in pain. Bad headaches. I'm sure he still has 'em."

"What was the truck loading thing?"

"They had just got a truck loaded. A log shifted and a chain snapped; it hit him in the head. They had to fix his skull with a metal plate . . . After that, his war dreams got worse. And he started drinking hard liquor, whiskey—a bottle a day, sometimes more. If he ran out of liquor on Sunday, he'd make this canned heat stuff. It made him insane. We had to call the cops—a lot. Mom got to where she just couldn't take it anymore. . . You know the rest of the story."

Filled with uncharacteristic empathy; shedding, for the moment, her selfish little ways; the whole of Rhonda's heart went out to her friend. Rare were the times she used her silver tongue to comfort rather than manipulate. She cried as she spoke. "Ohh, Connie, I feel so bad those things happened. I wish I could have known your family back in the old days. And I can see your dad having a good side—like a storm cloud with a silver lining. Sometimes you can see little glimpses of the dad he used to be."

"Finally, a doctor gave him some pain pills. It's strong stuff, but it helps." A warmth came into Connie's voice. "He always has been a joker though—always teasing and clowning around. Once he insulted Mrs. Agnew when she was visiting mom—something about her lazy son. Agnew got really mad and never came back to visit the house after that." Connie chuckled. "He told mom, 'I don't know what the hell was wrong with her—she ran off like a striped-assed ape'."

Rhonda laughed. "Yeah, I know, you told me that story before. I wish I could have been there." Rhonda tugged at the back of her hair. "Speaking of old lady Agnew, if I don't check in soon, she'll have some kind of witch fit."

"I don't think you have much to worry about. From what I've seen, she knits, watches soaps, reads detective magazines, then falls asleep with her mouth hanging open. She's probably snoring away. If not, she probably thinks you're still up in your room."

"No, she checks every couple of hours. The old bat actually cares about me. So, I'd better get home."

"Well, what's she gonna do when she finds out we left town?"

Rhonda closed Connie's jewelry box and gave her friend a long, kind, and loving gaze. "Connie, I know that you know we aren't really going to run away to California. You do realize that don't you?"

Connie opened her yap wide in protest, choked on her words, then broke down in tears. "Ohhh Rhonda." She went to Rhonda and gave her a bear hug, which seized her lungs and made her eyes bulge. "I know . . . I know we're not, Rhonda. I know we're not."

After Connie let go, and after she was able to breathe again, Rhonda said, "As awful as he can be sometimes, I know you could never run out on your dad. You could never leave your brother on his own. No matter how bad things get, or how much you complain, when it comes down to it, you'll always stand and fight . . . I wish I could say the same about myself."

"What's that old saying about a live coward and a dead hero?"

"You're neither one. You're a grumpy, crabby, punch-'em-in-the-face cowgirl who's gonna live forever!"

"Lucky me."

To redirect Connie's train of thought, Rhonda asked, "So what's gonna happen with the mill?"

"Dad'll have built it back up before Christmas—the main part anyway."

Rhonda put Connie's pink pull-over back in the closet. "Why don't we go down to the park for a while? We can get a pop and sit on the swings."

Connie's cyclone-struck room left her buried in a quandary. Torn between dismal druthers Connie acquiesced, "I can't let my dad see all this. He'll think I was—"

"We can have all this stuff put back in five minutes. Neat as a pin!"

The Hires Root Beer clock in the kitchen of the Rye Grass Cafe read 5:41 pm. Orrie, Lon, and Doug stood around a pinball machine called *Barnacle Bill*, a relic that had probably been manufactured during Prohibition. Doug pretended to play the silver ball, tapping the side buttons, and making sound effects—rings, dings, and tat-tat-tats. They had absent-mindedly set their sodas on the machine's glass top. When Wuzzie noticed, he went running over scolding like a harpy. "I told you guys a million times—keep your pop off the glass." They grabbed their pop, he wiped and polished the glass.

The boys quickly took their beverages to a corner table, then Lon followed Wuzzie back to the main counter. He asked,

"So Rhonda Stickle still wants that George Harrison card, right?"

"Far as I know. And she's still offering five bucks."

"She's rich. Why doesn't she just buy cards herself?"

"She has. She's bought a whole box once, and she's tired of having bad luck. She figured the odds would be better if she just offered five bucks. The George cards are hard to find. They'll really be worth something someday."

"Well, we made a pact. We wanna buy a skateboard."

"You guys are still battin' that idea around . . . But, come to think about it, they are getting pretty popular. I see lots of ads in magazines."

"We want to buy the one at Brownie's store, in the front window. Haven't you seen it? It's got a bunch of monster models around it."

Wuzzie started wiping the fountain area. "They've really got a skateboard?"

'Yeah, it came in last week?"

"I haven't been over to Brownie's lately. I'll take a look at it . . . maybe I'll buy it."

"No. It's ours!"

"Uh, it can't be yours 'til you have the money . . . I got the money . . . at least I think I got the money, how much is it?"

"Eight dollars and . . . maybe forty cents with tax."

"Yeah, I could handle that."

The wheels whirled in Lon's brain. "No, no, you should buy some models—like a Munsters Koach, or a Rat Fink t-shirt . . . Maybe that badminton game or the archery set."

"Maybe badminton would be OK, but I hate archery . . . And I wouldn't buy Rat Fink stuff if my life depended on it. That crap is for A-number-one dorks.

"Well, you're a dor—uh, I mean, there's other things too—like the croquet set."

"Nah, not for me. Anyway, do you guys *really* think you can find one of those Harrison cards? Rhonda's been trying all summer. And you already spent your measly quarter on Milk Duds. You might as well just let me buy the skateboard."

"No way! We saw it first. And you wouldn't even know about it if it wasn't for me."

"Face the facts. You, little guys, aren't ever gonna have the money."

Doug and Orrie walked up to the counter. Orrie felt around in his pocket and pulled out the five-dollar bill. "We got this from Ronnie."

Wuzzie's jaw dropped. "He actually paid you?!"

Doug said, "Yeah, we worked out a deal." The boys snickered.

Wuzzie could not believe his ears. "You took on Connie, and you took on Ronnie! Jeez, what's the world coming to! You guys are playing with so much fire—like nuclear-level atomic bomb fire!"

"We know," said Orrie. "Connie plans to grind glass in our faces and Ronnie plans to punch us in the stomach 'til blood comes out of our mouths. But buying a skateboard—that gives us something to live for!"

"With that board," Doug said. "We could have our last little bit of fun before we die."

Wuzzie gave the situation some thought and said, "I guess I could order a board from the Monkey Ward catalog."

"Yeah, do it," said Doug. "You could probably get a way better one from there."

Lon said, "We figure maybe buying some more of those Beatles bubble gum cards is our best chance."

"Dang, you guys got the cap from Connie, and you got the money from Ronnie—you've definitely got a lucky streak going," Wuzzie said. "And for little punks, you've got a lot of guts . . . Well for now you do, I think you're gonna get 'em all stomped out before long. But for now—you got my respect."

Lon looked hopefully at Orrie and Doug. "Come on, let's do it."

Doug was actually panting. Orrie scrunched his nose. He said, "Let me think for a minute." He studied the faces of his friends. He could not let them down. Begrudgingly, he said, "All right, let's buy a few cards."

Wuzzie said, "OK, you have my word, I won't buy the board at Brownie's until you guys have a chance at it. As you know . . . the cards are a nickel a pack."

"Let's get two bucks worth!" said Lon.

Orrie stroked his chin. Lon and Doug nodded approval. Orrie handed Wuzzie the five-dollar bill and said, "Give us three packs."

CHAPTER 22

Up a Tree

Ghostie, the shaggy white goat, took a slice of apple from Ronnie's hand. Toro, Wags, and Tiny rushed over to surround him, nudging and bleating. Ronnie started grabbing handfuls of fruit from the bag; he scattered the treats all around. "More than anything else, a guy's gotta take care of his family. Father Dom's a wonderful man and a good friend, but you crazy goats—you're my family." The goats lifted their heads and bleated joyfully; at least in Ronnie's mind, they did. Within seconds they had gobbled every bit of fruit. "Yep, that's you—my spoiled, little piggy family. And I'll always be there for you—just like you're there for each other."

Ronnie walked around the hilltop. He checked the water tub, feed bin, and took a look in the storage shed. The goats nosed at the shed door as he tried to close it. "Hey, hey, back off a little. There's plenty of feed in that bin over there; it'll hold you a couple of days. And those dumb little kids will probably be up here to check on you before then. Actually, they're not all that dumb; they teamed up and outsmarted me—at least a little bit . . . I gotta figure out what to do about that . . . Oh well, I'll give 'em some credit; they proved they have some guts." The goats bleated and nodded. "I'm glad you all agree." They bleated again.

The goats followed Ronnie under the horse-chestnut tree. He plucked one of the spike-covered nuts from a branch. "Man, these things aren't even half their normal size—shrivelin' up like everything else. This must be the hottest doggone summer ever. What's this world coming to? It reminds me of that song 'Green Fields'." The goats took turns bleating out a series of musical-sounding notes. "Nice song, but I didn't say 'Greensleeves'—I said 'Green *Fields*'." Ronnie sang a verse of the Brothers Four ballad.

When Ronnie finished singing, the goats bleated merrily and tapped their hooves against the ground. "Thank you, thank you. You guys have excellent taste in talent."

Ronnie stroked each goat on the back of the neck, then backed away, out from under the tree. He gave them a palms-out "stay" sign to keep them from following him down the hill. "I mainly came up here to tell you not to worry if you don't see me for a couple of days. I'm going to California—I'm an All-Star!"

The goats bleated in celebration, probably based on his expression and tone of voice, but Ronnie believed they understood every word. Wags and Tiny raised up on their hind legs. Ronnie had to hold up his palms again. "OK, OK. And I'm gonna bring you back some real California oranges—I'll pick 'em right off a tree!" More celebration. Their bleats rang like laughter. "I can't believe you guys are real. When I get old and tell this story, nobody in this whole round world will believe me. I almost don't believe it myself." Ronnie waved, turned, and headed down the grassy slope singing "California Here I Come".

Meanwhile, Orrie, Lon, and Doug had spent all the ransom money on Beatles bubble gum cards. A mountain of wrappers rose from the tabletop. Lon held up an unopened package. "Last pack, ladies and gentlemen." Wuzzie held up the empty display box and tapped the bottom.

Doug's eyes were hopeful and wide. Orrie exhaled, exasperated. He said, "Let's get it over with."

Lon peeled open the last pack as though it were a fragile heirloom. Wuzzie held a wastepaper basket while Doug and Orrie swept the wrappers off the table. Lon stacked the last set of cards face down and covered them with his hand. "We're doin' this surprise style—one at a time." Lon flipped over the first card; it showed Ringo sitting at his drum set.

"What a dud!" said Doug.

Lon said, "OK, Orrie, slip the next card out, but cover it up so we can't see it."

Stealthily, Orrie pinched the edge of the card and pulled it to his chest. He took a private peek and shrugged. He let the suspense build.

"Who is it?" asked Doug. No response.

"Is it a close-up?" asked Wuzzie. Orrie nodded *yes*.

"Does he have one of the Beatles coats with no collar?" asked Lon.

Orrie peeked again. "Yep." He waited for five seconds, then dropped the card face up.

The other three boys groaned. "Ringo!"

Lon said, "I can't believe we're getting all these Ringo cards! What a cheat!"

Doug took a turn, accidentally pulling out two cards. He quickly flipped them both. One card was a picture of the whole group jumping around in a field, and the other one showed John holding his triple-pick-up Rickenbacker. The final card lay forlorn under Lon's palm. Lon said, "Go ahead Orrie. And don't let us see it right off."

"Yeah," said Doug. "Let us venerate the moment."

Orrie and Lon looked at each other and said, "Venerate?"

Doug gave an affirmative nod. "Crossword puzzle."

As Lon lifted his palm, Orrie quickly whisked the card away and trapped it against his chest. With the card cupped in his hands, he took a good long look, then trapped it again. Orrie smiled and said, "It's another close-up. I'm not sure who he is, but it's *not* Ringo. He has a nice little smile, and he is wearing a suit, but not a regular Beatle jacket. And his hair is kind of short."

"They wear different kinds of suits, and sometimes turtlenecks," said Lon.

Wuzzie said, "George gets more haircuts than the others. Sometimes he jokes about it."

Three faces of great expectation looked on as Orrie slowly lowered the card and set it face down, very gently, on the tabletop. He counted backward from ten. As he said, "One," he quickly flipped the card. Three hopping-mad mouths exclaimed, "Brian Epstein!" Grumps and groans, gripes and moans, lots of pounding and laments.

At around 6 pm, at the Brayton berry fields, amid the cluster of tents, vans, and cabins standing alongside the fields, Father Dom approached Phil Trujillo. Phil and his children were washing their station wagon. Nearby, a field worker sat in front of his tent, strumming a guitar, and singing a beautiful rendition of the Mexican folk song *Cielito Lindo*. Children swayed in dance and sang the chorus. Father Dom set a small brown box on a picnic table and removed a bundle of white envelopes that were bound by a rubber band. He was surprised and very curious about seeing so many families washing and polishing their automobiles. The guitar player sang the familiar chorus:

Ay, ay, ay, ay
Canta y no llores
Porque cantando se alegran
Cielito lindo, los corazones

The children and Father Dom started singing along. Everyone cheered and clapped when the song ended.

"Gracious me," said Father Dom. "Is there going to be a car show tonight!"

Phil said, "A big car show, and a bigger party! It's payday, Father. Everyone is invited. Come and join us."

"Will there be root beer?"

"Si Senor, but mostly beer without the root." An amiable chuckle.

"Well, my heart and spirit go with you, but I'd better stay home and mend some of my stockings."

Phil rubbed lightly at his dry, scratchy eyes and tenderly touched the bee sting swellings on his face. He gazed at the sunset and noted a welcome change. "Look there, Father! I swear there's a cloud, a real cloud in the sky; it's moving in front of the sun."

"Goodness, it most certainly is. Getting a little cooler too—the first sign of fall . . . But maybe that's just my wishful thinking."

"No, no, I feel it too; and a nice little breeze every once in a while . . . finally, a little relief—we have waited so long."

A jovial little troupe had gathered about the table.

"Welcome—to my favorite day of the week, everyone," Father Dom said.

As the father distributed pay packets, the guitarist struck up "La Bamba". Father Dom found it odd that so many of the children were wearing their Sunday-go-to-meetin' clothes. The flowing skirts of the young girls twirled as they danced. The boys all seemed to know the traditional steps, arm stylings, and claps. For this song, everybody joined in on the chorus—*Bamba Bamba, Bamba Bamba.*

Fiddling with the tuning knob of her radio, Rhonda nearly tripped over a thick, gnarly tree root as she and Connie entered the west end of Rye Grass Park. Mighty oaks stood like pillars at each corner of the thigh-high stone wall. "Try that Canadian station," said Connie.

"That's what I'm doing. It usually comes in really good at this time of day, especially when the weather's hot and clear like this."

"I love that they play all that British stuff." Abruptly, Connie stopped in her tracks. "Hush. Turn it off." She rubbed the bruise on her thigh and went on point as might an Irish Setter. "The punks. Look at 'em . . . gettin' their kicks on the merry-go-round. Well, their good times are about to come to a merry little end." The girls casually strolled behind one of the big trees.

"Let's take 'em." Rhonda said. She extended her long, pink nails, scratching at the air like a cat raking a couch.

"Easy now, let's take it easy and hold off a minute. If they spot us, they'll scatter like mice."

Mid-park, not far from the angel and serpent fountain, Orrie, Doug, and Lon took turns pushing each other on the archaic merry-go-round. The treacherous toy wobbled and squeaked, making a terrible racket with every spin. When the pusher reached his top speed, he hopped up on the big toy and they all shouted, "We're flyin' saucer men from Mars—here we come and here we are!"

Rhonda tucked her radio between two thick tree roots and slipped out of her sparkly, silver pumps. She and Connie stayed hidden on either side of the oak tree, peering wickedly around the trunk. The boys were wholly occupied. The girls stalked like tigers. As the merry-go-round slowed, Doug pointed to some smashed, half-melted Milk Duds stuck to the wooden platform. Orrie wrinkled his nose. Lon seemed a bit tempted, looked closer, looked away, and said, "There's tobacco stuck on 'em." Doug used his fingernails to scrape up some of the chocolatey goo; he had a taste.

"It's good. The tobacco gives it a little extra flavor. Let me see if I can think of a good word . . . it's sweet and . . . uhh . . . *aromatic*."

As Doug reached for another dubious treat, Lon and Orrie said, "Don't!" With mouth-watering regret, Doug managed to resist. Suddenly, terror-filled his nine-year-old heart. He blurted, "C-c-c-Connie!" She and Rhonda charged like rhinos.

Orrie was off in a flash. Lon and Doug were still dizzy from the recent whirling. Doug fell to his knees. Lon helped him up, then sped off like a startled deer. Doug's fright-filled heart steadied his wobbly legs, and he lit out. Connie and Rhonda closed on him. Lon turned back to distract them with a taunt, "Hey, Constance, how'd that rock feel? You wanna shove glass in my face—well, here I am."

Doug fired his retros and headed for the tree where Orrie waited, ready to give him a boost. Lon made it to a ladder of old boards nailed to a nearby tree; the third board broke away as he climbed, but he managed to get beyond Connie's reach. Rhonda went after Orrie and Doug. With a strain and a heave, Orrie launched Doug onto a low branch, then jumped and pulled himself up. Rhonda grabbed his leg and a tug of war ensued. As her hands slipped, her sugar-pink nails raked Orrie's skin, but she managed to hold on to his foot. As she dragged him down, one of his fancy dress shoes came off. She fell hard onto the grass with an "umph". Lithe and quick, Orrie soon joined Doug among the higher branches. Rhonda fumed and threw Orrie's shoe into a distant barbecue pit. She tugged the back of her hair.

Treed like raccoons, the boys tried to find spots where the leaves and branches afforded the best protection. They saw the girls searching the ground and knew projectiles would soon be coming. Connie and Rhonda stood, hands-on-hips, and leered. Rhonda said, "I'm gonna run back and get my shoes and radio. I saw some really good rocks back there too."

"That's fine. These punks won't be goin' anywhere—except the cemetery."

Connie positioned herself with geometric precision exactly between the two arboreal sanctuaries. The boys cringed. Connie sang, "Three little monkeys sittin' in trees, k-i-s-s-i-n-g."

A breathless Rhonda returned with the radio and some golf-ball-size rocks. She adjusted the tuning knob in time to hear the DJ say, "By request, here's 'You Turn Me On' by Ian Whitcomb!" Connie picked up three formidable rocks and juggled them. Rhonda found a broken bicycle chain, whipped it against a tree trunk, and cackled. She circled the tree and quoted Shakespeare.

Double, double, toil and trouble
Fire burn, and cauldron bubble

Connie walked toward Lon's refuge and slung a rock; it hit him on the calf. "Oww!" He moved to another branch and curled up tight against the tree trunk. Closing one eye, Connie aimed another rock.

"That was just my warm-up pitch, Chief."

Rhonda started making a war drum sound and sang the introduction to the *Pow-Wow the Indian Boy* cartoon. After using the bicycle chain to slice away chunks of tree bark, Rhonda continued her "tribute" to Native American culture. She broke into an impromptu war dance and sang "Running Bear" the 50s hit by Johnny Preston. Connie winged another rock and hit Lon on the forearm. "Ow, yee-ouch!" Again, he adjusted his position.

Doug yelled, "Leave him alone, Connie. You stinky skunk!"

Orrie yelled, "Yeah, Constance, leave him alone, you skunk. And your haircut looks like Baby Huey's hairdo."

Doug laughed. "That's a good one, Orrie! She looks just like that big cry baby. Baby Huey, Baby Huey, Connie looks like Baby Huey!"

Connie and Rhonda snarled. In the boys' eyes, their mouths appeared to foam like rabid wolverines. They roamed and compiled an arsenal of minerals beyond compare. Then they limbered up their pitching arms. Connie said, "We're gonna knock your scrawny chicken butts out of those trees, you little *pudnuckers*! Pray for a quick death!"

Meanwhile, something far more sinister was taking place on the rocky banks of the Caulder River. The hillside fires had moved east, leaving black plumes of dissipating smoke. Toby Gussard admired the beautiful new bow he had stolen from Brownie's store. He pulled eight arrows from the archery quiver. Along the rocky dike, he spread out the arrows: some with smooth metal caps made for recreation, and some specifically designed for hunting. The hunting arrowheads were wide, interlocked triangles, with four well-honed edges—horrible, wicked-looking things. They were designed for cutting deep into an animal's muscle tissue. As the creature moved—the blades caused maximum hemorrhaging. The searing pain and profuse bleeding dealt by such an ungodly lance could bring down the strongest beast.

No better word than "ecstasy" could describe the look in Toby's eyes as he examined his prizes. Beneath an arrowhead, he wrapped a strip of bed sheet, then secured it with a piece of twine. He poured some kerosene into a tin can and dipped the arrow. He splashed a little more of the fuel onto a tuft of grass and lit it. Taking great care not to mash the feathers, he nocked the arrow and touched it to the fire. The soaked cloth burst into flame. He hooted wildly, "Woo-hoo! I say now boy, I say now boy, I say now boy, I say now boy—Woo-hoo!" Toby drew back the bow and let the burning arrow fly. It rose in a high arc over the water. He watched in wonder, as the arrow sailed, red-orange, through the swirling smoke. His keen and gawking eyes traced its path. "Wowee!" he hollered, as the fiery shaft dove into the river. Toby dropped the bow, then tipped back his head and gurgled, "Gog, gog, gog, gug, gug, gug." He rocked back and forth, screeched and prepared another arrow.

Back in the park, another rock left Connie's hand. With a grunt and a growl, she put on a good show as she hurled the stones; the effort behind her missiles was, in truth, half-hearted. Though Rhonda's rocks were hucked by a spaghetti arm, they hurt just the same. The real weapon here was fear, and it was working extremely well. Connie's next throw blasted through the leaves and ricocheted off a high branch; it finally dropped onto Doug's head. Showing Spartan fortitude, he made not a sound. Rhonda skimmed a saucer-like stone through the leaves; with a *thud*, it struck Orrie soundly on the left buttock. Feeling but a slight sting, he yelped, hoping to fox his captors and sate their vengeful fancies.

Connie cheered. "Good one, Rhonda! Nice butt shot!"

An old man using a walker doddered up and said, "You girls stop that, right now! You both know better."

Connie snipped, "Get outta here old man, or I'll twist your walker into a pretzel!"

"No respect," he grumbled. "No re—*goddam*—spect." He hoofed away in discretionary retreat.

At long last, the cavalry arrived. Leaping nimbly over the stone dike, Ronnie shouted, "Hey, you skags! Back off!"

All eyes fell upon the All-Star. "Back off—or pay the price!"

Connie said, "Mind your own *beeswax* Rix! This is none of your damn business!"

"I'm makin' it my business."

Rhonda cracked up and pointed to a spreading rhododendron bush. "Wrong Ronne. You do most of your business when you're squatting over there by the state flower."

Connie burst into laughter and said, "Maybe a couple of goldfinches will keep him company." The guys in the trees could no longer hold back; they laughed for the first time during their *neolithic* barrage.

Ronnie looked up into the branches and said, "You little pudnuckers wanna laugh at their skaggy jokes—I'll be glad to step off and let 'em have at it."

Lon quickly piped up. "No, no. We'll take your help."

"How 'bout you other two douchebags."

Orrie said, "Yeah, you bet—we *doofbags* want your help."

Connie reached down and pried a good-size rock from the hard-baked earth. Witnessing the prelude to a prehistoric standoff, the boys gawked with gaping gobs. At the foot of a fir tree, Ronnie found a rock the size of a ripe plum. Rhonda backed away. Connie mustered false bravado.

"You don't need *that* rock, Ronnie. Why don't you just use one of the rocks in your head?"

"You're real funny, Malman—lookin', actin', and smellin'."

"Hear that, Rhonda? Little weenie Ronnie is still in the third grade. Why don't you run home and play with your plastic dinosaurs?"

Rhonda covered her mouth with both hands. The boys bit their hands, suppressing rowdy cachinnation. Polishing the prune-like rock against his jersey, Ronnie did not disappoint the lads. He prepared for a wind-up. Rhonda and the boys held their breath. Connie held her ground.

Connie said, 'Whoa, you really got a big one there, Ronnie."

"Uh-huh, well, maybe I'll just bounce this big one, off yer big butt."

Connie said, "Blah, blah—if you think I believe that—you're *nuts*!"

"Yeah . . . what about 'em?"

When the retort sunk in, Connie blushed. Impulsively, Rhonda unchained her restraint and quipped, "Maybe he got 'em out of a box o' Grape Nuts . . . That about sizes things up."

Connie guffawed. Rhonda beamed. The boys among the leaves bit their hands once again.

Ronnie held his nose, reeled back, and pretended to waft away stench. "Why don't you skags just leave—you're drawing flies?"

Rhonda pulled Connie by the arm, and bellowed, "Let's get out here! Teeny Weeny needs some private time with his little friends!"

As the girls walked off, Connie yelled louder than a Viking horn: "It's been a real joy, little booger boys! Be seein' ya real soon! Have fun playing with the teeny-weeny skag boy, Ronnie! Maybe you can help him wash his panties!" As they sauntered off in revelry, Rhonda cranked her radio to full volume. They sang along with the Rolling Stones song "Get Off of My Cloud".

Ronnie looked up into the trees and said, "You little puds owe me. Remember that!" He walked to the low stone wall, did a scissor jump, then took off on his bike. Before descending, the boys examined their war wounds. There was nothing to be done but bear the pain. They waited and watched till their tormentors were completely out of sight.

CHAPTER 23

Belittle and Be Little

Being close to Rain, despite the heat and the hassles, comforted Ski. Few things comfort mind and spirit more than home and hearth. As he walked out of the prep room and into the kitchen, he found the love of his life scrubbing away with a grill brick. "Just got off the phone . . . Buddy Foley got locked up again. Doesn't surprise me a bit. He was out for less than a week—stole a car and robbed a filling station in Ritzville."

"What a fool. Did he get far?"

"State Patrol got him on a back road going to Idaho—you know, like they didn't know about that old trick—holy moly. My grandpa used to say, 'God have mercy on the dumb people'. That expression's been coming to mind more and more these days."

Rain sighed and said, "Any way you want to put it—this news is one big relief to me!"

"Figgs figured Buddy for both setting Lester's place on fire and breaking into the store. The fire possibly; he was on the loose at the time . . . He'll probably never get over Lester firing him.

And I'm sure he still holds Lester to blame for that first prison stint—nobody could ever tell him different. But the store break in doesn't fit the timeline."

"I've only heard parts of that story: something about throwing dynamite in the river and scooping up fish?"

"The crime was poaching. I think that's what they decided. Fall of '62, a few months before I took the deputy job, he stole a box of Lester's dynamite and threw it in the current when steelhead were coming up the Columbia. The concussion knocked out the fish. He'd net 'em up and sell 'em. He got 6 months in county for his trouble."

"What a stupid thing to do. As my mom would say, 'He ain't all there'."

"As long as he's locked up, it doesn't matter to me whether he's stupid, or all there, or had an unhappy childhood—just as long as he doesn't show his face around this town again."

"Actually, I think all three of those descriptions would fit the bill."

Ski took a close look at the French frier. He lifted the basket out of the grease. "I'll go ahead and change this stuff, Rain."

"I suppose we'd better. I was holding off cuz we're down to our last two cans."

"Yeah, I know. But if our ship's gonna sink, we'll go down selling some beautiful golden fries."

Rain laughed. "Our lifetime legacy."

"Anyway, back to the store break-in—that had to have been Toby. And when it comes down to it, Toby may have set that mill fire too. You do know that's why he was in the looney bin, don't you?"

"Yes, I knew. A terrible thing he did—just horrible. But the town council was told Toby had never given any sign of messing with fire. Matter of fact, the doctors at that hospital said he was afraid of fire."

Ski tightened his jaw and talked like the Frankenstein Monster. "Fire—bad! Bread—good. Grrr."

"It's not something to make fun about, Ski. I'm really suspicious about the whole thing."

"Sometimes a little humor helps. As crazy and out-of-whack this world's getting to be—sometimes you just have to laugh—we've all heard the line that it's 'the best medicine'. And as far as Toby goes, Father Dom would never allow him to have anything to do with matches, lighters, and so forth. They watch him pretty close out at the farm."

"True. But Toby's really sneaky, Ski. And a lot smarter than he lets on."

"I do agree with that. Give him an inch and he'll take a mile. I've seen that often enough. And *man*, did he ever tear up that store, but none of the matches or lighters had been touched, no charcoal fluids—Brownie and I checked that right off. If he had his mind on setting fires, he had everything right there at his fingertips . . . He didn't even touch any of the smaller valuables: bangles and baubles, trinkets to put in his bike basket; or the more expensive items like rings, watches, jewelry. Besides candy bars, all that's missing is some oddball stuff: a wiener dog toy, masking tape, lip stick, and some flashlight batteries."

Rain tipped her head and pondered. “How very strange . . . masking tape and lipstick—that makes no sense at all—there’s no connection. None of it makes any sense. Except maybe the wiener dog, it must run on batteries.”

“Nope, the wiener dog was a little pull toy. And that’s another reason I was thinking it was Toby. Figgs told me Toby shoves flashlight batteries up his rear end.”

“Oh, my Lord! You really didn’t need to tell me that . . . I can’t even imagine.”

“Yeah, I suppose I should have kept that to myself. It just sorta slipped out. But there’s not a darn thing anybody can do about it. I’m sure if it wasn’t batteries, it’d be something else . . . Anyway, as to the subject at hand, the break in, Brownie was still taking inventory when I left, so I’ll get an update and write up the report tomorrow.”

Rain yawned. “You know, we should close tomorrow and have a nice quiet Sunday at home.”

“You know, a little earlier I was thinkin’ about takin’ a day off. I don’t need to be concerned about Foley anymore. Toby’ll turn up at the chapel and we’ll get the goods back, at least most of the stuff. So, yeah, let’s do it. We can take a walk in the park, hold hands, and smell the roses, if we can find any that haven’t dried up.”

“How romantic. It makes me want to hear ‘Sukiyaki’—I don’t know what any of the words mean, but they sure sound nice.” She took a dime from the cash register.

While the song played, they wandered out the front door and stood beside Ski’s GTO. He pointed north. “What do you know, there’s a few honest-to-God clouds over there. And a lot of the smoke’s cleared off.”

"September's on the way. Hopefully, this'll be the last hot spell."

Ski kicked the gravel with the pointy toe of his cowboy boot. "We really should spread a new layer of rocks around. I could borrow a truck and do the work myself."

"When we get the dough, we'll get the rocks. In the meantime, people are just going to have to get stuck in the mud."

Ski glanced at his watch and called out like the town crier, "Ding, dong, ding, dong, six-twenty and all is well."

Rain shaded her eyes and looked down Main Street toward an empty town. "I haven't seen a car go by in hours." She sighed and yawned again. "Looks like the Trujillos won't be coming for dinner after all."

"I don't suppose they will. It was payday out at the farm today, so I think if he could have swung it, he'd have brought the family for dinner."

"At this point, I don't think it matters a whole lot. We'll be mostly out of supplies by Labor Day. No more leeway. No more credit. We've gotta decide on a back-up plan."

Ski put his hands on his hips and gave the GTO and long, last look. "I'll sell the car."

Rain's expression was a mix of hope and sorrow. "I can't let you do that."

"It's no big deal—it's a toy."

"It's your life's worth. You spent your army savings on that car."

"No need to remind me—stupidest move I ever made."

"It's your baby."

"You're my baby. You and Orrie are my life now. That's the way I want it and that's the way it's gonna be."

Rain folded her arms and struggled in thought. "Do you really think Ron Stickle would give you a fair price?"

"Two thousand bucks is what he said . . . What Rhonda wants, Rhonda gets."

"Except for what she needs the most—a little family time and a lotta love."

"Maybe so. But she turns 16 in October, and she adores the little GTO."

"She's so spoiled. And I can't help but wonder . . . How did Ron Stickle end up so rich? He seems like such a nimrod."

"The word is—he invented some kind of a gizmo that makes bombs blow up better—that's what I heard. Some electronic, transistor guided missile thing."

"A real humanitarian."

"Another rumor is the government's hiding him up here in boondocks so Russian spies don't steal his secret ideas and liquidate him."

"Ron Stickle, Agent Double-Oh-Zero. Our very own James Bond."

Ski mustered a little smile, but there was clearly a lot on his mind. He rubbed his brow and massaged the back of his neck. He leaned his head back, flexed his neck, smoothed his flat top fenders, and cracked his knuckles. "Who am I kiddin'? I can't take tomorrow off—not with Toby running around out there breaking into places. And, when it comes down to it, there's no telling whether he started that mill fire. The more I think about it, the more it seems likely." Ski pulled the deputy badge out of his back pocket and pinned it on his shirt. "No way around it—I'd better go out looking for him."

"Let me call Father Dom at the chapel—maybe Toby's already showed up out there."

"That'd be nice. It'd sure save me some time. I'll give Dom a call. Hard to believe Toby's been living here for less than a year and I swear he knows the town and the woods better than I do. And he also knows he's gonna be in hot water for tearing up the store . . . So, he'll be laying low for a while. I'll check out that chicken coop down by the feed store first, then maybe some of those shacks along Brayton Road."

"How long are you gonna be gone?"

"Couple of hours, more or less."

About ten minutes after Ski drove off, a shiny, red and white station wagon rolled grandly into the Thunder Burger parking lot. The Trujillo family had arrived for dinner. Carmalita and Juanita jumped out of the back seat, wearing their Sunday best. Running and laughing, Carmalita said, "Last one there is Frank Sinatra!" As they rushed past Rain, little sister Juanita got left in the dust. At the entrance of the restaurant door, Carmalita turned and teased, "You're Frank Sinatra, you're Frank Sinatra!"

In protest of the degrading moniker, Juanita said, "No I'm not! You're mean, Carmalita!" They continued their row inside.

Rain met Phil and Olive with open arms. "Hi, you guys. I was starting to think you weren't coming . . . The car looks beautiful!"

Phil smiled proudly and said, "I washed, she waxed, and the girls polished."

Olive said, "All for a special night with some very special friends."

Rain made a thumbing gesture toward the girls. "What's the Frank Sinatra contest all about?"

Olive laughed and said, "Oh, Phil sings 'It Was a Very Good Year' occasionally and they both just hate it. Getting called Frank Sinatra has become the world's worst insult. All the kids out at the berry farm have started saying it."

"Well, I like Frank Sinatra."

"Me too."

Rain gave the station wagon one last, appraising gander. "It looks like it just came out of the showroom of a dealership."

"Thank you. The old beater cleans up pretty good."

They headed into the restaurant and Rain led them to the table right in front of the jukebox. "I'll get you some ice water and glasses while you decide what you want. Fries are ten cents off today."

Just then, Orrie, Lon, and Doug straggled through the door. As Orrie approached Rain, she said, "I know—vanilla, caramel, fudge and pineapple."

"Exactly right," said Orrie as the boys hurried to the booth near the door. They glanced shyly at the Trujillo sisters.

Rain continued to the kitchen and laid four hamburger patties on the grill. While they sizzled, she dumped a bag of frozen French fries into a wire basket and lowered it into a vat of hot grease; it snapped and crackled, spit and spattered. She spread buns out on a tray and covered them with sauce and condiments. After flipping the burgers, she topped each with a slice of American cheese, then moved quickly to the ice cream fountain to switch on the clanky milkshake machine.

In the dining room, the Trujillo girls were reading the song list on the jukebox. They argued about the songs. Phil said, "If you ladies can't decide, I will sing you-know-what, and we can save some money."

"No!" they said, then pressed two buttons. A doo-wap song called "I Want to Love Him So Bad" by the Jelly Beans began to play. The sisters glanced at the boys, then quickly looked away; they giggled, swayed to the music, and continued to read the song list.

Lon said, "I never heard that song before."

"They just put it in there last week," said Orrie. "High school girls play it sometimes."

Rain set four milkshakes on the counter and asked Orrie to deliver them to the Trujillos. She followed with a tray of food, and said to Orrie, "Your sundaes are back by the fountain."

When Rain set the tray on the table, Olive said, "This looks wonderful. We won't need to eat for a week."

"Well, this is only the first course for me," said Phil.

Carmalita sat down and started singing a parody of "Frosty the Snowman": "Daddy the pigman, was a jolly, happy, soul."

Juanita said, "Oink, oink. Oink, oink."

The boys at the table laughed, then guiltily looked down.

Doug noticed a vehicle entering the parking lot. He did a double take. "Ahhh!" He ducked under the booth and whispered, "It's my dad! He's getting out of his truck."

"Curl up," said Lon. "We'll hide you with our legs."

The disheveled, unsteady figure of Lester Malman filled the doorway. He looked dizzily around and said, "Where's my damn kids! They in here?!"

With a slight stagger he approached the counter and laid his hands out flat. Rain was in the back room. Lester turned and saw Lon and Orrie. "Hey, you little injun buck—you seen my boy?"

"No, no sir," said Lon.

"Good. I don't want him playin' with your rotten little hide anyway." He hoisted up his pants. "Them kids ran off, dammit. They got chores to do. They ain't at the park, they ain't at the school, they ain't nowhere. Lester's blurry eyes noticed the Trujillos. He swaggered to their table and peered over Phil's shoulder. "You wetbacks lost?" He backed up and looked the whole family up and down. "I didn't know you pepper guts ate white man food." The little girls trembled.

Phil said, "We want no trouble, sir."

"Well, you got trouble, Poncho. Comin' into town stealin' and stinkin' up the place. You're all a bunch o' dirty Mexican dump rats!"

Phil looked up at Lester but kept calm. "We have worked hard all week. We just want to enjoy our dinner." Olive was clearly appalled but remained silent. She tried to settle the girls by mouthing, "It's OK."

"So, you want to enjoy your dinner, huh. Well, pardon me all to hell. Attention everybody, the beaners want to enjoy their dinner . . . fair enough, enjoy it off the floor!" Lester lowered his forearm and swept the food off the table. It scattered and splattered across the floor. The girls cried. Olive scooted them away, toward the corner of the room. Phil, a much smaller man, stood and squared up with Lester. Rain stepped out of the back room. Phil signaled for her to stay back. She was livid.

Rain rushed out of the kitchen blind with fury. She grabbed Lester's arm and spun him into a face slap; it rattled his drunken brain. She shoved him in the chest, and he stumbled backward. She yelled, "You get the hell outta here, Lester! You get out and stay out! You aren't welcome here anymore!"

Phil started to step in, but Rain waved him off. Clearly, she needed no help. Lester stood there stunned, dumbfounded, with a face drained pale and fluttering eyes. Rain chastised, "Whoa, what a *big, strrrong* man—scaring little kids! You're no big man, you're a little nothing bigot—a bug, an insect . . . turn around and start walkin', mister. Get out!"

Lester backed up a couple of steps and hesitated. With his mind in outer space, he wobbled toward the door. He coughed, glanced back once, then slowly headed for his truck. Rain followed him through the doorway with Phil at her side. Phil said, "This is a sick man. In much pain. The Devil claws at his heart and soul. He needs help . . . much help."

Olive approached and said, "A wound of the flesh may leave a scar, but wounds of the mind—they never heal . . . I will pray for Mr. Lester."

CHAPTER 24

Fiesta

The Trujillo family, along with Orrie, Doug, and Lon went right to work clearing and cleaning up Lester's mess. Rain went back to the kitchen to start cooking. Orrie swept, Lon mopped, Doug polished the tabletops.

The Trujillos walked outside and sat at a picnic table; they basked in the gorgeous sunset. "Look," said Phil. "The hillside—the fires have gone out." Unseen embers breathed their last; only smoky frills and curls lingered.

Ski pulled up beside the red and white station wagon. As he got out, the boys raced to meet him. Orrie said, "You should have seen it, Ski! Mom beat up Lester Malman!"

"Yeah," said Doug. "She slapped my dad upside the head!"

Lon said, "You should have seen it! It was great! And he really deserved it!"

Everybody was blabbing at once. The wordy bombardment made Ski's head spin. "Hold on a minute guys. What are you saying? Rain and Lester got in a fight?" Their clamoring was unfathomable.

"Come help me carry out this food!" Rain called from the doorway.

The boys quipped, quibbled, and babbled away. Ski had to shout them down. "OK, OK, tell me in a minute! Let's go help with dinner."

As the boys carried trays to the picnic tables, a line of cars flashed their headlights and rolled into the parking lot. Lots of cars. Lots of horns. Lots of people. A dozen radios blasted "Wooly Bully" by Sam the Sham and the Pharaohs.

Phil shouted, "Fiesta! Our friends have arrived!" Rain and Ski quick-stepped outside. Along with the boys they watched in wonder as the parking lot filled. When Phil spotted a '56 Chrysler Imperial, he called out to Ski, "Hey, Deputy, come take a look." Ski and the boys headed for the car. Phil opened the passenger door, pointed to the upholstery, and said, "Tijuana tuck 'n' roll!" Ski smiled. Phil said, "Why does everybody smile when I say *Tijuana*?!"

Ski gamely replied, "Whoa boys, look out—the joker is *wild* tonight!"

⚜

With the entire park to themselves, Connie and Rhonda sat on playground swings swaying from side to side. It was getting dark. Bats flapped and fluttered around the streetlamps, gobbling a feast of bugs. Not a car on Main Street. Frogs croaked, crickets chirped, birds roosted in the trees. An odd sort of evening: a little cooler, less smoke . . . an eerie lull suffused.

"It's a ghost town around here," said Rhonda. "Where do you suppose all those field workers went?"

Connie looked westward. "This time of night, the Thunder Burger's the only place I can think of. They must be having some kind of a celebration."

"I think there's still a few people at the Runnin' Bear."

"The regulars. They always park out back; except my dad, he parks right square in front of the place. Always wants people to know he's there. I wonder where the heck he is."

"I'll bet Mayor Figgs is *sooo* glad when your dad leaves. I'll bet he drives people away in droves."

"Nah, not the regulars. Being broke is the only thing that keeps *them* away. If they could afford it, they'd be there every night. Sometimes I think they go in there to see my dad the same way people go to look at the night creatures at the zoo."

Rhonda laughed. "That's one way to put it . . . a good way—mostly accurate."

Connie stood up and gave her swing a ghost ride; Rhonda started to swing in time. Suddenly, there was a rustling, shuffling sound in the dark. Something moved between the merry-go-round and the big slide.

"There's somebody over there," said Connie.

Rhonda dragged her feet and stood away from the swing. "Somebody—you mean a person?"

"Not sure. But I don't like people sneaking around spying on me." Though the noise had stopped, Connie still headed in that direction.

Rhonda pleaded, "What are you doing?! Don't. Don't go over there, Connie. There's somebody behind that tree!"

Connie kept walking. "Who's there? Who's out there?" She saw something move, crawling along the ground. A swaying shadow moved clumsily between the trees. In the darkness, red eyes glowed. There, foraging beneath the streetlamp, were two silvery shapes. "Possums," said Connie. "They're big ones . . . but they're just plain old possums."

Rhonda hurried to her side. "Are you crazy?! That could have been some killer, some escaped convict or mental patient."

"Somebody like that would have been quieter. And, like I said, I don't like being spied on. So live or die, come what may, I'll take on anybody."

"Yeah, I *saw* that—close-up, live, and in person. Let's get out of here before a convict does come. Or maybe some other creep like Toby Gussard, or even worse—your dad!"

"Ha, ha. Too bad that's not a joke . . . Around here—it's absolutely true to life . . . Let's go see what's happening at the Thunder Burger."

⚜

The mood lights in the dining area of the Rye Grass Cafe had been dimmed to a faint glow. Ronnie slid the tables to one side of the room, Wuzzie pulled a mop bucket out of the utility room. Wuzzie said, "After this, all we gotta do is polish the big mirror, the fountain, and the display glasses, then take out the garbage." The twelve-bar blues piano intro to Wilburt Harrison's "Kansas City" rock-and-rolled out of the radio. The guys briefly danced the Twist and threw in a few cowboy kicks.

Ronnie yelled over the music. "So, what do you wanna do when we get done?"

"I dunno, Marty? What do you wanna do?"

Ronnie laughed, "Go down to the Stardust Ballroom and meet some cute *tumaytuhs*!"

"That was a funny movie—especially Marty's mom."

"Yeah, I think I'll ask Father Dom to order it for the old folks."

"Invite me when it gets here."

Wuzzie used some Windex on the big mirror and Ronnie whisked the display cases with a feather duster. Ronnie said, "I got to watch the *Sound of Music* last week."

"How'd you do that since the theater's been closed? They're on vacation for another week."

"They loaned it to Father Dom so the nursing home people could see it. Best movie of the summer."

Skeptical, Wuzzie made a joke. "Did you get hit in the head with a ball today?"

"No, wiseacre. It's good. It's really good. Lots of good songs."

"Uh huh, baloney. You think I'm that gullible? You're the wiseacre—better yet, you're a wise guy from *Joyzee*."

"People from New Jersey don't say Joyzee, the say *Juhrzee*. They pronounce the R."

"OK, so now you're a speech pathologist."

"Not quite," Ronnie said and offered, "We'll go next week, when the Tanners get back from vacation. You'll see what I mean. No baloney."

"I still think you're kiddin' around. I saw the ads on TV . . . that is not your kind of movie at all."

Ronnie shrugged and said, "OK, you'll see."

Wuzzie removed his soda jerk hat and set it on the counter. "We're almost done . . . I'll clean the bathroom, you empty the garbage cans, and we'll be done."

When Ronnie picked up the wastebasket beside the ice cream fountain, he noticed a book. He read the title aloud: "*Relativity: The Special and General Theory*." He flipped through pages and read bits and pieces. "Einstein—do you really *get* this stuff?"

"Well, right now, I only understand about five percent of it—I figure I'll have to read it three or four times."

"Man, you're really serious about that physics stuff . . . Me, I'm reading *The Good Earth* by Pearl Buck."

"Is *The Good Earth* good?"

"Yeah, it's good. It's about farm life in China from around 1880 to the 1930s."

"Sounds boring to me, man. Real boring."

"No. It's really good. You should read it when I'm done."

"Sure: *The Sound of Music* and *The Good Earth*—I'll put those things *high* on my list."

"The biggest things in life are the little things we never did."

"Did you make that up yourself?"

Ronnie paused to wonder. "If I did—it was by accident . . . the biggest things in life are the little things we never did . . . I like it . . . feel free to quote me."

Wuzzie rolled his eyes. He scanned the room. His lips moved as he thought through the night routine checklist. "OK, I'll take your advice—let's do some little things—and for our *big* thing—we can lock up and go find out where all those cars went."

"Thunder Burger, no doubt."

"Had to be."

"Jeez, it looked like everybody and his brother's monkey's uncle headed down that way. And I swear, everyone dang one of those cars had been washed and waxed."

"Not to mention polished like mirrors. What the heck's that all about? But I'll tell ya one thing for sure—that Ford Customline—that thing was cherry, man."

"Yeah, there were a lot of nice ones. They'll be cool to look at. After that, I'd better hustle back out to the chapel and hit the hay."

"That's right, you'll be on the bus for *Californy* tomorrow."

"My dream come true!"

They finished their tasks and headed for the front door.

"Wanna take our bikes?" Wuzzie asked.

"Yeah. Then I'll ride back out to the chapel from there."

As they stepped onto the sidewalk, Wuzzie announced, "Everybody stand back! The big shot All-Star is comin' down the street!"

Ronnie started singing, "Here I come, Mr. Ameeer-ica . . ."

⚜

In the kitchen of the Thunder Burger, sizzling beef patties covered the grill. A bushel of golden fries soaked up the rays of a heat lamp. The entire countertop was covered with hamburger buns. Ski topped them with sauce, pickles, and onions. Field workers wearing starched white shirts and thin black ties carried tables and chairs from the dining room to the parking lot; this cleared the smooth cement floor for dancing. Out near Main Street, a string of firecrackers crackled and banged. Skyrockets, leftover from the 4th, whistled and exploded into stars.

Connie and Rhonda dodged diners and dancers as they made their way through the front door. They caught sight of Orrie, Lon, and Doug and gave them the stink eye. The boys averted their gaze and made themselves scarce. Rain appeared out of nowhere and grabbed each girl by the arm. "You've been drafted," she said, then dragged them into the kitchen.

"Drafted?" said Connie.

Rain barked orders. "Rhonda, you're on fries. Fill the small customer baskets as fast as you can and keep dunking new batches. Connie—you start flipping burgers."

"Burn 'em and turn 'em!" Connie said.

"No—don't burn 'em, but do add a slice of cheese. I'm counting on you both!"

Rhonda whined, "But I don't know how to—'

"Figure it out!" Rain said, then hurried to the ice cream fountain.

Ski continued dressing burger buns, adding tomatoes, and handfuls of shredded lettuce. Orrie filled cups with ice and soft drinks. Lon worked the milkshake machine. Every time Rain made a sundae, Doug carried it to the front counter where customers dropped cash into a box.

The joint started jumpin' when "Whole Lotta Shakin' Goin' On" by Jerry Lee Lewis began pounding eardrums. Phil met Olive at the center of the dance floor and the floor cleared. They treated the audience to some hip-flipping East Coast swing. Meanwhile, Orrie, Lon, and Doug were enjoying the shenanigans in the parking lot. Among other competitions, some guys were betting on who could walk the greatest distance with a beer bottle balance on their head. Watching and smiling a stone's throw away were the Trujillo sisters. After exchanging brief eye contact, the boys shyly looked away. Doug teased Lon. "Why don't you go over and introduce yourself?"

"Shut up!" Lon bristled and dodged behind an old Buick.

In the kitchen, beading with sweat, Connie and Rhonda laughed and jabbered away. They sang along to Petula Clark's pop hit "Downtown"; Rain added her voice. The burgers, fries, sodas, shakes, and ice cream sundaes moved down the assembly line. Ski motioned for Rain to join him in the back room. Hurried and harried, she followed and said, "We're swamped if you haven't noticed." There amongst the storage shelves, cardboard boxes, number ten cans, and onion peelings, Ski pulled a small box from his pocket. He carefully pried it open. The diamond sparkled, as did Rain's eyes.

Ski said, "I've been practicing, trying to find the right words."

"Those words are just fine, and the answer is *yes*!" After an impassioned embrace, Rain extended her hand and Ski clumsily placed the ring on her finger. Their kiss of eternal love lasted about ten seconds. "I'll jump for joy later. Let's get back to work."

Across the highway, in the woods, about 100 yards away from the Brayton chapel, Toby Gussard arranged a circle of ostrich-egg stones around a mound of pine needles—the foundation of his campfire. Within the lithic oval, he laid a pile of small sticks and a few broken branches. He dropped a match and laughed giddily as the makings combusted.

No mirror around, Toby never had the chance to admire his facial makeup and cranial adornment. Strips of masking tape secured a dozen chicken and crow feathers to his head. His lips were smeared with lipstick; his cheeks and jaw displayed war-paint stripes. Around the campfire he danced, chanting in the fashion of the half-naked heathens he'd seen on television.

Aligned with perfection on the forest floor were six arrows. All sported razor-sharp arrowheads designed for deer hunting. In a small box, were books of matches, cigarette lighters, a tin of lighter fluid, and long strips of cloth. Toby had improved his arrow modification technique. He crossed the ends of the fabric tightly around the arrows, following a figure-8 pattern. This allowed the cloth to be snugly drawn and secured. He prepared two arrows and gave each a touch of lighter fluid.

The flap of mighty wings and a swirling rush of air startled Toby. He watched an owl float silently away and land on a nearby treetop. Toby said, "Owl, owl. Hoo, hoo. *Owwwul.*" The bird flew a little farther on. Toby slipped his bow over his shoulder. Arrows in hand, he grabbed a lighter from the box and followed the creature. Reaching a sleepy glade, suppressing a squeal, Toby trembled in rapture when he saw the owl light upon a lofty branch. It was about twenty yards off, on the other side of the highway. Between the road and the bird were power transformers, electrical cables, and sagging telephone lines. Toby dropped one of his arrows, then touched the flaming lighter to another. Unslinging his bow, he grasped the handle and deftly nocked the burning shaft. Bow fully drawn, Toby closed one eye, adjusted his aim, and let loose. The shaft rose in a steep arc, well above the watchful bird, and landed in the distant woods. "Do be sine cup! Do be sine cup!" The next arrow grazed a power cable and impaled a dead tree instantly igniting the desiccated bark. The owl leaped, glided, and disappeared into the night.

Toby's first arrow had landed on the forest floor and bloomed into a wavering luminescence: orange, red, and gold. Flames from both arrows devoured the parched hemlock, pine, and fir. Toby whooped, hollered, and broke into a war dance. He brandished his bow, chanted in triumph, then lumbered back to his dying campfire.

Akin to this incident unfolded a parallel scene. On a dirt road in the woods near the Brayton chapel, Lester Malman slumped over the steering wheel of his truck. The ground aside was strewn with beer cans. A static-riddled version of the song "500 Miles Away From Home" by Bobby Bare leaked out of the radio. Lester stirred and flopped his arm out the window. He leaned back and twisted the cap off a bottle of cheap wine. He guzzled the nasty brine to the dregs.

Right then, a celestial spectacle revived his woozy brain. A shooting star he thought. But no; it was too bright and too low—and shooting stars don't land silently in the woods. He perked as another ball of flame sailed. He tumbled out of the truck, landing on his hands and knees. A flaming geyser appeared to spout; its flames undulated, like ocean waves spreading o'er the undergrowth. Adrenaline purged some of the poison from Lester's blood. He bolted for the chapel. "Fire! Fire! Fire! Fire!" Hellish branches crashed onto the telephone lines. The transformer on a power pole sparked and blew apart. Embers spread skyward like fireworks. Glowing bits and chunks of bark drifted in a tame breeze. The lights of the chapel, hospital, and rest home blinked once, twice, then went dark.

The brilliance of the flames rendered moot the flashlight held by Father Dom as he descended the chapel steps. From a distance of 40 yards, he could feel whips of the intense heat. Tongues of a thousand dragons lapped the darkness. Both Lester and Father Dom took panicked strides, meeting in the center of the road. Father Dom said, "We have no phones . . . I've got to start an evacuation . . . Good God, you smell like a wine vat! Do you think you can drive into town?"

Livened and alert, Lester assured, "I'm a trucker diver, Father. I could drive if I was dead."

"Then get going, Man!"

Lester's truck was a minute away. He ran like he was rounding third base.

At the fiesta, absolutely no one was aware of the Brayton inferno. In the restaurant dining room, the women greeted Rain with surprise-party congratulations. They called out for a glimpse of the ring. Phil beckoned Ski to the parking lot. He weaved his way past the ladies. Ski said, "Howdy!" to Ronnie and Wuzzie as they crossed paths. Curious, the boys ventured inside to investigate. Rain expressed words and smiles of gratitude as she made her way through the hugs, back pats, and handshakes of the many well-wishers.

In front of the restaurant, frothy beer doused Ski; it sprayed from all directions. Good-naturedly, the deputy endured his shower. The merry mob cheered with fervor. Several men threw towels; Ski vigorously dried his hair. His face was humble, grateful, and happy. "Man, oh, man," he said. "A beer shower can really cool a guy off—you all oughta try it."

Phil said, "A little too rich for our blood these days—we saved it all for you! This may be the biggest night of your life, my friend!"

As the raucousness died down, Orrie appeared, holding a football. With both hands, he tossed it end over end, to Ski. He yelled, "The Vince Lamborghini ball! Congratulations from Father Dom and the mayor!" Silence. Pondering. A burst of laughter. A baffled Ski tried to spin the ball on his finger, it stalled and plummeted." Accolades: All paid homage to the much-prized artifact. Ski retrieved the ball and tossed it back to Orrie, then went back to drying his top notch.

Inconspicuously, Phil headed for the dining room. On his way to the jukebox, he impishly declared, "We need a beautiful song of romance!"

"Don't you dare play 'Devil Woman'!" Olive playfully warned. And so, of course, Marty Robbins' yodeling voice soon told the tale of a bewitching seductress. Olive said, "Suuure, it's all that devil woman's fault! The weak little man has no blame at all!"

The women booed the song; some of the men sang along. Though none of the ladies were willing to dance, Connie sneaked up on Ronnie. She grabbed him by the arm and dragged him to the middle of the room. "This is gonna be *our* song, buddy." Beneath the spotlight, nowhere to run, self-conscious and blushing, Ronnie embraced Connie. They swayed back and forth in the good ol' high school tradition.

Meanwhile, Rhonda was manhandling Wuzzie. Like a cowgirl bulldogging a steer, she took him by the horns and swung him by the tail. "This is my version of the waltz," she said as she dipped her partner 'til his fuzzy hair brushed the ground. Revelers flocked to feast their eyes on the terpsichorean high jinks.

CHAPTER 25

Evacuation

As the music, madcap, and merriment beguiled, the horn of an approaching truck grew louder and louder. Someone was laying flat out on the warning button. Then the horn went into a Morse-like code SOS. And most everyone recognized Lester's truck. It barreled across the centerline and did a surf slide into the gravel. Lester leaped out, running and yelling like a wild man. "Fire! Fire! There's a fire at the chapel!"

Ski stepped out of the crowd and cut him off. He pointed and said, "You turn right around, Lester!"

Lester stuttered as he jabbered his panting, frantic plea. "Y-you gotta h-help! There's a f-fire in the woods!" He breathed in as he bellowed out. "A-at the chapel . . . Out in Brayton! It'll get to the nursing home! W-We gotta get out there!"

This was Lester. Ski was skeptical. "Fire? . . . Nobody called."

"Phone lines burned down. We gotta get out there—now!"

Mayor Figgs pushed through the crowd and marched up to Lester. He studied the tormented face. "You got a pickled brain, Lester?!" He saw panic in the man's eyes.

Lester laid digging fingers on the mayor's arm. "They need help out there!"

Figgs paled, his expression was grave as he turned to Ski. "He's telling the truth, Robert. I'll get the fire crew out there and put calls in to Wanoocha and Union City."

In a mad scramble, the crowd dispersed and rushed to their vehicles. Main Street seized up like a big city bottleneck. Traffic stayed congested all the way to the Brayton highway where trannies shifted to high and 90 down a winding road. The fire truck siren wound up and wailed. Bells rang. Gumball lights flashed as the truck passed everything in sight. Red taillights trailed off and vanished.

In the parking lot, Ski hustled to the GTO and opened the passenger door. Connie and Rhonda squeezed into the front seat. Wuzzie and Ronnie tried the back doors; they were locked. Ski said, "Sit this one out, Ronnie. You gotta stay here and watch over Rain and the kids. Toby Gussard's out there somewhere and I think he might be dangerous."

"I can handle Toby. But he's off hiding somewhere. These guys could keep all the doors locked just in case he came around. I should help with the fire."

"Nope. We need you more right here."

"But I—"

"No buts—we got this covered. There's gonna be dozens of people out there helping. I want you to stay here and stand guard, then be on that bus to Seattle in the morning."

Ronnie persisted, "I don't wanna let people down who need help. Those people out at the old folks home are my friends. Some of 'em can't hardly move."

Connie unlocked the back door for Wuzzie, then jumped out of the car bellowing, "Just shut up, Ronnie, and listen! Get in there and watch those kids! We don't need you out there! Get that through your head! If you're a no-show, you lose it all, so you better be on that damn bus in the morning!"

Briefly taken aback, Ski said, "I couldn't have said it better myself. Let's go, Connie!"

Ronnie envied Ski and Connie as they ran for the car. Ski spun out, throwing gravel twenty feet, while he stood alone, hands-on hips, feeling nagged by anxiety, fretfulness, and guilt. Rain and the boys walked out of the restaurant and sat at a picnic table. Rain said, "Come on over, Ronnie. Let's put a plan together."

Ronnie sat down and said, "I'll hang around, but I don't think I should leave in the morning. I'd be deserting you guys."

Orrie said, "But you're the *All-Star.*"

"Yeah," said Lon, "You, uh, you—" He looked at Doug for the right word.

"Represent?"

"Yeah, you represent us—the whole town."

"Protecting people and fighting a fire comes first."

Rain said, "You saw all those people tearing out of here to help with that fire. And Ski didn't really mean that warning about Toby. He just wanted you to stay with us. You know Toby; if he thinks he's in trouble, he'll hide *waaay* out in the woods somewhere."

"Uh . . . yeah, I guess that's probably what he'll do. But we'd better not take any chances. I doubt he'll come around 'til he gets really hungry, or wants coffee bad enough . . . Why don't I hang around out here for a little bit? You guys should go back in and lock the doors. I'll come inside in an hour or so."

Rain said, "Not until you promise you'll be on that bus in the morning."

Stubbornly mute; sour and sulky, Ronnie looked away and stared into the darkness.

"Promise. Promise as a man of honor—that eudaimonia thing you've been telling everybody about."

Begrudging, but coming around, Ronnie said, "Well, I don't think I'm much of a man of honor yet, but I guess this could be another crossroads . . . I guess I'll go ahead and go—as long as there's no other problems."

"It's OK, Ronnie," said Orrie. "Me, Lon, and Doug have been solving problems around here for the last three days. We took on both you *and* Connie."

Lon risked a little humor. "And don't forget—Doug is a Knight of the Templar!"

Ronnie smiled when he looked at the sleepy-eyed, chin-dropping Doug. "Yeah, he really looks ready to fight dragons."

Everyone but Doug chuckled. He roused and protested. "I could do it . . . I'm . . . uh . . . I'm resilient!" The others managed to suppress their amusement. Doug marched indignantly into the building.

Orrie's bright eyes flashed toward Ronnie. "So, for sure—are you're getting on the bus?"

Ronnie sighed. "Yeah, I'll keep my word. I'll get on the stupid bus."

The fire closed in on the chapel and neared a row of four Tudor cottages, which provided housing for hospital staff. A second burning path crept in the direction of the hospital. Sirens wailed as the Rye Grass fire truck rumbled down the rocky utility road; it crossed the grass between the fire and the structures. Firefighters, some dressed in jeans and pajama tops, rushed into well-trained action. Father Dom and the nursing staff escorted the old and frail toward the evac transport. The field workers drove cars and trucks past the wall of flame bordering the highway, parking on the soft shoulder. Oncoming headlights stretched along the highway for a quarter mile.

The woods crumbled and spread flaming debris generously. Heavy limbs and slender branches plummeted into a sea of fire. The firemen closest to the flames worked without masks. They coughed and choked, backing away often to draw a clean breath. Using axes, shovels, and rakes, they cleared the ground and started a fire line. Flames ran up the walls of a cottage. Four men with ladders and chainsaws ran toward the structure. Two men held the ladders, two men ascended with chainsaws; with skill and frenzy they cut vents in the roof.

Save for the dancing firelight reflecting against the windows and the feeble beams of a few flashlights, the hospital was totally dark. Nurses and attendants went from room to room in accordance with regimented practice. They wheeled and walked patients from the rooms, then directed volunteers to transport the non-ambulatory. Others guided the disoriented through the halls and into the parking area. Wuzzie pushed a rolling bed, trying to comfort a frantic patient. "Just pretend you're riding through the funhouse at a carnival." The patient started kicking her legs and swearing a blue streak.

As each room was cleared, the door was shut and marked with a strip of white tape. Every corner, cupboard, and closet were checked and double checked. Spoken instructions, crying, squawking, screaming, babbling, even crazy laughter echoed through the corridors. Several men entered the area with swinging lanterns—a more than welcome blessing.

With sirens wailing, two fire trucks from Wanoocha rolled in to do battle. Within seconds they had hoses flooding the woods and men shoveling on the fire lines. Field workers and townspeople pushed the frail and decrepit in wheelchairs and bed-like *banana* carts. Some carried patients on stretchers. An extremely obese man stumbled and fell hard; he floundered on the walkway. Nurses struggled to lift him into a wheelchair, but to no avail. Lester hustled to their aid, but the man's mass and unwieldiness defied their collective effort. Catching sight of Phil, he shouted for help. Phil arrived in an instant. Lester said, "Take hold up under his other arm, and we'll lift on three." With ample leg power and a well-timed effort, the men were able to wrestle the man into the chair. While an attendant rolled him away, Phil and Lester teamed up to relieve two nurses as they labored with a man on a backboard. They transferred him onto a banana cart. A few yards away, two knee-buckling nurses struggled with a screaming woman strapped onto a stretcher. Phil and Lester took over.

Attendants, nurses, field workers, residents of Brayton and Rye Grass helped patients into cars, trucks, busses, and vans. From the parking lot, Mayor Figgs beckoned Phil and Lester with a frantic wave. They jogged side-by-side and stood before the desperate mayor. "We've gotta get this ship moving faster," Figgs said. "I want each of you to take a bus into Wanoocha. We radioed ahead—they're waiting at the high school gymnasium. You'll see the place just as you get into town." Figgs pointed, "Go ahead and take that bus over there, Phil. Lester, you come with me." Briskly, they walked to the door of the other bus. "You're a good man, Lester. You saved the day here. Saved a lot of people. I haven't seen you like this in a long time."

"We're in a real battle here, Charlie. And I saw somethin' here. I started to feel some things. All these people in one place, working together, working for a common cause, with life and death on the line—it reminds me of a battlefield. I feel like I'm worth somethin' today . . . It takes a lot of people to make a world—we all count, and we all have something to offer."

"That's the old Lester I know, a young man ready to make a difference in this world. Come next week—you and me are taking a drive into Spokane—the VA hospital . . . We got a deal?"

Lester looked to the heavens. "That's a deal, Charlie. Let's do it—let's see what they have to say. I've got a family to raise, and I've got to start doing it right."

After a firm handshake, Lester boarded the bus. He scanned the grounds. The fires closed in on the buildings. Figgs said, "Get goin', Lester!"

Lester turned to the passengers. "Next stop Wanoocha!"

Ski, Rhonda, and Connie gathered around Father Dom, awaiting instructions. Father Dom said, "We think we've got everyone out. Attendants are still checking room by room . . . We still haven't located Toby though; he rode his bicycle into town at around noon and never came back."

Ski said, "I'm pretty sure Toby's the one who broke into Brownie's store."

Father Dom rubbed his temples and sighed. "I'll go out looking, once I know everyone here is taken care of."

"Me too. We'll split the town in half."

"He could be anywhere. He knows every nook and cranny for miles around."

With the greatest of urgency, Olive Trujillo ran up to the group. "The firemen say we must all dig. The fires nearing the church, they have branched toward the berry fields and are heading for where we stand. We need more tools, and we need everyone to dig."

Figgs said, "OK, Mrs. Trujillo. We can take it from here. Did Phil get that bus on the road?"

"Just as you asked. He is well on his way."

Ski said, "Rhonda and Connie, try to find some digging tools. Check the barn and sheds. Bring everything you can carry. Sharpen up some bean poles and broom handles if you have to." The girls took off.

Wuzzie ran up to Ski and said, "We got everybody out of the buildings. Some of the firemen with the hoses might be getting tired. I could go spell a one of 'em."

"OK, Wuzzie, go check with the fire chief. Do whatever you can."

Ski turned to Father Dom, but he was gone. In the blink of an eye, he had vanished. "Father Dom? Where the heck did he go?" Ski eyeballed the area. Only silhouettes could be seen against the flames. "He just disappeared. That's the darndest thing." Ski headed for the fire lines.

The chapel was now half-engulfed. The water tank of both the Rye Grass and Wanoocha firetrucks were almost dry; the refilling would take a trip back to town. If they were going to save the main buildings, shovels, axes, rakes, and dirt would have to do.

Flames crept through the chapel hallway. Smoke poured into the rooms. Father Dom was in his office, rifling through a desk drawer. He pulled a few items from the drawer and tucked them into his pockets. Half-blind he groped his way to the door, then did a military crawl toward the burning exit. He gasped, having too little breath to cough. He was trapped in an oven. Summoning a final burst of strength, he rose and tried for the door. Using the wall for support he slid until he was only a few yards away from the exit. He collapsed. Unable to stand, he squirmed and inched along on his belly. At the doorway of the front porch, he reached out, then passed out.

As Connie ran past the chapel, she glimpsed a white glove. She hurried past the flaming columns, up the steps, and saw the motionless body. The porch was an envelope of flame. Oblivious, she bent low and grabbed the shoulders of Father Dom's frock. She pulled and leaned back, but the body barely budged. As she fought to drag him out, her throat was spasming, seizing up. She squatted low to underhook an arm and a leg. "Father, you've got to help. Raise up just a little. Father!" He did not move. She repositioned herself and grabbed the collar of his frock. With her adrenaline surging and her athletic strength, she lifted and pulled. The body slid a few inches. Flames curled around the columns of the porch; they flared and singed her arms. Driving with her legs and leaning fully backward she gained enough momentum to reach the edge of the porch where she lost her balance. Blindly, she tumbled down the steps, dragging Father Dom with her. Her knees wobbled as she tried to stand. Her world went dark. The heat and pressure within the building rumbled. She and Father Dom lay on the walkway, both still, neither breathing.

With a rumble and a roar, the windows of the building shattered, a torrent of flame rushed through the door, engulfed their bodies, then was drawn back into a vacuum. When Connie's eyes fluttered open, Rhonda and Ski were pulling her across the grass. The smoke seizing her breathing passage loosened its grip. Her lungs fought for air. Ski and Rhonda knelt beside her.

Reviving just enough to turn her head, she watched a fireman's hands pressing and releasing over Father Dom's chest. Her breath was shallow but steady. Father Dom lay still.

Hemmed by the Brayton highway and bordered by newly plowed fields, the fires neared containment. The inferno had reduced two acres of woods to charred chunks and a layer of ash. Three fire trucks from Union City had crossed the Columbia River, traveling more than 20 miles in less than 20 minutes. Their fire hoses blasted the last of the flames and soaked the embers. The grass fires still burned and all four of the nearby cottages were ablaze.

The ground trembled. A volcanic blast ruptured the air and the ground trembled when the cottage next to the chapel erupted. A fireball burst forth in spherical form, then shrank into itself. The workers on the fire lines had dropped and covered their heads. Eardrums rang and painfully throbbed. Hurtling fragments and debris rained down. This shower was brief but injurious, as many were struck by glowing wood bits and fragments of glass. Ignoring minor wounds, workers sprang up and dug furiously. Flames ravaged the grass. Two fire trucks rolled up to the fire lines. Pressurized waves gushed from the huge nozzles. Quickly, the tide turned. The lawn fire became a lake. Though all the cottages were gutted they had been thoroughly drenched—no smoke, no embers lingered.

The valiant firefighters hailed their reward: time to rest and rehydrate. Admiration and congratulations all around. Eventually, these triumphant heroes straggled to the highway, curious to get a panoramic view of the aftermath. Details of the infernal fray would be branded in memories forever. Aside from minor contusions, blisters, and lacerations the folks were no worse for wear. Owing to the selfless acts of a community, a dire tragedy was denied. When impassioned people of common mind and spirit unite, miracles may abound. At four of the clock on that summer Sunday morning, even to the devout, the quality of mercy had not been strained. Drawn close for a time in those inky wee hours, the resolute at last dispersed. They wearily headed home.

Near the hospital, Father Dom rested in a wheelchair, upright and alert, holding an oxygen mask to his face. Across the way, the chapel lay blackened in ruin. Ski, Connie, Rhonda, and Wuzzie audited the fire chief's cursory assessment, which culminated in: "Well, as they say— 'It's all over but the cryin'."

Ski asked, "No ideas at all about the cause?"

"Father Dom told me Lester Malman had witnessed the start of things. At first, he thought he saw shooting stars—but then he started thinking about illumination flares over battlefields. His explanation doesn't make a whole lot of sense. But when you consider he'd been doing a whole lot of drinkin', I guess it made sense at the time . . . Right now, my thought is a power surge could be the culprit. They're rare, but when that transformer blew there was likely a flash and enough sparks to set off some dry grass and pine needles. When we start cleaning things up tomorrow afternoon—we'll get to the bottom of it."

Quickly hoofing up to the group was middle-aged shopkeeper Michael "Brownie" Brown. He was a middle-aged, wavy-haired man of average height and build. He owned the Rye Grass general store. As he drew near, he started talking loud and fast. His words were somber and worrisome. "We could have us a *reeeal* bad problem. When I finished up the inventory, I noticed the archery set from the display window was gone. So were about a dozen hunting arrows. The heads on some of those arrows are for deer hunting—wide-base, razor sharp—deadly as hell."

Panic filled Father Dom's eyes. He threw off the oxygen mask and sprang from the wheelchair. A little unsteady, trembling, he said, "The picture we showed Friday night—the Indians were shooting fire arrows! We've got to find Toby!"

Ski took charge. "Absolutely—no time to waste! We'll do a canvas and set up some neighborhood watches. Brownie, you take the highway and side roads from Maple Street to, say, halfway to Weston."

"You bet! I got a bone to pick." Brownie ran for his truck.

"Remember—he's got that bow."

"And I got a shotgun in my truck." Brownie headed for his ride.

"Charlie, you take Wuzzie with you—he'll be a good spotter. Cover the roads north and along the river. I'll take this facility and the berry fields. On my way back to town, I'll check the side roads and trails . . . Father, are you OK?"

"Fine. Fine. I'll take downtown, then go a few miles south. My truck is in the back. No time for talk!" Father Dom lit out like a man possessed. His pace was hurried, his gait hobbling, arthritic. After rounding the hospital complex, he took a private moment. Reaching into his frock he removed a little tin box and placed a small pill under his tongue.

Figgs, Wuzzie, and Brownie were already on the road. At the berry farm, Ski quickly sketched a grid search to cover the compound and fields. Connie and Rhonda were wringing their hands as they waited patiently. Finally, Connie spoke up. "What can *we* do?"

"Come on with me, girls, and stick close. Three pairs of eyes oughta be able to spot Toby—if he's even around—which I doubt. Just stay close, always within earshot."

Charlie Figgs, with his special assistant Wuzzie Washam, rambled along in a '38 Ford pickup. He turned onto the cracked, potholed road leading to the Caulder River bridge and stepped on the gas. He hung a hairpin louie onto the overgrown, rocky road that ran along the dike. At a reckless speed, he covered about fifty yards, then jerked to a stop. Figgs said, "It's gonna be bumpy, Wuzzie, but I need you to get into the back of the truck and stand, so you can see in all directions. Hold onto the cab and you should be all right . . . If you see something, you bang on the top of the cab."

"I got it." Wuzzie got out, walked behind the truck, and stepped up over the tailgate. From the moment the truck set sail, Wuzzie felt like he was rafting the Colorado rapids. With the eyes of a hawk, he surveyed the river and the woods. The old truck prowled along for nearly two miles before Wuzzie pounded on the cab. Abruptly, Figgs hit the brake, throwing Wuzzie well onto the top of the cab. Heart racing, he slid back onto the truck bed. Figgs met him behind the tailgate. On the ground, there was a rusty can and some strips of cloth. The fumes coming from the can were pungent. Figgs picked it up and swirled the fluid. Then he noticed some Snickers wrappers and said, "Toby's been here all right."

Wuzzie took a whiff of the can. "Kerosene."

"Yep, kerosene. It would make one *helluva* a fire arrow. We better find him fast."

"If Toby has a hideout around here, there'd be signs. Maybe he set up a campfire or some kind of shelter."

"Maybe . . . You look around down in that hollow and I'll follow the bank." Figgs' expression was grim, his voice nervous. "If you see his ornery hide, you get back up here. Get inside the truck, lock the doors, and blow that horn."

Ski, Connie, and Rhonda headed for the berry fields. Each carried a flashlight. The field workers mulled around the cabins and tents, trying to settle in for a long overdue trip to Morningtown. A young man approached Ski and asked, "Is there anything we can do?"

Ski said, "I didn't want to get you guys involved. We're looking for Toby Gussard. I think he's got a bow and arrows—deer-hunting arrows."

Three men stepped forward. One of them said, "Doesn't matter. We want to help. Give us a job."

"If you men could walk the berry fields, the girls and I can check out the barn, sheds, and then the woods across the highway."

"Sure, we'll search the fields—row by row, end to end." The men talked strategy as they headed toward the raspberry fields—six acres worth. Ski, Connie, and Rhonda walked the dirt road leading to the main barn.

Connie squinted at the tool sheds and broken hovels. She said, "Sorry, Mr. Welski, but those outhouses over there are all yours. I'll take the sheds."

Rhonda said, "I could look in that little room attached to the barn."

"OK, take a peek," said Ski, "but stay out of the main barn. There's too many places in there he could hide. Wait 'til Connie and I get there."

Connie said, "And yell, *really loud*, if you see something."

"Oh, you know I can yell loud. You'll hear me *just* fine."

Ski took a quick look in each outhouse, then walked the surrounding area. Connie, very cautiously, opened a shed door and shined a flashlight along the walls; she carefully inspected each corner. A little farther down the line, Rhonda warily entered the barn workshop. She twisted the knob of the light switch—eventually the bulb buzzed, blinked, and faintly glowed. Shining her flashlight under the workbench and counters, she saw two crudely fashioned arrows. "Eww! Toby Gussard crap!" She recoiled, then let the flashlight wash over the floor. She noticed a floorboard was slightly out of place. Curiosity piqued, she tip-toed across the floor and pried up the loose slat. Rhonda gasped when she discovered Toby's collection of incendiaries. As she lifted the box, the doorknob of the entrance to the main barn rattled. It made a rusty, grinding sound. Without a doubt, someone was trying to force their way through the relic of a door. Rhonda bounded outside and screamed, "Here, over here! Somebody's in there! In the big barn!" Ski and Connie ran all out.

In the thinnest of whispers, Rhonda said, "I found a bunch of matches and stuff in there—under the floor!"

Ski said, "You ladies step back—over that way. Stay where I can see you." Ski pointed his flashlight at the barn's double door. He approached slowly. One of the big doors eased open. A shadowy figure stepped into the light with a raised axe. Ski ordered, "Drop it! Drop the axe!"

The field worker tossed the axe aside. Jumpy and jittery, he said, "I was just putting tools away. I heard something—someone was inside the workshop, so I tried the door." After a brief pause, came three sighs of relief. The farm hand relaxed.

"It was me you heard in there," said Rhonda.

Ski said, "Stay right here. I'll take a closer look."

The field worker stayed with the girls until Ski returned. He carried the box of fire making odds and ends. "Let's head to the car. I want to get you girls home. Things are getting *waaay* too intense."

CHAPTER 26

Rye Grass Hill

At about 5 am, Ski stopped by the Thunder Burger. Looking through the window, he felt certain all were asleep. Silently he slipped in, woke Ronnie, and gave him the *shush* finger. They went outside and Ski said, "You'd better head down to the bus stop. I'll take care of this situation."

"What about Toby?"

"I've already got some guys helping with that. Just don't *you* miss that bus."

"No, I won't miss it. I'll just wash my face and get a couple of things, then I'll head right down there."

Ski decided to let the others sleep. He hung around outside long enough to see Ronnie on his way. Ronnie casually pedaled the three blocks to town in less than two minutes. The ornate clock on Main Street read five twenty-five. Ronnie's entire All-Star wardrobe adorned his frame—his baseball cap and uniform. The All-Star event spanned four days. He was grateful for the sack lunch Rain had prepared. He placed the sack and his mitt on a bench just outside the cafe, then chained his Harley-esque bicycle to the steel rack bolted to the sidewalk. He plopped onto the Victorian-era bench and inspected the seams on his mitt. Across the street, the park seemed haunted. Ronnie wondered about the long-forgotten lives of the idlers, lovers, day trippers, and dreamers of the past—perhaps their ghosts still roamed. Pretending to entertain these pining souls, Ronnie sang, at the top of his voice, "Take Me Out To The Ballgame" in the style of Dean Martin:

Oh, take me out to the ba-ha-hall game
Take me to that ol' crowd
Buy me zum beanuts and Graguh Jags
This guy don't gare if he ever comes back
It's a glass o' gin for the home team
If they don't drink it's a shame
And it's one, two, three and pass out
At the old ba-hull gay-ay-ame

He next entertained himself with a poetic tribute to the overdue bus driver:

He's late, he's late, for a very important date
Hello goodbye, hello goodbye
He's late, he's late, he's late

⚜

Back at the Thunder Burger, Doug and Lon slept soundly on the padded seats of a booth. Rain dwelled in slumberland, while resting her head and arms on a tabletop. Orrie walked past the dawn-lit windows and tapped lightly on Lon's foot. Lon stirred and curled onto his side. Orrie tapped him again and said, "Wanna go out to the hill. Nobody fed the goats last night."

Lon lifted his groggy head. "What time is it?"

"Almost six."

Lon snuggled against the back of the seat. "Nobody *in their right mind* gets up at six o'clock in the morning if they don't have to. We'll feed 'em later."

"That's OK. I'll just ride out there myself. They're probably hungry. Tell mom when she wakes up."

Lon snored. Orrie slipped out the door.

Parking himself on a seat in the middle section of the bus, Ronnie tried to relax. On the bus radio, the song "Follow That Dream" by Elvis seemed an apt send off. The bus driver stood on the sidewalk, looking every which way, waiting a few extra minutes for other passengers. Finally, he decided that Ronnie would be his only fare. As the bus pulled out, Ronnie saw someone riding a bicycle in their direction. The rider was about two blocks away. It was Orrie. He made a right turn at the sign pointing to Rye Grass Road. The bus driver shifted a few times, and the bus picked up speed. As they neared the Mobile filling station, Ronnie watched Orrie peddle on toward Rye Grass Hill. He mumbled, "What's that little idiot doing?"

"How's that?" said the driver.

"Oh nothin', I talk to myself sometimes."

"Don't we all."

At the crossroads, someone appeared from behind the filling station; it was Toby, standing next to his bicycle. A bow and quiver of arrows were slung across his back. He was watching Orrie, who had progressed about a quarter mile. When Toby straddled his bike, Ronnie stood and hurried to the back of the bus. When Orrie disappeared around a curve Toby started pedaling faster. Ronnie took note and the wheels in his head started turning.

The bus driver said, "Young man—you're going to have to sit down."

"Yeah, OK. Sorry." Ronnie sat down on the back seat. He kept his thoughts to himself: "That's weird. What the heck is going on? Maybe I should have stayed at the Thunder Burger. But I did promise everybody I'd get on the bus."

Congenially, the bus driver said, "You must be the kid on the All-Star team . . . I'll bet you're a little nervous."

"Yeah, I'm a little nervous. I've been dreaming about this day for a really long time."

"I'd have been dreaming about it too. And that scholarship they offer—that's one heck of a good deal . . . What are you gonna study?"

Ronnie squirmed. "I don't know. I've got a couple of years to think about it."

"Well, it's quite an opportunity, young man. And I wish you the best of luck."

Ronnie's voice quivered a little. "Thanks. Right now, mostly it's gonna be nice to get away from this boring little town for a while."

"I'll bet."

Ronnie stared out the back window, his thoughts: *Not my problem. Not my business. Not at all. I just wanna to go my own way . . . do my own thing. Not too much to ask. Not too much to ask at all. I earned this trip and I'm gonna enjoy it.*

As the bus left the city limits, Ronnie chewed on his thumbnail. He spit the bits from the tip of his tongue. More thoughts: *California here I come. It's gonna be so good to get a change of scenery and meet some new people.* He slouched in the seat and tried to relax. His foot started tapping. Suddenly, he grabbed hold of his mitt, jumped up, and ran down the aisle. "Let me off!"

"What's wrong?"

"Just let me off! Let me off now! Pull over and open the door!"

The driver slowed and stopped in the middle of the road. He reached for the door handle. "This is the last bus outta here today."

"Open the doggone door!"

Ronnie sprinted down the highway in fear and in fury. Catching up to Toby ruled his entire being; this was his only reason for existence. It was not fear, but terror he felt as he ran past the fields and barns. Entering the city limits, he flew past houses and fenced yards, finally reaching Main Street. Outside the cafe, he knelt at the bicycle rack and quickly dialed the lock combination. He tugged hard, but the lock stayed locked. Frantically, he spun the knob, then stopped and let the lock go. He cleared his thoughts, then dialed very slowly. The lock popped open, he pulled the chain away and rocketed off. Veering across Main Street, he cut through the park and flashed past the Mobile station. He passed the general store and shot right down the center of Rye Grass Road.

Rye Grass Hill stood three-and-a-half miles away, about a ten-minute ride. The endless fields and fences, telephone poles and mileposts, scrub brush and trees stretched on without horizon. Ronnie wheeled away, a tireless machine. His cap blew off, but he paid it no mind. Rounding each curve, he prayed he'd catch sight of Toby, but at the end of each curve he saw only the beginning of another curve. The instrumental tune "Pipeline" by the Ventures drummed in his head; its guitar rhythm stirred up waves of strength. Time stood still. It was all so frustrating. He ground his teeth; tears streamed back across his temples. As he huffed and puffed, his fears blew away. His steeled determination knew no bounds.

Up ahead, possessed by wanderlust, Orrie meandered the winding road, passing acres and acres of gently swaying ryegrass. The sun rose golden in the east. Toby pedaled steadily, staying one curve behind the boy. Warmth and joy touched Orrie's heart as Rye Grass Hill came into view. He knew his tail-wagging friends would be waiting. Not a hundred yards back, Toby's legs pumped away—Orrie had no idea. Finally arriving, Orrie rested his bicycle at the base of the hill and started to climb. Ominously, Toby rounded the final bend.

Father Dom cruised, a second time, past Toby's favorite haunts: the disintegrating chicken coop; the schools and youth counsel hall; the railroad tracks, flatcars, and boxcars; the park and the sidewalks of Main Street; the back alleyways; the Mobile station; the Thunder Burger; the movie theater and general store. He did a stop-and-go search of the neighborhoods. Finally, he rolled past the courthouse and parked in front of the post office. He paused to gather his thoughts. From behind, Ski came up in the GTO. He walked to the window of Father Dom's truck and said, "No luck so far?"

"Not a sign. I've been to every one of his usual spots . . . If he was hiding, I really do think he'd have come out when he heard me call."

"I reckon he probably would have. Just a minute ago, I ran across Brownie and sent him back for another drive around Brayton. I told him not to go any farther than the cemetery cuz I've heard Toby's scared of it."

"Yes, Toby will not go past the cemetery. Ronnie convinced him ghosts live there."

Ski nodded and said, "Figgs and Wuzzie must still be down along the river."

Father Dom added, "I've already talked with people in most of the neighborhoods. Nobody can sleep. And no one's caught the slightest glimpse of him. I don't think there's much of a chance he's hiding in town."

"At the nursing home, you told me his bike had been missing since noon. If he rode out of town, he'd have probably ridden west—I see him out along the highway pretty often. Brownie didn't see him earlier, but I think it'd be worth taking another look."

"Maybe so. But I've never known him ride all the way out to Weston."

"No, I agree. All that's out there in Weston is a phone booth, gas station, and an old man with a shotgun. We can be pretty sure he stayed a little closer to home."

"Agreed, Weston is, indeed, an uninviting port."

"No doubt Toby knows that just as well as we do . . . So, I'll just go down about five miles and re-check some side roads . . . maybe take a look in some of those ramshackle huts."

"I'll drive a little farther south, then circle back through the neighborhoods again."

"Sensible . . . After I dropped the girls off at Rhonda's, I stopped by the restaurant. Everybody was asleep. So, I just got Ronnie up and sent him on his way. He should be on the bus and gone by now . . . Could you check again on Rain and the kids?"

"Of course, I'll be passing right by there."

"Since I haven't heard from Figgs, the river is still an unknown. If he and Toby crossed paths, I believe Figgs would be able to coax him back to town with nothing more than the promise of some coffee."

"More truth than jest."

The men parted in opposite directions; both having grave thoughts, neither knowing where next to turn.

All four goats met Orrie at the top of the hill. "Roll call: Toro, *bleat*; Wags, *bleat*; Tiny, *bleat*; Ghostie, *bleat*." They all nudged him with their noses and bleated. "Settle down, everybody. I have no treats. You can't always have treats."

"Kill!" Toby yelled from the bottom of the hill. "Kill!" His shriek curdled Orrie's blood. He shuddered from head to toe. When he looked back, he saw Toby at the bottom of the hill, grinning and waving a bow and arrow over his head. "Kill you! Kill you! Toby Kill!" He followed these words with war whoops and did a little war dance. Toby started up the hill. "Shoot boy. Shoot goats." War whoops. "Fire arrow. Burn, burn, burn." Maniacal laughter. "Die! Die!"

The goats united on the crest of the hill. Toro dug a front hoof deep into the turf and lowered his horns. Orrie hugged his neck. “No, Toro! No! Run! Let’s run!” Orrie ran toward the wishing well. The goats stood their ground and tossed their heads. Orrie stopped, turned back, and hollered, “Come on goats. Toro! Tiny! Wags! Ghostie! Come!” He waved them forward. With considerable reluctance, the goats trotted to his side. Orrie pointed toward the fields below. “Run! Run down to the meadow!” He pointed and stepped toward the meadow. The goats did not move. Orrie pushed Ghostie and Wags. “Run!” They began to bleat fast and fearfully, but they would not leave Orrie’s side.

Toby appeared on the hilltop. He nocked an arrow. Orrie yelled, “Stop! Stop Toby! Get outta here!”

Toby smiled. His laugh was like the whinny of a horse. “Toby got arrow. Shoot boy. Kill goats.” Another whinny.

Orrie waved his arms. He shouted, “Go, Go!” He kicked at the goats.

Toby drew back an arrow and let it fly. It missed Wags by an inch and disappeared into the grass. Toby pulled another arrow from the quiver; this one was wrapped near the tip with a piece of white cloth. He dropped the quiver to the ground. From the pocket of his overalls, he pulled a cigarette lighter and a can of lighter fluid. He doused the cloth, lit an arrow, and slipped it onto the bowstring. “Look! Fire! Arrow! Look!” He shot the fiery shaft high into the air; it landed way out in the bone-dry meadow. He squealed and laughed.

Toby watched the dark smoke rise. As he prepared another arrow, Orrie gathered the goats and quietly led them toward the feed shed. He yelled, “Run goats, run!” But they would not go. Orrie stepped through the door of the shed and called them. They followed and Orrie slipped back out. He closed the door and leaned all his weight against it. The goats bleated and kicked.

When Toby turned his attention to the shed, Orrie said, "Over there, Toby. The goats. They ran down the hill. They ran down the hill to the big cedar trees. Leave me alone, go get them." Orrie pointed. "That way—past the big tree." Toby gazed intently toward the cedar trees; he tipped his head to the side and took a step, then the goats bleated and pushed at the door.

Toby narrowed his eyes. "Oh, you boy. Do be sine cup! Do be sine cup! Arrow! Toby shoot. Toby kill! You die!"

As Toby prepared another fire arrow, Orrie yelled, "You get away from us! Get away!"

"Boy go in. Go in house. Toby burn boy—burn!" The arrow flared. "Go in goat house. Kill you. Burn you. Burn goats." He pulled the bow to full draw, pointed the arrow at Orrie, slowly he lifted his aim and let the arrow loose. He watched it sail high over the shed and out of sight. "Look. Look. Fire! Arrow! Fire! Arrow!" He held his sides laughing and honked like a goose, then he used his Foghorn Leghorn voice. "I say now boy, I say now boy, I say now boy, I say now boy."

Coasting up on his bike, Ronnie saw the fire arrow strike at the base of the hill. Up the grassy slope he charged. Still unable to see Toby, he yelled, "Toby! Toby! Toby, come here! I want you! I have Snickers! Toby!" Though Ronnie was not yet in sight, Toby attended briefly, then focused on preparing another arrow.

Ronnie heard Orrie's voice coming from the other side of the shed. "Ronnie, watch out! He's got an arrow! It's real. It's sharp. He's lighting it!" The goats rammed the door and pounded with their hooves. Orrie glared at Toby. "You stupid, ugly monster! The whole hill is burning up. You better run!" Again, Toby pointed a hunting arrow at Orrie. The end of the arrow burned hungrily, just as did the hill.

Over the hilltop, Ronnie bounded and ran straight at Toby. Toby swung around and took aim at him. Ronnie yelled, "Run, Orrie! Now's your chance! Get those goats out of there and run!"

"He'll shoot the goats!"

Toby swung the bow back at Orrie. Ronnie stepped forward. Toby swung the bow back. Ronnie walked slowly toward the shed and stood in front of Orrie. Still the arrow blazed. Ronnie spoke quietly so Toby could not hear. "I'm gonna start closing in on him to block his shot. He won't shoot me. I can control him. I know what to say. Let me get a little closer, then let the goats out and run."

Orrie balked. "They won't run. They'll try to protect you. He's insane. He'll shoot you, Ronnie."

"He won't . . . The whole hill's on fire. We're all gonna burn up anyway . . . This is your only chance!"

Toby said, "Ronnie go! Go away! Do be sine cup!"

Ronnie stood tall—directly in front of Orrie. "If he shoots at me, you run. Hear me. You let those goats out and you run for all you're worth!"

"It won't work."

"It will! He's a bad shot and I can dodge the arrow."

"No, you can't!"

Ronnie put his hands on his hips like TV's Superman. "I'm Superman, Toby. You can't hurt me. Superman will punch you. Punch you hard in the face."

Though the flame of the arrow was fading, Toby continued to point it at Ronnie's chest. "Not Superman. Do be sine cup! Toby kill, Ronnie. Not Superman." With the strength of a madman, Toby pulled the bow string to its limit.

From the top of the rise came a booming voice. "Toby!" Father Dom appeared. Face grim, brow furrowed, he walked straight toward Toby.

Toby let up on the tension, but kept the bow pointed at Ronnie. In a flash, Toby's face contorted hatefully; he glared at Father Dom "No. No. Father. No. Do be sine cup! Father go! Go home!" Toby yelled at the top of his voice, "You stupid asshole!" A flash of fear, then a cloud of sadness came over Toby's face. His lips drooped in a pout. In the next instant, his face twisted hideously; his scream was terrifying. Pure insanity.

Father Dom reached into the pocket of his frock. He removed the *homerun* ball Ronnie had given him. With a mangled right hand, he formed a fast-ball grip. As he drew back his arm, Toby released the arrow, then the hardball blasted him in the chest; he dropped to his knees. The arrow struck Ronnie in the chest; he doubled over, then fell to his side. Hellish flames had reached the hilltop.

As Toby sat gasping on the ground, the four goats burst through the door of the shed. They fell upon Toby all at once. Raising on their hind legs they slashed him with their hooves. Toby curled up, covering his head with his arms; he screamed in rage and fear and pain. He writhed and wailed.

Orrie clapped loudly and called the goats. After a few last kicks, they heeded and gathered around the fallen Ronnie. Father Dom knelt and gently rolled Ronnie onto his back; he lifted the stubby, blackened shaft from the grass. Several inches, including the deadly arrowhead, had burned to ash, and fallen away. Ronnie sat up and rubbed at his breastbone. His hand was a smear of black soot. Ronnie reached for the arrow; the shaft crumbled to ash. Orrie and Father Dom helped Ronnie to his feet. When they looked around, they realized they were surrounded by flames. The air was as hot as a furnace. The goats panicked, bleating and scurrying around, looking to flee, but stymied by fear and confusion. There was no chance for flight. They circled, disoriented, strangely glancing at the sky. Repeatedly, they raised on their hind legs, tipping their heads as they came down. Through the thick smoke, Father Dom led the boys to the wishing well.

CHAPTER 27

The Wishing Well

Ronnie frantically turned the well handle 'til the bucket reached the top. From a snaggle of rope, Father Dom fashioned a harness and secured it under Orrie's arms. He disengaged the bucket and secured the harness to the well lanyard. "Hold on to the rope," he said. "Hold on tight." Father Dom cast a glance to the heavens. A rare hopelessness filled his eyes. Hypnotized, the goats also stared up at the heavens; their bleats were rapid but lulled and calm. Instinctively, they huddled together and lay down, somehow aware these were their last moments. Father Dom lifted Orrie to the opening of the well; Ronnie prepared to lower him. The smoke was suffocating. Their eyes burned and teared. They fought for each poison breath.

Most strangely, the ears of the goats twitched. They stood and looked toward the meadow. They bleated and circled the well, brushing against Ronnie and the Father. Somewhere in the distance came a faint rumble. Another rumbling sound—louder. A bright light flashed and tore through the smoke. In seconds, the sound of thunder rolled like boulders over boulders. Again, lightning flashed. Another bolt shot up from the ground, splitting a quince tree. Thunder roared, boomed, and crackled. Raindrops fell lightly, sparingly, and sparse. A sphere of blinding light burst before them as lightning struck and split another tree. Thunder rolled like a hundred drums and crashed like a thousand cymbals. Jagged bolts slashed and wounded the clouds. Rain poured. Rain pounded. Puddles became ponds, ponds became lakes. The sky cracked wide open—a watery deluge sloshed, splashed, and gushed.

Father Dom lifted Orrie from the rim of the well. While Toby sat on the soggy ground, bloody and battered, the goats danced and pranced in the silvery rain. Sunbeams brought back the morning. Vaporous ghosts rose from the cindery grass; they swirled around the charred harbingers of cherry and quince. The rain had vanquished the flames. Overlooking the valley, Father Dom, Ronnie, and Orrie, beheld the aftermath of a miracle. The thunder faded and the lightning retired. A lazy rain drizzled. Above, patches of a pale blue sky displayed the jigsaw smile of a rainbow.

Three soaked people and four drenched goats made their way to the feed shed. Inside the shelter, the boys found it odd that the goats were ignoring them to fuss and fawn over Father Dom. His disfigured hand gently kneaded their soggy necks. He went to one knee and let them nudge his face. With a wave of the Father's hand, the goats became calm and lay down. Ronnie and Orrie sat on bags of grain, smiling, and enjoying life itself. Father Dom stood, approached the boys, and tousled their dripping locks. He patted each on the shoulder. The rain pattered lightly on the roof. Through the open door they could see Toby sitting in a deep puddle. He was rocking in musical rhythm and babbling. "Muh-muh-muh-muh-mum."

Father Dom shouted, "Toby—go stand by the well!", which he immediately did. Orrie and Ronnie looked at each other quizzically. Most oddly, Father Dom's voice had lost its French accent; in fact, he sounded like a Midwest farmer.

Near the well, Toby muttered, "Do be sine cup." He slapped himself on the forehead—three slaps and a pause, three slaps and a pause . . .

Orrie looked Father Dom in the eye. "You just talked like an American, Father."

The French accent returned. "Yes, yes—I've found it helps Toby listen more carefully when he is upset."

Toby muttered, "Do be sine cup," over and over.

Father Dom switched back to an American accent. "Be still, Toby! You be still!" Immediately, Toby was silent. Leaning back against the well, he again began to rock. He looked up as the rain stopped and the sun reclaimed the sky. There was nary a wisp of cloud. The horizon was a deep blue. A full spectrum rainbow arced beyond the distant hills.

Ronnie asked," What is that Toby always says . . . something like 'do be zine gub'? Is it just baby talk?"

"Not baby talk—far from it. It's a foreign language. He is saying 'Du bist ein dummkopf'—German words. They mean 'You are a dumbhead' or as we might say, 'You're stupid'."

"Somebody must have said that to him when he lived at that hospital," said Orrie.

"I suspect many times, over many years," Father Dom replied.

Father Dom turned his attention to the patient goats. He playfully scratched each on top of the head. He stooped and gave each a hug around the neck. Intuitively, Orrie and Ronnie could tell he was saying goodbye. It was a final goodbye to cherished friends . . . a beloved family. The boys' eyes saddened.

"Dandy, you are still a good boy, a happy boy. Tinker, you be nice . . . and mind these two young men. Willow, ever true, I know you will keep watch over our family . . . and Henry . . . Henry—you will always protect your family and forever be their guardian. Henry snorted like a bull." The goats bleated and nodded. Ronnie and Orrie cheered them on.

"Why did you call them different names, Father?" Orrie asked. "Like Henry and Tinker?"

Father Dom placed a hand on his stiff back as he righted. "Oh goodness. I did do that, didn't I? My thoughts must have drifted back to goats I cared for at the monastery—I was a very young man—a monk and a shepherd. I do *so* miss the French countryside . . . those plush rolling hills."

"Why would you give French goats American names?" said Ronnie.

Father Dom chuckled. "Oh, that was not my doing. That was Father Gaston. He had spent several years visiting and working in Canada and the United States. He said he was christening them as honorary American goats."

"How did you hurt your hand?" asked Orrie. "Is that why you wear the gloves?" Ronnie elbow-nudged him.

"So, you've guessed the secret of my gloves. As the years have passed, I've found wearing them leads to far fewer questions." He cleared his throat. "Far fewer questions."

Interlacing their fingers on their laps, the boys awaited further address. Father Dom gazed through the open door. He watched Toby whose eyes were closed as he slowly rocked back and forth. "I'll be taking Toby away now . . . I need to find him a new home."

He saw questions in the boys' eyes and offered closure. "Quebec. Where I lived for a time before coming here."

"Canada," said Ronnie.

"Canada . . . Yes, and I know just the place. He'll be safe . . . And he'll never be able to harm anyone."

Father Dom reached into the pocket of his frock and removed a small plastic box. From it, he took two small plastic bags containing pieces of paper—they were cards. "I've had these for quite some time. There are no others like them in the whole world." He handed one to each boy. When Ronnie saw the image, his eyes glowed; he tried to hold back a mile-wide grin. A little short of breath he said, "Thank you, Father."

Orrie's reaction was subdued; unmoved, but polite. "Thank you, Father. It's a very nice card."

Father Dom's attention turned back to the goats. "We've said our goodbyes, old friends. The time to part has come again. But I'll be truthful—this will be the end for us. We've had a wonderful life together and my heart will always be with you." He backed toward the door. "Stay goats. Stay." The goats were silent, but only for a moment. One after another, they bleated softly. If goats could cry, they were crying.

As Father Dom helped Toby up out of the mud, the boys put their cards back in the sandwich bags and set them on top of the rusty oil stove. They knelt to comfort the animals. They took turns hugging and talking to each. When they glanced back through the door, Father Dom and Toby had gone, but the rainbow had expanded; framed by the door, it radiated, and it shimmered.

Orrie and Ronnie went back to looking at their cards. They sat back down on the sacks of grain and closely examined the gifts. Ronnie said, "Whatever you do, don't let anything happen to that card."

Orrie said, "It's a special gift. I'll take good care of it . . . but why do you think Father Dom wanted to give us a picture of a whiskey bottle?"

Ronnie took a long breath and sighed. "Turn it over, goofball."

"Hey! It's a baseball guy. An old-time baseball guy. But this is way smaller than a regular baseball card . . . and somebody scribbled on it."

"That's how they made the cards back then, fifty years ago. And nobody scribbled on it—that's an autograph."

Orrie scrutinized the signature. He turned it every which way. "El—eleus?"

"Elias . . . Elias Gussard."

"Gosh . . . that's Toby's grandpa." Orrie fell into silence. His expression was pensive. Soon a light came into his eyes. He looked at Ronnie and spoke as though he had solved the mystery of the pyramids. "Jeez, Ronnie—you think the guy in this picture is Father Dom, don't you?"

Ronnie choked up and nodded his head. His eyes watered. "I *know* it is."

CHAPTER 28

Cornfield Combat

Stopping the spread of communism justified just about everything in American politics, or so young people were led to believe in 1965. Most kids were so busy being kids that the content of the six o' clock news was usually faded, fuzzy, and fragmented. Communism was a monster more grotesque, more terrifying than the combined personas of Frankenstein, Dracula, The Wolfman, Godzilla, Mothra, The Thing, and Tyrannosaurus Rex. We *youngins* were led to believe communism was spreading across the Orient as once had the Black Death, and it was destined to contaminate the entire planet.

What did youngsters know of the Orient? Well, there was Japan. It was known for a huge city called Tokyo, kimonos, samurai, and a topographical outcropping called Mt. Fuji. The Japanese loved American baseball, but instead of hot dogs and popcorn, their concession stands sold boxes of noodles. We also knew the Japanese had suffered the horrors of the atomic bomb; and that for the most part, the Japanese government was ruled by an Emperor and had nothing to do with communism.

Then there was North Korea, which with the help of the Communist Chinese, fought America to a hard-to-swallow draw. China had a trillion-billion people who were all Communists; at least that was the word. They ate rice and fish-head soup and they shot off fireworks day and night for no reason at all. Another misconception was that Hong Kong was the capital of China. The people of Hong Kong were mostly known for making cheap plastic toys, which was dim-wittedly made sport of by this little rhyme:

If it's made in Hong Kong,
It will be made wrong,
It won't be strong,
And it won't last long.

Envy's green-eyed monster would have thumbed its nose at such trifling.

Finally, there was a newly discovered crop of *yellow* people dwelling in the rotting jungles of Vietnam. No one knew where it was or anything about the history or culture. Supposedly, North Vietnam was trying to force the people of South Vietnam to become communists and form a giant slave-labor country. Laos and Cambodia were scheduled to be the next stops. The French Army tried to protect the South Vietnamese but failed. So now it was America's turn.

A little different story was unfolding in Eastern Europe. They had a big, bad bully called Russia. Even though the region was called the Union of Soviet Socialist Republic, these hard-working farmers and factory workers bore the scarlet letter "C" for Communism: *Commies, Russkies, Reds*. Symbols of their nation included buildings that looked like Christmas ornaments, kick-dancing Cossacks, a flag with pictures of farm tools, the Sputnik satellite, and a crazy President who pounded on tables with his shoe.

Nikita Khrushchev struck fear into our hearts, saying Russia would *bury* us. Young and old alike thought he meant he was going to bury us under atomic rubble; few realized economic superiority was his true intent. In America, people were worried. Those who possessed the means constructed cement bomb shelters in their backyards, some reportedly lined with lead. A stubborn rumor held that if you weren't directly disintegrated by the bomb, you could protect yourself from the radiation by using putty around your doors, covering your windows with butcher paper, and wrapping yourself in a bed sheet.

Lastly, there was the Cold War. They knew things about us, we knew things about them, and both of us knew we knew things about each other. Pretty much every male between the ages of 14 to 54 cultivated the fantastical notion of becoming a suave and lethal secret agent who could charm beautiful women. They were also adept at utilizing ingenious miniature weapons to dispose of Russian spies. And they could fight adeptly using a top-secret version of the martial arts. As a side note: everybody, everywhere knew somebody who knew somebody whose hands were registered as deadly weapons.

While Ronnie and Wuzzie believed some of the misconceptions and propaganda anent communism, they made conjectures deemed advantageous to their militaristic survival. In the summer of '65, the two made a pact. They were going to dedicate at least one hour per week conducting Vietnam War practice sessions. Both agreed that if called, they would give their all to serve and defend their country, then come home and earn a college degree. The approval of the Readjustment Benefits Act was welcomed as a lucky bonus. It was unofficially called the Vietnam GI Bill and it restored educational benefits for veterans.

It was late August. The chapel had burned to the ground and the nearby cottages were crumbling frames of ash. But there was still a viable vegetable garden and a field of bright green corn kept up quite nicely by the dedicated people of Brayton. This flourishing garden had been seeded by residents, patients, and patrons of the church and nursing home complex. The well-sown crop would be prime to reap in September. The small plot existed as an island amid a sea of newly plowed soil that had spared it from the flames. To Ronnie and Wuzzie, the cornfield was a passable surrogate for the steaming jungles of Vietnam.

The first order of business was assembling a weapons arsenal: a bb gun with a hair trigger, a WW II Marine combat knife, a serrated gardening knife, a machete, and a hatchet. The hatchet was a point of contention: Wuzzie did not believe American soldiers carried hatchets; Ronnie convinced him that Army Rangers carried Vietnam tomahawks. This turned out to be true. For hand grenades, they hand-molded the rich soil to manufacture sun-dried dirt clods. They considered using a garden hose as a flamethrower but decided it would make too much of a mess. Finally, they constructed two scarecrows and covered them with t-shirts, which had been soaked in black dye to represent the Viet Cong.

During the last two weeks of August, Ronnie had double-day football practice, so Sunday was the only day they could conduct war exercises. The weather had cooled substantially, which was characteristic of the region in September. This was somewhat of a disappointment because they did not have the humid, stifling heat effect of the tropical subtropics. As goes the ages-old cliché: You can't have everything.

The first day of Vietnam War practice was the Sunday before Labor Day. At two in the afternoon, it was a comfortable 80 F;

the sky was clear except for some swirly cirrus clouds. The Viet Cong dummies were set up, side-by-side. All the weapons were at hand. Despite the careful planning, preparations, and discussions neither Ronnie nor Wuzzie believed Wuzzie could bring himself, under any conditions, to dispatch an enemy. For Wuzzie, this was his last best chance because he knew all too well pursuing some kind of deferment or running off to a foreign land were not options he could live with. Ronnie feared Wuzzie's humanitarian nature could very well lead to KIA status. It was essential Wuzzie be trained in the well-honed proclivities of a hard-boiled, rock-jawed snake eater.

The guys spent about twenty minutes taking turns shooting the VC dummies; neither were content with their marksmanship. Wuzzie said, "We've gotta get this trigger fixed. You just barely touch it, and it goes off . . . I mean, it's not even a hair trigger—the thing just goes off."

"Yeah, you can see it from the shot groupings . . . We're both missing high and to the right. The stupid thing goes off just a split second before we can get a fix on the bullseye. If that trigger would stay put, we'd be right on the money."

"We're gonna have to take it apart. There's a little catch that holds the trigger in place and it's probably worn down."

Ronnie looked at the lever and stock connection. "If we're lucky, we could sand it a little so it would grip better. But if the metal's worn down too much, we'll have to replace the whole piece."

"We might be able to put a little drop of solder on it."

"Maybe. But I don't think solder would hold for long. Too much tension. I'll bet Phil could weld it or heat it up and bend it. I'll ask him when I get a chance . . . It's good enough for now."

Tossing dirt-clod grenades at the cottage ruins lead to even more disappointing results. The blast radius of the clods was far less than satisfactory. While Ronnie could wing the grenades from 50 yards away, Wuzzie's range was only about 40 feet. But Ronnie was confident he could mold his buddy into a first-class dirt clod thrower. He decided they would start training with rocks, gradually increasing the size and weight to build up Wuzzie's throwing muscles. Ronnie said, "Let's finish up with some hatchet throwing. There's a dead tree on the main trail to the river. It's even shaped sort of like a person and about the same size."

"If you say so. But I still don't remember any soldiers in movies throwing hatchets."

"We need all the skills we can get, Wuzzie. We need to give ourselves every possible advantage . . . Anyway, it'll be a good challenge."

Wuzzie picked up the hatchet and took account of its weight and balance. It was very rusty, but Ronnie had sharpened the blade on the grinding stone at the big barn. The edge was shiny and razor-sharp. The handle had a deep crack, but Ronnie had bound it with electrical tape. Wuzzie inspected the "tomahawk" closely; he finally awarded his seal of approval. As they neared the woods, he began humming "The Snake Charmer Song". Ronnie added the lyrics:

There's a place in France
Where the women wear no pants
And the men go 'round
With their ding dongs hangin' down

Wuzzie questioned the lyrical content and offered an edit. "I thought it was 'With their ding dongs *danglin*' down'?"

"Yeah, a lot of guys sing it that way, but *hangin'* sounds better. With *danglin*' you kinda get tripped up—too many d's."

Wuzzie sang the two versions and said, "Yeah, *hangin'* is better. Definitely." He paused for thought. "I suppose there's lots of versions. I know a kid from Wanoocha who sings it: *There's a place in France, Where the naked ladies dance, And the men don't care, Cuz they'd rather see them bare.*"

Ronnie pondered this variant because he felt a fair assessment was warranted. After singing the alternative lyrics twice he said, "Nah . . . I'm gonna stick with our version."

Wuzzie pretended to throw the hatchet from various altitudes and angles. "When we're done, maybe we can take a little swim. The river's still gonna be warm for a couple of weeks."

"It'd be warm enough, but it's still so shallow right now—there probably won't be a place deep enough to swim."

As they neared the woods, Wuzzie asked, "Where do you think Father Dom took Toby?"

Ronnie kept his insider knowledge privy. "Nobody knows. And I don't think anybody is really looking. They just trust Father Dom to do the right thing." He stopped and pointed toward the woods. "See the tree? Right over there."

"Man, you're right—that thing really does look like a person."

"Let's chop on it a little first; try to shape the top so it looks more like a head."

"That'll be easy—like a knife through butter."

The following Sunday they had bayonet practice. They affixed the Marine combat knife to the end of the bb gun with their old standby—electrical tape. After each took ten thrusts, the Viet Cong dummies had been decimated. The guts had spilled out leaving nothing but shreds of black cloth and bean poles. Ronnie and Wuzzie spent the rest of the afternoon on dummy repair duty.

Wuzzie said, "Just having these things standing there isn't all that realistic. The enemy would be moving around, jumping out of nowhere."

Ronnie thought for a second. "We could hang 'em from a tree limb and get 'em swingin'."

"At least that'd be something, but we'd lose the jungle and the surprise effect."

"True. It wouldn't be a whole lot like real war action. I don't think it would be worth the trouble."

"Maybe we could get some guys from the football team to wander around out in the corn."

"Hah! When I told those guys about this idea, I got laughed at—so I told 'em I was just joking about it. They all think they're such tough guys . . . We play Union City on Friday—the Generals, they're huge! So, we'll see how tough they *really* are. And if any of 'em had any sense, they'd be doing what we're doing."

Once again, Ronnie and Wuzzie put their heads together. About a minute into it, there came a simultaneous epiphany, "The punks!"

As Orrie, Doug, and Lon sat in the Rye Grass Cafe sipping their complimentary Green Rivers, they felt like VIPs—all that was missing were the Cognac and Cuban cigars. Wuzzie gave Doug a dime so he could play his favorite song on the jukebox. While a rowdy, upbeat rock number was anticipated, it was a delightful surprise when "The Rebel" by Johnny Cash *scatter-gunned* out. Heads bobbed. They sang along.

Ronnie arrived a little late due to an extended football practice. He knew the boys looked up to him, idolized him in fact. So, he played it up and acted extra cool. "How goes the battle, men," he said while twirling a chair, so its back was against the table. He leaned on the top of the chair and assumed a teen dreamboat presence in the manner of Fabian, Pat Boone, Frankie Avalon. Wuzzie handed Ronnie a bottle of Coke and joined the group.

"The job pays four-bits each," said Ronnie.

"So how much is a bit?" Orrie asked.

"What?"

"A bit—how much is it worth?"

"There's no such thing as a bit," said Wuzzie.

"Then how can you give us four of 'em?"

Orrie, Doug, and Lon exchanged suspicious glances.

"Four-bits is fifty cents," Ronnie said, impatiently.

"Hmmm," said Orrie. "I still don't see why—"

Wuzzie said, "One bit would be 12 and a half cents. They don't make half cents so there is no one bit—it starts at two bits—two bits is a quarter."

"Yeah, I get it," said Lon. "Like the cheer: two-bits, four-bits, six-bits—"

"OK, OK," said Ronnie. "You get fifty cents apiece for doing the job."

The boys squirmed, still skeptical.

"Yeah," said Ronnie with a patronizing tone. "We'll really pay you—no tricks."

"In advance," said Wuzzie. Ronnie gave him a "shut up" look.

Ronnie clarified. "A quarter up front—now. And a quarter after you're done."

The boys held a sidebar. When they returned, Orrie probed, "So what do we do?"

"You gotta hide in the cornfield and jump out at us."

Wuzzie added, "And you gotta wear black shirts."

Lon rubbed his chin and said, "This is a joke, isn't it? You're gonna throw snakes on us or something."

Ronnie said, "No, we're not gonna throw snakes on you. But we're gonna pretend to shoot you when you pop out of the corn and you've gotta fall down like you're dead."

"No lie, it's the absolute truth," Wuzzie said with plausible sincerity. "We're practicing for the war; in case we have to go."

Doug said, "But you're not old—"

"Shut up!" said Ronnie. "Do you want the job or not?"

The boys nodded they were up for it. When Ronnie got up to leave, he said, "And don't forget—wear *black* shirts."

The Friday before the cornfield rendezvous, the Rye Grass Thunderbirds had a home game against the Union City Generals. That was also the day that Rain and Ski were authorized to be Ronnie's foster guardians. An after-game party was planned. Although Ronnie was just a sophomore, he had earned the spot of varsity tight end. His whole fan club was there: Rain, Ski, the boys, Connie, Rhonda, Wuzzie, Mayor Figgs, Phil and his family—and also, Lester, who was drunk, but had pledged to observe impeccable social etiquette.

After a brief stay at the VA hospital in Spokane, Lester came back with a notable change in philosophy and attitude. He'd been given some counseling techniques to help deal with his anger, which he learned was repressed, irrational fear. And being clobbered in the head by the snapping of a log-binding chain had definitely intensified matters. To cope with the alcoholism, he had been given a medication called Antabuse, which was supposed to cause nausea if he drank alcohol—but he wouldn't take it. Perhaps the best news about Lester was that he had become a friend to Phil and his family and had begun to socialize with a few of the Mexican field workers and their families. But *The Days of Beer and Roses* ended a year later when Phil and his family returned to California. They started an asparagus farm just outside of Fresno. It was very sad to see Lester slip back into his cave. More and more he hid within himself—not wanting to be bothered and not wanting to bother others. Mostly, he just sat at home and drank.

As for the football game: The Thunderbirds got their behinds kicked all over the field that night. But in the final minute, there was a redeeming moment of glitter and glory. Ronnie ran a quick out pattern, caught the pass, then rambled over two huge Generals for a touchdown. The red lights on the scoreboard glowed—Visitor 50, Home 6. The season went downhill from there. But that night, there were two walloping parties: one at the Thunder Burger, for the young with all the adventures of life yet to come; and another at the Runnin' Bear, for dead-horse stories of glory days and the one that got away. That was the last night this jolly gaggle ever spent together.

On Sunday, the *punks* showed up at the Brayton cornfield. They arrived in white t-shirts with black construction paper stapled to the chest area. They also had rubbed black shoe polish on their cheeks and noses. When Ronnie and Wuzzie beheld the sight, they were stupefied, completely lost for words . . .

Orrie apologized, "We couldn't find black shirts."

Doug piped in, "So I got some black construction paper from school."

Ronnie asked, "You stole school paper for this?"

"No, I asked my teacher for it."

Wuzzie said, "Why the heck would your teacher give you free school paper?"

Lon said, "He told her he wanted to get a head start on cutting out Halloween bats—that was my idea."

Ronnie gave Doug's Viet Cong outfit a keen appraisal. "You sure have a habit of wearing some weird stuff, man. What did you ever do with that gunny sack thing?"

"I hung it up in the garage and sprayed it with Aquanet."

Lon said, "We didn't have any Lysol, so Aquanet was the closest."

"Jeez," Ronnie sighed, "I don't think there's any hope."

"Maybe he wants to be a fashion designer," said Wuzzie.

"Yeah, I suppose—if there were fashion designers for lunatics."

While the comedy duo laughed, Lon complained, "You guys said you wouldn't pick on us."

"No," Ronnie said, "We told you we wouldn't throw *snakes* on you."

Wuzzie sternly issued instructions. "OK, from here on it's serious business. This is a live combat simulation. No laughing, no jokes, no comments, no questions."

At the edge of the cornfield, Ronnie said, "All you guys have to do is go in between the cornstalks and hide. Then when we get close, pop out like you're going to attack us. We'll point our rifles and say *dat-dat-dat*, then you fall down."

Lon asked, "Then we get the quarters?"

Wuzzie pulled a handful of coins out of his pocket. "Got 'em right here . . . So as soon as we're done, you get 'em."

Ronnie and Wuzzie turned their backs to give the boys time to hide. Wuzzie carried the bb gun and Ronnie carried a crude, plywood version of an M-16. They walked into the *jungle* platoon-style, with Ronnie taking point.

For the first three rounds of battle things worked out perfectly. During the fourth round, the hair-trigger bb gun went off and Lon was hit in the bicep. His feelings probably sustained more of an injury than his arm, but he did drop to his knees and cry. The most unfortunate victim of all was Wuzzie, who was mortified by this purely unintentional act. Lon was comforted by sympathy all around, and as final atonement, Wuzzie gave him an extra quarter.

CHAPTER 29

Nam

While the real Vietnam War dragged on, the days and years passed quickly in the small-town of Rye Grass. The nightly news reported battles and body counts, policies and protests. President Johnson left in exhaustion and dismay, President Nixon took office promising hope, unity, and an end to the war. In Rye Grass, all things considered, one of the biggest news stories between the fall of '65 and the fall of '68 was Ronnie Rix finally asking Connie Malman to go steady. But she didn't make it easy; he had to pursue her in earnest to make up for a history of torts and misgivings. Their senior year was a fairytale, true-love romance. Both graduated with honors, scholarships, and a passel of sports awards. Both decided to work a year before enrolling in college. By the fall of 1969, outrage against the war had reached a peak. In November, half-a-million protesters marched on Washington D.C.—pleading for and demanding an end to U.S. military involvement in Vietnam.

After graduating from high school, Wuzzie headed for college in Ohio under a science scholarship. Ronnie had received a scholarship from the VFW and the Rye Grass Senior Class Fund. He said he wanted to spend a year working at the farm in

Brayton to save some extra money for college—mostly, he didn't want to be away from Connie. He continued to live with Rain, Ski, and Orrie; they would not accept a penny from him. The Elias Gussard Foundation had granted the deed to the Thunder Burger restaurant to Rain and Ski—free and clear—in the interest of promoting the local economy; something Father Dom had mysteriously arranged before leaving.

On January 20, 1970, eleven days after his 20th birthday, Ronnie Rix received a government letter beginning with the words: "Greeting: You are hereby ordered for induction into the Armed Forces of the United States . . ."

Ronnie completed basic and advanced training at Fort Ord, California. He was allowed a 30-day leave before transport to Vietnam. On May 12, he was *boots on the ground* at a base near Da Nang. Deboarding the CH-47 Chinook, a thermal blast stole his breath, when it returned the smell of burning human waste hit him in the face like the flat blade of a shovel. His *in country* social calendar consisted of the standard *364 days and a wakeup.*

On February 14, 1971, nine months into his duty, his platoon along with a native interpreter headed out on a recon mission. His best buddy, Willy Brown, a 19-year-old black kid from a Chicago ghetto, laughed till tears rolled when Ronnie told him the story about the cornfield. Despite *yucking* it up, both hoped and prayed some of that cornfield training would pay off. And just as with Wuzzie back in the states, Ronnie and Willy made a few pacts.

The choppers put them down in a wide-open, grassy area amid some hills and heavy jungle. It was a pleasant, sunny morning as they humped their weighty rucks. They ascended a grassy rise where they blended in with another platoon. This was step one of their mission: establish a strategic vantage point. While the lieutenant and sergeants took turns with the binoculars, the men were at ease. Most of them had become experts at opening

K-ration cans. They compared and shared. Willy and Ronnie sat with their backs to a slab of rock. Willy acted like he had struck gold. "Beans and mutha fuhkas," he said. "Almost as good as back home."

"Those *are* good," said Ronnie. "All of this canned stuff is better than those powdered eggs and fake milk at the mess hall."

"Them things don't bother me. I grew up on that stuff back in Chicago. It's what I'm used to."

"I'm used to being surrounded by farms with regular eggs and milk. But I do agree this beans and ham stuff is mighty dang good."

Willy shouted, "Hey, man, I'll trade all my puddin' for a can of beans and muthu fuhkas!"

Five guys shouted, "You're crazy, Willy." Laughter rang.

Willy asked, "How much time you got left, Rix?"

"Three months."

'Might as well be three years . . . I'm down to 14 days and a wake up."

"Jeez, I didn't know you were that short. You shouldn't even be out here!"

"They don't care about my black butt. I just go where they send me."

"That's a bummer, man."

"Nah, it's OK. I been keepin' it quiet so not to jinx myself. Don't mean nothin'. Just two more weeks—two more goddamn bullshit weeks."

Ronnie looked down the hillside, across the grassy fields and up at the milky blue sky. He said, “This sort of reminds me of home, Willy.”

“This damn jungle?!”

“No, this spot right here. It reminds me of the spring when Connie and I graduated. We were walking along the creek out by Rye Grass Hill. The goats, I think I’ve mentioned ’em—all four of ’em were walking along with us. Sometimes they’d run and splash around. Ha! They were something. I really miss ’em.”

“Nasty ol’ goats?”

“Yep, but they weren’t nasty. They were really smart, and could do tricks—fetch sticks like dogs, and a whole lot more. I remember this one day, warm, a little breeze, the blossoms smelled sweet, and this song was playing on our transistor radio, “Save Your Heart For Me”, by Gary Lewis and the Playboys. I can hear it in my head right now. It was an older song, from like—’65 or ’66, but Connie and I both liked it, and from there on it was *our* song.”

“Kinda funny, a song like that’s perfect for you—you got somebody to go back to . . . The song that keeps goin’ through my head is “What Becomes of the Broken Hearted”, by Jimmy Ruffin. Must be cuz I lost a chance at love . . . I thought bein’ here might help me forget . . . but it don’t.”

“I love that song too.” Ronnie sang the first line.

Other guys cheered. They all joined in for a couple of verses.

Ronnie said quietly, “So what happened? Who’d you lose?”

Willy rubbed the end of his nose and sighed, “Somebody hangin’ way too high on the limb for somebody like me.”

"Ah well, it probably woulda been sour grapes anyhow—just like in that story about the fox and the crow."

Without hesitation, Willy said, "No. Nope, you're wrong on that—them would have been some mighty fine grapes."

Ronnie and the eavesdroppers offered some good-hearted consolation.

Sergeant Garcia strode among the ranks and issued sobering advice. "Rix and Brown, can that Top 40 crap. Get your head in the game."

They conveyed a double, "Yes, sir."

The command gave the order to move out. As they got their gear together, Ronnie and Willy's ARVN buddy Chinh, their platoon interpreter, dashed over with his brother, Due, for a quick introduction. Due was the interpreter for the other platoon. "Are you guy's twins?" Willy asked.

"Not twins," laughed Chinh. "But that's OK, I know you Americans think we gooks all look alike." Due smiled.

The comment took Ronnie and Willy by surprise. Willy started to apologize. "I didn't mean—"

Chinh deliberately butchered his grammar. "Hey Joe, you not like funny joke?" Ronnie and Willy couldn't help but chuckle. Chinh gave Due, what sounded like, a few words of advice in Vietnamese, then a brotherly hug.

"Good luck, today," said Due, then returned to his outfit.

The platoons split up at the bottom of the hill; the bush lay a half-klick down the line. In *The Nam* guys learned quickly to move with finesse through the trees and elephant grass. The trick was a slight twisting motion; it kept the rustling down and helped them avoid cutting their hands on the leafy blades. Small cuts on the arms and hands became inflamed within minutes and festered as the hours passed. Though most had never seen a jungle, American soldiers soon became adept at dissolving into the steamy air and becoming one with the dense web of tangled green.

The bush. Shadows blinked amongst glints of light. A kaleidoscope of browns and greens formed the jungle sky. Chirps and caws sang from the limbs and leaves. Moss and fungi, damp from jungle sweat, exuded the dank odor of a rotting cellar. Rucks sagged and snagged. The jungle got hotter, darker, and quieter the deeper they went. The going was slow; nobody said a word. The radio crackled. Everybody stopped. As he listened, Sergeant Garcia's eyes narrowed. He clutched the phone in a death grip. His voice was deep and low, his jaw tight. "What?! You're just telling me now!" Ire turned to sarcasm. "We got two hundred NVA behind us—only two hundred?!" Sarcasm turned to ire. He became louder, angrier with each word. "So, you're sayin' we're bait?!" He quieted quickly. "How far back . . . three klicks . . . you sure . . . a tree—just one?" Garcia rolled his eyes. "Yeah, yeah, same old, same old . . ."

Eleven men murmured. The sergeant's eyes lingered on each man. "We got NVA behind us; about 3 klicks back; they know we're here. King's whole platoon's been scattered— radio's out. We're supposed to meet up at an LZ about three klicks south. Should work out, but we gotta take a tree down." Mumbles and grumbles.

"Rix, take point. You go second, Chinh. People have been through here—maybe *Charlie*, maybe not. Look down, look close. Look for divots, packed leaves. Might be wires, maybe not. Just watch it. Watch it close. From here on—we're ghosts."

Private first-class Ronnie Rix moccasin-walked to the head of the line. His buddy Willy Brown brought up the rear. Ronnie gave a two-finger signal for all to scan the jungle: the ground, undergrowth, tree trunks and high branches. The faces of the men were gaunt foreboding masks. The smell of fear rising from brave men was sickening, but there was also a gut-knotted strength, brooding, and solemnity—courage was building. From about two miles back, came the pounding of an artillery barrage. With smiling eyes, the men raised and shook their fists.

The sergeant's voice was just above a whisper. "Maybe they'll take care of it. Keep your bungs wired tight—some of 'em *will* get through—that's a fact! Let's go, Ronnie. There'll be wires—almost for sure. Use that x-ray vision, Superman."

They trudged along, weaving through dense, unforgiving elephant grass and interlacing bamboo. The shelling stopped. The hollow silence was deafening. They listened for birds, not a peep. With great trepidation, they inched ahead. Tension torqued minds and twisted aching backs. After nearly a mile of snail-pace humping, Garcia rotated Ronnie and Chinh to the back of the line. Ronnie winked as he walked past Willy. The platoon was about a quarter mile from the LZ.

The bush gradually brightened. Up ahead was the jungle's edge. They could see the tall sawgrass of an open field; it was scattered with slender trees and bamboo. Abruptly, the point man stopped. He looked back and mouthed, "Wire." No time for disarming. One by one, the men stepped high over the tripwire. Suddenly, the point man tumbled forward; he went down into a shallow pit. The sergeant and medic moved up and knelt at the hollow. The man had been impaled by two, long punji stakes; each jutted through his back by nearly a foot. He had died instantly. The grunts gnashed their teeth; their eyes smoldered. Strangely, the ground around them swam. With a rustling and a whoosh, VC leaped from blinds and crawled from spider holes. They slashed, hacked, and jabbed with knives and machetes. Stray rifles ripped. VC fell. A severed head bounced, a neck spewed, a body dropped.

Ronnie was tackled from behind. His helmet bounced and rolled; his rifle launched into the undergrowth. He grappled with his enemy, rolling on top, using his elbow to smash-in the man's teeth. With a fulcrum-and-palm blow he broke the enemy's neck. Willy Brown grappled with two attackers, blinding one with an eye strike. As he head-butted the other in the face, a black-clad foe snuck up with a raised machete. A tomahawk flew from Ronnie's hand and split a skull; the enemy at Willy's back dropped dead. Ronnie grabbed his rifle. With a thumb jab to the throat and a head stomp, Willy finished his attacker. Ronnie retrieved his hatchet. Back-to-back they scanned the carnage. The VC had scrambled back into the trees. A massvie *blast*! Jolting concussions. Men dropped. Smoke rose. The fallen cried out. Lying flat, Ronnie, Willie, and Chinh waited, watched, rose to a knee, and aimed their M-16s. Chinh fired a burst; it merely shredded leaves. The enemy had simply vanished.

Men writhed and moaned. Some lay still. Sergeant Garcia had been gravely wounded. He fiercely fought back his screams as Ronnie dragged him from the bush. Chinh and Willy each dragged a man until they reached the clearing. Two bloodied Americans staggered from the trees; one fell dead. The able men pulled the wounded about twenty yards to the middle of a cluster of trees. Garcia's mouth was bleeding; he spit out each word, "Mister Rix, you're the senior. You need 30 yards square for the chopper. There's a spot southeast, pretty clear, you'll see it. You gotta take down a tree, take my machete and cut it low as you can . . . drag it out—"

"But I'm not the—"

"You got the job!" Garcia's eyes blackened; his body softened and was still.

Ronnie pulled the bloodied tomahawk from his belt. "Willy, go find that tree." He handed Willy the tomahawk and Garcia's machete. "You gotta chop like hell. The rest of us will catch up and help drag the thing out." Willy was reluctant to desert his friends. "Take off, man! We'll be right behind ya."

As Willy ran through the scattered trees and bamboo clusters, Ronnie and Chinh carried the last two bodies from the bush. With an M-16, a hobbling private covered their retreat. Only five men were left from a platoon of twelve. Bursting from the trees to the northwest, rifle in hand, was an American soldier. He waved and was acknowledged. He joined the group and helped cover the retreat. From the jungle, a shot rang out; from the sky, came the distant hum of a UH-1. Two NVA charged. A bullet from a Russian AK struck a nearby tree. The Americans set their wounded men down. Ronnie picked off the shooter. The other NVA zig-zagged back into the jungle.

Willy continued to hack away at the tree as the group arrived. One of the riflemen took over. "It's close," said Willy. "I tried pushing it, but it wouldn't budge." The chopper blades whirled louder, perhaps two minutes away. The man with the tomahawk looked up and nodded. Everybody pushed. The tree cracked and teetered; it crashed into the grass. An M-16 ripped through the tree's clinging pith and two of the men dragged it away. In the distance, along the jungle's tree line, at least a dozen NVA appeared. They charged; they fired. Leaving the wounded men, the Americans moved up, and from behind the trees, returned heavy fire. The rescue chopper approached the LZ. The enemy welled up at the jungle's edge. They attacked in staggered clusters, bursting, and dispersing at random intervals.

One after another, NVA soldiers dropped from rifle fire. But more filtered through the trees—a lot more. The enemy charged with abandon as their numbers grew. Overhead the chopper made a pass, strafed the NVA, then circled back. Protected by the trees, the Americans were able to fire at will, but they were too far outnumbered to hold their ground. The chopper descended. The sawgrass bent and flattened. The bird touched down. Two men jumped out with a stretcher. Ronnie, Chinh, and Willy kept up the fire as the others climbed aboard. Ronnie shouted, "Go, Willy—we got this." Willy kept firing; Ronnie shoved him. "Go!" Willy hesitated. Ronnie glared and waved him off.

The chopper pilot yelled, "Get on! I'm outta here!" He lifted the craft and hovered two feet above the ground. Willy costively hustled aboard. Ronnie and Chinh kept firing, slowly backing away from the charging horde. Chinh climbed on. Ronnie fired a few more rounds, then hopped on. The chopper slowly rose.

Chinh's face filled with terror. A South Vietnamese soldier was bouncing from tree to tree like a run amok pinball. He was obviously suffering from a leg wound. "It's Due! It's my brother, Due!" Chinh leaped, unarmed, into the grass. Bullets zipped past as Chinh raced to help Due. The chopper hovered at about the height of a basketball rim. Ronnie grabbed his rifle and started to jump out. Willy held him back.

One of the men said, "Ronnie—forget it! They're gooks."

"They're on our side, man! They're friends." Ronnie pulled away from Willy, grabbed his rifle and jumped. He landed hard and rolled through the grass. He crawled a few yards, then popped up and chased after Chinh. Ronnie provided cover as Chinh helped his brother. The chopper descended into the grass. The gunner continually sprayed rounds. Willy opened up with his M-16, picking off NVA left and right. Ronnie kept firing, taking down man after man. Chinh and Due were aboard. Ronnie ran backward, firing with every step. As he reached the side of the chopper, he was hit in the abdomen. He staggered backward. Willy jumped lifted Ronnie aboard, then followed. Under heavy fire, the chopper lifted. Taking hit after hit, the Huey tilted, dipped, and lurched, stalled, recovered, spun recklessly, then finally whirled up and away.

Surrounded by a pale-blue sky, the men surrounded Ronnie. His uniform was soaked with dark blood. Willy cradled him.

Pressing firmly on the wound, the medic looked at Willy, in sadness and in vain. Willy read his lips. "Liver shot—he's dyin'." Willy teared up.

Ronnie tried to talk. There was a film of blood on his teeth. "Did I make it, Willy? Did I make it?"

"What?" Then Willy understood. "Oh, that *yay-do-mony-oh* thing, a man of honor. Yeah, you made it, man—you made it and then some."

Blood leaking over his chin, Ronnie smiled and said, "Tell Connie . . . tell Connie I—"

"Yeah, I'll tell her, man. I'll tell her."

Ronnie coughed and swallowed blood. "Tell her I love her, Willy." With that, the young man smiled a peaceful smile, his eyes gently closed, his heart slowed, his soul rose. The men hung their heads and shed their tears.

CHAPTER 30

Night Lights

1918. The blast came in a blinding flash. The last worldly experience of Elias Gussard was hooking his thumbs into the eyes of a German soldier as the man was blown to bits. Slowly came an awareness, the feeling of floating within nothingness, no darkness or light, no sound, just the feeling of a warm, gentle wind. His thoughts sought his remains, which his mind saw strewn over the mud: blood, bones, intestines, heart, lungs, and brain. But there were no remains and there was no mud. Just a wind, getting warmer and stronger. The wind became hot—hot enough to melt the moon. And it became strong—strong enough to snuff the sun. Eli's essence, his soul, his physical being felt that God had passed through him.

Knowing the dangers of unexploded shells and arsenic fumes rising from the puddles and mud, French monks would routinely brave forsaken battlefields in search of fallen soldiers still clinging to life. In less than an instant, Elias was aware of the men. He saw them moving around, aimlessly, purposefully. He saw them from every angle and point of view. He heard their voices, read their thoughts, felt their feelings. These mulling men in hoods and robes scanned the muddy field and walked the broken forest. They looked at bodies and bits of bodies. Sadly, they shook their heads. One of the monks called out, "*Ici, ici*!" The monks gathered around the body. They talked. One of them knelt in the mud, then motioned for a stretcher. Up to their shins in mire, they labored with the body and placed it on a wagon. The gravely wounded American wore the Red Cross armband of a medic. He was their only salvage that day. Elias now felt the sensation of his physical body rolling along on the wagon. Its destination— a monastic, stone castle. At the same time, he was without a body, aware of everything, aware of everywhere, knowing everything that ever was and all that would ever be. Existence and infinity were one and the same. From the dark of death to the light of life, by both providence and willpower, an angel flew from Heaven and a man returned to Earth. There was work to be done.

On that dreary morning, in the French countryside, Elias Gussard died on the back of a horse cart and Dominique Toussaint was born. He had found a calling. The other monks bore witness and welcomed him into the fold, sharing their faith and vowing their guidance. The years passed. Another war came and went. Father Dom worked house and home; garden and field; river and pond. He kept watch on the sheep and herded the goats. He learned to heal hearts and to soothe souls. He formed friendships in towns and villages, factories and farms, along the borders, throughout the heartlands. His family was humankind. Like the friar in Sister Sourire's benevolent ode he sought to spread "the grace of love and simple mirth".

As the days passed and the seasons changed, Father Dom yearned to travel, to rove and roam; he yearned to spread *the word* in his own time, his own way. Like the jongleurs of lore, he found happiness in a simple life, a life of giving what he could and receiving what he needed. He offered the mercy of salvation and asked for nothing in return. This shepherd, this goatherd, had discovered an earthly enchantment, a blessing of the innocents, a oneness with the beasts. Together they toiled and tangled and taught each other how to listen with the mind, feel with the heart, and touch with the soul. For forty years, Father Dom and his generations of goats traveled far and wide. At last, the time had come for him to make the journey home. His American name would be Cal Brimiron.

In the fall of 1960, Cal Brimiron booked passage on a cargo ship from Liverpool bound for the city of New York. Cal had gone to great lengths to find a ship with a hold worthy of his family—Henry, Willow, Dandy, and Tinker. Cal spent most of his seven days in the bowels of the ship with the goats. This was where he slept. There was plenty of grain, and lots of apples, pears, and carrots. He maintained their quarters, keeping them ship-shape throughout. To pass the time, he told the goats tall stories and tiny tales. They listened, most politely, to his fond memories, his orders of business, his lofty dreams, and visions. Each day a seaman would accompany them on a walk around the deck. One sunny afternoon, they spent hours gazing in wonder at majestic icebergs—most of them far distant, some breathtakingly close. The voyage was a joy: a calm sea; a sky spangled by night and cloudless by day; a scalawag wind and a salty ocean spray. On day seven, October 9th at 7:07 am, they arrived in America.

With telephone calls, wires, and letters, Cal gained sanction from towns and hamlets to set up revival tarps, tents, and platforms. Thousands of miles they traveled in a pampered old truck, which pulled a cozy livestock trailer. Whether city, countryside, or somewhere in between, they were warmly welcomed and departed leaving truths of love, hope, and kindness. Like Methodist circuit riders of yore, Cal and the goats welcomed the food and shelter of the folks and families who dwelled along their path. Though they bid no coinage, contributions were never denied.

The shows were uniform but entertaining. Cal's opening sermon would be brief, light-hearted, occasionally poignant, always taking account of the labors and lifestyles of believers and non-believers alike. But the show was, for the most part, just a show—no preaching or piety, just the spreading of goodwill and a few words of good faith. At the opening, an old capstan-drive, reel-to-reel recorder played a merry tune, and the goats would dance. The music, a palatable variety: folk songs, barn dance fiddling, dramatic classics, some rock and roll, and of course, the traditional hymns. Then came the games—the goats played leapfrog, tag, and kick the can (at some point, chew the can—always good for laughs). They ran races, played tug o' war, nosed beach balls back and forth, and head-butted soccer balls into goals. For the finale, they would bleat a simple tune: each goat, in turn, bleated a pitch melodically complimenting the previous note: "London Bridge", "Old McDonald", "Greensleeves", and "Jesus Loves the Little Children" were the favorites; perhaps, this was the most amazing of all the amazing feats. In the end, Cal would offer final thoughts, and a final wise, often witty aphorism. The shows were fondly met; rare was dissent.

By the time they had crossed the borders of 48 states, nearly three years had come and gone. At certain stages the journey was exhausting. From time to time, setbacks befell, and perils arose, but the blessings were many. Each gathering offered comfort, redemption, joy, and inspiration. And while all good things do someday end, there are always new beginnings—a new beginning was just over the rise. Waterville, Kansas played host to the final performance of Cal Brimiron's Amazing Goats. Standing applause sent them on their way. As they rolled across the Idaho panhandle, their new home was just hours away: Washington State, near the town of Rye Grass, the flowering meadow, artesian stream, and placid hill where they would live out the rest of their lives.

It was a beautiful spring night, moving into the early-morning hours—warm and windless, the moon was almost full. A few ragged clouds drifted. The stars twinkled. A faithful truck and weathered livestock trailer lazily roamed a winding country road. The bittersweet lament "Dark Moon" by Bonnie Guitar drifted faintly from the radio. As the pickup eased to a squeaky stop the words on the trailer shone in the moonlight—CAL BRIMIRON'S AMAZING GOATS. Elated at having finally reached the oft-praised utopia, the four goats bleated in veritable throes of rapture . . . at long last, they'd found the promised land.

Revelations: If you haven't guessed by now—I'm Orrie, currently holding the title Father Orrin, caretaker, and minister of the Brayton Chapel—a quaint little church standing next to a row of rustic cottages, a retirement home and hospital, and six beautiful acres of Willamette raspberries. The buildings have been well maintained; in some cases, remodeled and rebuilt, by dint of the notorious fire of '65. Through the decades, these sanctuaries have most ably provided shelter, care, and comfort for numbers untold. And I am thrilled to say the current congregation is thriving. My unconventional approach to *apostling* has been working out very well. On Sunday morning it's standing room only. On Wednesday evening, young people from all around come to the recreation hall activities. We hold a dance on the last Saturday of every month and a box lunch social at the change of each season—homespun, old-fashioned . . . but sometimes that's a very good thing.

As the story began, I was looking at the statue of a man—a national hero. Now I'm looking at the statue of another national hero, a boy of 15, wearing a baseball uniform, a cap with an "M", and a first-baseman mitt. Ronnie Rix gave his life on a field of sawgrass, at the raw, frayed edge of an Asian jungle. He died bravely, sacrificing himself for the sake of others, and completing his quest to become the ultimate man of honor—undeniably attaining a glory the ancient Greeks called eudaimonia. So never to be forgotten, his high-school sweetheart Connie and I put together a beautiful shrine in the chapel showcase: his senior portrait, All-Star letter, sports trophies, the home run ball from the legendary Pemmican Pirates game, his autographed Eli Gussard baseball card, some news clippings, and his Silver Star.

As for Ronnie's monument in the park: Every time I look at the statue, I feel a chill cross my temples, get a lump in my throat, and try to fight back the tears. A big part of my job is assuaging and soothing emotional and spiritual suffering in others. Rarely, do I have the luxury of easing my own. But Ronnie was a friend, he was a brother, and he was among the best of men. Though I will always feel the presence of his soul, I do at times, mourn his earthly passing, and I can't help but cry. The Herman's Hermits version of "The End of the World" runs through my mind at these times. Somehow the song gives these memories a poignant depth. Until my dying day, once each year, on the date of the *big game* back in '65, I will visit a hill of tall ryegrass—a place where I, Father Dom, Ronnie, Toby, and four scruffy goats were embraced by Divine Love . . . where a blessed rain fell . . . where we all became part of a Miracle.

Traveling Rye Grass Road, the warm memories flowed, and though more than five decades had slipped away, these were the best times I've ever known. And as I thought about my friends and family, I felt certain they remembered those days just as fondly.

Suddenly, I was there again, on that old, cracked, and pitted road, the one I knew so many years ago. Ski and I were racing toward town in the GTO. For the first time in my life, I knew what it was like to fly. "Wishes are the wings of dreams", Mom once wrote. At last, I understood. And if I ever had a magical wish, it would be to spend one more hour, even a few minutes in that childhood paradise—a carefree, cotton-candy, ice-cream sundae world.

Returning to the present, the song "We'll Sing in the Sunshine" by Gale Garnett tagged along on the radio. The lyrics limned an idyllic love fated to fade. The beautiful melody summoned vivid images of old friends, familiar places, and once starry notions, compelling a yearn for compendium and closure. Connie's dad, Lester, mellowed out somewhat as the years passed. The legendary Gussard Memorial Baseball season of '65 marked the end of his baseball tutelage. Helping Ronnie earn that All-Star spot was one of the highlights of his life. In memory of Ronnie, Lester became a devout Los Angeles Dodgers fan. He made following the peaks and valleys of the former Brooklyn nine his life's major pastime, even after Washington had welcomed aboard the Mariners. Other than that, about all he did was watch the news and tons of movies from the 40s and 50s . . . Well, there was one other thing. In 1980 George Jones released a song called "He Stopped Loving Her Today". Every evening, right after the six o' clock news, Lester went into his bedroom, closed the door, and played the song three times—a heart rending ritual that helped him carry on.

He sold the mill and lumber yard in the early 80s for a reportedly hefty sum. Connie stayed close and visited him every day. With Connie twisting his arm, and twisting it hard, he was able to stop drinking hard liquor; but he made up for it by turning into what some call a *beero*. For him it was Oktoberfest 24/7. Drinking a full case a day was not unusual. Consequently, he gained a great deal of weight, 400 lbs plus. He passed away, with Connie and Doug at his side, in the Brayton hospital at the age of 69.

Lester had given Doug a grubstake, which he turned into a chain of hardware stores spanning the Inland Empire (Eastern Washington, Northern Idaho, Western Montana), which he eventually sold to a large corporation. He is amicably divorced and has a daughter named Connie. I see him at the chapel every Sunday and sometimes down at the Runnin' Bear. I'll be forever grateful to Doug for inspiring my love of words, which eventually evolved into a love of poetry—especially the alliterative classics (I suspect there's a nibble of a chance you noticed). In our school days, Doug and I religiously challenged each other to games such as Hangman, Bulls and Cows, Scrabble, Boggle, word search, and crossword puzzles. We still enjoy playing Scrabble online. Doug ended up fulfilling the life-long ambition of becoming a journalist—he runs a little hometown newspaper called The Paper Mill, which occupies the old Rye Grass Feed Store building.

Lon moved to Spokane and worked for quite a few years in the heating and air conditioning business. Eventually, he started his own outfit, creatively calling it "Lon's Heating and Air Conditioning". It was an extremely successful endeavor and he retired at age 55. He married his "soulmate". They raised three great kids, have a house with a white picket fence, and a little mongrel dog named Scooter—yep, the American Dream. During football season, he comes up north just about every weekend to watch the Seahawks game. After morning chapel, we meet at the Runnin' Bear. Beer and pizza are the usual fare.

Wuzzie finished college with a bachelor's in physics. He pulled a stint as a naval officer, and after ten years, went back to school and earned a—*drumroll*—PhD in Nuclear Physics.

After high school, Rhonda Stickle attended Pepperdine University, but did not graduate. Through the 1970s, she and Connie stayed in reasonably close contact, but by the 80s communication had been reduced to an exchange of Christmas cards. Ironically, Rhonda ended up spending a lot of her time doing what she despised her parents for—traveling. In January of 2000, Connie received a letter from Rhonda saying she was honeymooning in the Bahamas, her fourth marriage (all to rich guys). The fourth time was not the charm. Rhonda now lives in New York City and spends most of her time as a hospital volunteer and doing charity work.

Rain and Ski had always been young at heart. In the early 80s, out of their love for music and the restaurant business, they sold the Thunder Burger (which is still going strong) and started a restaurant/lounge in Union City. They called it *Lorraine's*. It soon became a real *hot spot*—less euphemistically—a meat market. Live bands on Thursday, Friday, and Saturday. Packed every night. Ski said the key to having a successful nightclub was security. If women felt safe, they would frequent a place, and believe it or not, men would flock to their banner. The 80s was a fantastic decade for music—clubbing was all the rage. After selling the club in 1996, they sailed the Caribbean, visited Hawaii often, and toured Europe several times. Not unexpectedly, they ended up spending most of their retirement years in the little town where they fell in love. Rain and Ski passed away in 2018, just a few months apart, as life-long couples often do. I'm still not over the loss—I never will be.

Ronnie left all his earthly belongings to his one true love. When I was a senior in high school, Connie was still living at home with Lester and Doug. One weekend I arranged to deliver all of Ronnie's things to their home. She asked me to stay and sort through it all. Connie became curious about a locked metal box made to hold manilla folders. She found the key and discovered some very unusual letters. The first was dated December 25, 1965; it was an unsolicited pen pal letter from a student in France. We immediately realized the letter was from Father Dom. There were fourteen letters in all. Although we were overjoyed with our find, Connie and I agreed to keep the letters a secret. Through these documents, I was able to piece together the story of Father Dom, most of which I relayed earlier. I eventually wrote to the monastery, but the letters came back RTS.

With a little further digging, I learned that Toby Gussard had spent the final years of his life as a groundskeeper at a French monastery. He passed quietly one night at the age of 51. As to the fate of Elias Gussard, there are, not surprisingly, some points of mystery and contention. There was an occurrence at Ronnie's memorial services at Rye Grass Park. Dozens of people attended including Wuzzie, who made it out from Ohio State; Allie Davis came up from Oregon; Kenny West surprised us with a visit (he did end up pitching for a few years in the minor leagues). Rhonda flew up from Pepperdine. She stopped her rental car in the middle of Main Street and waved. Connie and I ran over. When she rolled down her window, the tune "As Tears Go By" by Marianne Faithful was playing. The line about watching children play touched many a-heart—and sure enough, over by the merry-go-round, some young boys were engaged in shenanigans and tomfoolery. Nothing changes. Then, as might have been expected, Connie had somebody move their vehicle, so (spoiled girl) Rhonda could enjoy preferred parking.

And there was another attendee—a mystery man. He seemed harmless enough. From the way he walked, he appeared to be an older gentleman. Dressed in a long trench coat, wearing dark glasses and a black cap, he briefly spoke with Mayor Figgs, then wandered about, keeping to himself. I pointed him out to Connie, and she said she'd get around to talking with him, but she never did. I remember him paying respects at the flag-draped casket . . . but that was the last I saw of him. One has to wonder . . .

After the services, Willy Brown, Ronnie's army buddy stayed with my family for a few days. Earlier, he had given Connie and me a brief account of Ronnie's final hours. Before he left, I asked him for a few more details. Though this was extremely difficult for him, and he cried from time to time, he told me everything he had experienced during the horrific ordeal. In a way, it was a catharsis, an unburdening—but he said he would never talk about it again. Years later, Connie wanted to know the whole story. On a snowy December night, I relayed everything Willy had told me in as much detail as I could recollect. She listened stoically. The knowing had finally set her mind at ease. She once told me her favorite song was Simon and Garfunkel's "I Am a Rock". And a rock she is.

Then there's that old rascal Mayor/ Barkeep/Pawnbroker Charles William Figgs. One day, not long before Figgs passed away in '89, I got a phone call. He asked me to come down to the Runnin' Bear. It was late; the place was closed. I sat at the bar, and we had a few beers—quite a few. Figgs spent all night telling me one heck of a story.

Charlie Figgs and Elias Gussard had been childhood friends, best friends. After Elias' wife died in the influenza outbreak of '18, his son Virgil became executor and sole heir to the Elias Gussard Foundation. Shortly following the death of Virgil (auto accident), a New York legal firm informed Charlie that he had been designated to carry out the terms of the will—though there were quite a few stipulations, basically, Figgs had inherited everything. In addition, Figgs was the only person in the world who knew Elias Gussard was still alive. Charlie made the arrangements to bring Toby back to Rye Grass and he facilitated Father Dom's appointment to the Brayton chapel.

At some point after leaving Rye Grass with Toby, Elias had sent Figgs a letter instructing him to pass on the responsibilities of the estate to Ronnie and me. The Elias Gussard Foundation was worth, in rounded figures, eighteen-million dollars. Although stunned, I accepted the responsibility and told Figgs I wanted to transfer half of the estate to Connie in Ronnie's stead. He smiled and shook my hand. The whole affair was processed through the New York-based firm. Connie and I faithfully carry out our duties. The one loose end to the Charlie Figgs story was the mysterious man I had seen him talking to in the park. I almost brought it up several times, but in the end, I figured he had his reasons for keeping certain things to himself.

In 1973, Connie attended Eastern Washington State College and graduated with a bachelor's degree in Biology. She then moved to Spokane and enrolled in nursing school. Meanwhile, Doug remained at home with Lester and helped him run the mill. Connie chose to become an RN primarily because of her dad's compromised physical and mental health. She knew he'd be needing a lot of in-home living assistance. After graduating, Connie took a job at the nursing facility in Brayton. She is still employed there in an administrative role. Connie, along with her dog and cat, have a nice home in the ever-growing town of Rye Grass. She never married because the one man in her life still lived within her heart, and she knew they would be together—forever.

And so, I once again stood at the bottom of Rye Grass Hill, at the very place Ski and I had stood during that blazing summer of 1965. Throughout this writing, the songs of that era have provided sentimentalities and touchstones evoking memories, lucid and alive, allowing me to capture this chronicle's every event and every detail to the best of my ability. As a soft rain fell, "A Lover's Concerto" by the Toys came to mind. I walked to the song's 4/4 time as I climbed the grassy slope. On the hilltop, I paid my respects to one last group of friends; more of a family than friends, I suppose. Standing in the tall grass, I looked around at the quince and cherry trees; the little feed shed; the wishing well; the huge, horse-chestnut tree; and in the middle of it all, the bronze statues of four magnificent gifts to the world: Toro, Ghostie, Wags, and Tiny—The Goats of Rye Grass Hill.

So much of life comes down to faith.

ABOUT THE AUTHOR

Joe Don Roggins has lived in England, Scotland, New York, and San Francisco. He now writes from a small farm in the Cascade foothills of Washington State. Mr. Roggins started out in the field of agriculture picking strawberries and ended up in the field of literature spinning yarns. With a university degree in social science and one from the prestigious College of Bountiful Clouts, he has spent a great deal of his life working in the public arena.

Mr. Roggins has written extensively in the fields of technology, education, business, health care, and labor relations. Works of fiction include two novels, three screenplays, and a couple o' dozen songs; he always has a new project in the works. Pastimes include reading, movies, sports, live music and comedy, scenic excursions, and volunteer work. Currently, he participates in promoting climate change awareness.

www.joedonroggins.com

Rain Hill Publishing LLC

Made in the USA
Middletown, DE
20 November 2022

15280881R00246